MUTATION

The UNIT 51 Novels
by MICHAEL MCBRIDE

SUBHUMAN

FORSAKEN

MUTATION

MUTATION

- A UNIT 51 NOVEL -

MICHAEL McBRIDE

PINNACLE BOOKS
Kensington Publishing Corp.
www.kensingtonbooks.com

PINNACLE BOOKS are published by

Kensington Publishing Corp.
119 West 40th Street
New York, NY 10018

All Kensington titles, imprints, and distributed lines are available at special quantity discounts for bulk purchases for sales promotions, premiums, fund-raising, educational, or institutional use. Special book excerpts or customized printings can also be created to fit specific needs. For details, write or phone the office of the Kensington sales manager: Kensington Publishing Corp., 119 West 40th Street, New York, NY 10018, attn: Sales Department; phone 1-800-221-2647.

PINNACLE BOOKS and the Pinnacle logo are Reg. U.S. Pat. & TM Off.
ISBN-13: 978-0-7860-4601-0
ISBN-10: 0-7860-4601-5

First printing: October 2020

10 9 8 7 6 5 4 3 2 1

Printed in the United States of America

Electronic edition:

ISBN-13: 978-0-7860-4602-7 (e-book)
ISBN-10: 0-7860-4602-3p (e-book)

CROP CIRCLES
WILTSHIRE COUNTY, ENGLAND
JULY, 1990

#1: ALTON BARNES

#2: EAST KENNETT

#3: STANTON ST BERNARD

#4: ALLINGTON

MAPS:

MESOPOTAMIA

MESOAMERICA

ANTARCTICA

PROLOGUE

But Life, being Life, can never die at all.
—Frederick Tennyson

EVANS

Mosul, Iraq

The skeletal remains of Old Town intermittently appeared from the black smoke churning against the horizon. The ground trembled from the distant airstrikes, and the air crackled with automatic gunfire. U.S. Army Sergeant Luke Carmichael led the procession on foot through the ruins of the once-great city. The roads were filled with the rubble of the collapsed buildings, making them impassible by vehicle. Dr. Cade Evans followed closely behind him in his borrowed desert camouflage fatigues. A crust of dust had already formed on his lips and around his nostrils, and his skin felt like sandpaper. He'd never been to Mosul and couldn't picture how it must have looked before first the Islamic State and then al-Qaeda seized control.

A pall of concrete dust hung over the entire city. Power lines had fallen, their wires snaking lifelessly through streets where the charred husks of abandoned vehicles rusted. The façades of the few buildings that remained standing offered glimpses into the lives once lived inside them. There were no people on the streets, nor any sign that there ever would be again.

"How much farther?" Dr. Anya Fleming asked from behind him. She'd refused to don a burqa and instead wore her auburn hair tucked up underneath her helmet and fatigues that were way too large for her slender form. Her eyes stood out from her dirty face like emeralds stomped into the sand.

"It's just up ahead," Corporal Brian Lewis said. He brought up the rear so silently that Evans had almost forgotten he was there.

Carmichael moved through the haze like a specter. Evans followed him over a mound of rubble from which rusted lengths of rebar stood. Forty-eight hours ago, he'd seen a single picture of what awaited them ahead, and it had been all he could think about since.

A fighter jet screamed across the skyline a heartbeat before the ground shuddered and rubble rained down all around them. The shadow of a drone passed over him, but it was gone by the time he looked up.

The sergeant guided them through the framework of a building burned to the bare girders and into an alley clogged with debris.

"This used to be a school," Carmichael said of the demolished structure before them. It now looked more like a parking garage, with bare concrete floors and walls. Only the blackened metal frames of chairs and desks hinted at its former purpose. "There were children inside when they torched it."

Evans's boots left tread marks in the carpet of soot and ash. The rusted sprinkler pipes were still bolted to the ceiling, for all the good they'd done. Charcoaled wall studs framed corridors that funneled them deeper into the dark structure. Their military escorts switched on the LED lights mounted to the barrels of their M4 carbines and swept them through the vacant building. Carmichael offered Evans his mini Maglite and waited for him to turn it on before advancing.

The foundation was cracked in some places and entirely absent in others. They ducked in and out of what had once been classrooms to avoid pits that had to be a good fifteen feet deep. The sergeant stopped at the fractured edge of one maybe six feet across and shined his light down upon a ladder descending into the earth.

"You're on your own from here," Lewis said. "They don't pay me enough to go back down there."

"We'll stand guard up here," Carmichael said. "If either of us so much as senses anyone coming, we're out of here. All of us. You hear me?"

Evans stared at him for several seconds before nodding and starting down the ladder. Anya followed. The echoes of their footfalls on the aluminum rungs preceded them into the depths. The cool air was a welcome change and chilled the layer of sweat under his fatigues. The dirt floor at the bottom was hard and smelled of a bygone age.

He shined his light up the ladder until Anya reached the bottom and stepped down. There was an arched orifice behind him, near the ground. Not the traditional ornate Islamic pointed arch, but rather one chiseled from the bedrock itself. He crouched and peered inside. When he looked back at Anya, he couldn't hide his excitement.

"That good?" she asked.

"You have no idea."

Evans rolled onto his stomach and slid his legs through the opening. He pushed himself backward until he could duck his head under the arch before letting go and dropping into the ancient tomb.

There were only so many places in the arid Middle

East suitable for habitation. As such, countless civilizations had risen from and fallen on the very same land,
with new societies growing from the carcasses of their
predecessors. Discoveries like this weren't uncommon,
especially along the Tigris River and in what was known
as the Cradle of Civilization, although finding intact
human remains was an anomaly of the highest order. Entire peoples had come and gone without leaving any
posthumous evidence, at least not that the eternal desert
was willing to give up.

This part of Northern Iraq had been ruled through the
millennia by the Sumerians, Akkadians, Assyrians, and
Babylonians. While this necropolis could have been used
by any one or even all of them, the primitive stone arch
likely dated to ancient Sumer and a culture that thrived
thousands of years ago. The petroglyphs carved into the
walls appeared to reflect the Assyrian style, which reminded Evans of primitive Egyptian hieroglyphics, although it was hard to tell for sure through the eons' worth
of dust that had accumulated on them. And upon the
bones scattered across the floor amid the fallen boulders
that had once sealed the entrance of the necropolis.

A single opening branched from the rear of the antechamber. The passageway was ten feet long and led them
into the room where the picture had been taken. There
were skeletons in varying stages of articulation all around
them. Sprawled across the ground. Slouched against
walls adorned with elaborate carvings. All plastered with
dust and ravaged by age, despite which he could clearly
see the shapes of their elongated craniums and deformed
facial architecture.

"Classic abandonment context," Anya said. "They

were sealed in here and left to decompose where they
fell."

She drew her shirt over her mouth and nose, crouched,
and brushed the dust from the most complete set of remains she could find.

A narrow opening led to another chamber. Evans took
in everything around him as he walked toward it. There
were no stars carved into the ceiling as he'd seen at every
other similar burial site. No gouges in the stone where the
creatures had attempted to claw their way out. It was almost as though they'd acquiesced to their ultimate fate
without raging against it, which was totally out of character for this alien species.

There was another body wedged in the passageway.
He estimated that brought the total so far to nine, although
there was no way of telling how many of them were primary and how many were drones. He could only imagine
the horror the people who'd lived here must have felt
with so many of these monsters out there at once. They
must have existed in a constant state of terror.

The adjoining chamber was considerably smaller and
strung with cobwebs as thick as ropes, which nearly concealed the stone plinth in the center. And the hominin remains resting upon it.

Evans parted the webs, which made crackling sounds
as they fell away. For there to have been spiders in here,
there had to have been a means by which they entered.
Some sort of crevice or hole that reached the surface. And
any orifice, no matter how small, meant an influx of fresh
air, and yet the creatures had been unable to exploit it to
escape. There was obviously something he was missing.

"Cade?"

Anya's voice echoed from the chamber behind him. He couldn't find the words to respond as he stared down at the body on the plinth.

The dead man had to be close to seven feet tall. His skin was so desiccated and shrunken to his underlying skeleton that Evans could see all of the places where his bones had been broken. The tibias and femurs. The radii and humeri. The pelvic girdle and ribs. Whoever he was, he'd been beaten so savagely that he wouldn't have been able to so much as crawl, and yet still he was bound by frayed ropes that had eroded through his parchment-like skin.

"There's something wrong here," Anya said.

Evans swept the cobwebs away from the man's face and revealed an eagle mask, painstakingly constructed with real feathers and the hooked beak of a giant raptor.

Anya tugged on the back of his jacket.

"We have to get out of here right now."

He turned to face her and saw the fear in her eyes.

"What's wrong?"

She took him by the hand and pulled him back through the crevice and into the outer chamber.

"The bodies," she said. "Look at the way they're contorted. At the way their spines are bent backward."

Evans glanced at them as they hurried past. She was right. They were all twisted, with their knees bent and their upper extremities curled to their chests.

She hit the ladder ahead of him and scampered toward the surface.

"We need to seal the entrance!" she shouted.

Carmichael shined his light down on her.

"What are you talking about?"

"Hurry!"

Anya crawled from the hole and ran toward where an intact section of scorched paneling remained attached to the studs. She jerked on it until the nails pried loose and jumped back. It crashed to the floor at her feet.

Evans emerged from the hole and looked at the two soldiers, who could only shrug in response.

"Talk to me, Anya," he said. "What's going on?"

"Don't you see?" She positively trembled as she dragged the heavy sheet of wood across the room. "That posture is a result of contractures. I should have recognized it from the start. Every muscle in their bodies constricted. At once. *Before* they died."

"Okay. I'll bite. So what causes something like that to happen?"

He helped her slide the makeshift barricade over the pit. They dropped it with a booming sound that reverberated beneath their feet. She was so pale when she finally met his stare that the freckles on her nose and cheekbones stood out like constellations, even through the dirt.

"Disease."

BARNETT

The landscape was like that of an entirely different planet. Rugged lava fields gave way to sparse grasslands lorded over by towers of metamorphic rock. Green and orange lichen grew from jagged formations reminiscent of coral reefs. It had to be one of the most desolate regions on the planet, and yet still their prey eluded them.

Cameron Barnett, Director of Unit 51, crunched over the sharp, uneven ground. There were no trees or man-made structures, nothing at all to obscure his view of the horizon in any direction. If the creature was out there, he would have been able to see it.

He bellowed in frustration and listened to his voice echo across the plains.

There were only so many places it could have gone. The airplane upon which it had hitched a ride from Mc-Murdo Station in Antarctica had crashed near Rio Grande, Argentina, seventy miles to the south of their current location. He and his team had arrived within fourteen hours of the incident, the aftermath of which they'd watched on a live news broadcast. The pilot and copilot had been killed before the Basler BT-67 hit the ground. They'd found the cockpit spattered with blood and the seatbelts severed by the same implements that had been used on the men themselves, whose bodies had been thrown through the shattered windshield. There had only been two passengers, researchers returning to the States, and it was anyone's guess as to whether or not they'd still been alive when the rows of seats slammed forward upon impact and compacted against the rear wall of the cockpit.

Barnett didn't need to wait around for the National Transportation Safety Board's investigation. He already knew what had happened. He'd seen the damage to the door separating the cabin from the cargo hold. The passengers had never known it was back there and had surely been taken by surprise when the door suddenly opened and death came for them.

The few surviving footprints in the surrounding forest had led to the northwest before being lost to the bare stone and windswept snow. Remote tracking by satellite and drone had turned up nothing. It was as though the subject codenamed Zeta—after the sixth letter of the Greek alphabet and in reference to the alien species unofficially classified as Zeta Reticulans, but more commonly known as Grays—had simply vanished. There was only snow and ice to the south. To the east, the vast expanse of the Atlantic Ocean. And to the west, little more than a maze of frozen islands. North was the only direction the creature realistically could have gone as it led to the South American mainland, where if it could reach the deep Andes or the dense Amazon rainforest, it could potentially hide from them forever.

They couldn't let it get that far.

"Should be just over the next rise," Special Agent Rand Morgan said from behind him.

Barnett looked toward where a craggy formation serrated the skyline and nodded.

His men hung back from him. Not that he blamed them. He was in a vile mood and took it out on everyone within range. Or perhaps they simply wanted to have someone physically between them and Subject Z if they stumbled upon it.

Their black fatigues blended into the volcanic landscape, save for the red insignias on their shoulders, which featured the superimposed inverted triangles of Unit 51, the clandestine organization responsible for the investigation of arcane and inexplicable discoveries and events that potentially threatened national security. The unit was cofinanced by the estate of the late Hollis Richards—a venture capitalist who'd become obsessed with the alien phenomena that had ultimately cost him his life—and the Department of Defense. It was personally overseen by Grady Clayborn, the Secretary of Defense, who answered only to the President of the United States, a man who was growing increasingly distraught at their inability to find the creature responsible for slaughtering more than fifty men and women in Antarctica.

Their deaths weighed heavily upon Barnett's conscience. He wasn't sleeping and looked as though he'd aged a decade in the last week alone. Silver had crept into his dark hair at the temples and flecked his stubble. The lines on his forehead and around his ice-blue eyes were even more pronounced. There was a part of him that resented being burdened with this kind of responsibility, but there was no one else capable of bearing it. He hesitated to even consider the implications of failure. There were some things that the world at large could never know about, and it fell upon him to make sure they were able to sleep at night without ever learning of the horrors that lurked in the darkness.

Golden tufts of grass grew from soil as hard as stone. The blades were crisp and frosted and crackled underfoot. They formed a pattern like stepping-stones clear up to the point where the black escarpment jutted from the hillside.

Morgan caught up with him as they climbed over the sharp formation, from the top of which they could see nearly to the end of the world in every direction. There was no movement, no sign of life, least of all from the guanacos lying downhill in the weeds. The long fur of the orange and white camelids, which reminded him of a cross between a llama and an antelope, ruffled on the frigid breeze.

Barnett's team back at the Hangar, Unit 51's base of operations in Hampton, Virginia, had detected the dead animals by satellite and forwarded the coordinates to them in the field. He'd known the correlation between the dead animals and Subject Z had been a stretch, but they'd simply had no other leads.

They picked their way down the steep slope, through prickly groundcover that left burs in their laces. The two special agents bringing up the rear—Troy Brinkley and Saul Sheppard—drew their automatic rifles and pulled the charging handles. Of course, had Subject Z still been around, they would have already been in the same position as the guanacos, whose long necks had been opened with such savagery that it was a miracle their heads were still attached. They'd been cut from pubis to sternum and their abdominal contents disgorged onto the flattened weeds. Their carcasses were frozen to the ground, and a layer of frost had already formed on their distended skin.

The dirt had soaked up as much blood as it could hold and cradled dark puddles layered with ice. Their eyes were sunken and their noses gray and dry. At a guess, they'd been dead for somewhere between two and three days, which meant that Barnett and his men were rapidly losing ground.

"I've got something over here," Morgan said.

He knelt beside a carcass downhill from the others.

Barnett crouched beside him and followed his stare to the ground, where the mud had frozen and preserved a track he would have recognized anywhere. It was just the ball of a foot and the teardrop-shaped impressions of clawed toes, almost like the track of a bear, only rather than forming an arch, the digits tapered from medial to lateral. There was no mistaking Subject Z's footprint.

"There's another one over here," Sheppard said.

Barnett hurried to where the agent was already taking pictures of the track. It was a partial at best, but clear enough that he could see that it belonged to someone other than the creature, someone startlingly human.

"Zeta's not alone," Barnett said.

He stood and turned in a circle, hoping to see any indication as to where their quarry might have gone. The idea that someone was traveling with Subject Z through this wasteland made him uneasy, but not nearly as much as the prospect that the print belonged to someone who'd been dead for thousands of years.

JADE

"Let's start with a T1 sagittal," Dr. Jade Liang said. "I want a good look at what we're dealing with here."

From where she sat at the control console in the MRI suite, she could see the technologist's monitors to her left and the circular gantry housing the 3.0-Tesla magnet straight ahead through the soundproof window. The brain of Subject A—or Alpha, the codename given to the drone that had once been Hollis Richards—had been extracted and stabilized using a phosphate-buffered formalin fixating agent, chemopreserved with osmium tetroxide and epoxy resin monomers, and housed in a clear plastic casing shaped like the head inside of which it once resided. The MRI technologists had attached a series of electrodes designed to stimulate different areas of the midbrain, cerebellum, and cerebrum to determine the functionality of the various sections, assuming they remained viable this long after death.

U.S. Army Radiology Specialist Victor Dupuis used the scout images of the brain in three planes to program the system to virtually slice it, like a loaf of bread, from left to right in five-millimeter cuts. The mere fact that he was in the room with her meant that his security clearance was high enough that she could count on him not to tell anyone about what he saw. Jade had to wonder what all he'd dealt with through the course of his work that he had earned the trust of an agency that didn't trust anyone. He hadn't batted an eye when she arrived with the clear plastic head on ice. Neither had his partner, Jill Ervin, who positioned the phantom head in the domed electromagnetic coil and waited inside the room by the transcranial direct current stimulator she would use to deliver the electric shocks.

The MRI machine issued a throbbing techno beat as the changing magnetic fields caused the brain tissues to release characteristic signals that were then captured and translated into grayscale images—in this case, cross-sections of the elongated brain in profile. It looked like a football made of convoluted folds of putty, inside of which were structures completely different from those found in a normal human brain.

The brain stem, which regulated autonomic functions like heart rate, blood pressure, and breathing, was somewhat similar in appearance. The baseball-like cerebellum, responsible for motor functions and coordination, was wider and longer and cradled the brain almost like spread wings. The cerebrum had grown to fit the mutated skull, although it retained the same relative amounts of white and gray matter. She could tell right away that the pituitary gland and hypothalamus were easily twice their normal size, which made the corpus callosum look less like an inverted Nike swoosh and more like a tilted horseshoe.

"Look at the size of those temporal lobes," Dupuis said.

"Can you get me some T2 axials through them?" Jade asked.

"I can do anything you want."

He winked at her and set to work.

The increased dimensions of the pituitary gland and hypothalamus didn't surprise her. They produced the growth hormones that were responsible for the obvious deformations she'd noticed upon physical evaluation and subsequent autopsy. While the lab seemed to be taking its sweet time with the results of the blood and tissue assays, she was confident they'd show elevated levels of human growth hormone, HGH, and the insulin-like growth factor produced in the liver, IGF-1, which was capable of stimulating proliferation in a wide variety of tissues, most notably the osteoblasts and chondrocytes responsible for bone development.

Even with the lab results, she feared they wouldn't be able to determine the mechanism by which the skull elongated, the orbital sockets widened, and the jaws re-formed to accommodate the sharklike configuration of sharp teeth. These weren't random mutations, but rather specialized physical adaptations that followed blueprints coded into the RNA of the microscopic alien organism, which, like a retrovirus, replicated inside of an infected species and inserted its genetic code into the host's DNA.

"Check out the amygdala," Dupuis said. "I've never seen anything like it."

"That would definitely explain the aggression," Jade said. "And the increased size of the hippocampus and temporal lobes supports our theory about its long-term memory storage, if not its genetic memory."

"You mean like the way a monarch butterfly knows the exact route to take during its migration without ever having flown it before?"

"Essentially."

"In a human?"

"Trust me," Jade said. "There's nothing human about this thing."

Of course, that was a lie. She'd been with Subject A when it died in the field. In its final moments, it had spoken in the voice of Hollis Richards, who had warned her that it was up to her to stop the end of the world. There was a part of her that wanted to believe that conversation had never happened, that her mind and ears had conspired against her, and not just because the prospect of Hollis being trapped inside his own mind while the organisms used his body to commit horrible atrocities made her sick to her stomach. The idea of somehow being responsible for the fate of the entire world terrified her, especially considering she didn't have the slightest idea what she was supposed to do or where to begin.

"Can we move on to the functional imaging?" she asked.

"Give me a second."

Functional MRI, or fMRI, was a relatively new neuroimaging technique used to measure brain activity in response to various forms of stimuli, thus showing which parts of the brain were responsible for each function, like the temporal lobes and their increased activity in response to trying to recall childhood memories or the occipital lobe and its ability to distinguish visual phenomena. While a clinically dead brain wouldn't demonstrate actual functioning, electrically stimulating the corresponding parts of the brain allowed them to visualize the neural pathways that were already there. She needed to figure out how the parasitic organisms interacted with the host brain if they were going to find a way to prevent them from doing so.

"That's odd," Dupuis said.

Jade leaned closer to his monitor. He tapped the sagittal image, near where a blob of color had formed. It was gold in the center and faded to a deep red near the edges, and covered the thalamus, hippocampus, and vestibular nuclei. "Which electrode did you stimulate?" Jade asked.

"That's just it. We didn't stimulate any of them."

"What are you saying?"

"That area of the brain is responding to the static magnetic field itself."

Dr. Kelly Nolan, Jade's colleague who had solved the mystery of how Subject A had been able to travel from Antarctica to Mexico, believed it had done so using some sort of internal sensors that allowed it to detect the elevated magnetic fields aligned along the borders of tectonic plates. Not only did this prove her hypothesis, it potentially gave them the means by which to track Subject Z, assuming Barnett and his team hadn't already found it.

"Do you want to try to stimulate that area first?" he asked.

"Seems like a good place to start."

Dupuis brought up the visual representations of the electrodes surrounding the ghost image of the elongated brain on the monitor and programmed the system to acquire the images. He leaned forward, pressed the button to activate the speaker inside the exam room, and spoke into the microphone.

"Ready to get this show on the road?"

Jill turned toward the window and gave him the thumbs up. She wore powder-blue surgical scrubs and her blond hair in a ponytail.

"Target electrodes nine and eighteen," he said. "Let's start at one-point-five milliamps and seventy megahertz."

She set the system as requested and looked back at him expectantly.

"On my mark," Dupuis said.

He started the scan on his console and the machine on the other side of the wall started to thump. He held up three fingers so she could see them. Two. One.

Jill triggered the electrical stimulation and the brain on the monitor lit up. The golden aura raced outward from the central focus and struck like lightning bolts throughout the brain.

"What's happening?" Jade asked.

"I don't know."

A flash of light from inside the MRI tube. Jill shielded her eyes.

Dupuis attempted to terminate the scan.

"Make it stop!" Jade shouted.

"I'm trying!"

Arcs of electricity snapped and crackled from the plastic head inside the gantry. Jill rushed to the control unit and attempted to manually drive the table out of the magnet. The entire head glowed bluish-purple before suddenly shattering. Plastic shards and brain matter struck the window right in front of Jade, who flinched and pushed her chair backward from the console.

The thumping slowed, and the image on the monitor faded from gold to deep red to gray.

"What in the name of God was that?" Jade asked.

"Was there metal inside there?"

"No."

"There had to be."

"I'm telling you—"

"Well, something caused an electrical arc."

Jill stood with her back to them, her hands pressed to her face. Dark fluid spattered to the ground at her feet, but it wasn't until she turned around and Jade saw her face that she understood that it was blood pouring through Jill's fingers. The plastic shards had shredded her skin, exposing bone and embedding themselves in the soft tissue. She screamed and fell to her knees.

"Oh, my God," Jade said. She lunged to her feet, ran out of the control room, and into the hallway. The door to the exam room was closed and magnetically sealed. She jerked on the handle to no avail. "Open the door!"

An alarm klaxon blared and emergency lights flashed. Dupuis remotely drove the table out of the gantry.

"I can't!" he shouted. "It automatically locks if the sensors detect a biological contaminant!"

Jade ran back into the control room and watched help-lessly through the window.

Jill tried to push herself up from the floor, but only succeeded in smearing bloody palm prints on the white tile.

There was a drumroll of footsteps from the hallway as the emergency response team raced toward them.

Jade pressed the button and leaned over the micro-phone.

"Try to remain calm." Her voice echoed from inside the exam room. "Help is on the way."

Jill looked up, her wide eyes like beacons set into the

mask of blood. She struggled to her feet, staggered to the window, and leaned against it. Her molars were visible through a hole in her cheek. Her eyes sought Jade's and held them.

It wasn't fear Jade saw inside them, but rather something that raised the goosebumps on the backs of her arms.

An almost placid smile formed on Jill's face. Jade couldn't hear her when she spoke, but she was able to read the words on her lips.

Hello again . . . Dr. Liang.

"No . . ." Jade whispered. She stumbled backward and nearly toppled over her chair. "Please . . ."

The footsteps converged outside of the exam room. She heard barked commands. Dupuis rushed to join the rescue efforts.

Jill cocked her head first one way, and then the other, like a vulture. Jade could almost hear the deep, resonant voice of Subject Z inside her head when the woman spoke.

We are . . . free . . . thanks to you. Jill's pupils widened until they nearly eclipsed the irises. The vessels in her sclera ruptured and flooded the whites. *You will . . . live . . . this day.*

A pair of men in biohazard suits hurried past the doorway. Pressurized air hissed as they inflated the containment chamber outside the exam room.

Jill planted both palms against the glass, pressed her bloody forehead between them, and smiled.

But you will . . . die . . . with the rest . . . of your species.

She abruptly turned away from the window and walked across the room to where the shattered casing containing what little remained of Subject A's brain rested on the patient table. Shards protruded from the base of the broken cranium.

"Don't . . ." Jade whispered.

Jill looked back at her, smiled, and slammed her chest down onto the jagged plastic.

Jade turned away as the woman's blood overflowed the table and flooded onto the floor.

BOOK I

From each sad remnant of decay, some forms of life arise so shall his life be taken away before he knoweth that he hath it.
—CHARLES MACKAY

1
ROCHE

The events of the last year had changed Martin Roche, or maybe they'd simply served to return him to the path he'd been meant to travel. Either way, he didn't like it. He'd left the intelligence community and the national security apparatus because he'd lost faith in what he was doing and grown resentful of being made to spy on his own people, and yet here he was now, standing before a wall of monitors upon which played satellite, drone, and surveillance footage from all around the world.

He'd been trained to see the patterns that no one else could see and detect threats hidden in the chaos by the elite cryptanalysis unit of the U.S. Marines, from whose pocket he'd been picked by the NSA, who'd honed those skills to a razor's edge. Had he believed there was anyone better equipped to handle this job, he would have gladly declined Barnett's offer and walked away with a clear conscience. He'd seen glimpses of the fate that awaited them all if Unit 51 failed to prevent it, though, and couldn't abandon those he loved to it, even if it meant throwing away the life he had made for himself in England, the

countless hours of research he'd invested into deciphering the mysterious crop circles, and the burgeoning relationship with the woman who occupied his every waking
thought.

Roche cleared his mind. He couldn't afford to be distracted or he might miss something crucial.

"Transfer monitor six to the main screen," he said.

Three digital information specialists were seated at the
terminals in the front of the room. Each of them was responsible for acquiring and screening the incoming footage from various locations around the globe. In a perfect
world, there would have been a single technologist assigned to each source, but after losing nearly twenty percent of their total ranks to the feathered serpents beneath
the Antarctic ice cap, their numbers dwindled by the day.
They were running on a skeleton crew, and until they secured anything resembling an actual victory, they weren't
going to be able to lure quality applicants away from any
of the other branches. Assuming they even still had funding by then. As it was, Clayborn claimed it was becoming
increasingly difficult to appropriate any kind of budget
for his discretionary projects at the DOD, which was his
not-so-subtle way of saying that either they showed some
positive results or they were on their own.

Roche couldn't allow that to happen. Not with Subject
Z—and Lord only knew what else—out there on the
loose.

An aerial image appeared on the central monitor. A
jagged range of sharp, icy peaks rose from a seamless
field of white. It was all that remained of the ice cap
above the subterranean lake and Forward Operating Base
Atlantis, from which only a handful of them had managed to escape with their lives. With the feathered ser-

pents able to breed unchecked and with nothing to stop them from reaching the surface, a decision had been made to drop a bunker buster with a thermobaric warhead straight down the elevator shaft to collapse the entire ice dome. In theory, the detonation had sucked all of the air out of the caverns and used it to generate a high-temperature explosion that incinerated everything inside before dropping two vertical miles of ice onto the ashes, but if he had learned one thing during the past year, it was that nature always found a way to persevere.

"Give me a thermal overlay," Roche said.

The specialist toggled some keys and the image became pixelated. There were no heat signatures whatsoever.

"It's been six months," the specialist said. Lucas O'Reilly was his name. Or maybe just Reilly. That Roche didn't know the man's name spoke volumes about the situation and his state of mind. "If anything survived the blast, we'd have found it by now."

"We're dealing with an extant species of dinosaur capable of surviving for tens of thousands of years in a state of cryobiosis. You'll have to indulge my paranoia."

"Why don't you get out of here for a while?" a voice said from behind him.

Roche turned to find Special Agent Marc Maddox standing behind him with his hands clasped behind his back. He had brilliant blue eyes and wore his blond hair buzzed; his broad jaw was cleanly shaved. He wore the scars along the sides of his nose and from the corners of his mouth to his ears with pride. He'd earned them in Afghanistan, undoubtedly in a manner he'd rather not recount. The plastic surgeons had done such a miraculous job that what could have been a disfiguring injury merely added character to his face. With Barnett and Morgan in the field, he was in charge of operations, while Roche served as team lead for the scientific branch. They shared responsibility for tracking Subject Z and its traveling companion—officially classified as Unknown Subject, or UNSUB X—who continued to elude their pursuit.

"I was just about to check the drone footage from Colombia," Roche said.

"Do you really think it's possible that Subject Zeta and UNSUB X made it that far north?"

"We can't afford to assume they didn't."

"You and I both know that they could easily hide in the Amazon rainforest and we'd never find so much as a trace of them."

"If hiding is their goal," Roche said.

"What else could they possibly want? The moment they stick their heads out of that jungle we'll be right there to rain fire down upon them."

"They wouldn't have risked leaving Antarctica if they didn't have a destination. All signs support a steady northward advance."

"We've beaten this horse to death," Maddox said. "Have we heard from our men on the ground?"

"Both teams checked in right on schedule."

"And with the same reports, I'm sure."

"The northern unit will reach the coordinates first," Roche said. "Special Agent Staley estimated sometime around sunrise. Barnett said his team acquired a boat and shouldn't be more than four or five hours behind."

"You know as well as I do what they'll find when they get there."

"Maybe we'll get lucky."

"Unfortunately, at this point, that's what it's going to take."

"We will find them," Roche said.

"But not if we spread ourselves too thin. You should get some sleep. You look like you just crawled out of your own grave."

"That was the style I was aiming for."

"Go on, Martin. You're no good to anyone like this. We need you on top of your game if we're going to find them."

"It's a matter of *when*, not if."

Roche glanced back at the wall of monitors, nodded to himself, and clapped Maddox on the shoulder on his way out. The satellites would still be there when he returned, and there would be even more footage to evaluate. They would find Subject Z, whether tomorrow or ten years from now, and he would personally make sure that when they did, they obliterated it, right down to the molecular level.

He caught his reflection from the mirrored glass of the Arcade, as the drone room was known, and saw what Maddox meant. His hair was shaggy, his face unshaved, and his clothes were too loose. He'd let himself go and still hadn't accomplished a blasted thing, save for driving away the only person who truly mattered to him, but he couldn't bring himself to take a step back and let someone else do the job. He simply couldn't afford to trust anyone. As recent events in Mexico had clearly demonstrated, a shadow organization they'd taken to calling Enigma, because of how little they knew about it, seemed to always be a step ahead of them, which could mean only one thing: it had somehow managed to infiltrate Unit 51.

The office Dr. Kelly Nolan shared with Dr. Tess Clarke was near the end of the hallway. He stopped outside the open door and looked inside. Kelly had exchanged the red and green streaks in her hair for a completely new color, which appeared silver in some light and purple in others. Barnett had arranged for her to finish her doctorate at Oregon State via a remote-learning platform. After developing a system that predicted seismic activity and modifying the design from the ancient machine they'd discovered under the onion field in Wiltshire to produce a limitless amount of energy from flowing water, it hadn't taken a whole lot of convincing. She'd only just returned from defending her doctoral thesis and visiting her mother, who had begun displaying symptoms of Parkinson's disease. She'd asked Roche to go with her, but he hadn't even been able to do that for her.

She obviously hadn't arrived very long ago, as she was still wearing her jacket and hadn't even opened the bag of croissants on her desk, and yet she was already working at the digital touchscreen monitor mounted to the wall behind her desk. On the screen was a program of her own design that featured all of the tectonic plates with various overlays, from vague continental maps to precise images from Google Earth, which allowed her to evaluate seismic and volcanic activity, as well as the fluctuating magnetic fields they generated, in real time.

After the MRI revealed that Subject A had accelerated growth to the same parts of its brain that a homing pigeon used for magnetoreception, she'd set about isolating every single variation in magnetic field strength from the southern tip of Argentina all the way north to the Arctic Circle in hopes of determining every route Subject Z could take and every conceivable destination along the way. The problem was that there were simply too many possibilities. If the creature was as sensitive to subtle magnetic variances as a homing pigeon, it could utilize fields as small as fifty microteslas, which wasn't a whole lot stronger than the field generated by standard overhead power lines.

Her left hand fretted at her side. It was an unconscious tic that made her look like she was playing an air guitar. She was incredibly self-conscious about it, yet most of the time didn't even realize she was doing it. Roche wanted to go in there and take her hand in his, to reassure her that everything was going to be all right, but he was no longer sure that their relationship was such that he could. Nor did he believe that everything was going to be all right ever again.

She paused what she was doing and cocked her head.

Roche ducked out of the doorway before she caught him looking and headed toward the end of the corridor, where he'd taken to sleeping in the conference room outside of Barnett's office while the director was in the field. Roche couldn't remember the last time he'd seen the world above the underground bunker, which had been built as an emergency relocation center for the National Military Establishment—the precursor agency to the Department of Defense—in case of a nuclear attack, let alone the inside of the apartment he'd rented. He wasn't even sure if his key would still work in the lock. He'd sacrificed everything for the greater good and what did he have to show for it?

"Martin?"

Roche turned at the sound of Kelly's voice. She stood

outside her office with an expression of concern he could read from twenty feet away. He offered a half-smile and a wave, ducked into the conference room, and curled up on the couch.

Several seconds passed before he heard her footsteps retreat into her office and the door close behind her.

2
STALEY

Reserva Extrativista do Rio Jutaí,
State of Amazonas,
Brazil

They were closing the net; he could feel it.

Special Agent Shane Staley and his team slogged through the flooded jungle, negotiating the snaking roots of the mangroves, keeping to the cover of the rubber trees, and pushing through curtains of strangler figs. The soft mud sucked at his feet and released them with the vile stench of flatus. The shrieking of parrots and chittering of monkeys masked the sounds of their advance, at least until the racket suddenly ceased.

He held up his fist to halt his men, who were concealed so well that he could barely discern their silhouettes from the shadows and the whites of their eyes from their camouflage face paint. He stared up into the canopy. Everything was silent and still. No breeze ruffled the leaves and no birds jostled the branches. Even the sun, it seemed, was barely able to penetrate the upper reaches with more than the most ambitious columns of light. Only the mosquitoes whined around his head, their efforts intensified and frenzied as though somehow sensing their window of opportunity was closing.

Something brushed past his calf beneath the brown water. He turned around in time to see the furry body of a dead simian breach the surface before submerging once more and continuing its migration on the weak current.

Staley felt the weight of his men's stares upon him. They sensed it, too. The rainforest didn't fall silent without a good reason. It took something truly ferocious to quiet an environment accustomed to going about its business while jaguars hunted from the trees, crocodiles lurked in the shallows, and venomous snakes slithered invisibly through the detritus. He feared that they'd finally found exactly what they'd been dispatched to find, only suddenly he wasn't entirely sure that was a good thing. After all, he'd seen what their quarry was capable of doing.

He slowed his breathing and lowered his fist. No matter how vicious Subject Z might be, a bullet through the brainpan would put it down like any other animal, for that was how he had chosen to think of it. Calling it what it truly was only served to grant it a psychological advantage. When he had the animal in his sights, he would not hesitate. It was time to take this monster off the board, once and for all.

He seated the butt of his SCAR 17 assault rifle against his shoulder and started slowly toward the Rio Solimões. His men followed his lead, as he knew they would, with only the slightest hesitation.

The upper section of the Amazon River announced its presence with a thrum he could feel through the earth.

The brain trust back at the Hangar had discovered a method, however unscientific, of tracking their prey by satellite. While the satellites couldn't technically see the creature, or even the faintest hint of its thermal signature, through the impenetrable canopy, they could detect concentrations of carrion birds in the upper reaches and wheeling above the treetops. They were also able to extrapolate a line connecting documented signs of its passage with real-time imagery to plot the theoretical course of the creature's northward migration.

Staley and his team, who'd barely been given time to exchange names, let alone train together, had been airlifted to a point nearly twenty miles north of their current position with instructions to follow the winding course of the Amazon until they encountered Barnett's team. Or the creature. Whichever came first.

The rumble of the mighty river intensified from a subtle physical sensation to an audible one. The current against his legs grew stronger by the second, forcing him to work his way toward shallower water and the spotted stretches of dry ground from which dense thickets of ceibas grew. He crawled into the weeds and caught his first glimpse of the distant river—

A shrill scream erupted from somewhere ahead of him.

His men sought cover in his peripheral vision. The barrels of their rifles carved through the shadows as they attempted to get a bead on the source of the noise, which had sounded almost human—

Another cry echoed through the rainforest, pitiful and resigned.

Staley removed his global comlink from his backpack, but as expected, there was no signal. The satellite was generally only in range for a handful of hours every day,

and even then they were often forced to find an unob-
structed view of the sky.

They were on their own.

He caught the attention of Special Agent Todd Simmons and signaled for him to circle around to the right. A
heartbeat later, the former marine was gone, leaving little
more than shivering leaves in his wake. SA Ed Darling
recognized what Staley planned to do and was on the
move the moment their eyes locked through the underbrush. A glance confirmed that SA Don Koish was already falling back into containment position behind him.
They would drive their prey ahead of them and flush it
out into the open on the riverbank, closing in from three
sides as they approached, forcing it to either stand its
ground or attempt to get past them. Koish would serve as
the last line of defense. If it somehow eluded the three of
them, it was up to him to put it down.

Staley moved stealthily through the maze of buttress
roots and vines, never once taking his eyes from the jungle in front of him, despite the damp palm leaves and fern
fronds that grazed his face.

It was too quiet. Even his soft breathing and the faint
slurping sounds of his carefully placed footsteps in the
mud threatened to betray him.

He scanned the canopy for any sign of movement, but
the jungle might as well have been dead. Save for the infernal mosquitoes. He focused on anything other than the
sensation of the wretched insects crawling on his skin and
the instinctive desire to slap them.

Crack.

Staley froze.

The sound had come from maybe twenty feet ahead of

him, somewhere on the other side of a stand of rubber trees, between the trunks of which he watched the brown river racing past.

He lowered himself to all fours and crawled as close as he dared before flattening his body against the ground to minimize his profile. Although he couldn't see them, the subtle crunching of dead leaves and twigs announced the arrival of Darling and Simmons to either side of him.

Staley used his elbows to drag himself through the mud and studied the bank of the river down the sightline of his bullpup rifle. He saw some sort of animal. Four of them. Golden-brown fur, positively crawling with flies. Capybaras. Judging by the horrific smell and the bones protruding from beneath their pelts, they were already in advanced stages of decomposition, a state rarely seen in an environment like this with the preponderance of predators and scavengers, which never let a single morsel go to waste.

He suddenly recognized the implications.

The creature had used the carrion birds to lure them here.

Another cracking sound, barely audible over the rumble of the river.

It was a trap.

A shadow passed through the gaps between the leaves.

Staley swallowed hard. Concentrated on regulating his breathing. He was only going to get one shot at this. And if he missed . . .

He suppressed the thought and squirmed closer in maddeningly small increments. A gentle breeze ruffled the branches and he caught a glimpse of movement. A dark shape. Little more than a shifting of the shadows. It

passed through a pinprick column of light, revealing a
hint of pale gray skin. And then it was gone.

Crack.

Another few feet and he could clearly see the muddy
bank, bristling with wild grasses and ferns. The branches
of the trees on both sides of the river grew so densely
over the water that they shunted the sky.

Crack.

Staley looked to his right, through the proliferation of
leaves and vines, and saw it clearly for the first time. The
creature crouched at the edge of the forest with its hunched
back to him, balanced on its toes, its elongated skull
seemingly too large for its spindly form. It leaned forward and braced itself on its slender, sinewy arms. If ever
there had been anything remotely human about it, it was
long gone.

The creature stiffened. Raised its conical head. Cocked
it first one way, then the other.

It knew they were there.

Staley sighted down the base of its skull. A triple burst
from this distance and its cranium would simply vanish in
a red cloud.

The creature rounded on him, revealing a face out of
his nightmares. Its eyes were bulbous and round, a shade
of black so dark they appeared fathomless, and stood apart
from mutated features glistening with blood. Broad cheekbones tapered to a narrow chin. Its mouth formed a hideous expression reminiscent of a smile, only the teeth
resembled needles and were arranged in uneven rows.

Spread out upon the bloodied leaves and grass below it
were the carcasses of dozens of dead monkeys and vultures, their necks broken at obscene angles, their twitch-

ing appendages clawing and scratching uselessly at the ground. A black howler monkey with its mane torn away from a hideous gash on its throat looked up into the trees, its lips writhing as though trying to produce vocalizations that wouldn't come. It turned toward Staley and its spine realigned with a sickening *crack*. A rush of blood washed the whitish film from its eyes. It opened its mouth and issued an awful scream.

Subject Z spoke in a deep, resonant voice that seemed to echo from all around it at once.

"Have you come . . . to die?"

Staley shouted and pulled the trigger.

The creature moved in a blur and vanished into the foliage. Bullets pounded the bodies of the animals he was certain were dead, even as they struggled to rise from the ground.

Simmons yelled and fired a fusillade that shredded the vegetation. His war cry metamorphosed into a scream that abruptly ceased as his blood-spattered helmet rolled out from beneath the ferns.

"Fall back!" Staley shouted.

He turned and sprinted into the rainforest. Branches slashed at his face and chest, making it impossible to see. His foot snagged on a root and he went down hard. Pushed himself up from the slick mud, only to fall again.

Gunfire crackled from somewhere ahead of him, but when he looked up, it wasn't one of his fellow soldiers he saw.

A pair of long, thin legs protruded from the muck, their skin pallid and psoriatic, almost like the scales of a dead trout. The thighs and hips were corded with muscle. He followed the sculpted abdomen over a pair of bare breasts to the head of a stag. The deer's eyes had been removed, leaving ragged holes through which reptilian eyes with slit pupils stared.

A crashing sound from the underbrush beyond the figure. Koish screamed. His rifle clattered to the ground.

The woman looming over Staley had to be nearly seven feet tall. She reached up with her massive hands, curled her long fingers around the antlers, and lifted the mask from her head.

Staley's cries echoed through the jungle until, once more, only silence remained.

3
ANYA

The Hangar

The tomb in Mosul had been immediately sealed and the unknown biological agent determined to be "dangerous and exotic," a classification which meant that no one was taking any chances with it. Anya and Evans, along with every soldier who'd been within a quarter-mile of the scorched school, had been quarantined for seventy-two hours and subjected to a battery of painful and invasive tests, all of which had come back negative. During what Evans liked to call their forced vacation, the necropolis had been converted into a Biohazard Safety Level 4 containment facility and a hard-military cordon enforced at a one-mile radius. They'd been granted permission to return with the appropriate positive-pressure isolation suits, but only long enough to document the site.

In addition to photographing the underground cave from every conceivable angle, they'd used a FARO laser scanner to generate a perfect 3-D representation of each of the caverns, right down to the cobwebs hanging from the ceilings and the petroglyphs chiseled into the stone walls. They'd then sent the data files to one of Unit 51's

computer gurus, who'd spent the last six months converting their work into a virtual reality program that would
supposedly allow them to peruse the tombs at their lei-
sure.

Fortunately, they'd been allowed to collect various biological and bone-core samples that had survived the
sterilization process, which gave them something to work
on in the meantime. Had they known that the entire
necropolis would be subsequently "sanitized," which was
apparently the terminology used for obliterated from the
face of the planet, they would have been more aggressive
in their initial investigation. She understood they couldn't
risk an extremist faction like Al-Qaeda or a hostile state
like Iran gaining access to any kind of virulent biological
agent, although she couldn't help but wonder if it wasn't
all part of an elaborate cover-up to make sure that no one
found out about the nature of the bodies entombed within.

The Teleportation Room, as it was known, had been
constructed on the second sublevel of the Hangar specifically for VR viewing. There were four individual units,
each of which featured a circular railing and a treadmill-
like floor that moved in any direction to allow the viewer
to explore the virtual environment without worrying about
harming his or her corporeal form. The headset functioned in tandem with a rotating camera that detected the
viewer's movements, making it possible to incorporate
physical investigative techniques like crouching and leaning over objects. Everything about it was intimidating to
Anya, like voluntarily plugging herself into the Matrix,
until the goggles were on and she was magically transported into the Iraqi caverns.

Anya found herself in the antechamber. She could look
down and see the bones protruding from the dirt below

her where her feet should have been. The petroglyphs on the walls were even clearer than they had been in person, thanks to the various filters and digital enhancements the designer had applied. To say he'd done an amazing job was an understatement.

She exited the antechamber and passed through the room where the mutated remains lay contorted on the ground. The lab had been able to isolate a portion of the virus's DNA from bone cores, but the samples had been too degraded by the ravages of time to generate a complete genome. Based on what they could tell, however, the protein sequences were similar to those of hemorrhagic fevers like the Ebola and Marburg viruses. They'd been reluctant to commit beyond that, though. Of course, considering they'd finally discovered something capable of bringing down creatures like Subject Z, she had no doubt they were currently in a frenzy trying to revive and weaponize it.

Anya wanted no part of that. The mere thought of cooking up such nasty pathogens in a lab scared her on a primal level. There were undoubtedly countless similarly horrific primitive organisms frozen in the permafrost, just waiting to be thawed, though, so it was probably only a matter of humanity choosing the method of his demise. Her job was to determine the origin of the corpse entombed in the second chamber. Unlike those in the first, with their elongated craniums, bodily deformations, and clawed appendages, it was humanoid in form, if not dimension.

According to computer models, the man was a quarter-inch shy of seven feet tall. Based on the density of his bone samples, she estimated that his skeleton weighed nearly 150 pounds by itself. Assuming average human muscular proportions, his weight, while he was alive, had to have been at least 300 pounds. She wished she'd been able to run his mummified corpse through a CT scanner to provide a more in-depth analysis, but she was simply going to have to make do.

She felt oddly self-conscious turning sideways to squeeze through the crevice in the virtual wall and stepping over the creature's carcass. The remains tied to the plinth were so real she couldn't resist the urge to reach out and touch them, although her arm passed invisibly in front of her and her fingers grazed the safety rail. She leaned over the body and attempted to scrutinize it in the same manner as she would have in the field.

The man's joints demonstrated advanced cartilaginous wear with deterioration of the bones where they rubbed against each other, despite estimates placing him at some-where between thirty and forty years old at the time of his death, although any predictive models were based upon *Homo sapiens sapiens,* which this man, as evidenced by the sequenced portions of his genome, was clearly not. At least not entirely.

Anya spoke into a handheld audio recorder as she walked around the plinth. She hoped that articulation might some-how lead to the epiphany that had eluded her so far.

"The process of mummification has occurred by nat-ural means. There are no incisions in the vicinity of the abdomen to suggest evisceration or surgical excision of any of the organs." She crouched beside where the sub-ject's wrists and ankles had been bound to the floor by ropes. "The bindings have eroded through the flesh. Sub-sequent scoring on the bones themselves implies that the injuries were premortem."

"He was entombed while he was still alive?"

Anya shrieked and ripped off her goggles. Jade stood in the adjacent unit with the visor on and her arms stretched out in front of her. Anya had been so immersed in the virtual world that she hadn't heard the other woman enter.

"For the love of God, Jade. You nearly scared me to death."

She lowered her headset again and was transported right back to the tomb on the other side of the globe.

"Where are you looking?" Jade asked.

"On the right side of the plinth, where the wrist and ankle are bound."

"Good eye." It was strange to think that they were both crouching in the same place without being able to see each other. "Although I would be inclined to classify the injuries as perimortem based on the lack of callus formation."

Anya swelled with pride. Jade was their resident forensic expert and not one to casually offer a compliment, backhanded though it might have been.

"What brings you down here, Jade?"

"I was thinking about the contractures. They're caused by an attack on the central nervous system and aren't commonly associated with hemorrhagic fevers. Convulsions and contractures do accompany acute ventricular or meningeal inflammation, though."

"You don't agree with the lab's diagnosis?"

"I've studied their work. There are distinct similarities between the virus that killed these subjects and several modern hemorrhagic fevers; they just don't necessarily align with the physical presentation. Without the full genome, we can only speculate. And that's what worries me."

"The speculation?"

"The fact that somewhere out there is a disease capable

of overcoming nine of these creatures when we haven't been able to do that with the most advanced contemporary weapons at our disposal."

"The virus obviously didn't survive inside the necropolis or we would have been infected. It must have died with them."

"But if it didn't, there's potentially a virus out there capable of wiping out life as we know it."

"That's a pleasant thought."

"We need to figure out the mode of transmission. If it's blood-borne, then we can take precautions, but if it's airborne . . . ?"

She let the question hang between them. Anya fully understood the consequences if it were as transmissible as the common cold.

"This guy here didn't have it," Anya said.

"It's possible he died before the others were entombed in the outer chamber."

"It's also possible he possessed an immunity."

"Or he'd developed the antibodies," Jade said. "What kind of tests have they run on him?"

"You name it."

"Have they compared his genome against the sequenced portion of the virus's?"

"It's my understanding that they've compared it against every species in their database."

"And the results?"

"Ninety-nine-point-eight percent match with *Homo sapiens sapiens*. There are similarities in the remaining point-two percent to subspecies like *heidelbergensis* and *antecessor*, and archaic Ponginae like *Gigantopithecus*."

"But not the virus?"

"Not that I saw in the results."

"Have you dated the remains?"

"They're approximately three to four thousand years old," Anya said.

"What era is that? Sumerian?"

"More likely early Assyrian."

"And what happened to them?"

"They were conquered by the Babylonians."

"What about the hieroglyphics?"

"You'd have to ask Cade. Why? What are you thinking?"

"I'm not entirely sure," Jade said. "All I know for sure is that there has to be something we're missing."

Anya knew what she meant. This wasn't a traditional burial by any stretch of the imagination, even by the standards set by the previous discoveries of the tombs containing the remains of creatures like Subject Z, which spent countless hours carving the exact arrangement of the stars in the night sky into the walls and ceiling.

"Have they cultivated any tissue samples?" Jade asked.

"The skin's so desiccated you couldn't cultivate a pile of dust."

"What about the discolorations?"

"What discolorations?"

"Right there," Jade said, as though Anya could see her in the virtual world. "On his chest."

Anya leaned over the man's torso. The skin looked like greasy brown parchment paper wrapped over beef jerky. Jade was right. Some sections were subtly darker than others.

"I need more light," Anya said. She adjusted the dial on the side of her goggles, which brightened the overall picture, but washed out much of the contrast in the process. "I can't tell what it is."

"You saw the body in person, didn't you?"

"It was even darker than this, and we had people leaning over our shoulders the entire time, telling us to hurry up."

Anya dimmed the brightness again and used the adjacent dial to sharpen the contrast. The room around her darkened significantly, but the discolorations became just distinct enough that she could tell what they were.

"They're tattoos," she said.

"Are you sure it's not fixed hypostasis or pathologic process?" Jade asked.

"Dial up the contrast as high as it will go and see for yourself."

Several seconds passed in silence.

"Maybe," Jade eventually said. "If so, they didn't use ink."

"Back then they cut the skin with knives and rubbed charcoal into the wounds."

"You're sure of that?"

"That was the case with Ötzi the Iceman, the mummy they found in the Italian Alps in the nineties. His tattoos were so faded they had to use advanced imaging techniques just to differentiate them from his skin."

"What did they show?"

"The majority were just clusters of parallel lines."

"Did they determine the significance?"

"There are several theories. Why?"

"Because here we have a man of unknown origin bound to a stone altar in a chamber adjacent to a cavern filled with the mutated bodies of creatures killed by an extremely virulent pathogen. I would imagine that if this man were held captive down there long enough to worry the ropes through his flesh and into the bones of his wrists and ankles, he was probably alive long enough to be tattooed, as well. And if that were the case, then surely whatever design was permanently incorporated into his skin would be of no small significance."

Anya looked at the remains for several moments before taking off her goggles. When she turned, Jade was looking right at her.

"You just might be right."

4
TESS

Dr. Theresa Clarke couldn't get over how close she'd come to dying. It was a crippling sensation that crept up on her and brought her to the verge of tears when she least expected it. There had been a part of her that subconsciously believed she was invincible, or perhaps merely that she would be spared the fate that had befallen so many others. When Director Barnett had shown up at her door to recruit her, he'd laid all of his cards on the table so that if she chose to join his team, she did so with her eyes wide open. She'd understood that people had died where she was going, and yet the event had a historical quality to it, like the echo of a battle long since fought and won. Or maybe the prospect of working with an alien organism had been all she needed to blind herself to the fact that it had been directly responsible for the deaths of more than twenty scientists just like her.

And now it was out there on the loose.

She wasn't so narcissistic as to believe that any of the events culminating in the escape of Subject Z had been her fault, or even that there had ever been a point where she could have stopped them, but she had willingly taken on the burden of making sure that they captured it before it could inflict any more harm. Each passing day, however, brought her closer to conceding that there was nothing she could do to aid in its capture, despite her best efforts to predict its ultimate destination. There were simply too many variables, and for the life of her, she couldn't divine the one that would lead them to it.

Motive had to be the key.

Surely there was something it wanted. Otherwise, it could have just vanished into the wilderness and they never would have found it again. It could have easily slaughtered an entire village under the cover of darkness, yet it chose to subsist upon whatever animals it could catch and kill, and rather than creating a veritable army of drones, it had decided to minimize its numbers in an effort to travel largely undetected, which suggested that reaching its final destination was of the utmost importance. What was waiting for it there? Other creatures like itself or something more sinister? All she knew was that whatever it was, their primary imperative was to ensure that it never reached its goal.

And then there was the matter of its traveling companion, which no one seemed to want to talk about. What in the name of God had been inside that sarcophagus? How had Subject Z brought it back from the dead, and for what purpose?

In her previous life, she'd helped refine a system of remote sensing technologies that kicked open countless doors for the burgeoning field of satellite archeology. She'd discovered ancient ruins in some of the most remote regions on the planet, where no humans had ever been known to tread, and beneath the dense jungles that had grown over them. Structures that weren't even visible to someone standing right on top of them or were buried underneath the silt at the bottom of the sea. Every university had wanted her and every energy exploration company had bid on her services. She could have done anything she wanted with her life, but what had she done instead? She'd turned her satellites outward, toward other planets, and set about demolishing what had once been the most promising of careers. Worse, if given the opportunity, she would do the same thing all over again.

There were four touchscreen monitors mounted behind her desk, all of them larger than her television at home. She'd set up each for a specific purpose. The first showed the digital map of the constellations Subject Z had carved into the walls and ceiling of the cavern that served as its cage, only the actual stars had been subtracted, leaving those that didn't correspond to the sky on the night of September twenty-first of the previous year. It was among this remainder that she'd discovered the map that led them to Teotihuacan and a brush with Enigma— the heavily armed paramilitary organization that seemed to know far more about the events unfolding around them than they did—which had nearly cost Anya, Jade, and Evans their lives.

The second monitor featured an ordinary satellite photo of the Ecuadorian rainforest, beside which, on the third monitor, was an infrared image of the same terrain, to which she'd applied an algorithm that removed the jungle itself and revealed the shallow subterranean features buried beneath the soil. The fourth monitor utilized the same type of imagery, only applied to the surface of Mars, upon which she'd detected features strangely similar to those buried beneath the Antarctic ice cap.

And yet with all of this information at her fingertips,

she couldn't figure out where the creature was going. She could feel the answer staring her right in the face, but she couldn't make the connection.

"Tess?" She jumped at the sound of the voice behind her and turned to see Anya peeking through the door from the hallway. "I knocked, but . . ."

Tess recovered from the surprise and smiled.

"Lost in thought. You know how it is."

"I can't think without getting lost anymore. It's like for every problem we solve, we create a dozen more. Which is kind of why I'm here. I was hoping I might be able to pick your brain."

"Pick away," Tess said and plopped down in the chair behind her desk. She welcomed the distraction, if only because it reminded her that she hadn't touched her coffee.

Anya hovered in the entryway, staring at the monitors above Tess's head.

"I was thinking about how you use that program of yours to detect man-made structures that aren't apparent from the ground."

"It's really just a matter of combining magnetometry and infrared imaging to create a gradient scale of the superficial strata. The program assigns color values for each vertical increment, uses an algorithm to define them, and cleans the whole thing up. The computer does all of the work."

"Do you think you could use the same kind of algorithm to differentiate subtle discolorations on someone's skin that aren't readily apparent to the naked eye?"

Tess cocked her head and appraised Anya from the corner of her eye.

"Show me."

"Way ahead of you. I already uploaded the data and sent a shortcut to your inbox."

Tess opened her internal e-mail account, clicked Anya's link and found herself transported to a raw data file that looked like little more than an infinite string of numbers and incoherent commands.

"I'm not sure what you expect me to do with this."

"You said your program assigned color values to different gradients on a satellite image, right? Wouldn't it be possible to do the same thing with a three-dimensional laser scan?"

"How dark are the discolorations?"

"They were made by rubbing charcoal into lacerations on the skin."

"And the skin itself?"

"Not a whole lot different."

Tess closed her eyes to better appreciate the problem. If she substituted a shortened color scale for all of the values darker than that encoded for the skin tone, she ought to be able to create a veritable rainbow of colors distinct from it. She opened her eyes again and set to work running the data through a Fourier Transform and various filters before applying the final algorithm. The resulting data didn't look much different on the computer screen, but she had no doubt that the final image would be greatly altered. It took a few minutes to convert the massive data file into a visible image on her computer screen.

"Voilà," she said and spun the monitor around so Anya could see it.

The expression on the anthropologist's face changed from excitement to confusion.

"What is it?" Anya asked.

"I don't know."

Tess walked around to the front of her desk and took a seat beside Anya. The resulting image appeared in bright shades of orange and yellow. It had an iridescent quality, almost as though it shimmered with metallic blues and greens. While somewhat distorted by the uneven stretching of the mummified skin, the pattern was still largely intact, although what it was remained a mystery. To Tess, it looked like little more than a series of circles of varying diameter connected by a horizontal line. Some of the circles were contained within larger rings. Random designs protruded at odd angles from several: a trident, a bent tuning fork, and a three-toothed comb. If there were some deep symbolic meaning, it eluded her.

"Sorry I can't be of more help," Tess said.

"No, really. I appreciate everything you've done. We would never have been able to see this if it weren't for you." Anya sighed. "It's just . . . I don't know. Based on the way we theorize the subject was tattooed while he was restrained and entombed, we thought it might be a warning of some kind, a message pertaining to the disease that killed all of the creatures like Zeta."

"I'll run the design through the database and see if it turns up anything."

"Thanks," Anya said. She looked completely dejected as she rose and headed for the door.

"Anya?"

The younger woman turned and looked back at her from the doorway.

"We'll get Zeta," Tess said.

Anya smiled, but there was no warmth in the expression.

"Maybe, but how many more people have to die before we do?" She nodded and ducked into the hallway. "How many will die if we don't?"

5

BARNETT

Reserva Extrativista do Rio Jutaí,
State of Amazonas,
Brazil

Following Subject Z's trail through the Amazon rain-forest was an exercise in futility. The dense jungle made it impossible to move at a decent click, let alone see for any distance in any direction. The flooded wetlands concealed anything resembling footprints in the mulch, and every animal that crossed their path seemed to have a personal stake in their misery. The snakes they could handle—at least the ones they could see—with a machete and a flick of the wrist. The insects, however, were something else entirely. There was no break from their assault, not even while he and his team attempted to sleep inside the supposedly impenetrable netting. They ran fevers more often than not, although it was impossible to determine whether they were actually sick or merely overheating in their fatigues from the oppressive humidity.

Barnett had once believed that they would be able to find and eliminate Subject Z but now understood the reality of the situation: If the creature wanted to hide from them, there was no way on this planet they would ever

find it in the hundreds of thousands of square miles of im-
pregnable forests and swamps. There were still primitive
tribes and species of animals that had yet to come into
contact with modern man. Their best satellites couldn't
pierce the canopy with anything close to useful resolution, and even thermal imaging was limited to little more
than line-of-sight. They were practically flying blind and
falling farther behind by the day. Assuming they were even
still on its trail.

They'd lost Subject Z twice before, but ultimately
picked up signs of its passage from the air. While it could
conceal its tracks, it couldn't hide its appetite, nor could
the carrion birds that had ultimately drawn them to the
carnage left in its wake. It seemed to have developed a
taste for capybaras, or perhaps the dog-sized rodents
were the only prey large enough to leave behind carcasses worth the scavengers' time. There were any number of animals along the way that could be easily enough
caught and consumed, which meant that they couldn't entirely dismiss the idea that Subject Z was deliberately
stringing them along and could be lying in wait behind
the trunk of any tree they passed or preparing to pounce
from the branches overhead.

Barnett wasn't the only one who sensed it, either. He
could see it in the eyes of his men and in the physical toll
it was taking on them. They could only live like this for
so long. Sleeping in shifts. Subsisting on air-dropped rations and fruit they collected from the trees. Drinking by
the drop from wet leaves and trudging for days at a time
without seeing the sky.

They'd learned to be grateful for times like this, when
they could feel the movement of air beneath their damp
clothes and the caress of the sun upon their features. They'd

picked up the creature's trail near Jutaí and then again on
the northern bank of the Rio Solimões, a path that continued to lead them roughly fifteen degrees west of due
north, the same inclination as the arrangement of the
pyramids in both Teotihuacan and Giza. Extrapolated *ad
infinitum,* it would eventually take them through Ecuador
and Colombia, and into Panama, the gateway to North
America. Assuming it didn't reach its ultimate goal first.

With any luck, Staley's team would at least drive Subject Z back downstream toward them, if not outright
eliminate it, and they'd be able to put an end to it once
and for all. The thought of curling up in his own bed at
this same time tomorrow was almost more than he could
bear. The problem was that they were nearly to their rendezvous point and had yet to see the prearranged smoke
signal that indicated the other unit had secured the site.

The motor of the wooden boat chugged and issued a
steady stream of exhaust that clung to the brown water
behind them. The smell of petrol was thick enough to
make them queasy, but the ability to be dry and out of the
infernal jungle was worth infinitely more than the price
they'd paid for the decrepit vessel.

Capuchin monkeys chittered from the dense canopies
of the trees overhanging the winding river, which joined
with the Rio Negro near Manaus to become the mighty
Amazon. Macaws and chicken-like hoatzins screeched
from the upper reaches. Black caimans basked on the
muddy shores and drifted lazily on the current. Green
anacondas as thick as tree trunks slithered through the
shallows. They'd even seen one attempting to choke down
what looked like a small deer, judging by the hooved legs
protruding from its dislocated jaws.

Morgan monitored their progress via GPS on his tablet, which featured a satellite uplink that allowed them to remain in contact with the Hangar for several hours in the morning, while the satellite was still within range. For all the good it did them. The scientists back at Joint Base Langley-Eustis needed to earn their keep and figure out where the blasted creature was heading. Until they did, he was beginning to think that there was nothing any of them could do to stop it.

"We're close," Morgan said. He glanced at the map and then at the river ahead of them. "Looks like just around the next bend."

"And still no sign of our men," Barnett said.

Brinkley and Sheppard readjusted their grips on their bullpup assault rifles and watched the jungle pass down their short sightlines. Barnett killed the outboard motor. The boat drifted at the mercy of the current. The river narrowed, and the branches of the trees knitted together above them. The resulting shade was easily fifteen degrees cooler and emboldened the swarming mosquitoes, which swirled in the columns of light that pierced the canopy. The squawking of birds and chirruping of frogs diminished so subtly that he didn't notice until they were gone entirely.

Barnett shifted onto his knees to improve his range of motion and seated his rifle against his shoulder.

The river bent completely back upon itself, essentially creating an enormous blind spot. Satellite imagery had shown an unusual number of vultures perched in the upper canopy and wheeling above the treetops, as it had on several other occasions in the past.

This time was different, though. He could feel it. The hairs on the backs of his arms stood erect, and his heartbeat thumped in his ears. Something had frightened away every other animal in the forest, or perhaps it was merely the reek of death that hit him hard enough to make him wince.

The buzzing of flies guided them into the next bend, where furry carcasses stood out from the bank like ant-hills. The flies formed angry clouds above the remains, which had been there for some time judging by the amount of decomposition and the bones protruding from the sloughed flesh. The boat was nearly upon them by the time Barnett was able to tell that they were capybaras, or at least what was left of them, although with as many vultures as he'd seen on satellite, there shouldn't have been so much as a shred of skin remaining.

The flies.

They filled the air and crawled all over the surrounding ferns, and yet there wasn't a single one of them on any of the bodies. It was almost as though . . .

Something was wrong with the capybaras.

Barnett recognized their mistake too late. He looked straight up into the canopy. Dark, hunched shapes filled the interwoven branches of the ceiba, rubber, and mangrove trees. He could feel the weight of their eyes upon him, sense the sheer malevolence radiating from them.

There was no time to sound a warning.

He raised his rifle and fired up into the trees as they came to life with guttural hoots and avian screams. Black howlers hurled themselves into the open air and plummeted straight toward them. Vultures folded their wings to their sides and dive-bombed the boat.

The air rained blood as their bullets tore through the furry bodies and sent them cartwheeling into the water. Those that survived the fusillade landed in the boat and hurled themselves at the men with slashing arms and snapping teeth.

Barnett grabbed one by the scruff of its neck and pulled it away from Brinkley's throat. It rounded on him with a dark sentience in its eyes that Barnett would have recognized anywhere. Were it possible, the infected creature appeared to smile at him before he pulled the trigger and its head disintegrated into a crimson mist.

A buzzard struck his helmet with its beak and managed to carve through the meat of his shoulder with its talons before he snapped its wing and flung it into the river. It kicked a half-circle before a shot from Sheppard's weapon drove it beneath the surface.

Morgan caught a vulture by the neck and wrung it. He would have missed the howler monkey about to land on his shoulder had Barnett not put a bullet through its breast.

By the time they were able to catch their breath, the river behind them flowed red and spotted with feathers. Brinkley's cheek had been opened to the bare bone and Morgan wore a mask of blood from the parallel lacerations across his forehead. Outside of the stinging gouges in his shoulder, Barnett had to consider himself lucky to have only superficial wounds on his neck and face from those blasted monkeys, one of which had bitten off the first two fingers on Sheppard's left hand. He cradled it to his chest in an attempt to stanch the bleeding.

A roaring sound erupted from the upper canopy.

Barnett whirled to see a howler monkey staring down at him, its black mane flared and its wide mouth framing a belch-like howl. To either side of it, balanced on the branches, were the heads of the men who'd been sent to rendezvous with them. They'd never stood a chance.

Another being watched them through the eyes of the black howler until the boat rounded the bend and was lost to sight.

Subject Z had set a trap for them. It had lured them into a confrontation in an attempt to clear its path, but at least now they knew they were close. It couldn't have been more than four or five hours ahead of them, and, if Barnett was right, it just might have tipped its hand.

He cranked the outboard motor to life and accelerated out of the bend. They needed to take advantage of the speed with which they could travel on the river for as long as they could if they were going to catch up with the creature. There was no doubt in his mind that things were only going to get worse from here.

6
KELLY

The Hangar

Dr. Kelly Nolan went aboveground as often as she could. The deserted hangars and runways were deliberately left in a state of disrepair to maintain the illusion of abandonment. Weeds grew from the cracked tarmac, and vines had overtaken some of the smaller outbuildings. The astringent scent of jet fuel radiated from the ground itself, and the ceaseless air traffic provided a constant grating drone, but at least she could feel the movement of air and the warmth of the sun on her face. She was also close enough to the coast that she could smell the sea, if not hear its eternal restless movements, which was both a blessing and a curse.

It reminded her of home.

There were days when she wanted nothing more than to return to Oregon, where she could wander along the rocky shoreline listening to the waves break against the cliffs and the drizzle patter her windbreaker, to smell the rich brine and feel the buildup of salt on her skin. The sense of loss was a physical sensation that could never be fully dispelled, only minimized by her increasingly infrequent sojourns beneath the blue sky.

She arrived at the Hangar before the sun even hinted at its ascension and left under the stars, if she even left at all. While she loved her work, it wasn't enough for her. She needed more, and that's what she had expected when she'd made the decision to move to the East Coast. Roche had promised to be here with her, and while he hadn't technically broken that promise, the part of him that she loved, that saw her for who she truly was, had never arrived. She wasn't so self-centered that she couldn't see the pressure he was under, which he, in turn, amplified a hundredfold, but he didn't have to bear that burden alone. He thought he was protecting her, when he was really just driving her away. She wasn't sure who she was madder at: him for distancing himself from her or herself for letting him.

With any luck they would capture Subject Z before it caused any more suffering. And when they did, either the Martin Roche, who didn't even realize how deeply she'd fallen for him, would return, or she was going to have to make some hard decisions. Being so close to him only served as a painful reminder of what could have been.

Kelly allowed her gaze to linger on the dandelions growing from the tarmac before entering a hangar that looked like it would be leveled by a stiff breeze, assuming the rust didn't finish the job first. A maze of water-damaged wooden crates led to an interior wall that looked like any other, with the exception of the retina scanner concealed inside the rusted breaker box.

She allowed the laser to do its thing and stepped back. The false wall receded and slid to the side, revealing a stainless-steel elevator. There were no buttons, only a microphone that received voice commands and translated them into a digital sound wave on the embedded screen. Not only did the security system analyze the voiceprint as a secondary form of authentication, but there were also sensors in the ceiling that measured body heat and scanned for infectious biological agents. She didn't know exactly what would happen if someone were to trigger the fail-safes, but the aerial dispersion nozzles weren't so well hidden that she couldn't make an educated guess.

The door closed behind her. She turned to face the mirror-like surface and spoke to her reflection."Level One."

She still wasn't used to the silver-lavender hair or the brick-red eye shadow, but those weren't the only reasons she felt like she was confronting a stranger. It was almost a relief when the door opened upon the brightly lit, sterile corridor. She could hear Roche snoring from behind the closed door of the conference room, but headed for her office instead.

Tess was sitting on the wrong side of her desk with her back to the door when Kelly entered. For as much time as both of them spent down here, they were rarely in the office at the same time. Or maybe they were so lost in their own work that they didn't even notice when the other was in the room.

Kelly noticed the picture on the screen in front of Tess and couldn't help but smile.

"He got to you, too," she said.

"Who did?" Tess asked. Her eyes were bloodshot when she turned around.

"Martin."

"What do you mean 'got to me'?"

Kelly gestured to the monitor.

"Duh . . . the crop circle."

"That's not what this is. It's the tattoo from the body Anya found in the tomb in Mosul."

"I don't know about that, but I can tell you with complete certainty that what you're looking at there, that design? It's a crop circle from Alton Barnes, Wiltshire. Martin had pictures of all of them hanging on the walls of his workshop in England."

"You're sure it's the same design," Tess said.

"I guess I couldn't swear to it in a court of law, but I know someone who could."

Tess was already on her feet when Kelly turned and headed down the hallway toward the conference room outside of Director Barnett's office, which apparently moonlighted as Roche's new home. He didn't even stir when she opened the door. He was curled up on his side with his face to the cushions and his left arm pinning a pillow over his head. She felt awful about waking him since she knew how little sleep he was getting, but he was going to want to see this.

She placed her hand on his shoulder and gently shook him.

"Martin?"

Another shake and he rested his hand on top of hers. Softly. He mumbled something and rolled onto his back. A contented smile formed on his face, only the bottom half of which was visible beneath the pillow.

"There you are," he whispered and drew her hand to his chest.

"Martin?"

His expression suddenly changed, and he bolted from the couch so quickly he nearly knocked her over.

"What's wrong? Did they find Zeta?"

"No, nothing like that," Kelly said. "There's something we need to show you."

Roche nodded and followed them back down the hallway, rubbing his eyes the whole way. He recognized the design the moment they entered Kelly's office.

"Alton Barnes, Wiltshire. July 11, 1990."

"Was I right or what?" Kelly said.

"But what does it mean?" Tess asked. "That was thousands of years after the body was tattooed."

"What body?" Roche asked.

Kelly called down to the VR lab while Tess explained how she had isolated the tattoo from the raw data used to build the virtual re-creation of the tomb in Iraq and how Anya and Jade believed the design had been deliberately inflicted upon the remains as a warning to whoever discovered them. By the time she was done, Anya and Jade had arrived, with Evans in tow.

"We can only guess at its true meaning," Roche said. "It doesn't match the physical representation of a sound frequency, like the crop circles that helped open the temple in Antarctica, nor does it appear to be the key to solving a maze. Researchers have theorized everything from a form of communication similar to Morse code to a chemical formula of some kind."

Tess furrowed her brow for a moment, then rushed around her desk and printed out a copy of the tattoo. "What about a map?" She stood beside the monitor that showed the design Subject Z had carved into the walls of the cavern that served as its cage and held up the paper beside it, but there wasn't a match. "I thought maybe . . ."

She set the printout aside, returned to the monitor, and leaned on the backs of the chairs between Roche and Jade.

"What are your thoughts, Anya?" Roche asked.

"I've been looking into every style of writing from that time frame, but all of them are of a linear style derived from cuneiform. I can't find a single one that uses anything resembling circles, let alone different variations of them."

"Jade?"

"I'm convinced the design was tattooed within days— at most—of the man's death. The wounds appear to have been inflicted more recently than those on his hands and wrists."

"So you're convinced it's a message," Roche said.

"Stands to reason," Evans said. "What we don't know, however, is whether or not those remains were interred before or after the creatures were sealed inside with whatever virus killed them."

Kelly picked up the paper and stared at the design. Her left hand fretted faster and faster at her side, as though a physical manifestation of her thought processes. Previous crop circles had helped them decode special sound frequencies and guided them to a sarcophagus containing a potentially alien life-form nearly identical to the one in Iraq, and just like the one Subject Z had liberated from Antarctica upon its escape. The idea that this design might be a map wasn't so far-fetched, but she feared they lacked the skills to interpret it.

She tuned out the others and went to her workstation. The monitors still displayed detailed images of South America beside a map of various major and minor fault lines and areas of tectonic activity. She used the mouse to expand the map, highlighted an area over the Middle East, and zoomed in until she was able to see the city of Mosul. The screen was just bright enough to show through the paper when she pressed it against the monitor. She placed the largest circle over the city, but all of the other circles aligned with locations in the middle of nowhere. The slope of the horizontal line—straight in the middle and curved downward at either end—roughly approximated the course of the Zagros Mountains, which ran through northern Iraq and into southern Turkey. The same was true of the Bitlis Suture of the Arabian Tectonic Plate that had helped to form them. If she aligned the dots and the line connecting them with the fault line—

And then she saw it.

If she placed the smaller dot offset to the right—the one that looked like a bull's-eye—on top of Mosul, the remainder followed the fault line. One of the circles almost aligned with the city of Nusaybin, another with Gaziantep, but the remainder fell upon nothing. She'd been so sure . . .

"Can you bring up another map?" Evans asked from behind her.

Kelly glanced back and saw the excitement on his face.

"Of course. Anywhere on Earth."

"How about any *time*?"

She stared at him curiously for a moment before she realized what he was thinking and bent over her keyboard.

"How far back?" she asked.

"Jade?" Evans said.

"Three, maybe four thousand years," Jade said.

Evans turned back to Kelly, who was already typing. A search returned maps from ancient Sumer, Akkadia, Assyria, and Babylon. She clicked on the one closest to the time frame of interest and transferred it to the big screen.

The matches were apparent for all to see. She held up the printout, which, after shrinking the map just a touch, aligned perfectly.

The bull's-eye didn't correspond with Mosul, but rather the ancient city of Nineveh. The small dot beside it was Kalah. The larger circles represented Gozan, Haran, and Karkemish. The trailing dots at the far left aligned with Arpad, Ebla, and Charqar. Only the central circle inside the ring didn't match a city on the archaic map, which didn't seem to bother Evans at all. If anything, his smile had grown even wider.

"What?" Kelly asked.

"Anyone else up for a trip to Turkey?"

7

ARELLANO

22 miles south of Calamar,
Colombia

What passed for a road was actually a dry riverbed that became impassible by vehicle during the wet season. It was barely wider than the panel truck's tires, which bounced unevenly over the smooth stones. The suspension screamed and the overhanging branches scratched the sides of the cargo hold with a constant screeching sound. Precious little moonlight penetrated the dense canopy, barely enough to limn the damp rocks and the broad leaves of the rubber and palm trees with an almost ethereal glow. He'd driven this route enough times to know it by rote, not that it was really such an amazing accomplishment. Once the tires were slotted between the banks, there was nowhere to get back out until he reached the camp.

The men waiting for him were the reason Emilio Arellano had lost his faith in humanity. He was a minor criminal by comparison, an opportunist, little more than a scavenger picking at the carcass of their excess. These men, on the other hand, were a different breed of monster that had risen from the vacuum of power created by the

fall of the Medellín Cartel and the wars between the
Colombian military and various guerilla factions. Bloque
Meta had learned savagery from the Mexican cartels and
greed from the privatized corporations that controlled the
main shipping ports, a fact that necessitated a measure of
creativity when it came to the distribution of its product,
which was where Arellano came in.

There was really no such thing as interstate trucking in
this part of the world. Prohibitive taxes, geography, and
border hassles made it more trouble than it was worth,
except for the few Panamanian companies that imported
the American agricultural products that accounted for
nearly three-quarters of Colombia's imports. While the
majority entered by sea, a growing portion arrived via the
Panama Canal thanks to recent construction that increased its size to accommodate neo-Panamax bulk container carriers that could haul more than twice as much
cargo, which allowed for the consolidation of shipping
lanes between the American East Coast and Asia. The
massive ships barely paused long enough to unload a
fraction of their tonnage onto docks bristling with cranes,
where Arellano waited patiently with his refrigerated
truck.

He loaded the tripe into the back, drove to Colón,
where he boarded one of the RORO—roll-on/roll-off—
barges to bypass the Darién Gap, and delivered it to a
wholesale warehouse in Barranquilla. The men who un-
loaded his truck didn't even take the time to hose out the
bed before packing it full of coffee beans and bananas
and sending him on his way back to Cartagena, where he
would drive onto another RORO bound once more for
Panama. The overwhelming scents of blood and coffee
beans confounded the dogs in the port and the guards had

dealt with him so many times that they were on a first-name basis. There was no reason for them to open up the back and dig through the enormous stacks of beans and bananas for the bricks of cocaine hidden at the back, which would be halfway around the world in another seventy-two hours.

Arellano caught a flicker of light from the corner of his eye, but by the time he turned it was gone. He shouldn't have been close enough to see their bonfire yet. He was still at least five minutes out. Come to think of it, though, he should have seen the sentries posted beside the dry riverbed by now. Maybe they were getting better at hiding, although he'd always figured that the presence of hardened men with AK-47s was meant more as a show of force than an early warning system.

Another flash of light from the dense jungle.

It almost looked like the discharge of an automatic weapon in the distance. He rolled down his window and listened, but couldn't hear a blasted thing over the sound of the branches raking the sides of his truck. Firing off a few drunken rounds was one thing, but if they were executing someone in that camp, he wanted no part of it. He'd watched them flay his predecessor before dousing him with gasoline, setting him on fire, and kicking him while he crawled through the dirt, bleating like a dying goat. That had been more than enough to convince Arellano not to skim so much as a single gram. Hell, he didn't even pinch the occasional banana anymore, which was probably why they left him to his business when he arrived. Either that or they didn't want him getting a good look at any of their faces, which was totally fine by him. The less he knew, the more valuable he was.

He smelled the smoke from the fire before it material-

ized from the darkness. The surrounding rubber trees concealed the old guerilla training camp of the AUC—United
Self-Defense Forces of Colombia—until he was nearly
on top of it. The windows of the wooden buildings were
boarded over to conceal the electric lights inside. The
chugging of the gas generator sounded labored and issued a plume of black smoke that clung like a mist to the
bare ground at the bend. His tires thumped on the wooden
ramp, which always made snapping sounds, yet somehow miraculously held the truck's weight.

He pulled in beside the firepit, then backed around it
until his tailgate faced the door of the nearest structure.

"¡Hola!" he called out the window. He killed the engine, opened his door, and hopped down into the dirt.
"Estoy aqui para recoger mi entrega."

He closed his door. The echo sounded almost like a
gunshot. He walked around to the rear, unlocked the
hatch, and swung open the twin doors. Several bunches
of bananas fell to the ground at his feet. He brushed them
off on his shirt before returning them to their overturned
crates and once more stacking them neatly. He pulled out
the ramp, climbed inside, and made a path through his
cargo so he could reach the deepest part of the bed, where
the leftover blood had already summoned damn near
every fly in the jungle.

"¡Estoy listo!" he shouted.

Arellano was torn between wanting to make sure they
knew he was here and trying to keep from startling someone who might have had a little too much to drink and his
finger a little too close to the trigger. Between the women
processing the coca leaves, the guards, and the supervi-
sory honchos, there had to be at least a dozen people in
the camp at any given time, sometimes even more if he

counted the men he occasionally heard crying from the stables, begging for their lives to be spared.

Not tonight, though. Everything was silent. Only the crackling and popping of the logs in the firepit.

He didn't have all night. He needed to have his cargo in Colón in less than sixteen hours if they hoped to get the loads sorted and into the proper containers without arousing suspicion. He'd gotten used to making up the time on the road from Calamar to Cartagena, but this old truck could only go so fast. Probably best to just go ahead and start loading. Surely someone would return at any minute. The last thing he wanted was to go looking for them and stumble blindly upon them while they were immolating some poor bastard.

The door to the processing room was closed. He knocked and waited for a response. The women inside worked in the nude so they could be trusted not to steal from their employers, who deliberately hired the most unattractive specimens they could find to make sure business and pleasure never conflicted. The arrangement made him uncomfortable, even though he did his best not to let his gaze wander, which applied equally to everywhere in the camp.

When no one answered, he entered and immediately turned to his left, where the bricks were wrapped in duct tape, stacked from the floor to the ceiling, and sorted by load. Each had a series of numbers and letters for tracking purposes. He identified his load, grabbed as much as he could carry, and hustled it out to his truck. Thumped up the ramp, traversed the narrow aisle, and started stacking. Went back inside for more. One trip after another until each of the rear corners had a collection of bricks stacked ten wide, ten deep, and ten high. He draped the cargo nets attached to the frame over them and slid the bagged coffee beans up against them to hold them in place.

Arellano had thought for sure someone would have acknowledged him by the time he was done securing his load. He probably would have been fine just driving away, but he knew he'd spend every waking second between now and his next pickup stressing over the consequences of potentially having violated some unwritten protocol. Better to just track someone down now and hope to God they weren't in a trigger-happy mood. Surely, he could avoid any confrontation by simply asking one of the women laboring inside to pass along his message. The men would appreciate him not interrupting whatever they were doing. Or so he convinced himself.

He headed back into the building, only this time he passed the room filled with cocaine, turned right toward the production center—

And stopped dead in his tracks.

Crimson spatters stood apart from the scattered cocaine like roses in a snowstorm. The woman sprawled in the mess looked like she'd been attacked by a wild animal. Her back had been opened to expose the crescents of her ribs and the knobs of her spine. The curtains that served as a door to the storage room in the back stood open, revealing arcs of blood draining down the wall above the drums of caustic lime and gasoline.

He opened his mouth to cry out, but clapped his hands over it before he could do so. Whoever did this to her could still be nearby.

Arellano spun and sprinted from the building. He knocked over a stack of bricks and tripped over them.

Landed squarely on his chest. Pushed himself up from the stoop.

A man looked back at him from the shrubs to his left. His face was awash with blood from the parallel lacerations that divided it into sections of retracted skin and bare bone. Another man's legs protruded from the bonfire, where his Kalashnikov smoldered.

This time, Arellano couldn't contain his scream.

He scrambled back to his truck. Climbed in. Gunned the engine. Punched the stick into gear and stomped the gas to the floor.

The truck lurched ahead. Hit the ramp at an angle. Nearly toppled to its side before righting itself against the wall of trees on the opposite side of the riverbed, hitting them hard enough to knock a corpse from the underbrush. The rear tires bounced over it and his cargo slammed against the wall.

The tires caught on the loose stones and the rear doors slammed closed. The bumper careened from the bank and he entered the straightaway going way too fast, but he didn't care.

Behind him, the crates and sacks shifted and rocked and bounced from the floor and walls. And he heard scratching, which he tuned out as the branches scraping the sides of his truck while he prayed that the people who slaughtered everyone in the camp didn't come for him.

8
ROCHE

The Hangar

The virtual reality was hugely disorienting at first. Roche had been unprepared for the extent to which his mind bought into the digital world. It felt like he was actually inside the tomb in Iraq as Anya and Evans had originally found it, and yet simultaneously apart from it. When he looked down, he saw only dirt, rubble, and debris where his legs should have been, and nearly stumbled in real life trying to walk across what looked like an uneven floor. He had to resign himself to keeping his eyes straight ahead to prevent his primitive hindbrain from focusing on the details it couldn't rationalize. After a few minutes, though, he started to get the hang of it. The trick, he realized, lay in embracing the illusion.

There were a few spots around the room where the data was either missing or corrupted, leading to areas where there were simply black holes, but the remainder of the necropolis was nearly flawless. He found himself physically brushing away cobwebs that weren't there and ducking underneath overhangs where his head would have bumped against the stone roof in real life. It was almost impossible to believe that he could examine every detail in three dimensions and yet couldn't touch or hold it. He understood what the technology's detractors meant when they said people would enter these virtual worlds and never return. There would be whole generations that would willingly go down these rabbit holes and find realms far better than the one in which they lived, entire realities from which they had no desire to ever leave.

That wasn't why he'd come down to the VR lab, though. Nor was it just idle curiosity. The fact that the ancient tattoo matched a crop circle formed thousands of years later couldn't be a coincidence. If Jade was right about the tattoo being left as a warning to whoever had the misfortune of finding the sealed tomb, then it had to be more than just a map. There had to be some deeper meaning, and if anyone could find it, it was him.

Truth be told, he needed something other than tracking Subject Z to occupy his mind before he lost it.

He'd seen all of the pictures taken during the initial documentation, but there had been a sterility to them that vanished inside the virtual realm. The body was just how it had appeared on Tess's monitor, only seeing it in true-to-life dimensions reminded him of how tall the man actually was and how much pain he must have endured before his passing. Roche wished they could have removed the eagle mask so he could have seen the man's face, but he supposed that if he had found a corpse potentially riddled with disease, he probably wouldn't have been in any hurry to mess with it, either.

It served as a good starting point from which to begin his virtual exploration. While he didn't know much about ancient peoples specifically, he understood them well enough to know that the petroglyphs they carved into the walls of their tombs weren't just for decoration. They told stories in some way germane to the subject entombed with them. These were incredibly illustrative, although not so much in what they showed, but in what they didn't. The few designs on the sandstone walls were unevenly spaced and appeared rushed, as though whoever carved them had been in a big hurry to either get the tomb ready for its occupant, or to get the hell out of there. Judging by the bodies of the creatures with the elongated craniums, he figured it was most likely the former. He couldn't imagine anyone with big enough cojones to do his work with those hideous corpses lying at his feet, which meant the designs had been rushed to get the tomb ready for its occupant, or perhaps they'd even been carved while the tall man was tied up and dying on the plinth. Either way, the creatures had to have come later, which suggested they'd somehow been lured inside.

"Taking a break from the real world?"

Roche jumped at the sound of the voice and ripped off his headset. Maddox stood in the adjacent ring, his arms extended as he walked on the rolling pad.

"They should really make this thing like a video game so that if a new player enters, he appears inside the game," Roche said. "I didn't even hear you open the door."

"Dr. Nolan said she thought you might have come down here. I figured I'd let you know that the director and his team are aboard the chopper and heading north as we speak."

Barnett had sent them digital pictures of the dead monkeys and vultures lying in the bottom of their boat. Until that moment, Roche had never considered the prospect of Subject Z deliberately infecting animals with the microscopic alien organisms that not only formed its physical and mental being, but triggered the same transformation in other individuals, which allowed it to control them through some sort of hive-mind relationship. More frightening than the thought of being attacked by ferocious beasts beholden to its will was the idea that any single one of them, even something as benign as a field mouse could serve as a reservoir for the organisms. Even if they were lucky enough to kill Subject Z, it could always bide its time until the world forgot about it before respawning when they least expected it.

"How far north?" Roche asked.

"Panama," Maddox said.

"If they can stop it before it crosses the Darién Gap—"

"Assuming that's its goal."

"—then we can at least somewhat contain it."

"On a continent covered with tens of thousands of square miles of undeveloped and unexplored wilderness."

"I didn't say it was a perfect plan," Roche said.

"Have you notified the Panamanian authorities?"

"We made an attempt."

"And?"

"They were surprisingly unreceptive to the suggestion that there was an alien being rampaging through the jungle in their general direction."

"Did you tell them about the monkeys?"

Maddox raised his headset and gave Roche a look that let him know how he thought any sane person would respond to such a statement.

"Point taken," Roche said, "but we should at least dispatch another team—"

"With what men?"

"Tell Clayborn—"

"The Secretary of Defense doesn't appreciate being told anything. He's of the mind that this is our mess, so we should clean it up."

"Until we have a veritable army of monsters pouring across the Mexican border into Arizona."

"Those were pretty much his exact words."

Roche pressed the vein throbbing in his temple, which occasionally helped stave off the migraine he could positively feel building.

"Then I'm afraid that's exactly what he's going to get."

He pulled down his visor and welcomed the escape, essentially proving right all of the technology's detractors. He hated bureaucracy, but not nearly as much as the men who aspired to serve it. If this was Unit 51's mess, then he'd be damned if they weren't going to clean it up, which appeared to be the same thing the ancient Assyrians had done. Nine creatures like Subject Z didn't drop dead of their own accord.

The figures on the walls were either meant to represent the dead man on the plinth, or the mask had been fitted over his face so that he resembled the designs. In each depiction, he stood sideways with one foot in front of the other and one arm raised and extended. In the other hand he held some sort of canister by the handle. A tassel cascaded over his shoulder and wings grew from his back. In some depictions he had two wings, in others four, like a butterfly. He raised what looked like a pinecone in one hand and wore a bracelet reminiscent of a watch on the other. There were bearded men in some and griffons in others. Symbols with the wings and tail feathers of a bird. The only thing that remained unchanged from one picture to the next was the container he carried.

Roche scrutinized each depiction as he walked past, clearing his mind of conscious thought to allow his subconscious to interpret the meaning that had thus far eluded him. It wasn't what he saw on the walls that caught his attention, but rather what he detected on the floor from the corner of his eye.

He weaved through the contorted remains of the creatures and into the antechamber, where the upper crescent of the arched doorway granted a glimpse of what little data was captured in the adjacent sinkhole, at the bottom of the ladder. He knelt and felt as though he sank into the floor. He should have recognized it right away. The bones scattered throughout the chamber and nearly buried beneath the dust and dirt were different than all of the rest, but it wasn't until he found a recognizable piece of a decidedly normal skull that he realized that all of the bones belonged to an average human like himself, only one who'd been literally torn to pieces.

9

EVANS

***35,000 feet above the
Atlantic Ocean***

The Cessna Citation X had been fueled and waiting upon
their arrival and they'd been in the air less than an hour
after Evans's discovery that the central circle of the tattoo
corresponded to an archeological site known as Göbekli
Tepe, which predated the dawn of the Assyrian Empire
by more than 7,500 years. While only a relatively recent
discovery, the Stone Age site in the Şanlıurfa Province of
southeastern Turkey, near the Syrian border, had been
carbon-dated to the tenth millennium BCE, a time when
the region had been lush and known as the Fertile Crescent. The former Cradle of Civilization was now a vast
desert wasteland where proxy wars fought in the name of
oil threatened to erase the very history of mankind's gen-
esis. That Jade's theoretical warning led to the site of the
world's first temple wasn't surprising, especially considering it had been deliberately buried thousands of years
ago in the hope that it would never be found.

They needed to figure out exactly what they were walking into, which was why the three of them slaved over the

touchscreen monitors affixed to the armatures beside their seats instead of catching a little shut-eye or watching the pitch-black Atlantic roll restlessly past beneath them.

"No matter how long I stare at it," Anya said, "I can't figure out why the map would lead us to this place. It's a historical anomaly. I mean, it was built seven thousand years before the Pyramids of Giza and during the hunter-gatherer phase of our evolution. These guys were supposed to be painting on cave walls, not building"—she gestured at her screen in exasperation—"this."

Evans knew exactly what she meant. Göbekli Tepe was twice as old as Stonehenge, and yet the craftsmanship was on a completely different level, one that reminded him of the Mayans, who didn't appear until eight thousand years later. Massive T-shaped pillars up to two stories tall and ten tons each had been quarried from the bedrock, arranged in circles, and fitted together with walls of stacked stones. The primitive structures weren't arranged like a traditional village, but rather built one at a time and used for roughly a hundred years before each was completely buried and another built on top of it. Archeologists had used remote sensing devices to detect more than twenty structures buried underneath the man-made plateau that lorded over the flatlands, but they had yet to excavate beyond the five nearest the surface. All of them were essentially the same, with the exception of one subtle, yet striking difference.

At the center of each circular unit were two towering megaliths, taller even than the surrounding walls. Each was positioned parallel to its partner, fitted into a slotted stone support, and carved to resemble a giant man. They wore loincloths and belts and cradled their bellies with their hands. The tops of the T-shaped slabs represented their shoulders, while their heads were conspicuously absent. Animals had been carved in high relief on the sides of their bodies, predatory beasts theorized to be the protectors of these symbolic deities, but it wasn't the different animals that made the parallel pillars unique, but rather the minuscule difference in their alignment from one temple to the next.

Researchers believed they'd been designed almost like primitive picture windows to track a single star across the night sky, one that traveled low against the horizon and, thanks to the wobbling, top-like precession of Earth on its axis, only remained in the same place for a century before necessitating the construction of a new temple and twin megaliths with a slightly different orientation to monitor its progress. That star was Deneb, also known as Alpha Cigni, the brightest star in the constellation Cygnus, the swan with outstretched wings and a hazy body formed of distant nebulae. It was the head of the Northern Cross, one vertex of the Summer Triangle asterism, and the object to which mankind's first temple had been devoted, although archeologists could only speculate as to the reason why, which was of precious little help to them now.

"So what's your theory?" Jade asked.

"It obviously functions as a celestial observatory," Evans said, "but if there's a significance to their choice of stars, I can't see it. For all I know it's as simple as it was the brightest star in the night sky at the time. Then again, it's always possible they weren't tracking a star at all and we're simply trying to force a pattern where none exists."

"You don't believe that any more than you believe the map on the dead guy's chest leading to it was a coincidence," Anya said.

"And if the tattoo indeed serves as a warning," Jade

said, "then it stands to reason that the warning pertains to the disease that killed the creatures inside the tomb."

"Unless it has more to do with the creatures themselves than their deaths," Evans said.

"A distinct possibility; however, the physical remains would be a far more effective warning than a tattoo. Whoever ultimately discovered the tomb would essentially have to climb over their bodies to reach the tattooed man bound to the altar."

"Tell me about it," Anya said.

"No domestic refuse or hominin remains have been discovered at Göbekli Tepe," Evans said. "That suggests no one actually lived there, and that the complex was exclusively used for either worship or ritual."

"Which again flies in the face of conventional wisdom because our ancestors at the time were nomadic and didn't put down roots until the advent of agriculture five centuries later."

"So where did they live?" Jade asked.

"One can only guess," Evans said. "They built the temple complex long before any permanent dwellings. The only bones anyone has found so far belong to animals."

"Sacrifices?" Anya said.

"More likely food, based on the specific bones and the corresponding cuts of meat."

"So people showed up at this temple to eat and stare at a star through pillars shaped like giant headless men?" Jade said.

Evans had to admit it sounded ridiculous when she phrased it like that, but the simple truth of the statement was undeniable. There had to be something more to it than that, which brought him back to the carvings on the megaliths.

"It's possible there's a clue hidden among the petro-glyphs," he said. "I haven't had very much time to study them, but the only thing that strikes me as odd so far is the selection of animals. The majority of the carvings feature boars, snakes, vultures, and other native species like scorpions and foxes, but others depict species like geese and armadillos that aren't indigenous to the area."

"How would they know about them if they weren't local?" Anya asked.

"That's the point," Jade said. "What about the time frame itself? We know that crustal displacement fifteen thousand years ago was responsible for shifting Antarctica to the South Pole and causing it to freeze. That's not very far from the theoretical era we're dealing with here."

"You're right. In fact, 10,000 BCE coincides with the end of the Younger Dryas cold event, which was a mini ice age about three thousand years after the last glacial maximum."

"That would explain why they've located so many subterranean structures they've yet to be able to excavate," Evans said. "The underground cities at Derinkuyu and Kaymakli in Central Turkey date to roughly the same time and are theorized to have been carved to house entire populations during the Younger Dryas. There are actually more than two hundred Stone Age sites in the country with at least two sublevels."

"So you think what we're looking for is buried underneath two thousand years' worth of buildings essentially built one on top of the other?" Jade said.

"I suppose it's possible, but I'm inclined to think not based on the fact that the map was tattooed during the time of the Assyrians, more than five thousand years after its abandonment."

"Then what's there that we're flying halfway around the world to find?"

Evans switched to an aerial view of the site on his screen. There was nothing but open desert surrounding the man-made mountain of buried temples. If no one had lived there, then they must have traveled a considerable distance to reach their site of worship, the oldest in the history of the world. It would have been a sacred site, one the people of the time had apparently considered of greater value than their own homes to have invested so much time and effort into building the structures and then burying them. The temple would have served as the house of the first known gods, whose likenesses towered over each of the structures, cold and sightless. Whatever was housed there would have been of the utmost importance, even more important to them than their own lives.

"The next clue," he said. "But to what?"

10
BARNETT

22 miles south of Calamar, Colombia

"Over here," Brinkley said.

Barnett forced his way through the snarled branches of the ceibas and emerged to find the special agent crouched over a body lying prone on the detritus. Brinkley shined his handheld infrared beam onto the side of the man's face and checked for a carotid pulse, but it was obvious from where Barnett stood that there wouldn't be one. The flesh along the dead man's exposed back appeared green through the night vision apparatus. It had been opened from below his shoulder blades all the way up to the base of his skull, revealing a portion of his spine and the surrounding musculature, upon which the clouds of flies buzzing around the clearing had been feasting before their intrusion.

"He's still warm," Brinkley said. "Granted, it's the middle of the night and it's still eighty degrees, but I wouldn't guess he's been dead for more than a couple hours." He lifted the man's outstretched arm and let it drop limply to the ground. "Rigor mortis hasn't even begun to set in yet."

"Until now, Zeta's been avoiding overt demonstrations of brutality," Barnett said. "It knows we're getting close and doesn't have the time or luxury of being able to sneak through the jungle."

"It's possible it stumbled upon this guy and had no choice."

Barnett knelt beside the man, whose skin was dark, his face acne-scarred, and his eyes glazed. A loop of his shoulder strap protruded from underneath him. He rolled him over to reveal the AK-47 squashed into the mud and shined his light around the clearing until he caught the reflection of brass casings.

"He saw it coming," Barnett said. "He got off a handful of shots before turning tail and trying to run. It was on him before he took two strides."

"A man with a Kalashnikov doesn't wander off into the jungle on his own," Brinkley said.

"No, he does not."

The implication was clear. This man was part of a larger group, probably drug smugglers, which meant it was possible that not only were there more men to infect and turn into drones, there was also a potential means of transportation out of the Amazon.

What little breeze permeated the canopy shifted and brought Barnett a whiff of wood smoke. He stood and headed in that direction.

They caught up with Sheppard a hundred feet ahead through the underbrush, surrounded by dead men who looked like they'd been attacked by a herd of wild animals. The ground surrounding them was positively carpeted with spent shell casings. He glanced back at them and readjusted his grip on his SCAR with his bandaged hand.

"They died hard," he said.

"But at least it was over quickly," Barnett said. He stepped over the bodies, noting the expressions of sheer terror frozen on their lifeless faces. While their deaths might not have been protracted, there was no doubt their final moments had been excruciating. "Maybe twenty seconds. Start to finish."

Morgan emerged from the faint haze of smoke trapped beneath the lower canopy, beckoned them in his direction, and disappeared back into the forest.

Barnett followed him through a snarl of lianas and saplings. A faint glow materialized in the distance through the swaying branches, followed by a smell he associated with a luau. By the time the camp came into view, he already knew what to expect. They passed an empty stable, the weathered gray plank walls and the desiccated hay on the hardpan spattered with dried blood. The rusted shackles bolted to the posts set in the middle of each suggested something other than horses had been housed inside. The back of the main building was riddled with bullet holes. Through the open doorway he could see the bodies of naked women, their flesh savaged and their remains cast aside amid drums of industrial solvents and garbage bags full of coca leaves.

He signaled for Morgan and Sheppard to head around the side of the structure while he and Brinkley secured the interior, which took all of about thirty seconds. Beyond the storage room, the rear half of which contained an arsenal of assault rifles large enough to overthrow just about any government, was a production room overflowing with cocaine in various stages of manufacture, from a crust that resembled concrete to mounds of uncut powder worth millions on the street. Or would have been, anyway, were it not for the dead woman sprawled across them, her blood clotted into a red paste. Like the others, the wounds on her back had undoubtedly been inflicted by Subject Z, which, again, made no effort to feed upon her flesh. The victims had been dispatched in the quickest and most efficient manner possible and their bodies left to rot where they fell.

The front entryway was lined with bricks bound in duct tape. Several columns had been knocked over and scattered throughout the entryway. He followed them out the main entrance toward where Morgan crouched in the glow of a dying bonfire, which had dwindled to cinders crackling in logs the size of tree trunks and a charcoaled human skeleton. He fingered the edge of the tire tracks in the dirt.

"How long?" Barnett asked.

"Can't be more than a few hours." Morgan stood and surveyed the scene. "A single industrial transport vehicle arrived and backed around the fire to align its tailgate with the main entrance. The driver climbed out. Went around to the cargo hold of his vehicle, presumably to roll up the gate. Proceeded into the building. He appears to have been in the process of loading the bed when he realized something was wrong and got the hell out of here so fast he nearly went straight off the ramp and into the jungle."

Barnett followed the tracks to where the wooden ramp lay at the bottom of the dry riverbed. The ferns on the opposite bank were flattened where the right front tire rode up onto them. The trunks of the adjacent trees were either broken or scored from the impact of the bumper. He caught twin flashes of eyeshine from the shadows before a jaguar darted away from what was left of the man it had dragged into the brush.

He swept his infrared light across the rocky bed. Bunches of bananas were strewn across the ground amid coffee beans scattered from ruptured burlap sacks.

"His gate was still open when he took off," he said.

Morgan nodded. He understood the implications.

"If Zeta was on that truck, it could easily be a hundred miles away by now," he said. "We should call for aerial support."

"We have no idea what kind of vehicle we're looking for."

"The axles are too close together to be a semi and too far apart to be a pickup. And look at the way the branches overhanging the riverbed are broken to about ten feet in height. We're looking for a panel truck. No doubt about it."

"So where's it going?"

"Coffee beans and bananas are Colombia's chief agricultural exports. For my money, they're heading for the nearest port."

"Figure out which one that is," Barnett said and stared up the makeshift road to the point where it wound back into the jungle.

They couldn't afford to allow the creature to reach that port, where it could board a vessel bound for anywhere in the world. They needed to figure out the truck's destination and get there before it arrived.

If Subject Z managed to get off the continent, they'd never find it again.

11
TESS

The Hangar

Tess woke with a start. It took her several moments to realize she was still in her office and didn't have the slightest clue whether it was night or day. She'd fallen asleep clutching a printout of the tattoo, which she was convinced was more than just a map. There was something strikingly familiar about it, but she couldn't seem to put her finger on it. She'd printed out dozens of copies and scribbled all over them in an effort to figure out what nagged her about it, and yet she couldn't seem to scratch the mental itch. Hopefully a few hours of sleep would allow her to approach the problem with a fresh set of eyes.

She set the paper aside and rose from her seat. Yawned and stretched her arms over her head. Walked behind Kelly's desk and switched on the monitor displaying the old Assyrian map upon which the tattoo had been overlaid. There was something familiar about the size, shape, and relationship of the circles to one another, a pattern screaming to be recognized . . .

There was a coffee machine down the hall. Perhaps a little caffeine would get her sluggish neurons firing—

Tess was halfway out the door when she caught a glimpse of the monitor behind her desk from the corner of her eye and stopped dead in her tracks.

She turned and stared at the depiction of the night sky Subject Z had carved into the ceiling of the cavern that had served as its prison in Antarctica. The answer had been staring her right in the face the whole time. She couldn't believe she hadn't recognized it before now. She'd been so focused on finding the patterns among the stars that didn't correspond with the night sky on September 21 of the previous year that she'd failed to recognize the pattern in the space between them.

It wasn't simply that she'd been looking at the wrong thing, however, but rather from the wrong perspective. The stars representing the coastlines of South and Central America had been readily recognizable, as had those corresponding to the tectonic plates that led inland from the Pacific Ocean to the ruins of Teotihuacan. So recognizable, in fact, that she'd ignored their lack of precision, or perhaps she'd unconsciously chalked it up to Subject Z having been forced to fit the design into a fixed amount of space amid thousands of stars. The problem was she'd failed to take into account the curvature of the domed cavern ceiling. Her computer program had done a miraculous job of re-creating the creature's work, but had displayed it as a flat, two-dimensional image, which was all she'd needed at the time to determine the date in question since that data was also stored in two dimensions.

Tess sat at her desk and set to work. Without the precise measurements and angulations of the cavern now buried beneath countless tons of rock and ice, she was going to have to work backward. She brought up the AuthaGraph world map, which had been specifically designed to better illustrate the spherical planet on a flat surface. Traditional maps were all based on the Mercator projection, a sixteenth-century rendering that preserved navigational lines on a rectangular grid demarcated by latitude and longitude, thus distorting the true size and shape of nations and continents. Greenland appeared to be as large as Africa. Canada and Siberia were stretched and elongated. Antarctica covered the entire bottom of the map. The more accurate rendition presented Africa rotated forty-five degrees clockwise in the upper left corner and Antarctica, roughly the same size as Australia, in the lower right. In between were Asia, which appeared to twist toward the center of the map, and the Americas, which had been rotated counterclockwise a full forty-five degrees away from it.

She took a deep breath and laid the creature's star chart on top of it.

It took some manipulation and a few subtle distortion filters to align the path Subject A had taken from Antarctica to Mexico City with the coastline, but once she did, everything fell into place. All of the additional data points not corresponding to stars aligned with landmasses. Not a single one landed on an ocean. Her original attempts to plot the extraneous stars on the map had placed clusters in the middle of the Atlantic Ocean, the Caspian Sea, and northern Siberia. Now those same clusters fell squarely on southern North America, northern Africa, and western Asia; specifically the thin neck of Mexico along the Caribbean Sea, the Nile River Basin of Egypt, and a region in southeastern Turkey, respectively.

Suddenly, she was wide awake.

Tess zoomed in on the points of data that aligned with Turkey. There were dozens of dots arranged in a seemingly random manner, nearly all of them the same size, with the exception of nine that were not only larger but varied in size among themselves. A quick count and double-count confirmed there were a total of eighty-four points of data that must have taken Subject Z hours to carve in such detail. She might not have learned everything she wanted to about the creature, but she'd learned enough to know that it didn't do anything without a reason.

She glanced across the room at Kelly's monitor. The cluster of stars looked as though it corresponded to the same geographical location as Göbekli Tepe, but she didn't have nearly enough locational data to confirm her suspicions.

"There has to be a connection," she said and swiveled from side to side in her chair.

Tess abruptly leaned forward and started typing. She found an aerial photograph of the ancient Turkish site where her teammates were heading. There were several circular temples surrounded by square grids where excavation was only beginning, inside of which were the arcs of partially exposed outer walls. The T-shaped pillars were considerably larger than the other structural components and cut from stone a much lighter shade of gray, making them stand apart even from so far overhead, almost like the stars themselves.

"Well, what do you know?" she said and tilted her head to the side to view the screen from a different angle.

Tess closed the aerial image and opened the survey plans of Göbekli Tepe from the German Archeological Institute. The map had been created using a combination of ground-penetrating radar and magnetometer readings, and showed the temples that had already been excavated, as well as sections of those still buried underneath them. The way the walls of the structures overlapped at different depths made it difficult to determine how many there were, but it didn't matter. She'd seen what she'd needed to see.

The pattern of stars Subject Z had carved into the ceiling corresponded to the megalithic pillars buried at various depths both on top of and beneath the man-made plateau. All but the nine larger points of data, which corresponded to the precise center of each of the circular temples, labeled Enclosure A through I on the map. The structures formed a pattern that almost looked like a cross, only the horizontal bar was disproportionately long and turned upward at the ends.

She lifted her monitor from her desk and angled it until the cross stood upright.

The design was as clear as day.

It was more than just a cross. Along with the seventy-three smaller stars, it formed an unmistakable pattern anyone who'd spent as much time staring up at the stars as she had would recognize immediately.

The temples hadn't been built on top of each other; they'd been built on tiers and buried together as a whole, a primitive, five-story mecca that had been hidden beneath a veritable man-made mountain.

Take away all of the dirt, and from high above the site it would be clear that the pillars of the 12,000-year-old complex formed the constellation Cygnus.

12
JADE

***Göbekli Tepe,
Şanlıurfa Province, Turkey***

Not for the first time, Jade wondered what she was doing here. Archeology, specifically the speculative nature of it, was about the furthest thing from her specialty, and yet here she was on the other side of the globe, en route to one of the oldest historical sites known to man. The funny thing was a small part of her was actually beginning to enjoy it. At least the part where they explored the unknown and attempted to unlock its secrets, if not the part where they risked discovering the pathogen responsible for killing the creatures inside the tomb in Mosul, which was the whole reason they'd brought her along in the first place.

As the lone medical doctor among them, she was potentially the only one standing between life and death, assuming she was able to recognize the threat in time. After all, if Roche was right about the implications of the human bones he'd seen in the VR re-creation of the burial chamber, it wasn't just the creatures like Subject Z that needed to fear the virus. The acting director had called them several hours ago while their plane was refueling at Faro Airport in Portugal and explained his theory about the single set of human remains, which made total sense given the context of the situation. The creatures had to have been exposed to the virus somehow, and using an infected man as bait to lure them into the cavern meshed with the physical evidence.

The tomb had been created for just that purpose and then hurriedly sealed once the monsters were inside. The sacrificial offering, of course, had been ripped limb from limb in the most violent manner possible, but the pathogen had begun to work its magic before any of them could so much as attempt to find a way out, and, if that were truly the case, then they were potentially dealing with something even more insidious than Ebola, something capable of eliciting symptoms within a matter of hours.

They'd arrived at Şanlıurfa GAP Airport to find a Škoda Kodiaq waiting for them on the tarmac. The silver SUV was essentially the Czech version of the Volkswagen Tiguan, only bigger. The gear they'd requested had been loaded into the back, as verified by the checklist taped to the dashboard beside a GPS unit that had already been programmed with their destination, which lay somewhere ahead of them along the narrow road, the asphalt blurring past beneath them as they sped toward the unknown.

A flock of hairy sheep materialized to the right side of the road and faded behind them just as quickly.

"How much farther?" Anya asked from the back seat, where she reclined with her legs stretched across the upholstery and her shoulders propped against the wide window.

Evans glanced from the road to the GPS module.

"Four kilometers."

This part of Turkey reminded Jade of Wyoming, with vast stretches of yellow grasses and bare earth covering low, rolling hills as far as the eye could see, marred only by the occasional stunted pine tree. It was hard to believe this place had once been lush and fertile, harder still that anyone had ever chosen to live here. There was obviously a reason that places like this ended up abandoned. There was no shelter, let alone water, within walking distance in any direction.

"Have you determined what we're looking for yet?" Jade asked.

"I figure we'll know it when we see it," Evans said.

Jade rolled her eyes.

"Unlike any of the other archeologists who've been studying the site for the last quarter-century?"

Evans glanced over at her in the passenger seat and smirked.

"We have an advantage that none of them had," he said.

"And what, pray tell, is that?"

"We have the map."

"Assuming that's even what it is."

"Have a little faith, Jade," Anya said.

"I'd settle for the slightest proof we're not wasting our time."

The SUV pulled off the side of the highway and onto a gravel road that wended up the slope toward the plateau Jade recognized from the pictures they'd studied on the plane. They found a makeshift lot about halfway up and parked near the base of the railroad-tie staircase that led up to the archeological site. While theirs was currently the only one there, it was obvious from the crisscrossing tracks that this place hosted a reasonable number of cars. How were they supposed to find something that so many researchers and tourists had missed?

They climbed out, stretched, and mounted the uneven stairs. The cool air felt divine against her skin after being cooped up in first the Cessna, and then the Kodiaq, for so many hours straight. A churning mass of gray clouds scudded across the sky toward the ascending sun.

A figure appeared at the top of the plateau and beckoned them higher with a congenial wave. The man was sitting on the top step when they arrived and extended his hand to Evans, who helped pull him to his feet. He appeared to be in his early sixties, with a bushy white beard and curly hair poking out from beneath his field-wrapped turban. Sweat bloomed from his brow and ran down his plump cheeks. He wore sandals, dirty jeans, and an untucked blue button-down shirt that struggled to contain his girth.

"Dr. Ahmet Sadik," he said with an Arabic accent filtered through a formal British education. "Head of the Department of Protohistory and Near Eastern Archeology at Ankara University. And, for today, your humble guide back in time to the oldest temple known to man . . . Göbekli Tepe."

He gripped each of their hands between his sandpapery palms while they introduced themselves, clapped with apparent delight, and opened the security fence surrounding the excavation, which had been erected in response to the aggressive destruction of history by the marauding zealots of ISIS.

"Prepare to be amazed," Sadik said and guided them

toward the edge of a massive crater, at the bottom of which were the temples Jade had seen in photographs, none of which had captured a fraction of their true wonder.

She felt like she had when she'd first seen the ancient ruins beneath two vertical miles of ice in Antarctica. There was no doubting the authenticity of the ruins, let alone the veracity of the carbon dating, and yet all logic cried out for her to refute what her eyes were seeing. Loosely organized nomadic peoples didn't just one day decide to build such intricate and elaborate structures without first teaching themselves those skills through countless iterations of lesser structures, like the pithouses and primitive adobe structures that predated the cliff dwellings in the American Southwest. This was the architectural equivalent of man jumping out of the primordial ooze on fully formed legs and starting to run. It was a historical anomaly only now starting to give up its secrets, one of which, she hoped, was the key to stopping Subject Z.

The individual temples were built on tiers of different height, much the way artists depicted the Hanging Gardens of Babylon, only adorned with crowns of stacked rocks and T-shaped granite posts instead of flowering vines that spilled from one terrace to the next. It was impossible to appreciate the sheer enormity of the megaliths standing in the center of the rings until she descended the rickety wooden framework to the uppermost structure. How any number of people could have carried them up the hill before the advent of the wheel and the domestication of pack animals was beyond her.

A sloping ramp erected on stilts encircled the active excavation, which was already easily fifty feet down. As she descended in altitude from one tier to the next, she was reminded that the entire mountain had been formed by the act of burying one temple and then building a new one practically right on top of the old, a process that had been repeated for two thousand years.

They climbed down onto a section of flat ground and crossed a wooden plank to reach the edge of the nearest temple. Even standing level with the top of the outer wall, the twin megaliths still towered over them. They were much deeper than they were wide, with boars carved in high relief on the sides and the anthropomorphic figures on the narrow front sides, their hands cradling their bellies. Their forms were human-like in proportion, but terminated at the T-shaped shoulders.

"Where are their heads?" Jade asked.

"You are not the first to ask this question," Sadik said. "Many archeologists have pondered this very riddle."

"If you're waiting for a drumroll—"

Evans took her hand and gave it a gentle squeeze.

"What my colleague means to say," he interrupted, "is that the answer may be important to our investigation, especially if the heads are deformed in a specific way."

"That, unfortunately, is an answer I do not possess," Sadik said. "No one does. If ever these megaliths had heads, they are long gone. They have even been removed from the otherwise perfectly preserved idols we've exhumed."

"Why would they do something like that?" Jade asked.

"Perhaps because they did not want those who came after them to look upon the faces of their gods."

13
KELLY

The Hangar

Kelly strode into the command center expecting to find Roche standing on the bridge like the captain of a starship, overseeing the men charged with monitoring the various satellite feeds of the Amazon and the Middle East. The man standing with his back to her, however, was definitely not the one she'd come to find. Maddox sensed her behind him and turned to face her. The horizontal scars on his cheeks always made him appear to be smiling. She couldn't help but wonder what kind of nightmare he'd endured to get them.

"Good morning, Dr. Nolan."

Kelly smiled. She still wasn't used to people addressing her as "doctor." At least she no longer felt the urge to giggle or turn around to see if there was someone else standing behind her.

"Sorry to interrupt," she said. "I don't suppose you've seen Martin, have you?"

"Not since he briefed me on the mission to Turkey. Why? Is there something field operations should know?"

He glanced at a monitor displaying a desert location, but his stare didn't linger.

"Nothing like that. I just wanted to run something past him."

"If you find him, let him know that our team just arrived at its destination. He'll want to remain apprised."

Kelly nodded and headed back into the corridor. She was about to retrace her steps to the elevator when she noticed a faint aura of light coming from the computer lab. It grew incrementally brighter as she approached. The door stood open upon a room that appeared empty until she saw the lone figure seated at the workstation farthest from her, where four monitors had been pushed together.

She leaned against the doorframe and watched Roche turn from one screen to the next and back again. Every few seconds he lowered his head and raised his right shoulder, as though taking notes. From her vantage point, all of the monitors looked the same, only the background varied subtly in color. The scene reminded her of a different place and time, one she now thought about with as much regret as happiness.

Roche abruptly stiffened and turned around. He offered a weak smile and rubbed his eyes.

"Spare a few seconds?" she asked.

"Of course," he said. "Truth be told, I could use a fresh set of eyes, too. That is, if you don't mind."

Kelly weaved through the darkened stations, grabbed one of the empty chairs, and rolled it over beside his. At first glance, the images on the three screens to the left appeared to show the same crop circle from slightly different angles, but she quickly noticed the subtle differences

between them. The fourth, however, was completely unlike the others.

"Maddox wanted me to tell you that Evans's team just
reached Göbekli Tepe."

"Excellent," he said. "Did he happen to say if Evans
had figured out what they were hoping to find yet?"

"No, but that's kind of why I was looking for you. I
was wondering if you thought the fork-like symbols attached to the circles in the design might give us a clue."

"I definitely think we're supposed to recognize their
significance, like we did the cymatic expressions of the
sounds that helped us unlock the pyramid in Antarctica."

"So what's your theory?"

"See these crop circles?" He gestured at the monitors.
"They all appeared within days of each other in July 1990.
They were all roughly the same size and were found with-
in miles of each other in Wiltshire County, England, not
far from both Stonehenge and the Neolithic monument in
Avebury. The three on the left all feature the same circu-
lar designs, the only difference being their arrangement.
What do you see when you look at them?"

"I see variations of the map that led us from Mosul to
Göbekli Tepe."

"True, but take a step back and look at the designs from
the most basic perspective and give me your first impression."

"Linear alignments of approximately the same number
of circular shapes. Some have fork-like appendages. Others don't."

"Right, and the largest circles are in the middle. Why?
Are they more important somehow?"

"You're the one with training in cryptanalysis," she
said. "You tell me."

"That's just it. I think we've been looking too hard for a pattern that's been staring us in the face the whole time, something so simple even a child could understand."

Kelly was about to take exception to his statement when she experienced the revelation toward which he'd been guiding her.

"They're planets," she said. "The one we aligned with Ninevah isn't a bull's-eye, it's Saturn."

Roche smiled. It was the first time she'd seen him do so in months.

"Exactly. The sun's at the far left, followed by Mercury and Venus. I think the shorter lines between the next two in the series indicate an orbital relationship. The more prominent of the two, the one inside the circle, is Earth, making the other one the moon. After that we have Mars, Jupiter, Saturn, Uranus, and Neptune."

"So what do the longer lines mean?"

"That they're in direct alignment."

"Like an eclipse?"

"More like a conjunction."

"The Age of Aquarius."

He turned and looked at her with an expression of confusion.

"You know," she said. "The old song? When the moon is in the Seventh House and Jupiter aligns with Mars, then peace will guide the planets and love will steer the stars. This is the dawning of the Age of Aquarius."

"If I'm right, these designs portend an event that has nothing to do with peace and love. These aren't just maps—"

"They're dates," she finished for him.

Roche nodded.

"Two dates, actually. See how the moon is on the opposite side of Earth in the second and third crop circles? It's technically in conjunction with Mars and Jupiter, on the far side of Earth from the sun. The two dates are separated by fourteen days, half of the lunar cycle, the time it takes for the moon to move from one side of Earth to the other. And the forks stemming from the planets? I think they're like the hour hands on a clock. They mark the time, a different point on the planet's rotation. The time of day specific to each. So when Earth sits between the sun and the moon, it will create a lunar eclipse visible to the half of the planet experiencing darkness, during which time both Mars and Jupiter will be nearly right on top of each other in the night sky."

"But if the two that show the moon on the opposite side of Earth from the sun signify a lunar eclipse, why do they show two different times? It's not like an eclipse happens at different times on the same day." She realized as she said it how wrong she was. That was exactly what happened. Her hand fretted like crazy at her side. "The time difference signifies the point on Earth from which the eclipse is viewed."

"That's my thinking."

"But the second one places the tuning fork at nearly twelve o'clock, while the third one doesn't show it at all."

"I think whoever created the crop circle deliberately made the tuning fork of the second design a hair to the left of perpendicular to draw attention to the fact that it was shy of twelve o'clock, and omitted the fork entirely on the third to indicate midnight. A single day on the moon lasts 29.5 days on Earth, so a few seconds up there translates to hours down here. The problem is that we don't know how many seconds we're dealing with, which means we have to look to the other planets for clues." He pointed to the monitors as he spoke. "Each of the hour hands on Mars and Jupiter is in a different place, signifying some specific length of time, either earlier or later. A day on Mars is roughly twenty-four hours, while on Jupiter it's only ten. If we're looking at approximately a quarter revolution of Mars and a near-complete revolution of Jupiter, the time between them ought to be somewhere in the neighborhood of eight hours."

"So we need to find two locations that are roughly eight time zones apart and will both be experiencing nighttime during the lunar eclipse," Kelly said. "That only narrows it down to half the world. Even if we assume Göbekli Tepe is one of those points, the other could be anywhere from the Americas in the west to China in the east. Where do we even start?"

"That's what we need to figure out." Roche turned from the monitors and looked directly into her eyes. "Mars and Jupiter are in conjunction once every two years for a period that lasts forty-eight days and we're already nearly halfway into that window."

Kelly had a sinking feeling in the pit of her stomach. She didn't spend nearly enough time in the world outside the Hangar, but she vaguely remembered seeing something on the news about an impending solar eclipse and making a mental note to find a few free minutes to watch it, although with everything going on she'd forgotten pretty much right away. That felt like weeks ago now.

"How long ago was the solar eclipse?" she asked.

"Twelve days."

She closed her eyes and took a deep breath.

"So that makes the lunar eclipse . . . ?"

"Roughly thirty hours from now."

They were already nearly out of time.

Roche placed his hand on top of hers to still its relentless movements. A tingling sensation rippled up her arm. She opened her eyes and found him looking directly into them.

"What do you think it all means?" she asked.

"I don't know, but I have a feeling we're about to find out."

Kelly nodded and broke eye contact. She couldn't stand being so close to him and yet so far apart. Half of her desperately wanted him to take her in his arms, while the other wanted to lash out at him for creating the seemingly insurmountable distance she felt between them. She sympathized with the pressure he was under, but the way he chose to handle it was tearing her apart.

"What about the fourth one?" she asked. "It looks nothing like the others."

"It might be completely unrelated, but based on the date of its appearance and its physical proximity to the others—" Footsteps echoed from the hallway a heartbeat before Tess burst into the room.

"There you are!" she said and switched on the lights. "I've been looking for you for like twenty minutes."

Roche jerked his hand from on top of Kelly's and stood so quickly that he knocked over his chair.

"What's wrong?"

Tess held up an iPad.

"You have got to see this."

14
BARNETT

Colón, Panama

"*Los cuerpos están hacia atrás,*" the officer said.

"He says the bodies are toward the back," Barnett translated for his teammates.

He'd personally called the Secretary of Defense the moment he learned of the discovery and requested that he make arrangements with the Panamanian government to let his team be the first to examine the scene. If what awaited them inside was indeed Subject Z's handiwork and not that of either the Sinaloa or the Gulf Cartel, as the locals seemed to think, then the creature now had access to one of the busiest ports in the entire world, from which it could board a ship bound for any location on the planet, or continue its northward migration onto the North American mainland, which suddenly made things a whole lot more real for Clayborn back in Washington.

They followed the sergeant from the Panama National Police Force through the front door and into an ancient hangar made of corrugated aluminum, now more rust than metal. The dim interior was illuminated by what little sunlight permeated the dust-covered windows. Their escort wore drab olive fatigues, a black Kevlar vest, and couldn't have been more than thirty, which made him an old man compared to the unit outside, which guarded the crime scene and enforced a hard cordon at the end of the dirt road leading to the airfield. The place reeked of airplane fuel and pesticides, an old scent from a time when the facilities had serviced crop dusters, not smugglers. The massive fans in the wall vents squeaked as they turned ever so slightly on the gentle breeze.

Mountains of rubble rose to either side, collections of metal containers, wooden debris, and trash of all kinds. A table and two chairs sat in the center of the lone cleared area, where presumably business was conducted. The concrete was saturated with oil and chemicals, now furry with accumulated dust. An aluminum wall ran the width of the building. Based on the overall size of the structure, the space on the other side was a whole lot larger. The door that once fit the lone threshold jutted from the mound of junk beside it.

"Quien lo encontró?" Barnett asked.

"No sabemos. Fue llamado de forma anónima."

Barnett nodded. If he'd been the one to find what he believed awaited them on the other side of that wall, he would have gotten the hell out of there and reported it anonymously, too.

The sergeant stopped a dozen feet from the doorway.

"Estás solo desde aquí," he said and gestured for them to proceed. This was as far as he would go. *"Avisame cuando termines."*

Barnett left him behind and led his men through the doorway into the hangar proper. The smell hit him immediately, followed in short measure by the drone of flies.

"That can't be good," Sheppard said.

To the left was what remained of an office, its window shattered and desk overturned. Beside it were rows of shelves overflowing with rusted containers, water-damaged crates, and ripped bags of grain. To the right was a small plane that had been cannibalized for parts and its fuselage used for target practice. Several vehicles had been pulled into the space between them: an older model pickup stained red by dust, a Suburban with rusted wheel wells, a brand-new F-150 glistening with chrome, and a nondescript panel truck, its driver's side door standing open. The hangar doors remained closed behind them, all but the one on the far end anyway, which stood open just wide enough for a man to pass through.

Barnett weaved through the maze of parked vehicles until he reached the one he'd come to find. He rounded the open door and inadvertently kicked a brass casing underneath it. The tinkling sound echoed in the confines. Even more empty rounds glittered from the ground beside the cargo hold, behind which was pretty much exactly what he'd expected to find. Ruptured burlap sacks had disgorged a carpet of coffee beans down the ramp and onto the concrete, where the bodies of three men were sprawled in dried black puddles of their own making. The deep lacerations on their chests, necks, and faces were identical to those of the men back at the drug camp in Colombia.

His footsteps clanged from the ramp as he ascended into the cargo hold, the walls and ceiling of which were decorated with arterial spatters. Crates had toppled and broken open. Burlap sacks had been shoved aside and ripped with sharp implements. There was a conspicuous gap near the back where the cocaine had been stored and a mess of coffee beans had been trampled beneath the feet of the men unloading it. The dead man in the corner had been dispatched in a quick and efficient manner, yet with enough savagery to nearly separate his head from his shoulders. There was no mistaking Subject Z's footprints in the man's blood, nor those of its traveling companion, whose bare foot was human in shape and proportion, if not size.

Barnett recognized exactly what had happened.

"They buried themselves under the cargo to either side and waited patiently for the men to unload the truck before revealing themselves," he said.

"Poor bastards never saw it coming," Sheppard said from behind him.

Barnett beckoned his man closer.

"Document these tracks."

Sheppard removed a camera from his pack, stepped around Barnett, and placed his own foot beside the human footprint for scale. His size 11½ boots were almost exactly a foot long, but still four inches shorter than the unknown track.

"Whatever it is has to be close to seven feet tall," he said.

Barnett nodded. They'd been reluctant to draw a solid connection between Subject Z's counterpart and the body it had removed from the sarcophagus in Antarctica, but they were running out of excuses. The most glaring problem was that to do so they needed to accept the reality that the long-dead remains had been somehow reanimated after the creature drenched them with blood. Worse, they had to face the prospect that whatever this second being was, there was another one out there right now, in the hands of the masked forces of Enigma, who had retrieved the body from the tomb at the center of the maze beneath Teotihuacan.

"The skin's cool to the touch and rigor mortis has already set in," Brinkley said from where he crouched beside one of the bodies on the hangar floor. "I'd wager he's been dead for at least four hours, probably closer to five or six."

"We're losing ground."

"You don't know the half of it," Morgan said.

Barnett turned to see his second-in-command standing beside the column of light entering through the outer door. He looked up from the ground and met the director's stare.

Everything fell into place.

"Damn it," Barnett said and lowered his eyes to the bed of the truck.

Amid the scattered beans and squashed bananas were more footprints. They were nowhere near as distinct and looked almost like rust on the metal ramp. He descended and followed them into the mess of blood and bullet casings, from which they emerged on the opposite side, only farther apart, as though moving at great speed. The blood had transferred completely from their feet by the time he reached Morgan, who stared out across the dirt tarmac toward a runway overgrown with weeds.

The footprints were every bit as evident in the dirt as the tread of the tires driving into the building.

And those of the plane that was no longer there.

15
ANYA

Göbekli Tepe

"Each of these pillars stands two stories tall and weighs ten tons," Sadik said. They'd worked their way down to the floor level of the temple he called Enclosure C and stood before the twin megaliths, their heads barely reaching the stylized belts of the anthropomorphic figures. "They are colloquially known as the Celestial Ancestors, although they are called by many other names in as many different cultures. You will find idols crafted in the exact same proportions and style—what we call the 'birthing posture,' with their hands clasping their bellies in such a way as to frame the navel—all around the world. This specific symbolic gesture has appeared on statues from Mexico and Colombia to Tahiti and Easter Island, not to mention countless European and Asiatic sites, and provides what many believe to be proof that civilizations separated by seemingly insurmountable distances and geographic barriers must have come into physical contact with one another."

Anya walked a circle around the giant stone sculptures, which appeared fairly generic in design. Where else would someone carve hands in such a way as to be seen from the front of a narrow anthropomorphic construct? Of course, she couldn't deny the uncanny resemblance to carvings she'd seen firsthand in both Mexico and Russia. "What's the significance of the name?" Evans asked.

"They're called the Celestial Ancestors because all of the societies where these appear share a common belief that their gods descended from the sky. These are the beings responsible for their creation, hence the birthing posture. It was their way of saying 'This is where we come from.'"

"Surely there's a more logical explanation," Jade said. "One that requires fewer speculative leaps to get there."

Sadik smiled patiently.

"The people of Göbekli Tepe did not have the benefit of thousands of years of knowledge and accumulated history to draw upon, like we do," he said. "Where they saw the intervention of mystical beings beyond their understanding, we see the opportunity to impose science upon chaos. The two forms of religion are not necessarily so different. I find the truth generally lies somewhere in between."

Anya completed her circuit of the temple and returned to the others. If she stood on her tiptoes, she could see down into the adjacent temple complex. Something about their placement in relationship to one another nagged at her. The pattern in which they'd been built recalled another prehistoric site, but she couldn't seem to make the connection.

"And what is that truth?" Jade asked.

"The twelfth century BCE saw the arrival of a mini ice age known as the Younger Dryas, which reversed the gradual climatic warming that had occurred since the

Last Glacial Maximum and heralded the sudden onset of twelve hundred years of winter. While there are those who theorize that what we affectionately refer to as the Big Chill was caused by a comet striking the Laurentide Ice Sheet, the prevailing theory is that an ice dam containing a body of water trapped beneath that sheet—one the size of the Canadian provinces of Manitoba and Ontario combined—simply broke as a consequence of the warming, releasing all of that frigid water into the Atlantic Ocean, altering the circulation cycle by which warm water is gradually cooled on its way from the equator to the north pole, and causing flooding all across the globe. The influx of cold water pouring into the Arctic stimulated a cooling cycle that triggered the rapid expansion of ice across the northern hemisphere."

"Which wiped out the Clovis civilization and North American megafauna," Anya said.

"On your side of the globe," Sadik said. "On mine, it was the flooding that did the majority of the damage. Those who survived were afflicted with what modern psychologists have termed 'catastrophobia,' an extreme fear caused by abrupt physical upheaval and climatic chaos, both of which were common motifs in the artwork of otherwise disparate cultures. They saw the ending of the ice age as a form of rebirth, an archetype reflected in statues anthropomorphized with the universal symbol of birth. The flood motif is memorialized to this day in nearly every modern religion, the majority of which were conceived where we stand at this very moment, in the watershed of the Tigris and Euphrates Rivers."

The mention of flooding caused the tumblers to fall into place for Anya. That was what her mind had been crying out for her to recognize.

"The staggered construction of the buried temples reminds me of Derinkuyu and Kaymakli, neither of which is very far from here," she said. "We're talking massive underground cities carved into the soft volcanic rock, like human anthills. Both of them reach several hundred feet in depth and contain hundreds of miles of interconnected tunnels capable of comfortably housing tens of thousands of people. It was in places like these where we believe mankind rode out the Younger Dryas event in relative comfort."

"And not just the people," Sadik said, "but their animals, as well. In the ancient Iranian religion of Zoroastrianism, it is believed that the god Ahura Mazda descended from the sky with a dire warning. He foretold a coming cataclysm that would involve flooding and a winter such as had never been known. He instructed his people to build a Vara, an underground enclosure two miles long and two miles wide, and populate it with the fittest men and women and two of every type of animal."

"Like the Christian myth of Noah's Ark," Jade said.

"Which is theorized to be on Mount Ararat, just to the northeast of here. What you call myth others call fact, but is not all mythology rooted in fact? Is it so hard to believe that a Vara could be interpreted as an ark or that the two monotheistic religions share a common flood myth? Look around you. Do you not see the animals memorialized on all of these structures? They are an integral part of this metaphorical rebirth. All of them were there when man emerged from his underground warrens after countless generations and struck off to build his civilization anew, only this time under the sun. And it was on this very ground where he put to use the skills he had honed inside the earth to build upon it, where he erected the first monuments to the gods who saved them from the brutal winter and birthed them once more into a Garden of Eden."

"So they lived underground with their animals to ride out the ice age," Jade said. "It's a logical decision to make, one that any nomadic people would make under the same circumstances. It sounds like a nightmare of sanitation and disease, though. They're lucky they survived at all."

"But they did," Anya said, "and they tried to re-create the experience here. These temples exhibit the same physical configuration as the caverns underneath Derinkuyu, where the interior spaces were staggered to keep the honeycombed rock from collapsing upon itself."

"It was all they had known for more than a thousand years," Sadik said. "It makes sense for them to build a similar structure aboveground."

Evans walked around to the far side of the megaliths and stared up at the sky from between them.

"But what's the significance of aligning these giant idols with the star Deneb?" he asked.

"Everything!" Sadik said. It appeared they'd finally reached the part of the story he was itching to tell. "Where do you think Ahura Mazda came from?"

"Give me a break," Jade said.

"Whether you believe it or not is irrelevant. These people did. In fact, they believed it so deeply that they spent the next two millennia tracking it across the sky, even when the angle of the planet's precession changed and they were forced to start all over again. People traveled countless miles to stand right where you are now and look upon their god."

"Whose face they apparently didn't like."

"She's right," Evans said. "Without the faces, there's no way of validating your theory. I've studied dozens of temples, but none of them feature desecration of this nature. To mutilate the face of a god would be the ultimate sacrilege."

"As I said, this soil has given birth to many religions, some of which are outright hostile toward those whose gods they consider false, as you can see happening in this region even today. We had to erect the security fence around this dig for that very reason. There have been many days where we stood on this spot, watching the smoke rising against the horizon, feeling the ground shudder from explosions, wondering if that would be the day a caravan of Toyotas sped across the desert and destroyed this link to the origins of mankind."

"Where was Ahura Mazda when you needed him?" Jade said.

Anya discreetly elbowed her, but Sadik only smiled.

"Come with me," he said and led them down a wooden plank metered with horizontal boards that served as stairs. He gestured to a T-shaped stone only partially exhumed from the ground. It was covered with seemingly random designs and animals carved in high relief. "He was right here all along."

Anya recognized a vulture and a pair of ibises, a lizard and a scorpion. And at the very top, where the entire upper half had been broken off, were three canisters with arched handles. The central one clearly showed the hand holding it. She'd seen that exact same object before.

She looked at Evans, whose expression revealed that he'd made the same connection.

"Allow me to present Ahura Mazda," Sadik said.

He turned his cell phone around and held up the picture so they could all see. The screen displayed a petroglyph in the Assyrian style featuring a bearded man with a conical hat standing in profile. He had wings on his back and what looked like a watch on his wrist. In one hand he held a pinecone, while in the other he carried a container by the handle.

The design was nearly identical to the one they'd seen on the wall of the tomb where they found the remains of the tall man whose tattoo had led them here in the first place.

16
ROCHE

The Hangar

Roche ran into the command center. Maddox strode to meet him with a remote headset and the news Roche had been both expecting and dreading.

"Director Barnett confirmed that Subject Zeta managed to board a small aircraft and we have reason to believe it's already left the continent."

"Damn it," Roche said.

Now wasn't the time to remind everyone that he'd told them this would happen. They needed to figure out where that plane was going and have a team in place to intercept it.

He donned his headset and assumed his position on the bridge. The images on the screen scrolled frenetically as the communications specialists chased every possible lead around the world.

"What do we know?" he asked.

Kelly and Tess finally caught up with him and hovered at the back of the room. He could feel them behind him, but didn't turn to look. He was grateful for their presence; he was going to need all the help he could get.

"Our field team tracked the panel truck from Colombia to Colón, Panama," Maddox said. "They found it in the hangar of an abandoned airfield. The men inside the building had been slaughtered, but the cocaine was conspicuously absent. Our working assumption is that Subject Zeta and UNSUB X hid beneath the unrelated cargo in the truck, emerged once the cocaine had been loaded onto the plane, and mowed through the resistance to board the aircraft before it took off."

"No evidence of attempted consumption or conversion into drones?"

"Negative. The victims had been overwhelmed and dispatched in the same manner as those at the drug encampment."

"Have we established a time frame?"

"The condition of the victims' remains suggests between four and six hours."

"Jesus," Roche said. "They could be anywhere by now."

"True, but we're confident we have at least a general idea of where that plane's going," Maddox said. "The Sinaloan and Gulf cartels are the primary distributors of Colombian cocaine in the United States. The former controls most of the northwest region of Mexico, including the area bordering Arizona and California, while the latter controls the eastern side of the country, along the Gulf of Mexico, including the state of Tamaulipas, which borders Texas."

"That's nearly the entire country."

"According to the DEA, the Sinaloans dominate the trade, and based on their geographic location, receive the majority of their shipments directly from Colombia, either by plane or by boat. The Gulf Cartel has to be more creative to circumvent both the authorities and the Sinaloans, which means a truck bound for the northernmost city on the Panama Canal better fits its mold. A smaller twin-engine airplane could make it as far as Tabasco, the southernmost extent of their territory, without having to refuel. That would also be the perfect place to offload the product if their intention was to continue on to Neuva Loredo, the cartel's base of operations."

"So our working assumption is their goal is to reach Tabasco, one way or another," Roche said. "How long will that take?"

"Six to eight hours, depending upon their route," Maddox said. "If they're able to negotiate passage through Honduran and Nicaraguan airspace, they could potentially be there already."

"How quickly can we get a team there?"

"Barnett's unit is still our best shot. They just boarded a Cessna Citation X+, whose top speed is nearly 650 miles per hour, easily three times that of what we believe—based on the tire tracks and the distance between them—to be an older-model Piper Chieftain cargo plane. If they push it, they can be there in two hours."

"Then tell them to push it," Roche said. "In the meantime, we need a list of every active and decommissioned airfield within that Chieftain's range and satellites tasked to their locations. And contact the authorities in Guatemala, Honduras, and Nicaragua. Let them know what we're looking for and tell them to alert us the moment it hits their airspace."

"Assuming it hasn't already passed through."

"We'd better hope it hasn't," Roche said and turned to one of the communications specialists. "Bring up the satellite feed of Göbekli Tepe and get Dr. Evans on the phone."

"Transferring to the main screen," O'Reilly said.

A second later, Roche heard ringing in his headset. He was resigned to leaving a message when the call was finally answered.

"Evans."

"Where are you by now?" Roche asked.

"Right to it, huh?"

"We're in the middle of a rapidly devolving situation, and time is of the essence." The image on the screen switched to display the archeological site in Turkey. Four figures were clearly visible among the ruins. "Who's that with you?"

The miniature version of Evans on the screen craned his neck, shielded his eyes, and looked straight up at the satellite.

"The chief archeologist. Dr. Ahmet Sadik. He's in the process of explaining the history of the site."

"Tess discovered something you need to see. I'll have her forward it to you now." Roche glanced back at Tess, who'd already taken his cue and was in the process of sending the aerial images of the site with the matching overlay of the constellation Cygnus. "I'm not entirely sure what it means, but there has to be some significance."

"Give me a second to look at it," Evans said.

Roche covered the microphone and turned to Maddox.

"How are we coming on that list of airfields?"

"There are twelve commercial airports, although most of them hardly qualify as such, within the plane's range in the Mexican states of Veracruz, Campeche, Chiapas, and Tabasco," he said from where he leaned over the shoulder of the specialist charged with the task. "But that whole area's one big, sparsely inhabited rainforest. They could raze the trees, set up their own runway, and eliminate the risk of landing anywhere with a control tower."

"Then broaden the range of the satellites and look for anything that could serve as a makeshift airfield. They'll want to unload their cargo away from prying eyes, and they're going to need to refuel that plane, whether it's continuing north or returning to Panama. This setup has to be more than just a long stretch of dirt road."

"This is amazing," Evans said.

"Talk to me, Cade."

"This entire site was built with the intention of tracking a single star across the sky."

"Let me guess," Roche said. "It's one in that very constellation."

"Deneb, the head of the Northern Cross and the point dead center in the constellation."

"What's its theoretical significance?"

"It's where their god came from."

"Why am I not surprised?" He heard the sound of running footsteps from the hallway behind him but tuned them out. "Does the map overlay mean anything to you?"

"It means we need to find out what's waiting for us at the point where Deneb would be."

"Do you know where that is?"

"I'm sure I can find it."

A communications specialist burst into the room.

"I have an urgent call for the director," he said.

"Barnett's in the field," Maddox said.

"I told him that and he said to pass him down the chain to whoever's in charge. He has all of the proper security codes."

Maddox glanced at Roche and raised his brows.

"It's all yours," he said with a smirk.

"Let me know the moment you get there," Roche said to Evans. He terminated the call and turned to face the specialist. "Transfer the call to my com."

He heard a click, and then the hollow sound of an open line.

"Roche," he answered.

"Wait," the caller said. *"As in Martin Roche? You've got to be freaking kidding me."*

"If only I were."

"And you're in charge in Barnett's absence?"

"It was either Maddox or me, and apparently I drew the short straw," Roche said. "But I'm in the middle of something kind of important right now, so I really don't have the time—"

"Totally my bad. You just caught me off guard is all. You're about the last person in the world I expected to talk to. Not just there, but, I mean, ever again." The cadence of the caller's voice was familiar. Recognition dawned with a sinking sensation in Roche's stomach. *"I don't know if you remember me, but my name is Max Friden. Dr. Max Friden. From . . . you know . . ."*

Roche glanced back at Kelly, who appeared every bit as surprised as he was. Friden had been the resident microbiologist at AREA 51, the research station responsible for the discovery of the ancient civilization beneath the Antarctic ice cap and the subsequent creation of Subject Z.

"I take it from your silence that you do remember me," Friden said. *"But I'm not calling to catch up on old times. In fact, I'd really rather not. Like ever. I'm actually calling in my official capacity as director of the Special Pathogens Laboratory at the U.S. Army Medical Research Institute of Infectious Diseases."*

Roche stiffened. That was the lab where they'd taken the biological samples from the tomb in Mosul.

"What did you find?"

"Not over the phone. This is the kind of thing you have to see to believe."

17

TRUJILLO

**8 miles northwest of Chontalpa,
Tabasco, Mexico**

Gervasio Trujillo opened his eyes and raised the brim of his camouflage cap. It was about goddamn time. He unlaced his heels, rolled his chair back from the desk, and headed for the hangar door, where his men were already waiting. They wore the same camo fatigues with black balaclavas that concealed their faces, save for a narrow horizontal strip over their wide eyes. The way they clung to their Kalashnikovs reminded him how very young they actually were. Theirs was a business where few lived long enough to benefit from their experience, which was why Trujillo gestured for them to slide open the door and precede him into the clearing. He wasn't the slightest bit concerned that any of their rivals would be so bold as to make a move on the handoff, but he hadn't survived this long by taking unnecessary chances.

The assault of the heat and humidity was instantaneous and reinforced by the swarming mosquitoes. He waved them away, shielded his eyes, and looked to the southeast toward the source of the buzzing sound that had roused him from his siesta. The sun reflected from the fuselage of the distant plane through the gaps of the trees as it skimmed the upper canopy to keep from popping up on radar.

He whistled between his teeth and twirled his index finger over his head. His men took the cue and assumed their positions on either side of the narrow asphalt runway. A handful of snipers were already hidden in the trees, invisible to anyone who didn't know exactly where they were. Those in the open served as little more than a demonstration of strength, for he was prepared to lose every single one of them should anything go wrong. They all understood the risks, not just for themselves, but for their families, as well. Should any of them find themselves in the custody of the federales or, worse, the Sinaloans, whether or not they intended to cooperate, their loved ones would be dragged from their homes and executed in the most visceral manner possible for all to see. It was the kind of deterrent that guaranteed his men would fight to the bitter end, and the reason Trujillo had eliminated all personal attachments long ago. His allegiance was to his employers—more specifically, to the dinero they paid him—but should they ever fail to recognize his worth, he'd fall back on his training in Fuerzas Especiales, the naval special forces unit that had trained him in unconventional warfare tactics, and make them regret it.

The drone of the twin engines grew louder by the second, producing an echo from inside the corrugated aluminum hangar. The rumble of the fuel truck's engine joined it as the tanker emerged from the adjacent shed and headed toward the end of the runway, where the plane would pause only long enough for them to unload its cargo, refuel it, and load the waiting crates of cash.

Half an hour from now, they'd be on their way once more, all of them exponentially richer for their labors.

Trujillo strode toward where the fuel truck idled and turned to watch the plane approach. The airfield had been abandoned since long before any of them were born. It was invisible from the sky until you were right on top of it, and even then the pilot needed to make a perfect approach to hit the landing strip with enough space to decelerate before careening off into the dense jungle. There was a reason that people were only now beginning to find the old Mayan temples hidden around here. Much like him, the jungle took what it wanted and left no evidence behind.

The Chieftain was coming it so low he could barely see it over the treetops.

"Viene muy rápido," the driver of the tanker said.

Trujillo nodded. The man was right; it was definitely coming in too fast.

The plane disappeared behind the trees for several moments before appearing once more. It wasn't going to clear the canopy. The roar of the engines grew louder. Its flaps were up and its landing gear was down, but the approach sounded all wrong. The pilot wasn't making any effort to slow its descent.

Trujillo unclipped his transceiver from his hip and spoke into the microphone.

"Tenemos un problema. Mantén tus ojos abiertos."

The plane once more vanished, even as the engines grew louder. The men guarding the runway looked curiously at each other. Even they could sense that everything wasn't going as planned, but they held their positions.

Wind sheared from the wings with a high-pitched scream that reminded him of incoming mortar fire.

"*¡Huir!*" Trujillo shouted and sprinted away from the landing strip.

He heard the crashing sound of breaking branches and the shriek of wrenching metal as the plane burst from the trees. Its landing gear tore off and bounded onto the runway. One of its propellers flew off and chewed up the earth on its way through the side of the hangar.

His men didn't react fast enough. The plane hit the asphalt on its exposed belly and swung sideways, its wing cutting through those on the left side while its tail pulverized those on the right.

The engine of the fuel truck growled. It made a beeping sound as the driver threw it into reverse.

Trujillo caught a glimpse of the front windshield of the plane, the interior spattered with blood, as it skidded past, sparks flying from underneath it, straight toward the tanker.

The impact shook the earth.

A wall of superheated air struck him from behind. Lifted him from his feet. Hurled him ahead of it.

Trujillo rebounded from the turf, tumbled through the smoke, and smashed into the side of the panel truck containing crates filled with cash. A flaming tire bounded past in his peripheral vision.

He tried to get up, but the ringing in his ears toyed with his balance. Fires burned all around him. From the ground. The trees. He heard screaming through the smoke, the distant sound of gunfire. Not the rattle of AK-47s, but the booming thunder of long-range rifles. The snipers. Suddenly everything made sense.

The Sinaloans.

They'd shot down the plane and were about to swarm

the airfield. The hell if he was going down without taking them with him.

He followed the screams toward where one of his men lay facedown on the scorched earth, clawing his way toward where his weapon rested, beyond his reach. He appeared oblivious to the fact that his severed legs were still burning behind him.

Trujillo snatched the Kalashnikov from the ground and seated it against his shoulder. He'd lost his transceiver, but there was nothing he could do about that now.

A rapid series of gunshots. Screaming. Then, abrupt silence.

It struck him that he hadn't heard any return fire; his men were the only ones shooting.

They were in the middle of nowhere. The closest settlement was a dozen miles away and probably didn't even have a phone, let alone a police force. There was no reason for their attackers to be using suppressed weapons. Come to think of it, he hadn't heard whatever weapon they'd used to take down the plane, and while the front windshield had been covered with blood, it had remained intact.

More gunfire from the trees on the far side of the runway, somewhere deep within the roiling smoke. An errant shot ricocheted from the tarmac and struck the front tire of the panel truck.

He dove to the side. Scurried through the weeds. Pushed himself into a crouch and sprinted toward the burning plane. His employers would never forgive his failure, but salvaging what was left of the cargo might be able to buy him some leniency. Or maybe a new life where no one could find him, assuming such a thing was possible.

The fuel truck rested on its roof, canted sideways on a tank that had ruptured like a baked potato. Flames rose from what little was left of the fuselage beside it. The wings were nowhere to be seen. Smoke boiled from the open cargo hatch. The door was scored with deep grooves, presumably from the tree branches raking through the metal on the way down, although it almost looked as though they'd been inflicted in the process of prying open the door. The duct tape–wrapped bricks of cocaine inside were only beginning to smolder.

Trujillo pulled his undershirt up over his mouth and nose. Held it in place with his teeth. Slung the AK-47 over his shoulder, climbed inside, and started shoveling out the bricks as fast as he could.

Another scream. This time from the jungle behind the hangar.

He glanced in that direction, but couldn't see anything through the front windshield, now spiderwebbed with cracks and darkened by soot. The pilot leaned sideways from his seat, his neck torn nearly all the way through, leaving his head to dangle by tendons and broken bones. He couldn't have sustained an injury like that in the crash, which meant—

Again, he looked at the damage to the door. Long, deep gouges from an implement easily sharp enough to partially decapitate a man. And a partitioned area, beside the cocaine, someone could have hidden inside.

The hell with this. He was out of here.

Trujillo jumped out, gathered as many bricks as he could carry, and ran for the jungle. With his instincts and training, he'd be able to disappear and no one would ever find him. He knew how to live off the land, how to survive where no one else could.

An explosion behind him marked the passing of the plane. Flames washed over him from behind. He used the smoke to cover his escape and prayed his coughing wouldn't give him away.

He and his men had been set up from the start. They were being hunted by men with knives, men who hoped to throw the Gulf Cartel off their scent. Weapons could be traced and bullets could be matched, but if it looked like Trujillo's men had been slaughtered by wild animals—

A silhouette appeared through the smoke. Here one instant, gone the next. It was easily a full head taller than he was. Maybe more. It almost looked like a deer, rearing up on its hind legs, antlers protruding from its head, but its outline . . . appeared almost human.

Trujillo veered away from it and momentarily lost it to the smoke.

He felt a cold sensation across the backs of his legs and went down hard. Landed on his chest before he even knew he was falling. Ruptured several of the bundles. Coughed out the white dust. Spit the paste from his mouth, which was already beginning to tingle. Pain blossomed from behind his knees. Warmth poured over his calves. He tried to stand but couldn't seem to make his legs work.

The cocaine burned his eyes, his nostrils. He rolled over onto his back and saw his limp legs, only the upper halves of which rolled over with him. His heart jackhammered in his chest, so fast the edges of his vision shivered.

Something crouched over him from behind. He caught a glimpse of it from the corner of his eye—spindly appendages, a narrow chest, an elongated skull—but he couldn't bring himself to look away from the silhouette

approaching through the smoke. Its body was ensconced
in a gauzelike cloak, which did little to conceal the femi-
nine contours underneath. The woman reached up and removed what looked like the head of a stag from on top of
her own. Stared down at him for several seconds before
finally kneeling so she could get a closer look at him.

While human in form, there was nothing human about
her face. Her skin was psoriatic. Scaled. Like the flesh
sloughing from the body of a dead fish. Her pupils were
vertical slits, gecko-like, her teeth an amalgam of human
and serpent.

She spoke in a guttural language he'd never heard before.

"Zi dingir kia kanpa!"

Fingernails like talons struck his forehead. Lanced
straight through his skin, burrowed into the bone. Jerked
his head back.

He found himself looking up into the face of the being
crouching behind him. Pale gray skin, circular black
eyes, a conical head, and a smile knitted with needle-like
teeth.

Trujillo screamed until he felt the woman's teeth enter
his throat.

And then he screamed no more.

18
EVANS

Göbekli Tepe

Evans stood at the edge of the stone escarpment and consulted the image of the constellation Cygnus superimposed over Göbekli Tepe. If Tess's calculations were
correct, the point that aligned with the brightest star in the
Northern Cross, the one all of the observatories behind
him had been designed to track, was just over the next
rise. He stared out across the desolate valley toward a
limestone precipice from which a single twisted pine tree
grew.

"What's over there?" he asked.

Sadik shielded his eyes from the glare of the sun. He
was sweating even more now, if such a thing were even
possible.

"The entire plateau is composed of the bedrock from
which the megaliths throughout this site were quarried."

"You haven't found anything else over there?" Jade
said.

"As you can plainly see, there are no structures of any
kind."

"There has to be something," Evans said and commenced picking his way down the rocky slope.

"I assure you," Sadik said, "there is nothing of interest to you over there. In fact, we had to cordon off a large section after the most recent earthquake. We have strict instructions not to allow anyone up there until a geologist from the Ministry of Energy and Natural Resources has evaluated its structural integrity."

"Trust me," Anya said as she passed the archeologist. "There's nothing up there that could be half as dangerous as what we've been dealing with for the last year."

"We should at least return to the trailer and equip ourselves with the proper protective—"

"I just want to take a quick peek," Evans called back over his shoulder. "If there's anything up there that warrants further investigation, I promise we'll take all necessary precautions."

The loose sand and gravel gave way to sparse clumps of wild grasses and briars. He found it hard to believe that any number of people could have designed a settlement to match a constellation composed primarily of stars not visible to the naked eye, but considering he'd found the site using a map tattooed on the remains of a giant entombed three hundred miles from here, he was willing to set aside his skepticism, at least temporarily.

"They quarried the limestone from the ground directly beneath their feet," Sadik said. "The sharpened edge of a stone blade dulled as quickly as it cut, which means it took several months to chisel a single megalith."

"If each of them weighed multiple tons, how did they get them down one hill and to the top of the next?" Jade asked.

Anya answered for him.

"They laid logs side by side and used them to roll the stone blocks, almost like a primitive conveyor belt."

"Exactly," Sadik said. "Until recently there was a well-preserved megalith only partially carved from the bedrock. We believe they fractured it during the process of excavating it, so they were forced to leave it behind. Much to our good fortune. It is from this mistake that we were able to understand how the founders of Göbekli Tepe were able to accomplish such a magnificent feat."

They crested the rise to find random chunks of limestone protruding from loose soil barely deep enough to hold the roots of the wild grasses. It was a small miracle that the pine tree crowning the plateau had been able to grow at all.

Evans stared out across the vast expanse of weeds and exposed stone, beyond which gray clouds scudded across the sky. Metal posts had been staked in a circle around the central region. The yellow caution tape strung between them snapped on the rising wind. The ragged pine tree grew amid jagged stone outcroppings at the heart of the ring. Something about it nagged at him.

He glanced again at the image on his phone. If the GPS coordinates were accurate, the point corresponding to Deneb was somewhere within the cordoned zone.

"I didn't realize that Turkey was prone to earthquakes," he said.

"This region sits on the Anatolian Plate," Sadik said. "There are two major strike-slip fault zones to either side of us. Seismic activity is commonplace."

Evans couldn't seem to look away from the tree. Its sparsely needled branches were so thin that they hardly appeared strong enough to support the handful of pinecones that had managed to grow.

"Must have been a heck of an earthquake to cause

structural damage to bedrock like this," he said. "How strong was it?"

"Four-point-nine on the Richter scale."

He thought of the petroglyph of Ahura Mazda from inside the tomb in Mosul. The bearded deity had been depicted raising a pinecone in one hand, and holding a canister in the other, directly underneath it, the same canister that had been carved upon the megalith in the ruins behind him.

"Strange to think that this plateau withstood twelve thousand years of seismic activity only to be done in by an earthquake under five in magnitude. How long ago did it happen?"

"Just under two weeks," Sadik said. "I remember it specifically because it was the same day as the solar eclipse."

Evans glanced back at Jade, who read his expression and offered a subtle nod. He returned his gaze to the pine tree. He was by no means a botanist, but he did understand that a tree needed three things to grow: sunlight, water, and soil. No tree could grow without water, let alone in a few inches of loose dirt, which meant that not only was the soil underneath it considerably deeper, it either trapped some amount of precipitation above the underlying limestone, or the roots had found access to some other subterranean source.

He stepped over the caution tape and struck off toward the tree.

"What are you doing?" Sadik asked. "You said you would return to the trailer for protective gear. This area is too dangerous to proceed without it."

"You're probably right," Evans said, "but I didn't travel all this way to play it safe."

Besides, he didn't believe in coincidences, and arriving to find the specific area he was searching for cordoned off was a bigger one than he could swallow. He wasn't so far removed from the incident at Teotihuacan that he'd forgotten how an earthquake had exposed the entrance to the ancient subterranean maze and caused Enigma to emerge from the shadows. Was it possible that similar underground warrens awaited them beneath the superficial limestone? And if so, what did they contain? They needed to find out before the masked paramilitary group that had nearly killed them in Mexico to claim the mummified remains caught wind of their discovery.

"I must insist you turn around," Sadik called after him. "Mine is not the most forgiving government when it comes to violating its directives. Any perceived violation could lead to the revocation of our permit . . ."

The wind carried away the archeologist's words as Evans neared the tree. The surrounding limestone had been thrust upward at odd angles by the seismic activity, forming what looked like a jagged crown around its trunk. The stone that had been exposed to the elements for millennia was pale gray and covered with red lichen, while the undersides, which, until recently, had been lodged in the earth, were considerably darker and clotted with dirt. The tree itself leaned to the southwest, the roots on the opposite side pulled out just far enough to expose the rich, dark soil underneath them.

Evans crouched and dug through it, but only encountered more roots. He'd been so certain he'd find either a hidden orifice or the canister from the petroglyphs. They were going to have to remove the entire tree, which would probably cause Sadik to have a coronary, but they couldn't risk being beaten to the prize, especially if it had anything to do with the virus that had killed every living being inside the tomb in Mosul.

He stood and waved the others closer. They were already across the tape and halfway to him, treading carefully to avoid the crevices in the unstable limestone. If they wanted to get that tree out of there in a hurry, they were going to need help, specifically the kind that required some oil to grease the bureaucratic wheels of the Turkish government, not to mention some heavy equipment.

Evans walked several paces away and removed his cell phone from his pocket. He was just about to call Roche when he noticed the megalith Sadik had described earlier. The edges had been rounded by the erosive forces of nature, but the T-shape remained clearly defined. As was the diagonal fissure across the middle that had caused its makers to abandon it, only it was more than a mere crack now. The upper half stood at an angle to the lower, revealing a narrow opening.

"Guys?" Evans said and knelt on the ground beside it. "I think I found what we're looking for."

He tilted the screen of his phone to get a better look. It produced just enough light to reveal that the hole continued straight down, well beyond its reach.

The megalith hadn't been left behind because its builders broke it; they'd deliberately placed it over the hole to make sure that no one who didn't already know it was there would ever be able to find it.

Evans jumped to his feet, prepared to share his revelation with the others, only to find them facing away from him, holding their hands up at their sides. Sadik stood before them with a pistol in his hand. His face was positively dripping with sweat.

"I really wish you hadn't found that," he said.

19
TESS

The Hangar

Tess could feel all of the disparate events beginning to coalesce, and it was up to her to figure out what was about to happen. Or, more precisely, *where* it was about to happen. If they were right, the three similar crop circles represented not just specific dates and times in the planetary cycles, but locations, as well. The pattern from Alton Barnes had led them to Göbekli Tepe, where, theoretically, something had transpired to coincide with the solar eclipse nearly two weeks ago. While she had no idea what that might have been, hopefully their team on the ground would be able to solve that mystery any second now. In the meantime, it was up to her to determine the other two locations, and she needed to do so in a hurry, because in just over twenty-four hours, the Earth's shadow would eclipse the moon, triggering an unknown phenomenon with potential global ramifications.

She brought up the AuthaGraph world map, with its strangely contorted continents angled diagonally from the upper left to the bottom right, on the first of the four monitors on the wall behind her desk and overlaid the extraneous data points from the re-creation of the night sky

Subject Z had carved into the ceiling of its Antarctic cell. The cluster over southern Turkey was readily apparent, as were maybe a dozen others spread across the landmasses, too many to examine without something resembling a plan of action.

The three crop circles from July 1990, in Wiltshire County, England, were displayed on the adjacent monitors. She'd scaled the one from Alton Barnes—officially classified as CC1—to fit the map, and then adjusted the other two to match. While they all had the same basic elements, there were subtle distinctions between each of them. The Earth, the moon, Mars, and Jupiter all looked the same, with minor differences corresponding to the positions of their tuning fork-shaped appendages, which marked the time of day on each. The locations of Saturn, Neptune, and Venus varied, although not by so much that they warranted special attention. The only glaring variance between them—outside of the order of the Earth and the moon—had to do with Saturn.

The crop circle from Stanton St. Bernard—CC3—depicted Saturn with one ring instead of two, while the one from East Kennett—CC2—featured two Saturns: one exactly where it was supposed to be, between Jupiter and Neptune, and a second, inexplicable instance far to the right of all of the other planets. Curiously, the body of what she'd come to think of as Sat2 was larger than that of Sat1, and more closely resembled the Saturn of CC1, which had aligned with Nineveh.

"Could it be that simple?" Tess said aloud.

She zoomed in on the AuthaGraph map until she could clearly see the Middle East, from the Black Sea in the north to Ethiopia in the south, and Greece in the west to Afghanistan in the east. She overlaid CC1 so that it aligned with the cities from the ancient Assyrian map, placed CC2 on top of it, and then centered Sat2 over Nineveh, which caused the remainder of the crop circle, the portion that matched CC1, to slide across the Mediterranean Sea and partially off the screen to the left. Considering all of Subject Z's data points were on the land now, that couldn't possibly be right, could it? Then again, the continents had been steadily moving apart since Pangaea broke apart.

And then she saw it.

If she kept Sat2 on Nineveh and rotated the design roughly 40 degrees counterclockwise so that Neptune aligned with Kalah, just as it did with CC1, the planets ran diagonally down through Syria, Jordan, Israel, and Egypt.

"I need an older map!"

Tess rushed across the room to Kelly's computer, opened the map of ancient Mesopotamia, and forwarded it to her system. Dashed back to her desk. Brought up the file, adjusted the scale, and substituted it for the detail section of the Middle East on the AuthaGraph map.

The pattern was unmistakable.

Sat1 aligned with Palmyra, a primitive settlement in Syria. Neptune and Uranus matched Haræ and Oriza. Jupiter fell upon Damascus and Mars marked Jerusalem. The gap in the line connecting Mars to the moon signified where it crossed the southeastern corner of the Mediterranean, while the moon itself corresponded to Tanis. The bull's-eye of the Earth landed squarely on Giza, home of the pyramids and the Great Sphinx. Mercury and Venus coincided with Faiyum and Saqqara, respectively.

It made perfect sense. Göbekli Tepe and Giza were

two of the most important sites in the Old World and also the most inexplicable. Both were architectural anomalies, marvels of physics, and monuments to technology and skills beyond those of the people of the time. And if she was right, then the extra data points from Subject Z's carving of the night sky should line up—

"Perfectly," she finished out loud.

Tess switched from the ancient Mesopotamian map to Google Earth and zoomed in until she was able to clearly see the dots aligned with Giza. In fact, three of them synched perfectly with the pyramids of Menkaure, Khafre, and Khufu. It was only then that she made the connection.

Just as the pattern over southern Turkey had formed the constellation Cygnus, this one formed Orion. His belt consisted of the stars Alnitak, Alnilam, and Mintaka—the Three Sisters—each of which corresponded to a pyramid. The Sigma Orionis system and the Orion Nebula, which combined to form his scabbard, fell upon the mortuary temple and the tombs. The buildings that corresponded to the remainder of the constellation's primary stars—Betelgeuse, Meissa, Bellatrix, Rigel, and Siaph—were impossible to find, thanks to the constantly shifting desert and the modern city that had grown up around the—

"Pyramids," she said. She looked at the printout of the fourth crop circle, CS4. It was so different from the others that she'd unconsciously either discounted its significance or considered it unrelated, but now that she knew what she was looking for, she could tell exactly what it represented. The small, scattered dots outlined the coast of Antarctica, while the large circle with the fork-like extension marked the South Pole. The bull's-eye corresponded with what they theorized to be the lost city of Atlantis, where they had discovered the pyramid with the transformative powers. Was it possible the Egyptian pyramids served a similar function?

This was huge. She had to tell someone. They needed to dispatch a field team to Giza right now.

Tess ran out of her office and sprinted down the hall. Hit the stairs so she didn't have to wait for the elevator. Blew through the door and hurtled down the corridor. Burst into the command center.

"I figured out the second location!" she shouted.

Maddox whirled to face her, his eyes wide, his lips a grim line. His right hand instinctively sought the pistol holstered to his hip. His expression softened and his hand fell away from his weapon, but for the most fleeting of seconds she'd been certain he was going to draw it. "You startled me, Dr. Clarke." He offered an embarrassed smile, one she was more than a little surprised to discover made her lower abdomen tingle. Something about his scars made him seem vulnerable, and maybe even a little dangerous. She'd never thought of him in a romantic light, but perhaps it was high time she did. "Trust me when I say that's not an easy thing to do."

Behind him, the image on the main screen switched from an aerial view of Göbekli Tepe to a nondescript jungle. The shaky footage from the live drone feeds on the surrounding monitors made her queasy.

"Where are Martin and Kelly?" she asked.

"In the field," he said, "but I'd be happy to relay your findings."

She'd been so caught up in her work that she'd forgotten they were on their way to the medical facilities at

USAMRIID to meet with Dr. Friden, whose name she'd heard countless times while she was in Antarctica. He was the microbiologist who'd insisted upon bringing the mouse that had caused so much trouble.

"The second crop circle leads to Giza, which just happens to align with the constellation of Orion. Or at least part of it."

"You're certain?"

"One hundred percent."

Maddox smiled and turned to face his team of information specialists.

"Task another satellite," he said. "I need eyes on Giza. And find me the nearest drone."

There was a flurry of activity at the workstations below the bridge. Lines of code scrolled across several of the screens as his men performed their tasks. One jumped up from his seat and ran past her, presumably on his way to the Arcade, which housed stations resembling video game consoles from which to remotely control a veritable armada of drones.

"Excellent work, Dr. Clarke," Maddox said. "I knew you'd be able to crack the code. What about the other crop circles?"

"The fourth—the one that looks nothing like the others—aligns with Forward Operating Base Atlantis, which we probably should have recognized from the start."

"And the third?"

"I was just about to start on it. Now that I know what I'm doing, it shouldn't take too long."

"Perfect. Let me know the moment you decipher it." He offered a wink and a crooked smile. "If anyone can do it, Dr. Clarke, it's you."

Tess blushed and headed back to her office. All modesty aside, his sentiments reinforced her innermost feelings. This riddle seemed to have been custom-tailored to her skill set. If anyone in the world was equipped to solve this mystery, it was her.

20
KELLY

U.S. Army Medical Research
Institute of Infectious Diseases,
Fort Detrick, Maryland

It was a three-hour drive from Joint Base Langley-Eustis to Fort Detrick; the Black Hawk made it in under thirty minutes. Dr. Max Friden had been waiting in the front alcove when they landed and charged through the rotor wash to meet them, his lab coat snapping behind him on the hurricane-force wind. He looked just like Kelly remembered, with his round glasses and narrow face, but considerably healthier thanks to the exposure to natural sunlight he'd been denied in Antarctica.

Roche climbed out first and hopped to the tarmac. He ducked his head and jogged toward Friden, who had to shout to be heard over the whine of the engine as it ramped down.

"It's about time you got here. You absolutely will not believe—" He abruptly turned to look at Kelly as she rushed to catch up with them. "Hello. And just who is this divine—?"

"Stow it, Friden," Roche said. "You remember Dr. Nolan."

"Kelly?" he said. "My goodness, you've changed. And for the better, I might add. That silver hair really brings out the color of your eyes."

She rolled them for his benefit.

"Nice to know some things never change, Max."

"Are you through?" Roche asked.

"Oh, yeah," Friden said and snapped his fingers. "I totally forgot you guys were a thing."

As if sensing their discomfort with the subject, he looked at each of them in turn. "Does this mean you're not a thing?" He cocked his head and offered a boyish grin. "If you're not too busy, maybe afterward we could—?"

"You called us here," Kelly said. "Remember?"

"Right. We'll circle back to that topic later."

Friden led them up the walkway, through the entrance, and into a five-story atrium that reminded Kelly more of a hospital than a military installation. Everything was shiny and modern: from the polished tile floor to the vaulted ceiling, and all of the windows and sound-dampening panels in between. There was even a coffee kiosk surrounded by chairs that appeared as though a person could melt right into them.

"Don't let the looks of this place deceive you," Friden said. He guided them straight across the vast space toward a bank of stainless-steel elevators. "The scientists in these labs are working with some of the nastiest stuff you can imagine. I'm talking biological agents like anthrax and ricin, hemorrhagic viruses like Ebola and Marburg, staphyloccalenterotoxin B—I just love saying that one—plague, botulism. You name it, it's somewhere within these walls. Plus a few more sensitive projects, which is why you're here."

"Isn't all of that supposed to be housed at the CDC in Atlanta?" Roche asked.

They stopped in front of a bank of stainless-steel elevators, one of which was ready and waiting. Its door opened the moment Friden pushed the button, and they all stepped inside. He pressed his badge to the digital reader, which unlocked the access panel and buttons numbered one through five. An additional panel slid back and revealed a retinal scanner. He removed his glasses, leaned closer, and stared into the red light. The elevator doors automatically closed.

"That's the public health side of the coin. Those guys handle all of the touchy-feely outreach kind of stuff."

"Like trying to prevent and control our exposure to diseases?" Kelly said.

"Exactly," Friden said, oblivious to her sarcasm. "It's our job here to develop active countermeasures and figure out the most efficient ways of killing these bastards."

"Or weaponizing them," Roche said.

Kelly turned to face the doors as the elevator commenced its descent to an unlabeled sublevel. Roche's eyes met hers in the reflection on the stainless-steel panel. They both knew that if someone here was working with the alien bacterium that was responsible for the creation of Subject Z, they had a whole lot more to worry about than whatever virus had been contained in the Iraqi tomb, assuming that was even why they were here in the first place. The military applications of harnessing a hive-mind organism with such murderous potential were unlimited, as were the ways any kind of experimentation could go wrong.

"That's not my bag."

"Then what is your bag?"

"I get to work with the kind of cool things no one else can wrap their heads around. That whole mess at AREA 51 might have been the worst thing to ever happen to me personally, but definitely not professionally. Thanks to that alien organism, people figured that I knew all kinds of things that I didn't. It was like I woke up one day to find the government shoving security clearances in my face and begging me to work with stuff that would literally blow your mind. Why do you think you guys still send your samples to me?"

"I didn't know that we did," Roche said.

"Aren't you some sort of bigwig over there now?"

"I'm learning there's a lot Barnett hasn't told anyone."

"Why am I not surprised?"

The elevator dinged, and the doors opened upon a subterranean level that had to be more than fifty feet down, based on the duration of the ride. Everything down here looked a whole lot more intimidating. Gone were fancy chairs, picture windows, and modern décor. The walls were bare and utilitarian, the lighting cold and lifeless, and the dispersal nozzles blossoming from the ceiling the kind designed to expel highly pressurized, flammable accelerants that could be used to "sterilize" the corridor with a massive fireball should so much as a single viral particle escape the sealed labs.

At the end of the short corridor was a small reception area of sorts with a table and chairs, a coffee maker, refrigerator, and microwave. There were two doors on either side. Restrooms, a utility closet, and storage, or so it appeared. The lone door at the back of the room was different from all of the others. It was made of stainless steel and looked like a cross between a bank vault and the hatch on a submarine, only with a reinforced window at eye level. The lighted sign above it displayed the word CLEAR in red letters.

Friden walked straight toward it, opened it with a hiss of escaping air, and gestured for them to precede him into the pressurized room. Isolation suits hung from specially designed racks on the walls. Coiled tubing dangled from the ceiling beside each of them.

"All of the labs down here are biosafety level four, which means we have to wear positive-pressure protective suits. As soon as you put it on, hook it to the tubing. That'll fill it with oxygen and create a pressure barrier, so even if the integrity of the suit is compromised, air will be forced out instead of being sucked in."

Kelly was familiar with suits like these. The engineering team had worn them inside the submerged pyramid in Antarctica, for all the good it had done them. She elected not to share that observation with the others as she slipped into the smallest suit she could find, sealed it across her chest, and attached the air nozzle, which caused the plastic shield covering her face and upper chest to momentarily fog up. She glanced at Roche, who looked just about as nervous as she felt.

"Ready?" Friden asked.

Neither Kelly nor Roche could find the voice to respond.

"Oh, come on," the microbiologist said. "It's not that bad. Just don't fart in there or the smell will seep into your clothes and you'll be walking around with it for the rest of the day."

He unhooked himself from his hose and headed for the inner door. The sign posted on it read:

DO NOT ENTER
WITHOUT
VENTILATED SUIT
NO GLASSWARE
BEYOND THIS POINT

When he opened it, the door behind them automatically locked with a loud *thunk*.

The next chamber was barely large enough to accommodate all three of them at once. Friden again hooked his suit to the coiled tubing hanging from the ceiling and the others followed suit. Kelly noticed the grate in the floor and the nozzles overhead a heartbeat before chemicals poured down on them.

Friden raised his arms over his head and turned in circles to make sure that every inch of his suit was sterilized, then watched to make sure Kelly and Roche did the same. The lock on the inner door disengaged when the flow ceased. The hallway on the other side had bare white walls and blue doors with inset windows, through which Kelly saw clean rooms with hooded workstations, massive glove boxes containing Lord only knew what, and equipment ranging from test tubes and petri dishes to microscopes and centrifuges, plus countless devices so foreign to her that she couldn't even speculate as to their designated functions.

He opened the fourth door on the right, instructed them to attach the hoses hanging beside them, and led them into a lab that was the complete opposite of the one he'd shared with Speedy, the mouse he'd brought with him to Antarctica. Everything was spotless, from the work surface underneath the window running the width of the rear wall to the hooded stations to either side. There were computer monitors mounted to the walls and what almost looked like an arcade console with twin joysticks. The window offered a glimpse of the adjoining sealed room, where she saw a glove box filled with various instrumentation, only the attached gloves hadn't been designed for human hands, but rather the robotic armatures connected to the ceiling.

Friden assumed the stool closest to the joysticks and directed their attention to the monitor above the window. Kelly leaned closer so she could better see what almost looked like a honeycomb made from the tattered sails of a ghost ship.

"What are we looking at?" she asked.

"Those are desiccated adipocytes. Dried-up fat cells, if you will. They're some of the largest cells in the human body, which helps to illustrate what I'm about to show you." He toggled the joysticks and a whining sound emanated from the adjacent chamber. The armatures on the other side of the window advanced into the glove box, toward what she assumed to be the microscopic array responsible for the image on the screen. "As I'm sure even you know, adipocytes form a cushioning layer underneath the skin to both protect the underlying tissue and store energy reserves. When a body dies, these cells essentially liquefy and the greasy fat drains out. That's one of the most important factors in the process of mummification."

Kelly suddenly understood where the sample had come from. She glanced at Roche, whose expression remained guarded, but she knew him well enough to see through it. He recognized the source, too.

"The sample is from the body in Mosul," she said.

"Um, yeah," Friden said. "It would have been nice if

you guys could have offered a little more information than that. Might even have saved me several months—"

"What did you find?" Roche asked.

"Check this out." He looked back at Kelly, winked, and manipulated the joysticks. "Prepare to be amazed."

The image on the screen simultaneously darkened and blurred. When the details resolved, the honeycomb was already well into the process of regeneration. The empty cells refilled and plumped up. The formerly ragged edges became smooth. Within a matter of seconds, it appeared to be a completely different sample.

"What did you do?" Roche asked.

"That, my friend, was a single drop of hemoglobin. Those fat cells not only absorbed it, but incorporated it into their biomass. I tried the same experiment with tissue samples collected elsewhere in the body. Skin, nerve, viscera. The same thing happened to each and every one of them."

"That's impossible," Kelly said, but she knew that wasn't the case at all.

She'd seen the footage of Subject Z slitting a man's throat and bleeding him onto the remains in the stone sarcophagus, remains it had subsequently stolen and taken with it to the South American mainland, where those remains now left the footprints of a human being close to seven feet tall.

BOOK II

Hard light bathed them—a whole nation of eyeless men,
Dark bipeds not aware how they were maimed.
—C. S. Lewis

21
BARNETT

8 miles northwest of Chontalpa

"**F**an out," Barnett said. "They can't have gotten very far."

The landing of their Cessna had dispelled a good amount of the deep black smoke, but the flames still lapping at the ruptured fuel tanker and the carcass of the wingless Chieftain just kept churning out more. The sun permeated the roiling clouds as little more than a vague aura, hardly brighter than the crackling flames. He could barely see more than a dozen feet ahead of him and his men were already well outside of visual range, although he could hear them through the comlink in his ear.

"There's another one over here," Morgan whispered. *"Looks like he was cut in half by the wing of the plane. His body's still warm, though. And his blood has barely begun to coagulate. We can't be more than an hour behind them. If that."*

"Then we can't afford to waste any more time here," Barnett said.

Their course had taken them roughly fifteen degrees west of north this entire time. It stood to reason that unless Subject Z had overshot its destination, it would likely continue in that direction. They needed to know what was out here.

He removed the satellite phone from his pack and called the dedicated line at the Hangar. Maddox answered on the first ring, his voice made hollow by the acoustics of the command center.

"We're on the ground, but they're already gone," Barnett said. He caught a glimpse of a body through the smoke, crumpled on the ground. Crouched and felt the heat of the dead man's neck, if not his pulse. Retracted his hand bloody and wiped it on his pants. "We're right behind them now; we can't afford to give up any ground by running off in the wrong direction. I need to know what all is out here in this godforsaken jungle."

"Give me a few minutes," Maddox said. *"I'm out of men to assign."*

"Where's Roche?"

"He took a chopper to USAMRIID"—he pronounced it you-SAM-rid—*"to meet with Dr. Friden."*

"Friden?" Barnett's heart rate accelerated. He'd been waiting for the microbiologist to make a breakthrough for months now. "Did he say what he found?"

"Negative. He declined to divulge any details over the phone and insisted on sharing whatever he'd discovered in person."

"When Roche checks in, tell him I want a status update."

The dead man's face was covered with a paste of blood and cocaine the consistency of mud. There were vertical lacerations on his forehead, the skin parted and puckered where claws had gripped it hard enough to score the underlying frontal bone. His neck had been ripped open by teeth. No doubt about it. Subject Z's teeth were sharklike in their configuration and resembled needles, though. The edges of this wound demonstrated dramatically different dentition, more gripping and tearing than cutting and slicing, closer to what one would expect from a wolf or a coyote. Or a human being.

"Dr. Clarke figured out that the second location is in Giza," Maddox said. *"And if we're right about the importance of the lunar eclipse, we have just about twenty-four hours to get someone there."*

"Dispatch a unit—"

"Unless you want me to dispatch our command team, we're out of bodies."

"Damn it." Barnett stood and headed toward the wreckage of the Chieftain, inside the cargo hold of which was a burning tower of bundled cocaine that had to be worth millions of dollars. At least someone out there was having a worse day than he was. "Get ahold of Dr. Evans and make sure he's on the next flight to Sphinx International. And contact Clayborn at the DoD. Tell him to ready a tactical unit. I've got a hunch we're going to need it."

"Yes, sir."

"I've got clear tracks over here," Sheppard said through the comlink. *"Leading into the jungle to the north."*

"Transfer me to Dr. Nolan," Barnett said. "I need her to evaluate our location in relation to variations in the magnetic fields. If Zeta's using them for navigation, then we should be able to find a way to head it off."

"She left with Roche," Maddox said.

Barnett bared his teeth in frustration and narrowly resisted the urge to spike the sat phone on the turf.

"Here's what I need you to do: comb through those satellite feeds, determine every possible destination within a day's walk, and get drones over those locations as quickly as possible."

"I anticipated your order," Maddox said. *"We're in the process of executing as we speak."*

"Excellent. Let me know the second you find anything. Now transfer me to Dr. Clarke."

"Dr. Clarke?"

"You said she deciphered the second location. I need her to decipher the third. Right now. And surely she can access Dr. Nolan's system and forward a map of the magnetic variances in this area."

"Good luck, director," Maddox said and with a click, he was gone.

"More dead to the east," Brinkley said. *"They had snipers set up in the trees. For all the good it did them. Looks like they were fed through a wood chipper. The savagery gets worse with each encounter."*

Barnett had noticed the same thing. It appeared as though UNSUB X somehow grew stronger with every confrontation, but he chose not to share that observation with the others.

He left the wreckage behind and entered the dense rainforest. The smoke seemed to be trapped beneath the canopy, unable to filter through the branches. He barely saw the trunk of a massive kapok tree in time to keep from walking into it and had to duck underneath a head-hunting bough. Something warm grazed his cheek, leaving behind a sensation of dampness. He turned around and saw first a hand, its curled fingers dripping with blood, and then the rest of the body, hanging upside down from the upper reaches.

The dead man was tethered to a harness, which was hardly able to contain his ravaged torso. A sniper rifle lay at Barnett's feet amid a scattering of brass casings. He crouched beside it and identified fresh footprints in the soft loam.

"Zeta definitely came through here."

"I've got their trail," Morgan said. *"Heading north-northwest of the clearing. Maybe a quarter-mile in."*

Barnett struck off in that direction, shoving through vines and lianas and swatting aside saplings and thorny branches.

"This is Dr. Clarke," Tess said from the sat phone.

"Director Barnett," he said. "Tell me you're in your office."

"Yeah, but—"

"Good. I need two things from you, Dr. Clarke, and I need them right now."

"I'll do my best."

"I need you to get into Dr. Nolan's computer and send me a screen-grab of the lines of magnetic variance along the Gulf of Mexico. Everything from Tamaulipas to Tabasco."

"That shouldn't be too hard."

"And I need you to crack the code of the third crop circle design and tell me where it leads."

"That might be a little more problematic. I've been trying to align it with the others, but I can't seem to match it to any of the ancient Mesopotamian maps."

Barnett stopped in his tracks. They were less than five hundred miles from Teotihuacan, where the mummified remains of the man with the feathered serpent mask had been discovered at the heart of the subterranean maze. Was it possible Subject Zeta and UNSUB X were heading back there, or were they—?

Suddenly, everything fell into place.

If the tomb in Mosul served to lead to whatever awaited them at the end of the map, then did the tomb beneath Teotihuacan serve a similar function? Was the body Enigma stole right out from under them similarly tattooed? And if so, was it also a map, and where did it lead? He needed to know what the hell he and his team were about to walk into.

"Try using ancient Mesoamerican maps instead. Aztec, Maya, Inca, Toltec. Whatever you can find. I'll lay odds that Teotihuacan aligns with one of those planets and wherever Zeta's heading is at the other end."

"*I'm on it.*"

Barnett caught up with Morgan, who knelt on the muddy detritus, tracing the edges of the clearly defined footprints with his fingertips. They were evenly spaced and measured. Full heel contact. Their prey wasn't in a hurry, but rather settling into a comfortable pace.

"That destination is within a day's walk from where I'm standing right now," he said. "We're talking no more than thirty miles. Maybe as little as twenty in this jungle. Coordinate with Maddox. Figure out what's waiting for us and work your magic with the satellite footage. Use whatever remote sensing tools you can access. I need to know everything possible about this place before we stumble blindly into an ambush. Let me know the moment you have something useful."

He terminated the call and looked at his men. The four of them had been fighting their way through one hostile environment after another for the past six months, always several steps behind their quarry, but this was the endgame now. He could positively feel it. Everything had been building up to a final confrontation beneath the lunar eclipse, and it was only a matter of time before Dr. Clarke deciphered the location of the battlefield.

By tomorrow night, their ordeal would finally be over and the bullet-riddled carcasses of Subject Z and UNSUB X would be in boxes on their way to USAMRIID for dissection.

"Come on, men," he said. "This is the home stretch."

"If you're right," Morgan said, "they're going to be ready for a fight."

"I'm counting on it."

22
JADE

Göbekli Tepe

Jade stared down the barrel of Sadik's pistol. While she was by no means an expert on firearms, she recognized it as a semiautomatic, which meant he could fire as fast as he could pull the trigger. Assuming it was loaded, anyway. Based on Sadik's posture and the way his hand shook, she was confident it was loaded, but questioned his marksmanship. At ten feet, however, they'd be hard to miss.

"Why are you doing this?" Anya asked.

Sadik wiped the sweat from his brow with the back of his free hand.

"You would not understand," he said.

A rooster tail of dust rose over the adjacent plateau. Sadik followed her gaze and noticeably relaxed, which could mean only one thing.

Reinforcements had arrived.

They needed to extricate themselves from this situation before whoever was in that car arrived, because, unlike Sadik, they likely weren't the kind to hesitate when it came to pulling the trigger, which was the very weakness they needed to exploit right now. It didn't take a tremendous amount of courage to draw a weapon, but actually using it? That was another thing entirely.

She glanced back at Evans. He appeared to have recovered from his initial surprise. She could almost see the wheels turning in his head as he tried to formulate a plan.

"Turn around!" Sadik snapped.

The rumble of the engine grew closer. The parking lot was maybe half a mile away. At the most. They needed to get out of here in a hurry, which meant she was just going to have to handle matters herself.

"Let me guess," Jade said, her tone one of mockery. "This isn't about the money. It's about answers, right? You're just trying to solve one of the world's greatest mysteries, but you can't do so on your own."

"You do not know anything about me."

"There's nothing special about you. You're just answering a higher calling, aren't you? We've heard your story before. And, believe me, it sounded just as trite when the lead archeologist at Teotihuacan told it. Did your friends back there happen to tell you what they did to Dr. Villarreal? That cavalry you're so anxiously awaiting? They put a bullet through his head. He never saw it coming."

The distant grumble of tires on gravel faded and the dust trailing the vehicle diffused into the sunset.

"You still have a chance to survive this confrontation," she said, "but you're running out of time. Once the men back there see that hole and realize they can reach whatever's buried underneath this plateau, they won't have any further use for you."

Sadik appeared momentarily confused, but the expression slowly gave way to one of amusement.

"You think you just now found the entrance? The cavalry, as you called it, isn't here for the artifact. We retrieved it nearly two weeks ago. No, my dear. It's here for you."

The sound of the car doors closing echoed across the valley like the twin blasts of a double-barrel shotgun.

Sadik instinctively glanced over his shoulder and Jade lowered her hands to shoulder level.

"They won't leave any witnesses," Evans said from behind her. He moved to his left. Slowly. Sadik's eyes tracked him toward Anya. Away from Jade. "That's not their style. They used you to lure us out here, and they'll kill you with us, tying off all of their loose ends at once."

"You have no idea what is down there, do you? Our ancestors lived inside the catacombs below us for twelve hundred years. While the world above was frozen, they dwelled in darkness, generation after generation. This is the Vara of Zoroaster, the metaphorical Ark of Noah. Beneath our very feet is more than just a wealth of artifacts; it is a perfectly preserved time capsule predating the dawn of the Stone Age. What is down there changes everything we know about the history of our species."

A silhouette crested the adjacent plateau, above the ruins of Göbekli Tepe. Followed by another. And another. "Those men don't care about history," Evans said.

"That is where you are wrong," Sadik said. "History is the only thing they care about, for it is in the dust of history that the seeds of the future are planted."

At least four men were picking their way down the excavated hillside to the ramp that would guide them around the stone temples. Just over a quarter-mile away. And closing at a rapid pace.

It was now or never.

"And just what future is that?" Evans asked.

Sadik stared him dead in the eyes and smiled.

"One in which the gods of man once more walk among us."

Jade lunged forward and hit Sadik squarely in the shoulder, causing the barrel of the gun to swing past Anya and out over the plains. He lost his footing and fell to his side, absorbing Jade's weight on top of him with a grunt. He tried to bring his pistol to bear on her, but Anya kicked it out of his hand. She stomped on his arm to keep him from reaching it before Evans could grab it. He pointed it down at Sadik's face and tightened his finger on the trigger.

"Do what you must," Sadik said. "Events have already been set in motion. The prophecy is at hand."

Jade brought her elbow down as hard as she could, striking his temple and hammering the opposite side of his head into the exposed bedrock. His eyes rolled up into this skull, and he was out cold before the rebound.

She glanced up in time to see the men across the valley break into a sprint. They wore tactical masks and black fatigues, just like the team that had ambushed them in Mexico. She caught a flash from the barrel of an automatic rifle as bullets ricocheted all around them.

"Go!" Evans shouted and fired off a few rounds toward the men.

He lifted her from on top of Sadik and shoved her toward the hole in the ground. Bullets pounded the upthrust stone and filled the air with limestone shrapnel. She contorted her body and entered feetfirst. Felt nothing underneath her. A vastness confirmed by what little light reached past her into the narrow shaft.

A bullet screamed past her ear, and she dropped into

the pit. She felt a momentary sensation of weightlessness. Her stomach rose into her—

Impact.

Her heels struck. Knees buckled. Legs crumpled underneath her.

She let out an involuntary shout and barely had the presence of mind to roll out of the way before Anya landed where she'd been a heartbeat prior.

The younger woman whimpered and tried to stand. Jade grabbed her by the back of her shirt and dragged her from the vague aura of light.

Evans alighted gracefully behind them and stepped away from the wall, a beam of light streaking from his cell phone.

"Why didn't you guys use the toe trail?" he asked and shined the built-in flashlight toward the staggered holes chiseled into the wall.

"You could have said something, you know," Anya said.

"Save it," Jade said. She removed her own phone from her pocket and switched on the beam. "We have to find another way out of here in a hurry."

The stone ceiling was coarse and uneven, the walls of pitted limestone scored black by carbon from the torches that had once burned in the recesses. A single arched doorway opened upon darkness deeper than her light could penetrate. She took off at a sprint and nearly flew out over the abrupt ledge. Twisted to the side at the last possible second and stumbled down the uneven stone steps lining the cavern wall. To her right was a pitfall straight down into darkness, on the far side of which was the landing awaiting her at the bottom of the primitive spiral staircase.

Uneven columns carved from the earth itself partially enclosed the stone platform on both sides. She took the first passage she saw, her light barely outpacing the shadows. A rounded chamber opened to her left, inside of which were countless human skulls, stacked from the floor to the ceiling and encircling the entire room, at the heart of which was a sunken firepit. The bones were the same color as the walls, as though the deceased had become one with the earth through the millennia.

"My God," Anya gasped from behind her. "We've never encountered such perfectly preserved remains from the Stone Age. This civilization must have practiced some form of ancestor worship. Imagine how much we could learn—"

"Imagine our skulls joining theirs," Evans said. "Because that's what's going to happen if we don't pick up the pace."

Automatic gunfire crackled from somewhere behind and above them. Their pursuers were firing blindly down the shaft to clear the way.

They were gaining on them.

Jade rushed through the narrow corridor, blowing past smaller chambers from which her footsteps echoed back at her. She caught fleeting glimpses of stylized paintings on the walls, of desiccated animal pelts and carcasses decomposed to jumbled piles of bones, of the occasional wall discolored by algal and bacterial growth, where surface water leached through the bedrock.

The blood, however, was far newer. Maybe a couple of weeks old. High-velocity and arterial spatters, definitely fatal amounts, but no sign of bodies.

"Careful!" Anya yelled.

Jade looked down in time to see a circular hole. Nearly

stepped right down into it. The scent of dust and age emanated from it, beneath which she detected a biological smell, almost like—

"A stable," Anya said. She shined her light downward at an angle that revealed individual stone partitions filled with dust. "They kept livestock down there."

"Which means there has to be a way to get animals in and out of there," Evans said. "And they're definitely not herding anything up those stairs."

A thumping sound echoed from behind them. The first of the masked men had descended into the warrens.

"We need to distance ourselves from them," Evans said.

He lowered his legs through the hole, drew his arms to his chest, and slid over the edge. The floor was maybe ten feet down, half the initial drop from the surface, but being able to see the bottom somehow made it worse.

Jade helped Anya work her legs through the hole and brace her elbows on the rim. "I've got you," Evans said and gave her a reassuring squeeze on the ankles.

Anya released a high-pitched shriek when Jade let go. She glanced back in the direction from which they'd come. She heard the distant thrum of footsteps, but as of yet couldn't see any sign of movement or approaching lights.

"Come on," Evans said.

Jade sat down, scooted over the hole, and dropped through the ground into the room below. Evans caught her around the waist and drew her tightly to him, his face buried between her breasts.

"You can put me down now," she said.

He released her, and she landed off-balance, toppled

backward, and alighted unceremoniously on her rear end. He offered his hand and pulled her to her feet.

"Sorry about that, but you did say to put you down."

Jade jabbed her index finger in his face and prepared to let him have it, but Anya cut her off.

"Over here," she said. "You guys have to see this."

A ramp led downward from the stable to a level metered by rough-hewn limestone columns. The ground was rocky and uneven around the circumference of the circular cavern, the center of which was several feet lower. It was almost as though the outer ring had been designed to function as a gallery that offered a better view of the cleared section. There were more blood spatters on the wall, and brass casings and long feathers hardened into the congealed mess underneath them.

Something had definitely been alive down here when Enigma arrived, quite possibly the same extant species of dinosaur that had been left to guard the maze underneath Teotihuacan.

Jade strode out into the open and joined Anya beneath the domed ceiling. What had looked like pillars were actually freestanding megaliths resembling those from the temples being excavated from the hillside. These, too, were anthropomorphized, only they had something that none of the others aboveground had.

Their heads.

23

ROCHE

Friden led them down the sterile corridor toward the genetics lab. Roche watched the researchers through the windows of the doors on either side. None of them so much as looked up from their work as the procession passed. He saw a glove box swarming with mosquitoes in one room and another overflowing with cages full of venomous snakes and screaming primates.

"What in the name of God do you do down here?" he asked.

Friden opened the door at the end of the hallway and admitted them into a lab containing equipment the likes of which Roche had never seen before. He looked at Kelly, who appeared every bit as overwhelmed as he felt. Her gloved hand was squirming at her side, the material too stiff to allow her fingertips to tap the pad of her thumb with their customary rhythm.

"Funny you should mention God, because if you were

to find a way to sequence his DNA, I'd imagine it would look a lot like that of the sample you guys sent me." Friden stopped in front of a series of three computer monitors displaying vertical bands of colors reminiscent of the badges worn on military dress uniforms. "What you're looking at here is the visual expression of the genomes of three distinct species. On the left you have a common chimpanzee, *Pan troglodytes*. In the center, *Homo sapiens sapiens*. That's us. And on the right, a hominin species the likes of which I've never seen before."

"The sample from the man entombed in Mosul," Kelly said.

"There's nothing manlike about him. Check out the human genome. Each of these bands represents a single chromosome, forty-six in total, between which there are more than twenty thousand genes. This is humanity boiled down to its most basic ingredients, the fundamental building blocks from which each and every one of us is constructed."

"Each of those colored lines represents a gene?" Roche said.

"Do try to keep up," Friden said and gestured to the screen on the left. "Compare the human genome with that of the chimpanzee. They look pretty much identical, don't they? The chimp actually has forty-eight chromosomes—two of which combined down the evolutionary road to help create us—but express roughly the same number of genes. Now check out the one on the right. The one you sent me."

Roche stared at the screen. It looked like there were the same number of vertical bands, but so many more horizontal colored lines packed into the same amount of space that they were nearly indistinguishable. "It has the same number of chromosomes," Kelly said, "but twice as many genes."

"More than that," Friden said. "We're talking forty-seven thousand genes. That's nearly as many as a grain of rice."

"Rice?" Roche said.

"You know, the white stuff they serve with Chinese food?"

"I'm familiar with rice, Dr. Friden, but I don't have the slightest clue what you're trying to say."

"All living beings have chromosomes," Friden said. "Even plants. A species like rice might have fewer chromosomes, but there are variants with upwards of fifty thousand genes, largely because, evolutionarily speaking, rice has been around a heck of a lot longer than we have. It's been forced to adapt to all kinds of environmental conditions in order to survive. Temperature, climate, sunlight, darkness, different types of soil. You name it, and rice found a way to beat it. Its advantage is that its life cycle is measured in seasons instead of years, giving it the ability to adapt much more quickly. Considering the weather changes dramatically, often from one year to the next, plants have to basically evolve on the fly, which means that a new adaptation is beginning to kick in even as the current one is in full swing and the one before that isn't even out the door. All of these minuscule changes start to stack up, one on top of another on top of another."

"But that's not how we work," Kelly said. "Our genetic code is more like a hard drive in the sense that it essentially rewrites the new data over the old very slowly over millions of years."

"Which is precisely why it took millions of years to

develop an opposable thumb. Meanwhile, rice just keeps piling on the new genes, because at the end of the day, rice is always going to be rice. It's not going to magically grow legs or wings or anything like that, but all of those genes, with all of their subtle variations, serve to make it one of the hardiest organisms on the face of the planet, one capable of surviving environmental cataclysms that'd kill off even the cockroaches."

"So what's the significance?" Roche asked.

Friden turned to face him and smiled patiently, as though preparing to address a child.

"Look at it this way," he said. "Despite tens of millions of years of evolution, we're really not all that much different than the chimpanzee. We share ninety-six percent of our DNA and have the same chromosomes, if not the same number. If this were a simple mathematical equation, you'd be able to round up a chimp and call it a man. Now look at the one on the right and apply everything I've been telling you."

"This sample comes from a hominin species countless millions of years older than ours," Kelly said.

"Try billions," Friden said. "This is a species evolved to the umpteenth degree, one capable of surviving any number of extinction-level events that would wipe us all out."

"You're suggesting it could even survive death," Roche said.

"I just showed you how it could do just that. Those fat cells? They weren't merely desiccated; they were outright dead."

"And yet you were able to use blood to refill them."

"It's doesn't work like a sponge. You can't just pour blood on it and expect it to soak it all up. I mean, I guess that's exactly what you can expect, but it isn't that simple. We believe it utilizes regenerative capabilities similar to those of a zebrafish."

"A fish," Roche said.

"Or a flatworm," Friden said. "I figured a fish would give you a better visual, but I'm flexible. Heck, a salamander might even work—"

"The zebrafish will be fine," Kelly said.

"Okay, so *Danio rerio* is a common aquarium fish you can buy at just about every pet store in the world. It's incredibly common, and there's really nothing extraordinary about it, outside of the fact that it can regrow just about anything you cut off of it. You can blind it, deafen it, sever its spinal cord, or lop off its fins. Whatever you want, really, and a process called histone demethylation will occur at the site, essentially causing the cells of the damaged tissue to revert to a stem cell–like state. These cells are undifferentiated, and thus have the potential to be any part of the body, be it retinal cells, the lateral line hairs of the ear, the neurons in the nervous system, or the structural components of the fins. They aggregate into masses called blastemas, which contain the blueprints for every type of cell in the entire body. You'll find them in the embryonic stage of every animal species before they begin the process of specialization and form the different kinds of structures and tissues."

He suddenly turned and strode back down the hallway to his lab, disconnecting and attaching air hoses as he went. It was all Roche and Kelly could do to keep up with him. He passed through the door and veered immediately to his left, where a scanning electron microscope was set up at its own station. The sample on the monitor beside it was stained purple and resembled a long-abandoned spiderweb, the pattern broken in spots and stretched in others.

"This is a blastema we collected from the same adipocytes you see on that screen over there. Our working theory is that they circulate throughout the specimen's body in its blood, most likely attached to the surface of the red blood cells themselves. You have to understand that blood interacts with every cell in the body, whether directly through the cellular membrane or indirectly via the interstitial fluid, so these blastemas are literally everywhere in the body at once. Anyplace you find blood, you'll find them, too."

"The tissue sample came from a mummified corpse," Roche said. "There wasn't a drop of blood in it."

"But there *was* at one time, right?" Friden said. "In a living specimen, that blood flows from the heart throughout the body and then back again, delivering oxygen and removing waste by-products. It's a closed system, at least until something traumatic happens to open it, like, say, someone slits your throat and severs your carotid artery. The loss of blood is copious and fatal within a matter of minutes, but it's not like every drop of blood evacuates your body through the hole in your neck. Once your heart stops beating, the residual blood lingering within that formerly closed system stops flowing and begins to settle, the cellular membranes rupture, and the fluid leaks out, leaving behind these blastemas like grains of salt from an evaporated pond."

"The same would hold true during the process of mummification," Kelly said.

"I'd go so far as to say the same thing would happen with any form of death. These blastemas are essentially aggregates of hematopoietic and mesenchymal stem cells capable of restarting the entire embryonic process. Producing blood cells, stimulating nerve cells, regenerating dead tissue. All they would need is the right catalyst to come along, one possessing what we theorize to be a protein called IGF-1, an insulin-like growth factor present in human blood, which researchers believe plays a role in triggering cancer cells to begin proliferating. The same thing happens here. The blastemas react to the IGF-1 in the blood and start rapidly differentiating into various tissues and red blood cells. We're talking complete cellular regeneration."

"So without the IGF-1 from the donor's blood, the body could essentially linger in a state of physical death indefinitely," Kelly said.

"As long as those blastemas remain intact and viable . . . which brings us to the whole reason I called you out here."

Friden returned to the station at the back of the room, through the window of which Roche could see the glove box containing the regenerated fat cells. He recalled something the microbiologist had said when they first arrived. *It's our job here to develop active countermeasures and figure out the most efficient ways of killing these bastards.*

"So how do you kill something that can't die?" he asked.

"Aye, there's the rub," Friden said. "I can't tell you how long I've been waiting to use that line."

"So what's the answer?"

Friden smirked.

"We're still working on that, but what I can tell you— thanks to this miraculous specimen here—is how to wipe out the organisms that produce those gray bastards once and for all."

"Gray?" Kelly asked. "You mean like Subject Zeta?"

"You're kidding, right? That's just about the lamest name I've ever heard."

"Focus, Friden," Roche said. "How do we kill them?"

"A better question would be: How do we kill them without wiping out humanity in the process?"

24
ANYA

Göbekli Tepe

Anya didn't know what she'd expected the faces of the gods represented in these primitive sculptures to look like, especially considering the lengths those who worshiped them had gone to aboveground to eliminate all traces of them, but she certainly hadn't expected something so . . . plain. The craniums were somewhat conical, although they tapered more toward the face than the vertex, upon which had been carved what almost looked like a hat. The eyes were long and slanted, the nose and mouth represented as little more than two dots above a horizontal line. The features didn't even remotely resemble those of Subject Z, as she'd half expected. If anything, they appeared almost reptilian.

"We don't have time for this," Evans said. "We have to keep moving."

She knew he was right. The men with the assault rifles were still coming, and if Sadik had been telling the truth, they'd been down here before, which gave them a distinct advantage. She quickly snapped off several pictures with her cell phone and hurried to catch up with the others, who were already ducking into the passage at the far side of the cavern.

This place was just like the underground cities of Derinkuyu and Kaymakli. It had been built like an anthill, with sloping walkways connecting one spherical hollow to another. Carbon scoring lingered on the walls to mark where torches had once burned. The ceiling was similarly blackened where the smoke had traced the contours of the rock toward small chimneys that served to funnel it all the way up to the surface. It was impossible to imagine human beings living down here in the flickering glow of flames they required as much for their heat as for their light. Raising children among animals, in filthy conditions rife with disease, while outside raged an apocalyptic blizzard they feared might never end. Generation after generation, for 1,200 years, the same length of time, historically speaking, that separated the Viking Age from the Space Age. The sheer terror that defined their daily existence must have been a physical presence stalking the darkness, their only hope the prayers to the very gods who had consigned them to this fate in the first place, to whom they would build temples when they eventually emerged, temples devoted to tracking the star Deneb, from which they believed these gods to have come.

Anya's breath caught in her chest. It looked like Evans was sprinting straight into a dead end, but he turned at the last possible second. Jade ducked around the corner behind him, and Anya followed her down a set of narrow, uneven stairs into another circular chamber from which arched doorways branched like the spokes of a wagon wheel. There was more blood on the ground in here, smeared where the body of the feathered serpent had been dragged away. She prayed that there weren't any more of them down here, lying in wait.

"Which way?" Jade asked. A note of panic had crept into her normally level tone. The clapping footsteps of their pursuers were still distant, but they were definitely louder than before. "We can't afford to guess wrong."

Anya shined her beam across the ground. Twelve centuries was more than enough time for the tread of the people who lived down here to wear through the limestone, like traffic patterns in carpet.

"That way," she said and pointed toward an opening ahead of them and to the right. It suddenly struck her that they were descending in a specific pattern. "They built this place in a spiral to keep the chambers from collapsing under the weight of the bedrock."

"But that doesn't mean there's a way out at the bottom," Evans said.

Anya could only hope that these warrens had been built like the other underground cities and somewhere down there was another tunnel that would lead them back to the surface. Of course, if the men trying to kill them already knew about it, there could be a second team working back toward them from the other end. They couldn't worry about that now, though, at least not until they escaped the hunters she could positively feel gaining on them with every passing second.

The tunnel wound downward toward a circular cavern that appeared to be a communal living space, with rooms framed by earthen pillars to both sides and a walkway running straight down the middle. The orifice on the far end led to another descending corridor.

They had to be close to a hundred feet down by now.

She wished she'd been paying closer attention to this plateau on their way in. For the life of her, she couldn't seem to remember how tall it had been, but surely they had to be close to the level of the surrounding plains, which meant that if there was a tunnel leading away from here, like the three hundred miles of interconnected passageways beneath the majority of the Stone Age sites in Central Turkey, it couldn't be much farther ahead.

The tunnel opened onto a narrow ledge enclosed by a partial retaining wall and columns carved from the limestone. They were far more elaborate than those elsewhere in the subterranean mecca. They'd been sculpted into anthropomorphic figures with their backs to the ledge, like gargoyles watching over the chamber below them. They wore loincloths and cradled their bellies with their arms, like the megaliths in Göbekli Tepe, but each was depicted with the head of a different animal. One had the face of a bull, another that of an eagle. She saw a snake, a lion, a deer . . .

Anya was struck by a sudden realization that brought her momentum to a standstill. This prehistoric site was linked to the pyramids beneath the jungles of Mexico and two vertical miles of ice in Antarctica in ways she would likely never be able to comprehend.

"They're the same," she said.

"Come on, Anya!" Jade said.

"Look at their faces. They're the same as those on the statues we found in the gallery inside the pyramid in Antarctica."

"You're right," Evans said, "but there's nothing we can do about that now."

He rushed back to her, grabbed her by the hand, and pulled her around the circular ledge to where a series of irregular ledges descended to the chamber, at the center of which was a stone sarcophagus. It looked just like the one at the heart of the maze in Teotihuacan, only much smaller. So much smaller, in fact, that nothing larger than a newborn could have been buried inside.

"We have to open it," she said. They all knew that this was what they'd come here to find. Whatever the map tattooed on the body from the tomb in Mosul led to was inside this stone container.

Evans glanced nervously back toward the entryway above them, from which the drumroll of approaching footsteps grew steadily louder. His stare rose to the domed ceiling, where it lingered for several seconds. Anya followed his line of sight and saw the tattered remnants of massive nests, like those of paper wasps, hanging from the ceiling. Several still contained the remains of long-dead animals, their hooves, paws, and horns protruding from the sides. Too bad the men who'd discovered this place had been better prepared for the feathered serpents this time.

"Then we'd better do it quickly," Evans said and pushed against the lid, but it didn't budge.

The footsteps became steadily louder. She could have sworn she heard voices.

"Hurry!" Jade said.

Evans put his shoulder into it and shoved the lid several inches. Anya joined him, and together they moved the lid back far enough to see that there was nothing inside. Where she'd expected to find a mummified body, there was only a circular cutout about six inches wide and just as deep. Anya knew exactly what had been inside

Sadik had been telling the truth; they'd already collected the artifact.

"They're coming!" Jade said.

"Keep pushing," Anya said.

"There's no time!" Evans snapped.

"I have to know for sure."

"Know what?"

"Just, please, help me push this off."

Evans again glanced back toward the sound of approaching footsteps, then leaned into the lid and drove with his legs. Anya groaned with the exertion. Jade moved in beside her and pushed—

The lid slid over the opposite side and clattered to the ground with a thunderous boom that echoed throughout the warrens.

Anya ran around the base and knelt beside the lid. It had cracked down the middle, where an arch had been carved into the underside. She traced its smooth contours with her fingertips. She'd been right about what had been sealed inside for millennia, and now the canister was in the hands of the last people in the world they wanted to have it.

A faint aura of light limned the mouth of the tunnel above them.

They were out of time.

"Go!" Evans whispered and shoved her toward the lone exit branching from the far side of the room.

She sprinted toward the arched doorway and hurtled through the narrow tunnel. The passage constricted until it was barely wider than her shoulders and continued to wind downward into darkness that grew colder by the second. They had to be below the level of the surrounding desert now, and yet still the passage descended. She was on the verge of panicking when she finally saw the end.

Anya burst from the confines into a large cavern unlike all of the others. It was a natural formation hollowed from the limestone by eons of running water. The ceiling was spiked with stalactites, many of which reached the ground, forming columns that looked like they'd been molded from candle wax.

She shined her light from one side to the other and back again.

Her heart pounded in her chest.

This couldn't be right.

Evans and Jade caught up with her and added their lights to the search, which only confirmed the grim reality of the situation.

There was no way out.

25
TESS

The Hangar

Tess was so frustrated she could have screamed. She'd looked at countless Mesoamerican maps, both pre- and post-Columbian, but couldn't seem to match the third crop circle, CS3, to any of them. The problem was that unlike the Fertile Crescent, where one civilization had been built on top of another, the indigenous peoples of Mexico had largely colonized different parts of the country, even though few of their cultures had existed at the same time. The Olmec civilization had lasted clear up until the Zapotec appeared in the Valley of Oaxaca to the south, which they'd ultimately ceded to the Mixtec. The Maya had risen from the Yucatán Peninsula around the same time the Teotihuacan had staked their claim to the Valley of Mexico, only to give way to the Toltec. They were eventually succeeded by the Aztec, who, for all their might and ferocity, had been no match for the Spanish.

One civilization didn't suddenly become extinct at the same time that another spontaneously materialized from thin air, though. There had to be a certain amount of spillover from one to the next, whether as a result of conquest, integration, or migration, which meant there had to have been a time when the maps of the various cultures overlapped, at least to some degree.

The Olmec had been the first, so she started there. They'd inhabited the modern-day state of Veracruz, along the Gulf coast, around the same time the Assyrian Empire ruled Mesopotamia. No one knew why their civilization failed, but archeologists speculated that some form of catastrophic natural disaster, be it drought or the fallout from a major volcanic eruption, altered the climate to such an extent that an agricultural society like theirs was no longer able to sustain itself and was forced to either re-locate or perish. Some went south and joined the Zapotec, with whom they already had a fruitful trade relationship, while others headed to the east to seed the Maya popula-tion or to the west to found the Teotihuacan civilization. It was this last group she followed, since she had to be-lieve that the bull's-eye representing Saturn on CS3 fell squarely upon the Temple of the Feathered Serpent, where they'd discovered the mummified remains entombed at the center of the maze, just as it had marked the location of the body in nearly identical condition in Mosul on CS1 and CS2. When she placed it on Teotihuacan, however, none of the remaining planets aligned with any ancient sites. The planets stretched across the mountains and des-ert to reach the Pacific Ocean and a part of the country that didn't see many permanent settlements until the nineteenth century.

Either they were wrong about the map coinciding with Mexico or she was missing something crucial.

The third map was the anomaly among the three, the one with only a single ring surrounding Saturn, while the others featured twin rings to identify Nineveh. It stood to reason that the distinction would serve to differentiate this crop circle from the others, but not so much as to obscure the overall relationship between them. Did that necessarily imply that she needed to look on the other side of the world, though?

If Roche was right about the prongs on the planets functioning like the hands of a clock, then that was exactly what it meant. The majority of Mexico was within the Central Time Zone, which was eight hours earlier than the Turkish Time Zone, so she was definitely in the right place, she just had to be—

"Looking at it wrong," she said out loud.

She stared at the map on the monitor above her desk and nibbled on her lip as she followed that line of thought. The design that had led them to Göbekli Tepe had started with Saturn to the east and used Earth to indicate the destination to the west. The same held true of the map to Giza, except that it was the second instance of Saturn, Sat2, on CS2 that coincided with the ringed planet of CS1. Now she was dealing with a different variation of the same element, only this time on the opposite side of the world.

"Opposite, opposite, opposite," she said as she spun around in her chair.

Mesoamerica and Mesopotamia weren't technically on opposite sides of the globe; they were more like a quarter turn apart. They were metaphorical opposites, though. The Old World and the New World. The East and the West. A matter of perspective.

Tess abruptly stopped spinning, stood, and looked at the map.

"Could it really be that simple?"

She grabbed the printout of CS3 and held it up against

the resized map of Mexico on the screen. She scooted
Saturn until it was directly on top of Teotihuacan, held it
there with her finger, and twirled the paper 180 degrees
so that Saturn was now to the west and the planets stretched
away from it to the east. They weren't in reverse order,
but rather in the order in which they'd be viewed on the
opposite side of their orbit, or perhaps merely from the
perspective of the other side of the sun. It still wasn't
right, though. Several planets fell upon the Gulf of Mexico. She dialed the design clockwise, slowly, until she
was roughly thirty degrees south of horizontal, and suddenly she recognized the pattern.

Her idea about tracing the migration patterns had been
spot-on. The new alignment of planets ran straight from
the heart of the Toltec Empire, through the Olmec, and
into the Mayan.

She taped the paper in place, overlaid the maps of all
three civilizations on the monitor, and stepped back to ap-
praise her work. They weren't discrete cultures, but
rather one in the process of evolving into three, its prog-
eny sprouting across the countryside like aspen saplings
from the colonial roots of a dying parent tree, its centers
of influence separated more by distance than by time.

Neptune corresponded with Tula, the capital of the
Toltec Empire after the fall of Teotihuacan, diagonally to
the southeast. Jupiter aligned with Hueyatlaco, while
Mars matched La Mesa. The moon fell upon the last great
Olmec city, Tres Zapotes, and Earth aligned with its seat
of power, La Venta, from which people had migrated east-
ward to Comalcalco and Palenque, respectively, where the
Mayan influence became readily apparent.

She'd done it. She'd cracked the third code.

Tess brought up the map of the state of Tabasco and

pinpointed the location from which Barnett had contacted her. La Venta was just about twenty-five miles to the north-northwest. She compared that route to the lines of magnetic susceptibility she'd downloaded from Kelly's system and confirmed that it ran straight through the Mexico-Yucatán suture zone. All that was left now was to match the coordinates to the extraneous data points from the ceiling of Subject Z's cage in Antarctica, which had already given them the constellations Cygnus and Orion at the previous sites.

The scattering of dots was easy enough to find along the curvature of the Gulf of Mexico. She magnified them until she had a clear image of a total of fifteen stars, fewer than either of the previous constellations. There was no readily identifiable pattern, like she'd seen with the Northern Cross and Orion's belt, which had practically jumped off the screen and bit her. The stars were clustered to the left side in what almost looked like three distinct down-turned arches: one above the other two, which were aligned nose to tail. The dots to the right formed a half-circle, from six to twelve on the face of a clock. Since she didn't recognize the pattern, she was going to have to backtrack and subtract the smaller stars, which were rarely bright enough to contribute to the formation of the name-sake constellation. She adjusted the tolerances until roughly half of the stars disappeared, leaving behind what almost looked like a vertically oriented trapezoid or a—

"Rhombus," she whispered. "Oh, no."

Tess hurriedly brought up an aerial image of La Venta. The majority of the site was covered with jungle so thick that the camera couldn't penetrate it. There was a vaguely triangular-shaped clearing to the left with a conical mound overgrown with foliage near its apex. Without being able to visualize the primitive structures, the blasted image was useless. She closed it and searched until she found a map of the buildings she hadn't been able to see from the air. Like the constellation, they formed an elongated diamond shape, inside of which were complexes lettered A through H, a necropolis, a central plaza, an acropolis, and the buried pyramid she'd seen in the clearing.

She quickly compared the layout to the constellation, with its four main and eleven lesser stars, which were named using the Bayer convention, a process by which each was assigned a Greek letter followed by a genitive form of the parent constellation, which, in this case, had been originally named Rhombus upon its discovery in the seventeenth century, before being renamed Reticulum a hundred years later. The brightest star corresponded with alpha, followed by beta, which formed two corners of the trapezoid, but this time it was two of the lesser stars she was looking for, two tiny dots that sat nearly right on top of each other in the night sky and somewhere beneath the jungle on the ground, two stars that actually formed the basis of a binary star system nearly forty light-years away. Together they carried the name Zeta Reticuli, and they were where the alien species known as Grays supposedly originated.

Tess knew exactly where Subject Z was heading.

"It's going home," she whispered.

26
EVANS

Göbekli Tepe

"There has to be a way out," Evans said.

He rushed past Anya and Jade, weaved through the maze of speleothemic columns, and scoured the rear wall for any sign of an exit. Water had to have been able to find a way in and out of here to create this cavern in the first place. They just had to find the source.

The footsteps behind them grew louder, the voices more distinct.

He swept his light across the ceiling. Nothing but stalactites, the shadows from which made the limestone appear to writhe. He was just about to move on to the floor when his beam disappeared into the ceiling. It only lasted a split second, but he'd definitely seen it. Somewhere up there, hidden amid the jagged protrusions, was a way out.

It took him several seconds to locate the hole. A ring of stalactites had formed around the man-made chute, concealing it from just about every angle. He got as close to it as he could and shined his beam diagonally through a gap between stalactites. It looked almost like a well, with a toe trail leading up into the underground city, far beyond the reach of his light. Air moved through it with a faint whistle that suggested it terminated somewhere near the surface opening. He thought of the pitfall near the first staircase and wondered why the inhabitants would have sunken a hole straight down into this cavern.

"They're coming," Anya whispered.

"I hear at least three distinct voices," Jade said. "How many bullets are left in that pistol?"

Evans didn't have the slightest idea and couldn't afford to waste any time checking. He hoped to God they didn't have to find out.

The formation of the stalactites meant that some amount of water had been leaking down the chute for millennia, carrying with it the minerals that had accreted to form the earthen spikes, which glistened in his light. He watched a droplet swell from the tip. It shivered momentarily before falling onto a stalagmite formation that looked like a miniature mountain of termite mounds.

". . . dort gefangen."

They all turned toward the tunnel behind them and the source of the disembodied voice. While still distant, the sound of footsteps had slowed. The men were approaching more cautiously now. They knew there was nowhere left to run.

The ceiling was easily ten feet high. Maybe if he was somehow able to balance on top of the stalagmites, he'd be able to boost the others up far enough to reach the lowest rungs, but there was no way of knowing how deep the toeholds were. The water that helped form the stalactites had undoubtedly filled them with some amount of flowstone on its way down.

Something about the toe trail bothered him, but he couldn't quite put his finger on it.

Evans climbed up onto the formation, wrapped his

arm around the thickest stalagmite, and leaned around the other side so he could shine his light straight up into the hole. He retraced his mental steps until his conscious mind finally caught up with his unconscious. No one would have built a toe trail where they couldn't reach it, especially when there was a tunnel leading directly to the destination, one that eliminated the risk of falling and breaking open his skull. The trail had been laid for the people who created the well, which was exactly what it was. Where else could they have gotten potable water when the entire world above them was frozen?

The presence of a karst formation like this one meant there was an aquifer somewhere beneath their feet, some body of water where the fluid leaching through the limestone accumulated.

He readjusted his grip on the damp stalagmite and shined his light straight down. The stalagmites had partially grown over the matching hole in the floor, leaving a crescent-shaped opening through which he could see only darkness.

"Come out, come out, wherever you are."

The voice spoke with a thick German accent and seemed to originate from all around them at once, cruel and taunting.

"Hurry!" Evans whispered, waving the others toward them.

He offered his hand to Jade, who climbed past him and onto the other side of the stalagmites. She was practically straddling the hole in the ground when she realized what he wanted her to do. Her eyes widened when she looked up at him.

"There's nowhere else to go," he whispered.

"How far down . . . ?"

"There's only one way to find out."

Jade visibly swallowed and slid down the slope of the speleothem. Lowered her rear end to the rock and slid her legs down through the crescent.

"I'm going to give you to the count of three," the voice boomed, "and then we're coming in after you."

"Kill your lights," Evans whispered.

He switched off his beam and jammed his phone into his pocket. Anya whimpered when she did the same. Her hand was trembling when she gripped his shoulder.

Jade shined her light down between her knees one final time before killing her light and abandoning them to darkness marred only by the faint golden aura coming from the tunnel.

"There's a toe trail," she whispered. "On the opposite side of the stalagmite."

Evans wished he could have gone first to make sure it was safe, but they were out of time and someone needed to cover their escape. Jade was as tough as they came, though, and it still remained to be seen if he could even fit through the opening.

He heard a scrabbling sound, followed by the tap of Jade's shoe striking one of the tiny ledges.

"One!" the man shouted.

"Go," Evans whispered.

He guided Anya over the stalagmites and did his best to help her balance on the damp surface. She clung to his forearm so hard that his fingers started to tingle.

"They're too slick," Jade said. "I can't get any kind of trac—"

She gasped and slapped the limestone.

Evans heard a rush of air, then only silence.

"Jade?" He scrambled over the rock formation. Slid down to the edge beside Anya. "Jade!"

A soft splash. Distant.

If anything had happened to her, he'd never be able to forgive—

Coughing and sputtering from what sounded like fifty feet down.

"I'm okay," she croaked.

"Two!"

Evans glanced toward the tunnel leading into the room. The light had brightened and taken on a crimson hue from what he could only assume were the laser sights of the men's rifles.

"You can do this, Anya," he whispered.

She released his wrist. He felt her inching away from him in the darkness. Scooting out over—

A squeal and she was gone.

He held his breath until he heard the splash, then rolled over onto his chest, stuffed the pistol under his waist-band, and squirmed backward through the orifice. It was going to be one hell of a tight squeeze.

"Three!"

Evans wiggled his hips. The ledge scraped his pelvis, bit into his stomach. The pistol pressed into the small of his back. He wasn't going to make it, but maybe there was still a chance he could hold them off. He pushed himself high enough to grab the gun, draw it, and—

His hips passed through the hole. The limestone lip scraped straight up his belly and chest. It caught his pectoral muscles and felt like it nearly ripped them off, but they bought him just enough time to turn his head and raise his arms—

A sensation of weightlessness.

He instinctively braced for impact, but only succeeded in banging his knees against one side of the stone chute and smacking the back of his head against the other.

The pressure abruptly released and the walls fell away.

Evans was still taking a deep breath when he hit the aquifer and went under. The frigid water caused every muscle in his body to clench. His heels grazed the slick bottom and swung back over his head. He pushed off and swam in what he hoped was the right direction, the urge to cough more than he could bear. He was already retching when he breached the surface.

The crackle of automatic gunfire was deafening. Discharge flickered from the tube overhead.

He half-coughed, half-vomited until he expelled the aspirated fluid and paddled away from the light, which abruptly darkened when the shooting stopped.

Brass casings tinkled to the limestone, followed by a palpable silence.

"Ziehe heraus, was von ihnen übrig ist." The strange acoustics made the man's voice sound as though it came from miles away. *"Sie werden eine visuelle Bestätigung wünschen."*

Evans treaded water as quietly as he could, every subtle splash amplified tenfold by the acoustics of the cavern into which they'd fallen. A faint current pushed past him beneath the surface, carrying him ever so slowly with it.

"Sie sind nicht hier drin," a second voice said.

"Was meinst du?"

"Genau das, was ich gesagt habe. Es ist niemand hier drin."

"They figured out we aren't in there," Jade whispered.

Evans's eyes had adjusted to the darkness just well

enough to get the impression of the massive space surrounding him, which brightened incrementally as the lights
of the men searching the cavern above him passed through
the hole. The walls were jagged and uneven, striated with
sharp ridges that memorialized the high-water levels
through the eons. The ceiling had to be a good fifteen feet
up, far too high to reach, even had there been any visible
means of scaling the concave rock. He saw the silhouettes of the others, their heads barely above the bitterly
cold water, which eddied around them as they struggled
to remain afloat, unable to control the clicking sounds of
their chattering teeth.

"Sie konnten nicht an uns vorbeigekommen sein," a
third voice said.

*"Bist du sicher, dass du gesehen hast, wie sie den Tun-
nel hinuntergehen?"* the first said.

"Ich habe nichts gesehen, ich hörte—"

The first man bellowed in frustration.

"Geh zurück an die Oberfläche," he said. *"Stellen Sie
sicher, dass sie ihr Fahrzeug nicht erreichen."*

"They think we m-must have somehow g-gotten past
them," Jade whispered. "They're heading b-back to the
surface to intercept us b-before we reach our c-car."

The light dimmed and once more Evans heard the
sound of footsteps, only this time heading in the opposite
direction. None of them spoke until the darkness was
complete and even the echo of the footsteps was a memory.

"We n-need to g-get out of the w-water," Evans whispered.

He'd already lost feeling in his fingers and toes, and he
hadn't been in the water as long as the others. Soon their
bodies would start to shut down. Worse, their cell phones,

regardless of how waterproof their manufacturers claimed they were, had been submerged for too long to turn on, let alone power the flashlights. It only took a few seconds, even with as badly as his hands were shaking, to confirm as much.

"I c-can't do this again," Anya whispered.

"You c-can and you will," Evans said, but he was already experiencing his own doubts.

The water inside the flooded maze in Mexico had been considerably warmer. They were working against the clock down here. If they didn't get out of the aquifer soon, they might not be able to at all.

At least there was a current, weak though it might be, which indicated the water flowed from one place to another.

An inlet and an outlet.

There was a way out somewhere down here.

They just needed to find it.

27
KELLY

U.S. Army Medical Research Institute
of Infectious Diseases,
Fort Detrick, Maryland

Friden highlighted a segment of DNA on the monitor, isolated it, and brought it to the forefront. Two more strands appeared below it. The points of similarity between the three were marked, leaving only a handful of nucleotide pairings on each to distinguish one from the other.

"What you see here is a comparison of three sequences of DNA," he said. "The first is a section I snipped from the genome from the tissue sample you sent us. The computer identified it as a ninety-nine percent match to the partial sequences of the genomes below it, both of which are textbook examples of viruses in the Filoviridae family."

"What do they do?" Roche asked.

"They're just about the nastiest viruses on the face of the planet. We're talking the kind of hemorrhagic fevers that practically turn you inside out. Ninety-plus percent fatal. These two here? You're looking at the Ebola and Marburg viruses, which disable your immune system first,

then begin to replicate unchecked. Your body temperature rises. You experience the mother of all headaches.
Every joint and muscle in your body starts to burn. The
virus eats away at the collagen in your connective tissue,
causing your organs to sink into your abdomen. Your skin
essentially floats on a layer of liquefied tissue. Blisters
form, then tear. You spontaneously start bleeding from
your eyes, ears, and mouth. Your red blood cells coagulate
in your vessels, causing the linings to rupture. There's no
stopping the internal bleeding. You can't circulate enough
oxygen to your organs, so they start shutting down.
Shock sets in. You pray for the release of death, which is
now a foregone conclusion."

"You're saying this . . . man . . . was infected with the
virus?" Kelly said.

"Maybe at one point in his distant history, but he wasn't
actively infected, if that's what you're asking. It's what's
called an endogenous viral element—an EVE—because
its genetic code has been incorporated into that of its host
species. What doesn't kill you makes you stronger and all
that. It's the same thing with our own genome. Eight percent of the genetic code that makes us human beings
comes directly from viruses we've fended off through the
course of our evolution."

"And this virus is what killed the creatures like Zeta?"

"Without a doubt," Friden said. "Red blood cells are
primarily produced in your long bones, specifically in
your marrow. You know, the spongy tissue running through
the core? There are tons of small blood vessels leading
from the marrow, through the honeycombed cancellous
bone, and out of the hard cortex. When the virus causes the
blood to clot and these vessels burst, the pressure inside the
bones increases exponentially, causing microfractures of

the trabeculae that form the walls of that cancellous honey-comb, which is precisely what we found in the bone core samples you sent us."

"So this virus killed every living being in the room except for the man from whom we collected the tissue samples," Roche said.

"Exactly!" Friden beamed and looked at each of them in turn. His expression suddenly faltered. "You don't get it, do you?"

He sighed and brought up an image-capture of a stained microorganism under intense magnification. To Kelly, it looked like a long, convoluted worm covered with wart-like bumps.

"This is what the Ebola virus looks like," Friden said. "I see it practically every day. Trust me when I say we've got enough of it down here to wipe out half of the country by dinnertime tomorrow, but it's not just the nastiness that makes it so cool; it's the fact that it has somehow figured out how to completely shut down the human immune system. By the time your body figures out what's going on, without radical emergency intervention, it's already too late. This bugger's a part of you. It's already transcribed its RNA into the DNA of every one of your cells, which are constantly replicating as it is, only now they're producing new cells that contain more than just copies of your DNA, they're producing copies that incorporate the viral DNA, too. They're trying to save your skin, literally, by making more and more of it, even as the virus is killing them from the inside out."

"Then how does anyone survive it?" Kelly asked.

"Some people have a variation of the human leukocyte antigen-B gene, which codes for a protein that helps bolster the immune system to fight off the infection, but for

our purposes we're concerned less with how the host survived than the consequences of it having done so. Those
cells that were replicating with the altered DNA continue
to do so. Not only does this new genetic code pass from
one cell to the next, it passes from one generation to the
next. So if you have the residual viral DNA and you're
exposed to the virus again, your cells are like 'Ha-ha. I already have that sequence, so there ain't shit you can do
to me.'"

"It becomes an immunity," Kelly said.

Suddenly, the condition of the remains they'd discovered in the tomb made total sense. The infected human
had been sealed inside the tomb, where the creatures tore
him limb from limb, contracting the disease in the process, a disease so deadly they didn't even have time to
find a way out. The masked man on the plinth, however,
had survived because he possessed an immunity, which
allowed his body to enter a state of suspended animation
until he could be reawakened with an influx of blood.

"So all you have to do is work backward from the
DNA in the tissue sample to re-create the virus," Roche
said.

"It's not that simple," Friden said. He switched back to
the program that compared the three strands of DNA. "As
you can see, we only have a partial genome. The remainder has either been incorporated elsewhere in the host's
genetic code or simply dropped through the natural course
of time. All that's left is a partial blueprint. We could try
to splice it together with segments of another filovirus,
but who knows what kind of monster disease we could
inadvertently make in the process. Without the rest of it,
there's absolutely no way of accurately reproducing it."

"So how were people without the benefit of modern technology able to do it?" Kelly asked.

"They had to have found an existing reservoir from which to extract the live virus. You find that and you find your disease."

"Surely one of the other filoviruses, like Ebola or Marburg, would serve our purposes," Roche said.

"You'd think so, wouldn't you?" Friden said. "But you'd be wrong."

"You've already tried them," Kelly said.

She thought about the monkeys down the hall and quickly suppressed the image of primates being deliberately infected with the symbiotic microorganism that had turned Dale Rubley into Subject Z and then subjected to a hemorrhagic virus the scientists hoped would make them die in the worst possible manner.

"That was the first thing we tried, but the alien organism recognizes the virus and stimulates the host's immune system to fight it off before it can even take root. Whatever this disease is, it works a whole lot faster than any hemorrhagic fever we've encountered."

"It's the combination of the alien organism and the host's immune system that fights it off?" Roche said.

"Yep. It's like the organism can detect everything we throw at it and manipulate the host's antibodies to fight it off. We've found that nothing short of spontaneous brain death is able to effectively kill it, and it tends not to oblige us by holding still long enough for us to put a bullet through its head. And even then, it takes a whole lot more than that to kill an organism capable of outliving its host. As you both well know, it can survive for thousands of years without one. The bone core samples you sent us, though? The practically fossilized alien organisms inside the trabeculae were as dead as dead gets. The virus ruptures its cellular membranes every bit as easily as it does the host's."

"So it's all or nothing," Kelly said. "Either we find the source of a virus last encountered millennia ago or the alien organism will continue to respawn until we do."

"That about sums it up, but don't forget that this virus has the potential to wipe out the global population in the process. If you do find it, you'd better be really careful or it won't matter if we're able to figure out how to kill this other hominin species or not."

"That's not especially helpful," Roche said.

"Not helpful? I just told you exactly how to destroy an organism that was nearly able to kill all of us using a single host, and you call that information not helpful?"

"If a disease like this still existed, we would have definitely encountered it by now."

"There are all kinds of nasty pathogens frozen in the permafrost, just waiting for a good thaw."

"You think we should just start digging up permafrost until we find it? That's your solution?"

"That would certainly be a whole lot more productive than standing here arguing with me."

Kelly tuned them out. She thought about the design that had led them from the tomb in Mosul to Göbekli Tepe. The tattoo had been left as a map for whoever found it, someone who would recognize its significance and use it to find something of critical importance, something hidden at an even older site. She recalled the image on the wall of the tomb, of the man with a pinecone in one hand and a canister in the other.

"I know where it is," she said. Roche and Friden stopped

arguing and turned to face her. "We have to warn the others before they accidentally release it."

"I need a phone," Roche said.

"Yeah . . ." Friden said. "That's not the kind of thing we keep down here in these labs, for obvious reasons."

Roche disconnected his hose, turned without a word, and headed for the door.

"While you're at it," Friden called after him, "tell them the most recent set of samples yielded the same results as the others. The contamination has to be at the source."

"What do you mean?" Kelly asked.

"Whoever's responsible for field collection screwed the pooch in a big way."

"How so?"

He brought up a split screen featuring what at first appeared to be three identical bar codes. It took her a moment to realize they were actually PCR DNA profiles, which were commonly used to establish basic genetic characteristics for purposes of identification and comparison, like establishing paternity or matching physical evidence from a crime scene to a suspect. The first was labeled 51TEO327-1X, the second 51TEO327-2X, and the third 51TEO327-3X. She cracked the code right away: Unit 51, Teotihuacan, March 27, unknown subjects one, two, and three. The samples belonged to the bodies of the masked men who'd stolen the mummified body from the maze underneath the Mexican pyramid and would have killed Anya, Evans, and Jade had it not been for the intervention of Subject A, the creature once known as Hollis Richards.

"They're not simply mislabeled," Friden said. "Unless these guys just happen to be triplets, someone lost the other two samples and tried to cover his ass in the dumb-est possible way. If we did that kind of thing down here people would wind up dead."

"What kind of samples?"

"Human tissue. Here, I'll send the data to the printer so you can pick it up on your way out."

"What were your instructions?"

"Just to generate a standard DNA profile that could be run through the ABIS."

Kelly furrowed her brow. It wasn't like any of the specialists at Unit 51 to make such a boneheaded mistake, especially one that would be a source of embarrassment when it was flagged by the DoD's own Automated Biometric Identification System. She remembered Jade saying something about all of the assailants having the same blue eyes, though. Was it possible there was more to it than that?

"I'll make sure to pass it up the chain," Kelly said. "In the meantime, can you do me a favor?"

"If it's take you out to dinner, it would be my pleas—"

"Run the samples again. And try any other tests you think might help differentiate them."

"Need I remind you of Einstein's definition of insanity?"

"Please?" She batted her eyelashes. "For me."

"You're not playing fair."

"Call me the moment you're done," she said and hurried to catch up with Roche.

28
BARNETT

16 miles northwest of Chontalpa

Barnett led his team across a field overgrown with chest-high weeds that shimmered in the moonlight and onto the first road they'd encountered in hours. It was little more than twin ruts separated by a stripe of wild grasses, on the far side of which was a fence made of weathered gray boughs held together by rusted lengths of barbed wire. The pasture beyond was mostly dead, save for patches of green that had been grazed nearly to the bare dirt by what he suspected to be either goats or sheep, based on the size of the desiccated droppings, although he had yet to either see or hear any livestock.

"Fan out," he whispered into his comlink. "We're too exposed out here."

Sheppard headed to the left, back out into the field, while Brinkley hopped the fence and crossed the pasture toward the distant wall of ceiba, kapok, and palm trees, which curved around a stable made of scrap wood and swallowed the road a quarter-mile ahead. He was certain he saw several small structures situated among the trunks. Morgan must have noticed them, too, because he slipped off the far side of the road into an overgrown drainage

ditch and vanished into the weeds. Barnett did the same
thing on his side of the road.

His satellite phone vibrated and he transferred the call
to his com.

"Barnett," he whispered.

Those were definitely houses out there in the middle
of nowhere. They might have lost their prey's trail several miles back, but they weren't the only monsters out
here. He and his team couldn't afford to waste any time
or manpower stumbling upon an encampment of heavily
armed drug smugglers.

"Director?" Tess said. *"I can barely hear you."*

"Now's not the best time, Dr. Clarke."

"But I figured out where Zeta's going."

Barnett slowed his pace and concentrated on her
words through his earpiece. She had his complete and un-
divided attention now.

"You deciphered the third crop circle?"

*"It's heading for an ancient Olmec city called La
Venta,"* she said. *"I'm sending you the coordinates right
now. It's twenty-five miles north-northwest of the last location you sent me, straight through the Mexico-Yucátan
suture zone."*

"You're certain?"

*"Not only does the design align perfectly with the map
of the main cities of the Toltec, Olmec, and Maya civilizations during the time of the Assyrians in the Middle East,
the location matches another constellation I was able to
identify from the star chart in Subject Zeta's cage in
Antarctica, and you'll never guess which one it is."*

The road forked ahead. Based on the patterns of wear,
both branches experienced relatively equal use. One branch
continued straight ahead through rows of trees that ap-

peared to have been deliberately planted, while the fork to the right wound back toward a single-level house and an outbuilding.

"Reticulum," Tess finally said when it became apparent he wasn't going to play along. *"You know, like Zeta Reticuli, the star system we named the creature after?"*

Barnett didn't need to have the significance explained to him. At the University of New Hampshire, he'd studied the Hill Collection, which included extensive notes and tapes created by Barney and Betty Hill, who claimed to have been abducted by aliens in September 1961. Among them was an audio recording from 1964 of the psychological examination of Mrs. Hill, who, under hypnosis, described her traumatic ordeal, otherworldly technology, and the alien species that would come to be known as Grays. She also drew a star chart, which an amateur astronomer named Marjorie Fish later recognized as the Zeta Reticuli system.

"We need to know what kind of snafu we're walking into," he said.

"I'm in the process of sending you a map of the archeological site. The majority of the structures fall within a trapezoidal shape. The points representing Zeta Reticuli, however, are off in the jungle to the southeast, but aerial images don't reveal anything beneath the canopy."

"What *can* you see?"

"Very little. A clearing with a buried pyramid and maybe the entrance to a tomb. Like I said, everything else is hidden beneath the trees."

"Work your magic with the satellite GPR and magnetometer. Get me every last bit of information you possibly can."

"I have the satellite scanning as we speak. Once I've

collected the raw data, I'll run it through my program, filter the resulting imagery, and send it to you."

"How long will that take?"

"*Best-case scenario? A couple hours.*"

"We don't have that kind of time."

"*It's outside of my control. You have to take into account the physical distance between the satellite and the surface of the earth. The time it takes the signal to cover that distance, there and back. How badly it's degraded by the time it passes through the upper strata, rebounds from buried structures, and returns to the satellite. We're talking a fraction of a percent of the original signal reaching the receptor array. Imagine how many times the process needs to be repeated to gather enough data for the reconstruction program, especially through all those trees. It's like making a sandcastle one grain at a time.*"

"Can you set the reconstruction to download at intervals and send the imagery directly to me so I can at least get a general idea of what we're up against?"

"*I've never tried, but I suppose it could work. In theory, anyway. The complete reconstruction will probably take twice as long, though. Maybe even longer with having to compress the data to send it to you.*"

"If anyone can do this, Dr. Clarke, it's you. I have complete confidence in your abilities."

Barnett terminated the call before she could raise any further objections. He needed to focus on the task at hand. Something wasn't right here. He could feel it. The air was too still, the area too quiet. Whatever animals were out there in the fields were not only hiding, they were completely silent. No crickets chirped or birds called. The only sound was the crackle of the detritus underfoot and the shushing of the tall blades of grass against their fatigues.

He crouched at the edge of the weeds and tried to get a look at the homestead through the surrounding trees. The white house had been sandblasted to the bare wood by the wind, which had scattered the thatch from the bare boards of the roof. The barn on the far side of it had been assembled from warped gray planks. A fenced pasture surrounded the buildings, inside of which were rows of crops, fruit trees, and several large brown and white mounds.

"Keep your eyes open," he whispered into his com. He seated his rifle against his shoulder and surveyed the pasture through the scope. Just as he thought. The mounds were the bodies of horses, their throats opened and their blood pooled around them. If he held his breath, he could hear the drone of flies. "They definitely passed through here."

"I picked up their trail," Sheppard whispered. *"Heading in your direction from the west."*

"Morgan: check out the house," Barnett whispered. "Brinkley: you take the barn."

There was another homestead farther down the road and on the opposite side of the road from the first. The house appeared nearly identical, only rather than a barn, there was a haphazard plywood structure built up against the back of the main dwelling.

"Sheppard," he whispered. "There's another house up ahead. Take a western approach and come in from the back. I'll take the road and enter through the front."

"Do we have a visual on any of the occupants?" Sheppard whispered.

"Negative," Morgan replied.

Barnett figured if any of them were still here, they were long past the point of caring about trespassers on their property.

He walked straight down the road, sighting his rifle from one side to the other, taking in everything around him as quickly as he could. A clothesline had been strung from the side of the house to the nearest palm tree. The shirts and pants hanging from it were large, colorful, and in the local ethnic style. Rubber trees surrounded the entrance from the road, simultaneously concealing his approach and hiding his destination.

"No movement around back," Sheppard whispered.

"Hold your position," Barnett whispered as he stepped over the barbed wire fence. He cut across the windswept yard toward the front porch. Pressed his back against the wall. Tried to peek through the window, but couldn't see a thing through the drawn curtains. Listened for even the slightest sound to betray the presence of anyone inside. "Wait for my mark."

"The door to the barn's standing wide open," Brinkley whispered. *"There's a lot of blood inside. Something was recently slaughtered in here. Several somethings by the look of it, but outside of some baled hay, the place is empty."*

"No bodies?" Barnett whispered.

Brinkley's hesitation was all the answer he needed.

"No, sir."

"There's a truck between the house and the barn," Morgan whispered. *"The keys are still in the ignition. Whoever drove it here either must not have been planning to stay for very long or didn't have to worry about it being stolen."*

"Brinkley and Morgan: take opposite sides of the house," Barnett said. "We hit them both at the exact same time. Hard and fast. Watch your crossfire."

He stepped away from the wall. Planted his feet. Shouldered his rifle.

"Everyone in position?" he whispered and waited for a chorus of assent before giving the order. "Go!"

Barnett kicked in the front door and was already across the threshold when he felt the rebound against his shoulder. To his left, a broken rocking chair. To his right, an overturned couch. Arcs of blood decorated walls overburdened with framed images of Jesus Christ and shelves of candles. The smell was of fresh meat, of the counter in a butcher's shop. The people who lived here hadn't been killed very long ago. Assuming killing them had been the creature's objective.

"This place is empty," Morgan whispered from inside the house across the road. *"Definite signs of a struggle, though. The table's broken and there's blood all over the floor."*

"Damn it," Barnett whispered.

"There's blood in the pen back here," Sheppard said. *"It looks like someone was dragged through the dirt and gutted—"*

His voice cut out.

"Sheppard?" Barnett whispered.

No answer.

Barnett passed through the main room and entered the kitchen. The lone window offered a glimpse into the structure built onto the back of the house, where Sheppard should have entered. The wooden door stood open, admitting just enough moonlight to separate mounds of hay from the darkness. He detected movement in the deep shadows, felt unseen eyes upon him.

There was no sign of Sheppard.

He heard the crunch of dry straw beneath stealthily transferred weight. Something was definitely back there.

"All this blood and no bodies . . ." Morgan whispered.

Barnett kept his sightline affixed to the kitchen window as he backed into the main room. A shadow passed across the glass. He heard a thump from the other side of the wall to his right. There were at least two sources of movement. He suddenly understood what had happened to the inhabitants of these houses.

"Zeta's building an army." A crashing sound from the kitchen. Glass spread across the floor. Footsteps clamored from the adjacent room. "Get the hell out of there!"

A portly man slid through the broken glass on his side. Rolled over onto his hands and knees. Looked up at Barnett through eyes positively filled with blood. A mask of crimson covered his face from the torn skin along his hairline, through which his elongated frontal bone showed.

"Director . . ." the man said in a voice and cadence Barnett recognized immediately.

He shouted and pulled the trigger. Hit the man in the upper chest. Sent him sliding backward through a wash of his own blood. He was already trying to get up when Barnett spun and fired at the woman emerging from the adjacent room to his right. She ducked back inside before he could get a clear shot.

Barnett whirled and shot straight through the open front door to clear his path. Sprinted out into the yard. Footsteps drummed the wooden floor behind him. Silhouettes raced through the jungle in his peripheral vision.

He heard the rattle of gunfire from across the road, saw the strobe of discharge through the trees.

"They're all around me!" Brinkley shouted. *"I can't get—!"*

His words degenerated into cries of agony.

Subject Z had lured them into another trap. It had waited until it was nearly to its final destination before infecting the people who lived here in an effort to prevent Barnett's team from stopping it. Lord only knew how many people were now at the mercy of the alien organisms spreading through their bodies, in the process of physically transforming into drones at the creature's command.

"Get to the road!" Morgan shouted.

Barnett veered to his left and sprinted toward the fence line.

A blinding light burst from behind the other house. An engine roared.

He hurdled the fence, stumbled through the drainage ditch, and propelled himself to his feet.

A silhouette emerged from the trees ahead of him. He shot it at center mass, sending it tumbling into the weeds. He saw its face in the flash of discharge. The deformed architecture of its features. The sentience behind its eyes.

Barnett ran past it before it could regain its feet.

A pickup truck streaked across the field to his right, its headlights flickering through the maze of tree trunks. It angled toward the road. Tore through a wall of shrubbery. Destroyed the fence. Bounded over the drainage ditch. Launched up onto the road.

"Get in!" Morgan shouted.

He slammed the brakes and the rear end skidded sideways.

Barnett lunged. Planted one foot squarely on the fender. Dove over the tailgate. Hit the bed on his shoulder and pushed himself right back up. Fired at the shadows materializing from the jungle.

The tires spun in the dirt before finally catching and sending the truck rocketing away from the silhouettes converging on the road through the cloud of dust behind it.

29
JADE

Göbekli Tepe

Jade had lost all sense of time and direction. Worse, she'd lost the feeling in her hands and feet. It was all she could do to keep her head above the water, a terrifying sensation that was still fresh in her mind after nearly drowning in Mexico not so long ago. Finding herself in the same situation again, especially so soon, caused her to experience panic beyond anything she'd ever dealt with before. She wanted to cry out for help, to swim as fast as she could in any direction that offered the elusive promise of salvation, and yet she knew that once she embraced her fear, all hope would be lost.

The water rose over her mouth, entered her nose. She sputtered and rolled over, tried to float on her back, let the current carry her. She wanted to call out to the others, to make sure they were still with her, but she feared even that slight exertion might send her under. Only the subtle splashing sounds echoing from the darkness assured her that she wasn't alone.

The logical part of her, the part that understood the physiological stages of hypothermia and the mechanisms of drowning, urged her to accept the inevitability of her demise. And still the irrational part of her raged against her fate. She wasn't ready to die. Not here, not like this, although perhaps it would be a more merciful end than the one the virus offered the outside world. Better to drift off into a dreamless sleep than suffer through the contractures and crippling pain—

She again tasted the water and thrashed in a vain attempt to raise her head. She opened her mouth to cough, but only succeeded in inhaling another mouthful.

Evans wrapped his arm around her from behind and pulled her onto his chest in an effort to use his body as a floatation device for both of them. His breathing in her ear was ragged and labored, his skin so cold against her she felt it radiating into her chest.

"Stay w-with m-me," he whispered through chattering teeth.

He needed to let her go or she'd only take him down with her. One of them needed to survive. If they were right about what the missing canister contained, the consequences of all of them dying down here would be catastrophic.

The temperature seemed to drop by the second, the air on her face growing so cold she had to close her eyes against it and pray no ice formed in her lashes. It took her far too long to understand that the rapid cooling was because of the increased flow of air across her wet face. The current was growing stronger, propelling them faster and faster through the darkness. She sensed the walls closing in to either side, the ceiling lowering to within inches of her face. The sound of the water changed, too. What was once the gentle shushing of fluid against stone had become a growl.

She'd learned in medical school that the flow rate of

blood increased as the lumen of a vessel constricted and feared they were hurtling into a choke point in the aquifer. Considering she hadn't seen a single body of water during their drive into the barren desert, she had to believe that wherever the water went from here, it remained entirely underground. All thoughts of crawling onto dry land died with the scream trapped in her chest.

"L-let me g-go," she whispered in a voice so soft she couldn't be sure she'd spoken out loud.

Her knees bumped against the low ceiling. She barely turned in time to spare her face. Evans went under. It took so long for his head to break the surface again that she worried it might never do so again. He coughed aspirated fluid onto her cheek.

They were both going to die.

Anya was their only hope now. She was the best swimmer among them; hopefully, she'd be able to survive—

Something grazed Jade's shoulder. She felt the cold flesh of the younger woman's shoulder, the tickle of her hair trailing her beneath the surface. By the time she reached for her, Anya was already gone.

The roar grew louder. The ceiling flew past, so close it grazed her cheek. The flow of the current changed, sucked her under. She raised her head, only to smack her forehead against the limestone.

"T-take a b-breath," Evans whispered. "H-hold it as l-long as you c-can."

Jade gasped—

That was all the air she got. The water pulled her under and impelled her even faster.

Her skull ricocheted from rocks. As did her hips. Her knees.

Evans's arm slipped from her chest.

She tried to grab it. Missed. Accelerated away from him.

The back of her head passed his feet and struck the ground. Stars exploded from the darkness. She resisted the urge to cry out.

Pressure built in her chest, her mouth, behind her lips.

The walls tightened against her shoulders. She was going to get stuck. This was where she was going to die, where her body would remain until the flesh sloughed from her bones—

She lurched forward. The walls fell away. Her legs swung up over her head as she tumbled into a larger body of water. Unable to tell up from down.

Air leaked from her nostrils. She struck something hard, felt consciousness beginning to slip away. She bounded along the bottom, hammering one rock after another, until her head emerged from the water. A split second later it was submerged once more.

She'd felt it, though. The air on her face. If only she could find her way back to it, she could—

Impact to her chest. Her stale breath burst from her lips.

She was momentarily pinned against a stone outcropping before the current dragged her downstream. Her diaphragm spasmed, but she fought the reflex to inhale. Drove her legs straight down. Pushed off with everything she had left.

Her head breached the surface. She gasped. Desperately attempted to grab anything she could hold on to. Her forearm struck something hard. She secured just enough of a grip on it to halt her progression. She used the momentum to raise her legs. Shift her hips. Get her left knee onto the rocky crest. Prayed to God it stayed there. Felt movement against her flank.

"H-hold on," Anya whispered and wrapped her arm around Jade's waist.

Something struck Jade's right leg. Underneath the water. Snagged the pocket of her jeans. Nearly pulled her back under.

Violent coughing. A gasp.

"Cade?" she whispered.

He let go of her pants and she thought for a fleeting second that the current had whisked him away, at least until he rolled over her and vomited onto the limestone.

"G-gross," Anya whispered.

Jade dragged her other leg from the water and hugged the younger woman as tightly as she could. Rolled over onto her back and felt Evans beside her. Found his hand and squeezed it. She lay on her back, shivering, while she tried to catch her breath and let her eyes adjust to the darkness.

She could almost make out the shape of the cavern surrounding her. The rocky ceiling was at least fifty feet up and jagged, as though chiseled by primitive stone tools. The aquifer flowing beside her traced a course toward the wall to her left, where it once more disappeared into the earth. It suddenly struck her that for her to see even such faint, vague details, there had to be some small amount of light entering the cavern.

And where there was light, there was a way out.

"G-get up," she whispered, as much to herself as to the others.

Jade's hands were shaking so badly she could hardly push herself up from the cold limestone. Her frozen feet felt like they were made of lead, and her trembling legs barely seemed capable of supporting her weight, and yet somehow she managed to stagger away from the water and toward the cavern wall. It was covered with markings. No, carvings. She traced them with her fingertips while her eyes separated the details from the darkness.

The style was the same as the petroglyphs on the walls of the Iraqi tomb she'd explored virtually back at the Hangar. Men with helmets and beards. Chimeric creatures with the heads of animals, the bodies of humans, and the wings of birds and butterflies. While ancient, they were considerably more modern than the images painted on the walls of the subterranean city they'd just escaped.

"T-they're Assyrian," Evans whispered. "If t-they c-could find a way in h-here—"

"Then we c-can find a way out," Anya finished for him.

Jade frantically smoothed her palms across the stone, praying for anything resembling a ladder or a toe trail, any mechanism by which they could reach the light. While she couldn't see its source, she could positively feel it drawing her toward it with its promise of survival.

She clipped her shin on an outcropping and went down hard. Her frozen bones felt like they shattered when she landed on another rocky protrusion. She palpated its contours and gasped in recognition.

"S-stairs," she whispered and crawled upward.

The steps were rough-hewn and uneven, some natural, others chiseled by long-dead hands. They wound steeply upward until they passed through a narrow recess in the wall itself, where they became even steeper, forcing her to stand to ascend them. The passageway constricted to such an extent that she had to turn sideways and duck her head. There was a natural opening in the wall to her left, offering a glimpse of the cavern far below, but she didn't even look. She was far more interested in the faint aura of light emanating from above her.

She scrambled up the narrow staircase, stumbled through a short tunnel, and nearly ran headlong into a wall of rock. Cold air flowed through the crevice to her left. She scooted sideways through it and found herself on a ledge halfway up a stone escarpment, a deep valley sprawled below her in the darkness.

The wind rose with a howl and threatened to pry her from the ledge.

Jade knelt for balance and waited for the others to catch up with her. She leaned as far as she dared over the edge, but couldn't see a way down. Their only option was to follow the two-foot-wide trail leading diagonally upward toward the edge of the rock formation, beyond which she could barely see the rounded wall of what appeared to be a man-made structure. Shadows scrabbled on its uppermost edge, flapping their massive wings for balance. She hadn't even taken her first step toward it when she was accosted by a stench so awful she instinctively clapped her hand over her mouth and nose.

She recognized it immediately. She'd smelled it twice in Nigeria: at the village where Boko Haram dumped its victims in a mass grave and, later, at the camp where the marauding Islamic army had slaughtered a missionary group. It was a scent she'd never forget as long as she lived, nor any of the memories associated with it.

It was the smell of death.

30
TESS

The Hangar

Tess returned to her office with the biggest mug she could find and an entire pot of coffee. Programming the system to reconstruct the data from the ground-penetrating radar and magnetometer at more frequent intervals had taken longer than she'd anticipated, but things were actually progressing faster than expected. The combined data had already produced the first digital elevation model, which was little better than a photograph of television static, although it would gain more and more detail with each subsequent reconstruction. She only hoped Barnett's team in the field had enough patience to wait it out. While she understood the need for speed, there was only so much she could personally do to expedite the process. That didn't mean she was going to sit on her hands while the program ran, though.

It would help if she knew what Evans's team had found in Göbekli Tepe, assuming they'd found anything at all. If there was nothing there, then the whole theory about the map leading to something of great importance didn't necessarily fall apart, but it meant they were going to have to check all of the other locations corresponding with the various planets, which would take time they simply didn't have.

She sat in the chair behind her desk, poured herself the first of what would likely be several dozen cups of coffee, and speed-dialed Evans. The call went straight to voicemail. She tried Anya and Jade, too, but achieved the exact same result. Considering they were thousands of miles away and in the middle of nowhere, she wasn't overly surprised. She debated calling Maddox, but figured she'd be heading down to the command center with what she hoped would be useful information in a matter of minutes anyway. While she didn't like the idea of plowing ahead without some form of confirmation, it was a million times better than doing nothing.

The map of Giza was still on her primary computer screen. Because it was one of the most famous archeological sites in the world, she was certain the entire area had been studied with every scientific instrument known to man, and was rewarded when her search returned both GPR and magnetometric surveys. In combination, the two produced a grayscale map of the entire city, from the modern aboveground structures to the ancient ones buried underneath up to fifty feet of sand. The resulting three-dimensional digital elevation model always reminded her of scarring on human skin. Terrestrial buildings like the pyramids and contemporary houses appeared white and raised, while those buried beneath the gray earth were as dark as bruises. Where an aerial photograph showed only sand and the general shape of the structures that breached the surface, the digital elevation model revealed the entire buried city as it must have looked five thousand years ago.

There were hundreds of square and rectangular dwellings surrounding the pyramids, packed tightly into grids separated by archaic roads that now registered as little more than ghostly lines, smudged away by the wind that had ultimately buried them beneath the desert. She recognized the Sphinx facing a pair of large square ruins and a slew of buildings reminiscent of apartment complexes. The contemporary neighborhoods encroached upon the site from all sides, forming a backward C-shape around the pyramids.

She opened the file containing the scaled image of the constellation of Orion and laid it over the map. The majority of the stars aligned with houses that had been built upon ground containing history the world might now never know. The star corresponding to Rigel—Orion's left foot—fell upon an area of open desert to the northwest. It almost looked like something was buried beneath the sand. A structure of some kind, roughly the same size as the largest of the pyramids. Its walls were defined by charcoal lines, barely discernible from the surrounding gray sand, easily missed by someone without her experience and highly trained eyes. Only two sides of the construct remained, forming a right angle. She recognized part of a third, which confirmed her assumption that it was built to form a square, but she could tell little beyond that. The sand covering it was a mere shade of white brighter than the surrounding desert, which meant it had some amount of height to it, like a low-lying plateau, possibly little more than a gentle rise.

Whatever it was, that was where they needed to go.

Tess saved the image, uploaded it to the working database, and sent it to the printer so she'd have a hard copy to show Maddox. She was just about to grab it when the digital elevation model of La Venta refreshed. Gone was the pixelated black-and-white chaos; in its place was the faint outline of what was once the seat of power for the oldest known civilization in the New World. The pyramid took the form of a gray square with a white peak. The neighboring structures were outlined by ghostly dots. She could easily pick out the walls of the acropolis, the basalt columns that defined the plazas, and the massive stone altars and monuments. And there, off to the side, nearly blending into the gray mass of trees, was the dotted outline of a black rectangle, a buried structure right where Zeta Reticuli should be in the constellation Reticulum.

She sent the image to the printer with the other one, grabbed both, and ran out of her office. Down the hall and the stairs. Her adrenaline kicked in, and she practically flew down the corridor to the command center.

After nearly getting herself shot bursting onto the bridge unannounced last time, she had the presence of mind to approach at a more measured pace. It also gave her a chance to fix her hair in the reflection from the window of the Arcade, through the tinted surface of which she could see the faint outlines of the drone stations and the operators manning the controls. There was no harm in making herself presentable, just in case they somehow prevented the end of the world.

She strode confidently onto the bridge, the printouts clasped at her side. This was her moment of triumph. She and she alone had cracked the code. Assuming Evans's team had solved whatever mystery awaited them at the end of the map, for this first time since this whole mess started, they held the advantage. Slim though it might be.

Maddox stood with his back to her, his hands clasped behind his back, his deltoids testing the strength of the material of his uniform top. Below him and on the other side of the railing, the information specialists toiled at their stations, flipping through the aerial, satellite, and drone imagery faster than she could keep up with. She recognized the circular ruins of Göbekli Tepe, the modern and ancient buildings juxtaposed at the heart of Giza, and the dense jungle surrounding the buried pyramid at La Venta.

Tess looked down at the printouts in her hand. While she'd told him about deciphering the second crop circle, she had yet to tell him that the third led to the primitive Olmec site. He obviously could have learned of her accomplishment from Barnett, but she'd only just talked to him and it hadn't sounded like he was in a position to turn around and start making follow-up calls.

She again glanced at the live footage from Turkey, where several figures picked their way through the stone temples. There were two cars in the lot and a third parked across the dirt road leading into it, blocking access to the ruins. Granted, it was dark and the resolution was somewhat pixelated, but they all appeared to be wearing black.

It was already nearing dawn on the other side of the world, and they hadn't heard from their team in the field. Or at least no one had told her if they had. And there'd certainly been no mention of a second team being dispatched to the site.

Maddox must have sensed her presence. He stiffened and turned to face her.

"Dr. Clarke," he said. "Tell me you have some good news."

Tess smiled and prayed her expression looked more genuine than it felt.

"I wanted to let you know that I cracked the code of the third crop circle. I have my program collating remote sensing data and generating a three-dimensional model as we speak. We ought to have a pretty good idea of what we're looking for within a matter of hours."

"You're referring to La Venta, correct?"

"Director Barnett already told you?"

"Of course," he said. "We've piggybacked on your satellite feed and are in the process of dispatching drones to the site. Everything should be in place by the time his team arrives." He nodded his head toward the papers in her hand.

"What do you have there?"

"Oh," she said. "This is a preliminary reconstruction of the subterranean structures at La Venta. You can't see very much detail yet, though."

He walked toward her and extended his hand. She passed the printouts to him and discreetly watched the main screen over his shoulder while he perused them. None of the black-clad figures looked like Anya, Evans, or Jade, but if they weren't her teammates, who were they?

"What's this other one?" Maddox asked.

Something inside of her cried out for her to be careful how she answered. It was an irrational reaction, but one she knew better than to ignore.

"Just an aerial view of Giza, but I can see you've already got a handle on that."

The image of the screen was centered over the pyramids. The swatch of open desert that corresponded to Rigel wasn't even in the picture.

"We have imagery of the site," he said, "but we still don't know which structure to target. I was hoping you were here because you'd figured it out."

Tess was a terrible liar. He'd be able to see right through her if she so much as tried, so she chose her words carefully.

"It would help me if I knew what we were looking for," she said. "What have we heard from the team at Göbekli Tepe?"

She watched the dark forms swarm the stone ruins over his shoulder. There was an urgency to their movements, an order, almost as though they were searching for something.

"They found an underground system of caves the size of a small city," Maddox said. "They're still in the process of exploring and outside cellular communications range. Updates are infrequent at best, but I anticipate hearing from them soon."

It was a reasonable explanation, but it didn't sit right with her. They knew that satellite archeology was her specialty; even if the satellite over the ruins wasn't equipped with remote sensing devices, she could have tasked one to their location and produced a detailed map of the hollow spaces within a matter of hours.

There was no doubt in her mind that he was lying to her.

She concentrated on controlling her facial expression and tone of voice and prayed that neither betrayed her.

"Any idea when Kelly and Roche are getting back?"

"They just boarded a chopper at Fort Detrick," Maddox said. "They should be here within the hour."

"You can recycle those printouts." She made eye contact and smiled, then turned and headed toward the hallway as nonchalantly as possible. "I'll have a more detailed DEM by the time they arrive."

Tess maintained a steady pace all the way down the corridor and waited until she was inside the stairwell to remove her cell phone from her pocket. Opened her messenger. Selected Roche's number. Started typing as fast as she could. She didn't know exactly what to say, but she needed to warn him, and she needed to do so in a way that wouldn't give her away if her communications were being monitored. Something was definitely wrong here. And if she was correct, it was only a matter of time before—

The door to the stairwell burst open. Slammed her against the wall. She cried out. Dropped her phone, which clattered to the ground at her feet.

"It was the live feed that gave it away, wasn't it?" Maddox said. "No matter. We'll just have to accelerate our timetable."

Tess lunged for her phone, but he caught her by the hair and jerked her backward. Her feet went out from underneath her. She hit the ground. Pulled free. Rolled over, tried to crawl. A blow came to the back of her head and her arms gave out. Her chin rebounded from concrete dotted with the same blood she could taste in her mouth.

She saw her phone from the corner of her eye. Reached for it. Closed her hand around it and dragged it under her chest. Hoped to God she hit the SEND button in the process. "What do we have here?" he asked. He pulled her arm out from underneath her, pried the phone from her grasp, and read the outgoing message. "When Aldebaran sees red, two-twelfths minus two zeroes equals one. What's that supposed to mean?"

Tess smiled and felt the warmth of the blood dripping

from the corner of her mouth, where it pooled against her cheek. If anyone could decipher the code, it was Roche.

The pain in her head metamorphosed into numbness and spread throughout her body. She welcomed the release.

Maddox dropped the phone in front of her face and crushed it beneath his heel. Grabbed a fistful of her hair and jerked her head backward.

"Are you talking about the star Aldebaran?" he shouted. "That name has never once appeared in our research. What does it mean?"

Her eyes rolled up into her head.

Maddox released her hair, but the darkness claimed her before her forehead hit the floor.

31
ROCHE

**10,000 feet above the
Pamunkey River Basin, Virginia**

"Can't this thing go any faster?" Roche shouted into the microphone.

"Not in this wind." The pilot's voice sounded tinny through the headphones. *"At least not without spreading flaming wreckage across the valley floor."*

Everything was finally coming together, but it was happening too quickly. Roche needed to coordinate with his various units, but he couldn't reach his team at Göbekli Tepe, and all of the incoming lines at the Hangar were being diverted to the message line.

Something was definitely wrong.

Whatever semblance of control he'd once maintained was lost; all he could do now was try to make sense of this new information before it was too late. If Kelly was right about the source of the virus, then Evans and his team were in serious danger. Assuming they hadn't already released it under conditions they had no hope of controlling.

"Try the Hangar again," Roche said.

"Yes, sir," the copilot said.

Roche glanced up from the lab results Friden had given to Kelly and caught his reflection in the window. He didn't think it was possible to look worse than he felt, especially with how his head throbbed in time with the thumping of the rotors, and yet here was proof to the contrary. The world beyond passed in a blur of greens and browns, while the Pamunkey River snaked through golden reeds and flooded marshlands below.

"I'm telling you," Kelly said through the headset. *"Whether literally or metaphorically, the virus is inside the container the god in the petroglyph is carrying. Between that image and the map tattooed on the dead man, it's like the ancient Assyrians left a message saying 'Here's what you need, and here's how to get it.'"*

"You're putting a lot of faith in a five-thousand-year-old carving."

"It's not just that one," Kelly said. *"I've found multiple variations of this same deity from the same time frame in our database alone. He appears across many cultures and goes by many different names."*

She gestured toward the screen of her laptop. Roche leaned closer to get a better look.

"This is a photograph of the petroglyph from the tomb in Mosul," she said. *"Here's another depiction of him, only facing forward. Still holding a pinecone in one hand and a canister in the other. He has the same beard and hat, the same wings and watch-like bands on his wrists. Here he is again, standing sideways. And again. He appears in at least fifty carvings from ancient Mesopotamia alone, from the ancient Sumerians, who knew him as An, to the Akkadians, Babylonians, and Assyrians, who called him Anu. To them, he was the god of all creation, the personification of the sky."*

"So what's his significance?"

"I'm still trying to work that out, but if you look here, this same deity with his pinecone and canister appears in later carvings as the Zoroastrian god Ahura Mazda, who looks an awful lot like how the Egyptians depicted their god Ra in these hieroglyphics, only with his beard bound at his chin and holding an ankh by the handle instead of a canister, and even the customary Christian portrayal of Jesus Christ. We're talking about five thousand years of worshipping this one being."

"All religions are derivative to some extent. It's possible they envisioned their god looking the same because that's how the ideal man looked at the time, especially considering they originated in the same general area. Or maybe he's based upon an actual person who traveled the area—"

"Or maybe his body is sealed in a stone sarcophagus like the others."

Roche looked out the window while he gathered his thoughts. They were searching for a canister from an ancient petroglyph they believed contained a virus capable of wiping out mankind; was it so hard to believe that the man depicted carrying it had been real as well?

"Walk me through it," he said.

"This god you see here is nearly identical to the first," Kelly said. *"He has the same pinecone, the same canister, the same bands on his wrists. The Assyrians called him Nisroch and portrayed him with the head of an eagle."*

"Like the man from the tomb in Mosul."

"Exactly. In Sumer he was known as Enki; Ea in Akkadia and Babylon. The son of An/Anu. They believed he lived in the abzu, *the ocean underneath the earth, upon*

which the city of Babylon itself was built. As the 'god of subterranean waters,' he was supposedly the one who saved his people from the Great Flood."

Roche glanced up at Kelly in surprise. It wasn't the first time he'd heard those names.

"The crop circle from Poirino, Italy, in 2011 was encoded with a message in a binary language used for electronic communications called ASCII. It read ENKI EA. While I've always searched for a rational explanation for such phenomena, there are those within the field of crop-circle research who genuinely believe that ancient astronauts came here from other planets long ago, beings so advanced they were believed to be gods and incorporated into primitive pantheons."

"After everything we've seen, nothing sounds as insane as it once did," she said and offered him a smile from behind her microphone. *"He was also known as Set to the Egyptians and Brahma to the Hindu."*

"What about this one here?" he asked and tapped the thumbnail image of a man identical to the others, only wearing the head of a fish and a cape made of scales.

Kelly maximized the image and skimmed the attached documentation.

"That's Enlil. At least to the Sumerians. Ellil to the Akkadians and Babylonians and Ashur to the Assyrians, none of whom anthropomorphized him, for whatever reason. They envisioned him wearing a crown of seven pairs of superimposed ox horns. It was the Phoenicians and Philistines who depicted him with the skin of a fish, only they called him Dagon, in which form he made an appearance in the Bible. The Egyptians called him Set. The Hindu knew him as Vishnu. His likeness even appeared in

the Americas, where he was known as Quetzalcoatl to the Toltec, Kukulcán to the Maya, and Viracocha to the Inca."

"How did we get from Mesopotamia to Mesoamerica?" he asked.

The mere mention of the god Quetzalcoatl recalled the terror of being hunted through the Antarctic ruins by an extant species of dinosaur, the very same creature the Teotihuacano had used to guard the alien body entombed in the maze beneath the Temple of the Feathered Serpent. *"I'm not entirely sure, but all three incarnations are associated with the various 'flood myths' of their respective people."* She switched screens to reveal dozens of pictures of statues, petroglyphs, and reliefs in the unmistakable style of the ancient Mexican civilizations. *"These images are from the ruins of the Toltec in Tula, the Olmec in La Venta, and the Maya in Chichén Itzá, where he'd been depicted wearing the mask of the feathered serpent god and still carrying that infernal canister."*

For the life of him, Roche couldn't envision the implications of what she was saying. There were simply too many seemingly disparate thoughts running through his mind at the same time, all demanding his full attention, and yet simultaneously crying out for him to recognize the connection between them.

"I know you're searching for a way to rationalize what I'm telling you," she said, *"but maybe we should consider the irrationality instead. We're dealing with ancient cultures with no scientific knowledge and belief systems built upon superstition. These people literally thought of these men as gods, regardless of whether or not they were real, or if they were even men at all, but for the sake of argument, let's say they were. This bearded man with*

his pinecone and canister, his sons with their eagle and feathered serpent masks. Masks like we've seen on the bodies inside the sarcophagi in Antarctica, Teotihuacan, and Mosul. Bodies we've since learned have regenerative properties that allow them to survive thousands of years in a state of suspended animation. Imagine these giant advanced beings with their animal masks walking among much smaller, intellectually inferior humans with no understanding of the natural world. Superior physical specimens that have been memorialized at some of the most architecturally advanced structures known to man. What if these aren't just mythical beings, but rather gods that physically lived in their midst?"

Roche thought about the megaliths at Göbekli Tepe and Tula. The henges of England. The pyramids in Egypt, the Yucatán, and Antarctica. The ziggurats of the Middle East. They were all structures primitive men should never have been able to build, not even with modern technology at their disposal.

"The presence of a godlike race with superior intelligence would theoretically explain how they were able to build some of these monuments, and maybe even why they entombed these beings instead of killing them."

"Who's to say they didn't try?" Kelly said. *"The man bound to the plinth in Mosul, the one with the eagle mask? Nearly every single one of his bones was broken. The other masked bodies were sealed inside stone sarcophagi with lids too heavy to lift. And it can't be a coincidence that all three of them were among the statues inside the pyramid in Antarctica, the pantheon of gods worshipped by the people who built it."*

"What do we know about the one with the stag mask?"

"The Sumerians called her Inanna, but the Akkadians,

Babylonians, and Assyrians all knew her as Ishtar. She was Sauska to the Hittites and Astarte to the Phoenicians. Goddess of fertility and war, rebirth, and destruction. Daughter of An/Anu. Half-sister of Enlil and Enki. Twin of Utu/Shamash, god of justice. She's often depicted with the skin of a fish, riding a lion, and with antlers on her head or an eight-sided star behind it."

Roche understood the connection Kelly was attempting to make, but couldn't comprehend what could possibly be so important about the mummified remains of a supposed goddess to a creature like Subject Z that it had risked its life to save them.

"We've seen the evidence of these beings in the flesh," Kelly said. *"And while the historical correlation is anecdotal at best, you can't deny there's a certain logic to it."*

"So then what's the significance of the pinecone and the canister?"

"Can you think of a better weapon to maintain control over the masses than a deadly hemorrhagic virus?"

He closed his eyes and concentrated. Something she'd just said had brought him to the brink of a revelation he could positively feel building inside of him.

"We still can't raise the Hangar," the copilot said through the headset, *"but we'll have you on the ground in fifteen minutes."*

Roche couldn't respond for fear he'd lose his train of thought. He thought back to Antarctica, after he and Evans had narrowly escaped their encounter with the drone inside the clean room, when they'd first discovered Hollis Richards was missing. They'd followed his trail into the stone passageways leading deep into the heart of the Drygalski Mountains, where the creature had brought the remains of its victims. He'd emerged from the tunnel and heard a conversation he would remember to his dying day, one between the monster that would come to be known as Subject Z and an old man desperate to prove mankind wasn't alone in the universe.

All . . . species . . . serve.

Serve what?

God.

You're saying God is real?

Many.

So both of our species serve these gods.

In . . . different . . . capacities.

Yours is to destroy us when we evolve beyond the limits of our usefulness? And what is ours?

Build.

Build what?

What . . . is . . . required.

Was it possible these beings were indeed the physical manifestations of primitive deities, a race of superhuman, godlike entities? Everything Friden had shown them confirmed theirs was an advanced species, even more advanced than the symbiotic organisms that formed Subject Z. More advanced than any species he'd ever seen before, one so advanced the only word he could use to describe it was alien.

Thinking about AREA 51 reminded him of the Nazi relics they'd discovered beneath the ice, from the listening station at Snow Fell to the sunken submarine in the channel below the pyramid. Anya, Evans, and Jade had independently described their masked assailants from Enigma as having the same blue eyes. While such a detail could prove entirely coincidental, there had to be a reason they all wore masks. Until now he'd assumed it was to prevent them from being identified, but what if they needed to conceal their faces for an entirely different reason? What if it was because they were all the same?

One could certainly make that case with the results of the DNA tests he held in his hand. While the odds of the three masked men Subject A killed in Teotihuacan being triplets were by no means astronomical, the chances of Unit 51 botching the collection and handling of the blood once, let alone twice, were incalculable, which left him with two realistic alternatives: either these men really did have the exact same DNA or someone within the organization deliberately sabotaged the samples. He'd suspected there was a mole inside Unit 51 ever since their unknown adversary had appeared in Mexico six months ago, but he simply couldn't see any of the people he worked with every single day betraying them when there was so much at stake. And even if the three masked men were triplets, was there any significance?

Roche's cell phone chimed to alert him to an incoming text. He removed it from his pocket and glanced at the screen. They must have been out of cell range for a while, because several messages all came through at once. He'd missed two calls from Maddox, who'd left a voice mail his phone had converted to text:

POWER OUTAGE ON JBL-E. ON BACKUP GENS UNTIL
ARMY REPAIRS. NOT LIKE WE CAN CALL TO COMPLAIN.

It felt like a weight had been lifted from his shoulders. He'd known there had to be a logical explanation. He almost laughed out loud before he read the text message he'd received from Tess.

WHEN ALDEBARAN SEES RED, 2/12 − 00 = 1.

He read it three times before handing his phone to Kelly.

"I don't get it," she said. *"When Aldebaran sees red, two-twelfths minus two zeroes equals one?"*

"It's a coded message. She's trying to tell us something no one would understand if the message was intercepted."

"Why would she need to do that?"

Roche shook his head, and the weight settled onto his shoulders once more.

"Aldebaran's the brightest star in the constellation of Taurus," he said. "It's literally the bull's eye."

"Taurus is one of the twelve signs of the zodiac."

"The second, but Aldebaran's orange, not red."

"Maybe it's in reference to the color of the cape that causes a bull to charge. Then again, she could mean the metaphorical definition of seeing red. Like it's angry. What else could make a bull see red?"

And then it hit him.

"Those aren't zeroes. They're balls."

"I don't . . ." she started, but quickly caught on. *"Oh. I can definitely see how losing those might make a bull angry, but I still don't get what she's trying to say."*

The answer struck him with the force of a physical blow.

"Damn it!" he shouted. "How long until we're on the ground?"

"Ten minutes," the pilot said.

"That's too long!"

He suddenly understood why they hadn't been able to

reach anyone at the Hangar, why Enigma seemed to know their every move.

Unit 51 had been compromised at the highest level.

"What is it?" Kelly asked.

"A castrated bull is an ox. If you cut off its balls, you'd have one very mad ox."

"Jesus," she whispered.

"Maddox is the mole."

32
ANYA

Göbekli Tepe

Anya pressed her back against the escarpment and scooted sideways as fast as she dared. Loose pebbles skittered from the ledge and plummeted into the deep chasm, through which the rising wind screamed. She did everything in her power to keep from looking down for fear her legs would turn to jelly. The bottom was so far down she couldn't even see it, the wall of the opposite cliff so close she could have almost reached out and touched it. How anyone could have built the structure nestled like an Anasazi cliff dwelling inside the cave across from her defied the laws of physics, but why they had done so was obvious from the stench, which she could smell despite pulling her wet shirt up over her mouth and nose and biting it to hold it in place.

The construct reminded her of the tower of a medieval castle, only broad and squat, with walls made of stacked stones. Swatches of the brittle, clay-based mortar that once formed a smooth outer layer remained. The vultures perched on the top ring flapped their massive wings to maintain their balance as Jade passed within mere feet of them. They huffed their indignation at Anya, who followed Evans and Jade up a series of staggered, steplike ledges until she could see over the wall and the filthy birds and into the primitive structure.

It was what the Zoroastrians called a Tower of Silence, a circular building designed for the sole purpose of excarnation, a practice of using carrion birds to deflesh human remains known as a sky burial. While the rationale for disposing of the dead in this manner varied from one religion to the next, the act was essentially the same: the body was prepared in a ritualistic manner and laid out for consumption by scavengers, leaving behind only the bones to be shoveled into the central pit. She'd studied the remains collected from a Parsi tower in Mumbai back in grad school, but they'd had a whole lot less flesh on them. In fact, it looked like these bodies hadn't been touched at all.

"Jesus," Evans said through the hand holding his shirt over his mouth and nose.

"The bodies have been out here in the elements for at least three days," Jade said. "If it was an airborne virus that killed them, it couldn't have survived outside of a host for more than forty-eight hours in this climate. Of course, a hemorrhagic fever like Ebola can remain active inside a corpse for more than a week, so don't even think about touching them."

"The thought never crossed my mind."

"Are you certain that's what killed them?" Anya asked.

She climbed carefully upward until she could clearly see into the tower. The inner ring was maybe six feet down, six feet wide, and slanted subtly toward a hole roughly six feet in diameter, around which at least a dozen corpses had been arranged in a radial pattern. Their skin was black and distended, their clothes discolored by putrefaction, a greasy stream of which coated the stone and clung like wax to the inner lip. The blood had settled into their feet, making them appear disproportionately large.

"Without a doubt. See those black spots all over their skin? Those lesions are the result of subcutaneous petechial hemorrhaging. That's why the lips and eyelids look like the skin of a burned hot dog. And you can tell by the pattern of bruising, the way it almost mimics the shape of the ruptured vessels underneath, and the suffusion of blood in their eyes that this is definitely the work of a virus from the *Filoviridae* family."

"They tested the virus here," Evans said. "They needed to make sure it worked."

"Which means we're too late," Anya said. "It could be anywhere in the world by now."

"They obviously have access to the same intel as we do. I get that they beat us here because they already had a man inside the dig, but how is it they seem to know everything we're going to do before even we do?"

The question hung in the air between them before being swept away by the wind. The implication was clear: Enigma had infiltrated Unit 51. Someone within their organization—possibly someone they saw every day—had betrayed them.

Jade scooted around a blind corner and was halfway up a series of stair-like ledges by the time the others caught up. When she reached the top, she peeked out across the rock formation, then slowly climbed out of sight. Evans followed, with Anya right behind him, the desire to feel solid ground beneath her overwhelming.

Her arms and legs were trembling so badly that she collapsed onto her chest the moment she was away from the deep crevice.

They were on top of a plateau overlooking a vast expanse of desert spotted with a handful of trees, patches of wild grasses, and, at the very edge of sight, an arrow-straight canal where the underground aquifer had been tapped for irrigation. She had no idea which direction she was facing, let alone what they were supposed to do next. Their only means of transportation was back at Göbekli Tepe, and they'd be visible for miles from every direction walking across the open terrain.

"Over here," Evans whispered in a tone that made the hairs rise on the backs of her arms.

She crawled away from the precipice and toward a white limestone formation that looked like it was made of chalk. Evans leaned around the side, his attention focused on the valley on the opposite side, beyond which she could see the megalithic ruins of Göbekli Tepe carved from the hillside and the adjacent plateau concealing the subterranean caverns. A narrow dirt road cutting through the desert had served as a landing strip for an olive-green cargo plane. It reminded her of the kind the Army used in Vietnam, with twin propellers set close to the fuselage and a ramp that opened from the rear, under the tail fin. There was a cluster of tan Jeeps behind it, surrounded by a gathering of men dressed in all black.

"What are they doing?" Anya asked.

"Accelerating their timetable," Evans said. "You think the virus is on that plane?"

"I can't think of anything else so important they'd need to get it out of here in such a big hurry."

"You don't need a plane that size to transport a virus," Jade said. "They plan on taking everything of value, which means they have no intention of ever coming back."

"If that plane gets off the ground, we'll never find it again."

They all knew exactly what that meant. This was their only chance to prevent the release of the virus.

"There have to be at least a dozen men down there," Anya said.

"I count thirteen," Jade said. "Wait . . ."

The men in black parted to make way for someone to descend the ramp from the plane. The person was considerably shorter than all of the others and undeniably female. She wore her long blond hair in a ponytail and a golden mask that glimmered in the sparse sunlight permeating the cloud cover. Even from a distance, the black Celtic cross design was unmistakable. There was no doubt in Anya's mind that this was the same woman who'd escaped from Teotihuacan with the body that had been entombed at the center of the maze, the mummified remains wearing the mask of the feathered serpent—

She instinctively gasped when another figure started down the ramp.

"It can't be," Evans whispered.

It wore a long black cloak that trailed behind it on the ground and a hood that concealed everything but the crocodilian face jutting from the inside. It was so tall it had to duck its head to step out from underneath the plane, where it stood, towering over the assembled men, who gave it a wide berth.

The woman strode into the heart of the gathering. Her body language left no doubt as to who was in charge. She pointed to the Jeeps and made a sweeping gesture toward the hillside. Her voice carried across the plains, but not well enough that Anya could make out her words. The drivers returned to their vehicles, turned around in the open desert, and disappeared beneath a cloud of dust as they headed back toward the ruins, leaving behind a half-dozen men to guard the plane.

"That can't possibly be the same man from the sarcophagus," Jade said. "He'd been dead for five thousand years."

The woman turned in their direction, almost as if she'd heard them, and shielded her eyes from the glare.

Anya ducked behind the rock formation and found her face inches from those of the others.

"You saw the tracks Barnett's team found in Chile," Evans whispered. "It can't be a coincidence that Zeta escaped Antarctica with the mummified body of a giant, only to reappear with a traveling companion whose footprints suggested he had to be nearly seven feet tall."

"There's no possible way it survived thousands of years of entombment," Jade said.

"The feathered serpents sealed inside the maze with it did."

"That was a dinosaur capable of cryobiosis; we're talking about a hominin species."

Anya risked a glance around the side of the rock formation. The woman had turned away, but the giant behind her continued to stare in their direction. Parrot feathers bloomed from inside the hood, to either side of the crocodilian snout. She felt the weight of the man's stare from behind the hollow reptilian eyes, where before there had been only empty sockets, and sensed a dark sentience that positively terrified her. If ever she'd doubted the willingness of their adversaries to release the virus, its desire to exterminate the human race, she no longer did. This was a being without mercy or conscience, an entity that needed to be more than entombed within a stone sarcophagus. It needed to be wiped from the face of the earth.

She remembered what the creature that had once been Hollis Richards had said to Jade with its dying breath.

You must . . . stop . . . the end . . . of the . . . world.

"We can't let that plane take off," Anya said, "or all is lost."

33
BARNETT

5 miles southeast of La Venta,
Tabasco, Mexico

The old F-150 Ranger bounded down a dirt road that looked like it hadn't seen use in decades. A stripe of waist-high weeds separated the tire ruts, which were considerably narrower than the vehicle. They frequently vanished altogether where stormwaters had eroded through them, exposing massive stones that made the vehicle rock on its creaky suspension. The strain showed on Morgan's face as he tried to navigate them without the benefit of power steering, although he wouldn't have to worry about it for very much longer. They'd torn out a solid chunk of the truck's undercarriage during the escape from the creatures and watched helplessly as the engine temperature rose and the fuel gauge fell.

They were at the mercy of the jungle, which dictated their course through fallow fields and dry irrigation ditches as they struggled to keep heading north. If they strayed too far from their course, they risked sacrificing whatever lead they'd opened. At a guess, they were maybe ten miles ahead of the army of drones, but with their destination in sight, there was no longer any need for discretion, which meant the creatures would be coming, and they'd be coming fast.

"How many did you see?" Barnett asked.

"Four for sure," Morgan said. "I hesitate to speculate beyond that. There was a lot of movement in the forest."

"Same on the other side of the road, so we have to assume we're dealing with a minimum of eight."

"Then I guess we're just going to have to hope the jungle slows them down."

Barnett said nothing. There was no point. They both knew the odds of surviving a direct confrontation. Their only option was to reach the ancient Olmec site first and find whatever the creature had traveled all this way to get before it did. And considering neither of them had definitively identified Subject Z among the creatures at the homestead, they could only assume that the drones had been deliberately left behind to spring a trap like the one with the monkeys and vultures back in the Amazon Basin, while Subject Z and UNSUB X had pressed onward toward their goal. Surely they were several miles behind by now, too, but neither of the men could afford to take anything for granted.

Something under the hood made a loud clunking sound, followed by a metallic rattle. Faint fingers of smoke reached up from the grille and traced the length of the hood.

The surrounding trees drew contrast from the impending dawn, little more than shadows against the transition zone where the stars slowly faded out of being.

Barnett returned his attention to his tablet and studied the map. They were roughly five miles southeast of La Venta, with the Tonalá River basin and a seamless stretch of rainforest standing in their way. There was no way they were getting through there with the truck, even if it did manage to last that long, and the only way around would take them at least ten miles out of their way. They were rapidly approaching the point where they would be forced to make a decision.

He returned the tablet to his backpack and tried to call the Hangar on the sat phone. Again, he was unable to raise anyone on the other end. They were nearly to the southern rim of the Gulf of Mexico, so uplinking with a satellite shouldn't have been so difficult, assuming that was even the problem.

The rattling sound metamorphosed into a vibration that shook the entire cab. Smoke gushed from beneath the hood.

Barnett glanced at the temperature gauge. The needle was well into the red.

It appeared as though they might not have to make that decision after all.

A loud thud, then the scream of metal tearing through the undercarriage.

The steering wheel locked up. Morgan fought against it, but ultimately failed to keep the truck on the road. Its momentum carried it off into the high weeds and toward a stand of ceibas. The bumper hit the trees going fifteen miles an hour. Their seatbelts bit into their chests and hips. The impact split the trunks horizontally and dropped the upper halves down onto the hood. Cracks spread across the windshield, through which they could see only leaves.

"I guess this is where we get out," Morgan said.

Barnett unfastened his seatbelt and tried the handle, but the warped door didn't open. He had to put his shoulder into it several times before it finally swung outward.

He stepped down onto the damp detritus and seated his

rifle against his shoulder. Listened for any sign that they weren't alone, but couldn't hear a blasted thing over the hissing of fluids under the crumpled hood.

Morgan rounded the back of the truck and walked backward toward him, sighting the field behind them down his barrel.

"We cut through the jungle," Barnett whispered. "It's a footrace from here."

"That's not very reassuring."

"It wasn't meant to be."

Barnett led Morgan into the darkness beneath the lower canopy and set the fastest pace he dared. They remained in tight formation as they traversed the dense rainforest, drawing reassurance from the cawing of birds, the chittering of monkeys, and the rustling of lizards scampering through the underbrush. The jungle had no fear of them. It was when those sounds suddenly ceased, they knew, that they would be in serious trouble. That didn't mean that either of them was going to lower his rifle for a second, though. There were more animals out here that wanted to kill them than not, and they were the only ones standing between Subject Z and whatever awaited them beneath the ruins, something so important that the creature had crossed thousands of miles, and at considerable risk, to find, something related to the impending lunar eclipse and its unknown significance to beings not of this world.

Barnett signaled for Morgan to stop and cover him while he looked to see if Dr. Clarke's program had updated the satellite imagery of La Venta. When last he'd checked, the subterranean features had been only marginally better defined, with faint structures just beginning to materialize from beneath the trees. If he understood the way the combined GPR and magnetometer imagery worked, those buildings were buried under several feet of soil and thousands of years of tangled root growth. Even if they were able to identify what they were searching for, he had to wonder if they'd be able to reach it without earthmovers and with as little time as they had left before the onslaught commenced.

He was surprised to find considerably more data this time. The rhomboid pattern of the constellation was even clearer, with the peripheral dots representing Zeta Reticuli drawing increased definition from the jungle. There were two buried structures, square in shape and aligned almost like a figure eight made of straight lines and ninety-degree angles. They overlapped just enough to intimate a physical connection between them. Other darkened sections hinted at the presence of subterranean constructs, only hazier and less distinct, which presumably meant they were even deeper underground.

"What do you suppose is in there?" Morgan asked.

Barnett could only shake his head. He speculated it had to be a weapon of some kind, either one capable of destroying the creature, like the virus that had killed its brethren in Mosul, or one designed to eradicate those who stood in its way. Then again, he'd seen the machine that had created Subject Z inside the pyramid in Antarctica and realized there were potentially far worse things than disease waiting for them.

He used the opportunity to try contacting the Hangar again, but there was still no answer. His device was obviously linking up with the satellite just fine. The problem had to be on the other end, although he didn't know if that made him feel better or worse.

"Still nothing?" Morgan asked.

"We should pick up the pace while we can. We're going to need all the time we can get."

Barnett consulted the GPS one final time before returning the tablet to his pack and setting off at a jog. The ruckus of their passage silenced the animals in their direct vicinity, robbing them of their early-warning system. Trees blew past to either side as they weaved between trunks, ducked underneath branches, brushed saplings out of their way, and swatted mosquitoes from their faces.

He'd learned in the military how to set his mind to run like a computer program in the background so his subconscious could work through his situation while ignoring the protests of his tiring body. There was something about Dr. Clarke's map crying out to be recognized, but every time he came close to identifying it, his mind conjured images of dozens of creatures like Subject Z descending from the trees in a flurry of snapping teeth and slashing claws. They had neither the men nor the firepower to survive a full-frontal assault. They'd barely survived a bunch of monkeys and vultures a fraction of their size.

The rising sun pierced the canopy in slanted columns of red light and he realized, with a start, that this would likely be the last sunrise that either of them saw.

34

TESS

The Hangar

Tess awakened to throbbing in her forehead. She tried to reach for the source of the pain, but couldn't seem to make her arms move. The muscles in the back of her neck ached from the way her chin rested against her chest. She tasted blood and, for the briefest of seconds, wondered why.

The memories assaulted her. She opened her mouth to scream, but no sound came out. Only a trickle of blood that dribbled onto her thighs and pattered the floor between her feet.

Maddox.

She remembered the live satellite feed from Göbekli Tepe and the men in black fatigues swarming the ruins where Evans's team had fallen out of contact. Remembered him cornering her in the stairwell. Trying to escape. Pain in the back of her head as he caught her by the hair, then in the front when he slammed her face into the ground.

Then, only darkness.

She moaned. The noise sounded small and pitiful. Like

a wounded animal, which, she supposed, was exactly what she was.

"Tell me about Aldebaran," a disembodied voice said.

Tess tried to raise her head to see who was talking but couldn't seem to coax her body into following even that simple command.

A fist knotted in her hair. Jerked her head back. Blood flooded the back of her mouth, her throat, forcing her to sputter.

The warmth of breath on her ear. A voice.

"Aldebaran."

She gagged and gasped for air.

The hand released her hair and let her head fall.

She coughed the blood onto her lap. Struggled to keep her eyes open. Focused on the floor, where the Rorschach pattern of blood stood apart from the white tiles like a rosebush in a snowstorm. She needed to concentrate on her situation if she was going to figure out a way to survive it. If she didn't clear the fog in her head—and in a hurry—this was where she would die.

Maddox walked around in front of her. She watched his shadow pass across the floor, followed by his boots. He planted his feet to either side of the crimson spatter, crouched, and tipped up her chin so she could look directly into his eyes, which were a dramatically different shade than they'd been previously. He'd obviously removed the contacts he used to alter their color, revealing irises an intense shade of blue unlike any she'd seen on another human being.

"I'm going to ask you nicely one last time," he said. "I suggest you tell me what I want to know or you'll leave me no choice but to ask in a less-friendly manner."

While his eyes were unsettling, what she saw behind

them terrified her. She broke his stare and tried to gauge
her surroundings over his shoulder. Despite her eyes focusing in and out with a will of their own, she could tell
she was in the command center. She identified the various locations on the screens right away. The ruins of
Göbekli Tepe no longer crawled with men in black fatigues, while another angle showed what looked like a
military transport plane shrouded by a cloud of dust. The
central column featured aerial views of Giza. The pyramids. The Sphinx. Unrecognizable ruins protruding from
the eternal white sand. And, beside it, La Venta, with its
buried pyramid, massive stone altars, and the encroaching jungle.

She only recognized one of the men manning the stations beneath the monitors. O'Reilly. The other two wore
black fatigues and worked on consoles still spattered with
blood from the information specialists whose bodies had
been dragged to the side of the bridge, heaped into a pile,
and draped with a tarp. A man's hand poked out from underneath, the outermost fingers amputated at the first
knuckle.

"We know about Cygnus, Orion, and Reticulum, but
this is the first we've heard anyone refer to the constellation of Taurus," he said. "We need to know the significance, and I've already run out of patience."

Tess realized that the message she'd sent to Roche was
the only reason she was still alive. Had Maddox cracked
the code, she probably never would have woken up at all,
and her body would likely be under the tarp with the others. She needed to string him along and hope to God he
didn't see through her deception.

"I don't . . . know," Tess croaked. She tried to swallow
to clear her throat. "I haven't figured it out."

"Oh, I think you have."

Maddox smiled in a predatory manner, one with which he appeared intimately familiar. Nothing about his face had changed, and yet it somehow looked completely different, as though he'd relaxed the muscles he used to make himself blend in with the rest of them and allowed his true monstrous self to emerge. The scars on his face made him look like a scarecrow, as though his face had been poorly stitched back together. His blue eyes hinted at the kinds of horrors he was prepared to inflict upon her. That he was eager to inflict upon her.

"Aldebaran is the bull's eye," she said. "Like Saturn in the crop circles, I believe it serves as a target, although I don't know whether it's meant to be literal or metaphorical."

"Taurus is adjacent to Orion in the night sky," he said. "Aldebaran lies in the same plane as his belt and aligns with his shoulders, as though he's looking directly at it. If it's part of the riddle, then we need to know now or we'll waste what little time we have left searching in the wrong place. We can't afford to wait another twenty-seven years for this celestial alignment to occur again."

"I told you—"

His hand moved so quickly she never even saw it. Her head snapped back and her lower lip burst. She toppled backward in the chair. Watched her feet rise toward the ceiling. Landed on her shoulders. The base of her skull ricocheted from the floor. Colors flashed before her eyes.

Maddox stepped over her legs, straddled her chest, and stared straight down at her.

"You need to think long and hard about how you answer my next question," he said. "Lie to me again and I won't be so gentle."

Blood welled in the back of her throat. She struggled to cough it out, to turn her head far enough to the side to let it drain, but failed. The prospect of drowning in her own blood was more than she could bear. She thrashed against the restraints binding her chest, arms, and ankles to the chair.

Maddox watched the panic form in her eyes. Let her struggle until she was on the verge of inhaling one final time before grabbing the chair and rolling it onto its side.

Tess barely staved off hyperventilation as the fluid drained from the corner of her mouth.

He again crouched in front of her. She could see past him into the hallway, where several men in tactical masks strode directly toward them. One broke away from the others and warily approached Maddox. The urban camouflage design stood apart from the white walls but concealed his face.

"The contact lenses and voice modulator subverted the security system in the elevator, but we can't find a way to circumvent the electromagnetic seal at the bottom of the shaft," he said.

"Have a little faith," Maddox said. "Just be ready to move when it opens."

"What if there's nothing down there?"

"Trust me, it's down there."

"And if you're wrong?"

"Then we'll turn this entire base into a flaming crater!" Maddox shouted.

The man in the camo mask took an involuntary step backward.

Maddox straightened his jacket and took a moment to compose himself.

"I know Barnett," he said. "There's no way he allowed

it to be incinerated. It has to be here somewhere, and you and I both know the original blueprints show more than three sublevels."

"And just how do you propose we reach the fourth?"

"Use your imagination," Maddox said. He turned to face Tess with that horrible smile on his face and a knife she hadn't seen him draw in his hand. "After all, there's more than one way to skin a cat."

35
KELLY

***Joint Base Langley-Eustis,
Hampton, Virginia***

Kelly's cell phone rang. She glanced at the caller ID but didn't recognize the number. She was about to send the call to voicemail when she recognized the area code as one corresponding to Maryland. She removed her headset and answered on the third ring.

"That was fast," she answered. She had to shout to hear her own voice over the thunder of the helicopter. "Tell me you have good news."

She nudged Roche, who was still on the direct line with the Secretary of Defense, although he hadn't done much of the talking since informing him that Unit 51 had been compromised, and mouthed that she had Friden on the line. *"Where are you, Yemen?"* Friden asked. *"It sounds like you're in the middle of a freaking war zone."*

"Still on the chopper," she said. "What do you have for me?"

"So the PCR test produces a basic genetic profile, right? It breaks down sections of DNA, amplifies them, and forms a kind of bar-code design unique to every indi-

vidual. These bar codes are useful in court because they're not only accurate but cheap to produce in cases where there are a lot of potential baby daddies, if you know what I mean. Assuming the samples weren't contaminated, all we'd really done is establish that all three men had the same father. That's our Western morality, for you. We just assumed that meant they had the same mother."

"I take it they don't."

"Not even close. I could tell just by looking at their mitochondrial DNA that they all had different moms. So I ran a more detailed analysis, worked a little magic, and isolated several sequences that I recognized right away. I don't have an eidetic memory per se, but I do have a pretty fantastic—"

"Max."

"Remember that genome I showed you earlier? The one with all of the extra genes?"

Kelly's hand fretted at her side. She knew exactly which genome he was talking about, but the mere mention of it left her reeling.

"You ran their DNA against that of the body from Mosul," she said.

"Yeah," he said. *"You kind of jumped the gun on the big reveal."*

"He's their father?"

"Not even close, but they have enough of the same genes that you can tell they share some amount of blood. With more time, I could probably determine how much and the extent of their relationship, but I figured you'd want to hear this right away."

"I could kiss you, Max."

"Can I make a suggestion as to where?"

She terminated the call, put her headset back on, and glanced out the window as the Black Hawk banked out over the Back River, offering her the briefest glimpse of Plum Tree National Wildlife Refuge and Chesapeake Bay before heading back inland toward Joint Base Langley-Eustis. *"Yes, sir,"* Roche said. *"I'll contact you personally once the Hangar has been retaken."*

He swung the microphone away from his lips and blew out a breath he'd been holding for too long.

"Friden confirmed the samples belong to three distinct individuals with the same father, but different mothers," Kelly said.

"So they weren't mishandled or contaminated."

"Worse. They share genes with the man in the eagle mask."

Roche flinched but quickly recovered.

"We'll have to deal with that later," he said. *"Right now, we've got more urgent matters that require our attention, namely taking back the Hangar."* The chopper streaked toward a small airfield surrounded by squat industrial buildings. Clayborn had ordered the immediate enactment of a contingency plan designed during the Cold War for the extraction of senior military officials from the fallout shelter and revised after the renovation of the secret base, transferring operational control to a central command center capable of coordinating all of the various moving parts involved in the tactical response. She'd overheard something about a training facility but hadn't expected anything as ordinary as this. There were no other helicopters or airplanes on the tarmac and nothing in the adjacent fields. Four men jogged away from an aluminum structure toward the helipad.

"The drone's in the air," a voice Kelly didn't recognize said through the headset. *"Two miles and closing. ETA: five minutes."*

Roche swung the microphone back in front of his mouth.

"Copy, Command."

The Black Hawk descended so fast that Kelly's stomach fluttered. She feared it wouldn't be able to pull up in time, and while a fiery crash would be a fitting end to the day, they had people inside the Hangar and field teams in both Mexico and Turkey who were counting on them. For all the good she was doing. She felt helpless. Her expertise was in geothermal forces and tectonic activity, not . . . whatever this was. The speculative nature of her current inquiries into ancient religions and mythology made her somewhat uncomfortable, but she was grateful for the opportunity to utilize her skills as a researcher to help, even in such a small way.

"We've identified the GPS beacons of your men in Mexico, roughly three miles southeast of their destination," Command said, *"but we're unable to locate your team in Turkey. We do, however, have visual on a cargo plane in a field near their last known location."*

"Damn it," Roche said. *"Can we keep it from taking off?"*

"Negative. By the time we negotiate penetration of Turkish airspace, it'll be long gone."

"Then track it. And for God's sake, don't lose it!"

"What's going on?" Kelly asked.

"Our team was ambushed," Roche said. *"Presumably by the same group that attacked them six months ago in Teotihuacan and used Maddox to infiltrate Unit 51, which means that if they found the virus—"*

"It's on that plane," Kelly finished for him.

The rotors screamed as the chopper pulled up and settled to the ground just long enough for the special ops team to throw open the sliding door and climb inside before taking to the sky once more. The soldiers wore black from head to toe, with night vision apparatuses protruding from their foreheads like horns and semiautomatic rifles with laser sights and infrared beams clutched to their chests. Their eyes passed over Kelly and Roche, but no introductions were made.

"Thermal imaging of the site is negative," Command said. *"And there's no movement whatsoever aboveground."*

"Do you have access to satellite footage from the last three hours?" Roche asked.

"We're already going back through it in an effort to determine if an incursion team penetrated the base and the size of the force you're potentially up against."

The chopper streaked toward the Hangar, staying just above the treetops to avoid detection for as long as possible. Maddox knew everything Roche did, if not more. He had to know they were coming and had undoubtedly already implemented countermeasures. Kelly couldn't quite imagine what these four men could possibly do to retake a bunker that had been designed to survive a nuclear detonation and upgraded to withstand a siege, but she had to believe they knew what they were doing.

"Why would they risk an assault on the Hangar when it's in the middle of one of the largest military bases on the planet?" Kelly asked. "They have to understand there's no way they're getting out of there."

"I've been asking myself the same question," Roche said. *"The information in our database would be priceless to the right people, but Maddox has had ample op-*

portunity to download everything in our system. He could have walked right out the door with it and no one would have known."

"What about the technology?"

"While the tech down there has to be worth billions, it would take a team of engineers weeks to disassemble it and even longer to transport it out of there. It would be easier to just download the plans and build copies somewhere else. We have to be missing something."

"Like another way out?"

"Possibly, or perhaps Barnett keeps more than just information down there."

Kelly suddenly understood what he was suggesting.

"You mean like the collection of artifacts Hollis Richards brought with him to Antarctica," she said.

"With as many secrets as Barnett was keeping, it wouldn't surprise me to find out there was a veritable treasure trove hidden somewhere down there."

"We've practically lived in the Hangar for the last six months. Surely we would have come across it by now, but even if you're right, what could possibly be valuable enough to justify the risk?"

"That's what we need to figure out," Roche said. *"I have to believe that if Maddox knew where it was, he would have simply taken it when the opportunity presented itself."*

"Assuming it was small enough."

"Even size wouldn't be an impediment if, as I suspect, he managed to get a team into the base. As long as it fit inside the elevator, they could have loaded it into the back of a truck and drove off with it while we were gone."

"Which brings us back around to them taking an unnecessary risk."

Roche leaned back and chewed on his lower lip, an affection Kelly knew meant he was trying to chase a thought that continued to elude him.

"We have imagery of three men entering the decommissioned airfield on foot precisely fifteen minutes after you left," Command said. *"We're still working backward to determine their point of origin, but I can tell you they walked straight into that hangar like they owned the place."*

"There are countless cameras throughout the complex," Roche said.

"Disabled fifteen minutes after you left and within seconds of the appearance of the men."

"I just talked to Max," Kelly said. "There's no way he's in on it."

"We've dispatched a team to Fort Detrick to interview Dr. Friden, but I'm inclined to agree," Command said. *"He would have bolted the moment you took off if he was an active conspirator. It looked like these guys simply seized the opportunity when it presented itself, but they were prepared to make their play regardless."*

Kelly understood the implications. Had she and Roche been inside the Hangar when Maddox put his plan into effect, theirs would be the same fate as the men and women trapped inside, assuming they were still alive.

"The timing has to be the key," Roche said.

"You mean the lunar eclipse," Kelly said.

"It can't be a coincidence. The only other time this faction risked stepping out of the shadows was when our team discovered the maze under the Temple of the Feathered Serpent in Teotihuacan. They already knew what was hidden at the center, which was why they co-opted the site archeologist in the first place."

"They wanted the body."

"Exactly."

"You don't think . . . ?"

"It's not like Barnett to allow anything as valuable as the body in Mosul to be destroyed. And he certainly wouldn't have told us if he'd brought it back to the States instead of having it incinerated."

"That would certainly explain why Max had access to so many samples, even after the remains had supposedly been destroyed," Kelly said. "These people must be after it for the regenerative properties of its tissues."

"If we assume the body they recovered from Mexico has the same abilities, then surely they have access to all of the samples they need," Roche said. *"This has to be about the body from Mosul specifically."*

Kelly glanced down at the images of the gods on the screen, at the analogous beings who formed the foundation of nearly every extinct and modern religion.

"What if they genuinely believe that these are the bodies of ancient gods?" she said.

"I've heard of stranger things."

The men crouching near the sliding door tensed and readjusted their grips on their weapons. She followed their lines of sight to where the abandoned airfield materialized from the horizon.

"If there's another way out of there," Command said, *"we can't find it on the blueprints."*

"What about an additional sublevel?" Roche asked.

"The original blueprints have a fortified bunker another sixty feet down, but I show it was sealed off when the substructure was modified."

"What if it wasn't?"

"It was designed to withstand a nuclear detonation directly above it. We're talking fifty feet of reinforced concrete surrounding it in every direction."

"Then how were they planning to get out?" Kelly asked.

"I assure you," one of the men beside her said. *"There's no way they're getting past us, let alone off this base if by some miracle they do."*

Maddox had to know that, so why had he taken such an extreme gamble? If she was right and he was part of an organization composed of zealots who believed they were recovering the physical bodies of their gods, then the traditional motivations didn't necessarily apply. Perhaps these men never intended to escape in the first place and they'd willingly undertaken their assignment knowing it was a suicide mission. What if their sole objective was to attempt to resurrect a being they thought of as a god? Kelly thought about the mummified bodies they'd discovered so far and the masks in which they'd been entombed— the eagle in Iraq, the feathered serpent in Mexico, and the stag in Antarctica—and recalled a carving she'd seen during her hurried research. She scrolled back through the various searches until she found what she was looking for: a detailed image from the Seal of Adda, a greenstone cylinder used as a formal signature on a clay tablet, like a stamp in a wax seal, that dated to 2300 BCE. It featured four figures—the bearded god, An, and his children: Enlil, with his symbolic fish; Enki, with his eagle; and Inanna, with points jutting like antlers from her triangular hat— surrounded by symbols of ritualistic importance to each. These four formed the upper echelon of the pantheon that had been passed from the Sumerians to the Assyrians, provided the foundation for the religious beliefs of the ancient Egyptians, and found modern representation in Zoroastrianism, Hinduism, and, some would argue, even Judaism and Christianity.

Was it possible Enigma thought the body wearing the eagle mask—a being they believed to be the god Enki—was hidden inside the Hangar and that they could somehow revive him? Had they already succeeded in doing so with the man wearing the mask of the feathered serpent, the Mesoamerican representation of the god Enlil?

"They couldn't bring themselves to kill their gods, so they entombed them where they hoped no one would ever find them," she said. "Or maybe they knew there was no way of killing them because they kept coming back."

"What are you talking about?" Roche asked.

"The ancient Assyrians, the Teotihuacano, and the Atlanteans. They were so terrified of these beings that not only did they hide the bodies, they completely abandoned their civilizations at the height of their prowess."

"And you think people like Maddox are collecting their bodies with the intention of bringing them back to life?"

"I know how it sounds, but after what we saw at US-AMRIID, you have to admit there's a certain logic to it."

"So what's their endgame? Bring them back to life, and then what?"

Kelly closed her eyes and tried to piece it together. If her theory was correct, the body Subject Z revived in Antarctica wasn't that of a man at all, but rather that of a woman known as Inanna to the Sumerians, Ishtar to the Assyrians, Isis to the Egyptians, and Ishvara, or Shiva, to the Hindu. Goddess of war. Goddess of death. Goddess of rebirth. Goddess of destruction. Depicted with either the antlers of a deer, an eight-pointed star behind her head, a figure eight of twined cobras on her headdress, or with eight arms. She was the half-sister of the gods Enlil and Enki, Dagon and Nisroch, Osiris and Set, and Vishnu and Brahma. The daughter of Anu, god of all creation. The sky god. The sun god. The giver of life.

Suddenly, everything made sense.

The crop circles showed where the gods were entombed. The first map marked the location of the necropolis buried beneath the streets of Mosul. She could only assume that one of the others led to the Temple of the Feathered Serpent, where Enlil's body was hidden at the heart of the maze. Another surely identified the cavern at the bottom of the world where Inanna had been interred. But the fourth was the most important because, if she was right, it led to the burial site of the supreme being upon whom most religions were based, a deity whose prophesied return heralded the apocalypse about which Hollis Richards had warned Jade.

Kelly opened her eyes and turned to Roche.

"They're trying to bring about the end of the world."

36
EVANS

Göbekli Tepe

Evans skidded down the loose talus and scurried behind a rock formation. Crouched and peered around the side. It didn't appear as though anyone had noticed him. The plane was still thirty feet down and roughly three hundred feet away across the flat desert, with only a dry riverbed in between to conceal their approach. Not that he had any idea what they were going to do if they were even lucky enough to make it that far. It wasn't like any of them had the ability to commandeer a plane or the tactical skills to prevent what appeared to be a small army from taking off, but they had to try something. Anything. The consequences of failure were simply too great.

Jade and Anya slid down beside him. Rocks clattered over the edge and bounded down the steep hillside.

Evans ducked back down and held his breath. Waited for a distant shout of recognition or fusillade of bullets to strike the stone around him. When nothing happened, he risked a quick glance.

The woman in the golden mask was already halfway up the ramp, while the tall man with the cloak and feathered serpent mask stared through the dust toward Göbekli Tepe and the source of a faint rumbling sound. Several seconds passed before a convoy of panel trucks materialized from the dust, speeding straight toward the plane.

"We're only going to get one shot at this," Evans whispered. "We go on my mark. Keep your heads down and follow this ravine all the way to the bottom. We'll be totally exposed once we break cover, so get to that dry riverbed as fast as you can."

The moment the masked man turned around, Evans gave the signal and jumped out from behind the rock. Dropped into a crevice he prayed was deep enough to at least minimize his profile and worked his way down the escarpment. Clung to the cover of the ravine until he reached the edge of the open desert and surveyed his surroundings.

A pair of men wearing tactical masks and black fatigues assumed their posts beside the ramp and awaited the trucks barreling toward them. Behind them, the twin engines grumbled to life and the propellers slowly started to turn.

This was it. Now or never.

Evans cast a quick glance over his shoulder to make sure the others were still with him, then sprinted across the plains toward the dry riverbed. Sand pelted him in the face, forcing him to lower his head and shield his eyes. He listened for the crack of gunfire, watched for bullets chewing up the ground in front of him. As soon as he was within range, he dove into the shallow trench, scrambled to the far side, and peeked over the bank. The caravan slowed as it neared the plane. Up close, the panel trucks looked like crosses between moving vans and troop transport vehicles, with beds made of canvas stretched over boxlike frames and held in place with bungee cords. Their desert camouflage blended perfectly with the swirling dust and the rocky terrain.

"What now?" Jade whispered.

The engine of the plane roared, and the propellers became a blur, kicking up even more dust. Evans had to raise his voice so she could hear him.

"You two stay here."

"The hell we will."

"If something happens to me, it's up to you to contact Roche and make sure he doesn't let that plane reach its destination."

"And just what do you intend to do?"

It was a good question. One, unfortunately, for which he didn't have an answer.

The lead truck eased to the edge of the ramp. Its tires spun in the sand until they gained traction, then launched the vehicle upward. It barely fit into the cargo hold of the plane.

And just like that, Evans had a plan.

"Stay here," he said and crawled over the bank, into the open.

He paused only long enough to make sure he hadn't attracted anyone's attention, then pushed himself up and took off like a sprinter from the blocks, heading straight for the third and final panel truck in line. The wind from the propellers threw up so much sand that he could barely see a thing, and it forced him to lean into it to maintain his course. Dust found its way into his mouth and sinuses, clung to the undersides of his eyelids like sandpaper. Filtered into his chest.

The plane was little more than a vague black shape, the men guiding the second truck onto the ramp mere silhouettes. Its taillights produced an amoeboid red aura. The driver's-side window of the third vehicle was opaque with dust, the driver invisible behind it.

Evans heard men's voices, shouting to be heard over the engines. The few words he isolated from the tumult were in German, the same language spoken by the men who'd tried to kill them in the cavern and six months ago in Mexico.

Enigma.

The second truck crawled up the ramp, its canvas siding flapping in the gale, tearing loose from its tethers in back and exposing the wooden crates inside.

This wasn't going to work.

The third truck started forward.

Evans waited until he was on the road behind it to correct his course and then ran straight toward the tailgate. Had the side mirrors not been completely coated with dust, he would have been clearly visible to the driver.

He was within five feet of the truck when he realized that the bed could very well be packed with an entire unit of armed soldiers. And while he might have the element of surprise, it wouldn't take them very long to recover.

He grabbed the middle bungee cord. Unlatched it. Lifted the canvas just far enough to squeeze underneath. Scurried inside and took in everything around him at a glance.

There were no troops staring down at him, but that was about all he could tell for sure. Scant light passed through the canvas, barely enough to offer the faint impression of the crates stacked all around him. He wriggled between them and drew his legs inside. Turned around and reached back to reattach the bungee—

Jade's face appeared within inches of his and he nearly shouted in surprise.

"Move," she whispered and crawled in right on top of him.

"I told you two to—"

Anya grabbed him by the arm and used him as leverage to pull herself inside.

The truck jerked forward and nearly sent them tumbling right back out.

"What are you doing?" Evans whispered.

"They would have caught us for sure out there," Jade whispered. "Besides, where were we supposed to go?"

"Someplace where you could contact the Hangar—"

"This plane would have already reached its destination by the time we got there," Anya said.

"You two are going to be the death of me."

A voice. On the other side of the canvas. Mere feet away.

Evans scooted backward and watched the rear, where the canvas remained open just far enough to reveal a crescent of the road behind them. It was too late to strap it back down now. If either of the men outside decided to take a quick peek, they were screwed.

The guard pounded the driver's side door and the truck juddered up the ramp.

Evans felt the crate behind him start to slide and braced his feet against the tailgate. Strained to keep it from shoving him toward the opening, through which he saw the legs of a man walking up the ramp behind the truck. Evans was certain he'd been seen and prepared to hurl himself at the guard before he could raise his weapon, but the man simply pulled down the canvas and secured it to the frame once more, stranding them in darkness.

The truck leveled off and sat there, idling.

Evans released a shuddering breath and slumped back against the crate. Felt around him until he found a gap and inched deeper into the cargo to find a less visible location.

The ramp rose behind them with a hydraulic whine, and the plane started to roll.

Jade bumped into his knees. He spread his legs to accommodate her hips and she scooted right up against him.

"This was a really stupid idea, you know that?" she whispered.

He wrapped his arms around her and rested his chin on her shoulder. She placed her trembling hand on his forearm, revealing just how scared she was.

"We're going to get through this," he whispered into her ear.

She turned as best she could. Her lips found his, and he kissed her with an urgency that surprised even him. There was nothing like being in the jaws of death to remind one how precious life was.

Her teeth struck his and he recoiled.

"Sorry," Anya whispered and practically climbed into both of their laps.

Evans gave her shoulder a reassuring squeeze and tried to settle into a position he could maintain for an extended period of time.

The plane accelerated until the nose tipped up and he felt the ground falling away below them. He heard the scream of wind shear, the whine of the landing gear retracting.

And prayed no one decided to check on the cargo.

37
BARNETT

La Venta

The rain had started as a drizzle that barely penetrated the canopy but had quickly escalated to a torrential downpour. Fog had settled into the treetops, a smothering mist that crept lower with every passing mile, descending upon them like a deflating parachute. The animals that had served as their early-warning system had taken to the trees or scurried into their burrows to ride out the storm. Only the occasional bird cried out in distress at their intrusion, while they passed drenched monkeys clinging to the boughs without raising an alarm.

Barnett could think of nothing worse than navigating hostile and unfamiliar terrain under such claustrophobic weather conditions. Other than being hunted in the process, of course. The creatures racing through the jungle in their direction might have been their greatest concern, but they weren't their only one.

They'd been trying to reach the Hangar for several hours and had yet to talk to anyone on the inside. The bunker had been designed to outlast an extended nuclear winter and, as such, had been equipped with countless redundant measures, including both internal and external backup generators capable of powering all subterranean equipment and communications systems, for a full week and essential life-support functions for ninety days after that. It had been set up on a completely separate grid from the rest of the base and grounded in a way that blocked catastrophic electrical surges from any external source, everything from the main power lines to a low-altitude electromagnetic pulse. Even the worst-case scenario promised a delay of fewer than three seconds between the termination of the main power and the reserve generators kicking in, which registered as little more than a blip on any of the computer screens. A prolonged silence like this could mean only one thing . . .

The Hangar had fallen.

That revelation brought with it a new set of problems. The fact that their adversaries had chosen this of all days to go on the offensive confirmed that tonight's lunar eclipse was of paramount importance to them, and despite its vast resources and brainpower, Unit 51 had yet to determine why. They'd been at a distinct disadvantage from the start, especially when it came to intel, seemingly two steps behind at any given juncture, but now things had become exponentially worse. Enigma now possessed every iota of information Unit 51 had amassed, including the data that had led them to Göbekli Tepe on the other side of the world and the ancient Olmec city just ahead of them through the trees. He and Morgan needed to be prepared for a decidedly more human threat, as well, one that could very well have access to Dr. Clarke's remote sensing data and a helicopter, which could be thundering toward them with a heavily armed tactical team at this very moment.

And while he was confident that their adversaries were raiding their databases, he had a feeling that wasn't why they'd chosen today to make their move on the Hangar. He didn't know how they'd found out about it, but he was certain they'd come for what he had locked in the vault, presumably for the same reason Subject Z was bringing UNSUB X to La Venta on this specific day. Something big was about to happen and he couldn't have been more poorly prepared.

The terrain grew steeper, forcing them to use the trees for balance to keep from slipping in the mud. At the crest of the hill, they were afforded a decent view of the valley below them from the anonymity of a wall of shrubbery. The archeological site stretched out ahead of them, a narrow, mist-shrouded meadow struggling to hold the encroaching jungle at bay.

He recognized the buried pyramid and the various monuments from the satellite images. To the north, the nine-foot-tall colossal stone heads watched over the collapsed basalt columns that had once formed Complex A. In its prime, the ceremonial center had been paved with ornate serpentine stones that glimmered like emeralds and housed the earliest known carving of the feathered serpent god, a deity venerated throughout Mesoamerica. And, as Barnett knew all too well, a species of dinosaur capable of surviving in a state of suspended animation for millennia. But it wasn't the creature in the primitive carving that had summoned them to this place; it was the figure depicted alongside it: a stylized man holding a canister identical to those memorialized in petroglyphs throughout Mesopotamia. And if their assumptions about the crop-circle maps were correct, then that canister, whether literally or metaphorically, represented an object of great importance, one he desperately needed to find.

Of course, that sculpture, like most of the other artifacts, offerings, and grave goods exhumed from this site, had found its way into a museum, taking with it whatever clues it might once have held as to the location of the canister, which, he sincerely hoped, contained the means of eradicating Subject Z and its drones. "The city was designed to align with Polaris, roughly eight degrees off due north," Barnett said. He consulted the GPS map on his tablet. "So we need to head down . . . there."

He pointed at a dense section of rainforest to the east.

"Do we have any idea what we're looking for yet?" Morgan asked.

"I'll let you know when I figure it out."

Morgan nodded and turned away, presumably so his expression didn't betray his growing concern. Barnett switched to Dr. Clarke's remote sensing map. He could easily pick out the shape of the forest below him as well as the subterranean features buried underneath it. There were definitely man-made structures down there, and what almost looked like passageways connecting them, although their borders were still poorly defined. He couldn't tell how far down they were, whether they were hollow or filled with earth, or even how the hell they were supposed to get inside. Chances were when the Olmec abandoned and buried this city, they hadn't anticipated anyone ever finding it or trying to get inside. And they certainly hadn't planned on a bloody jungle growing on top of it.

He wiped the raindrops from the screen with his forearm, tucked it inside his jacket, and shouldered his rifle.

"Let's get this over with."

The two of them worked their way down through the trees, conscious of every sound: every twig snapping underfoot, every branch raking their fatigues, every sigh of the wind through the canopy. They were fortunate the rain had driven away whatever tourists might have lingered in the ruins through the afternoon. They had enough on their plates without having to worry about civilian casualties. Not that there was really anything they could do about it anyway. Subject Z could easily mow through any number of unarmed men by itself, and their adversaries had already demonstrated their willingness back in Teotihuacan to slaughter everyone in their way.

The jungle provided cover all the way down the mountainside and to the fringes of the ancient mecca, where Barnett again consulted Dr. Clarke's map of the subterranean structures. Another update had defined even more detail of what appeared to be a veritable underground city beneath their feet. It must have taken the Olmec decades to bury their entire civilization, leaving behind cryptic altars and giant heads that served as a warning to people so far removed from this primitive society that they could no longer understand the warning well enough to heed it.

They couldn't see the main ceremonial complex that formed the trapezoid shape of Reticulum to the northwest, but the rain striking the open field instead of the ceiling of leaves created a sound differential, a blank space they kept to their left as they searched through the trees, brushing aside palm leaves and ceiba branches, shoving through saplings and chest-high weeds, navigating buttress roots, vines, and lianas until their GPS coordinates aligned with the location corresponding to Zeta Reticuli.

"This is it," Barnett said.

"I can't see a blasted thing through all of the trees," Morgan said.

Barnett realized how ridiculous the notion of arriving and immediately finding some major archeological discovery that had somehow eluded everyone else for nearly three millennia sounded, but no one else had ventured into this rainforest armed with such advanced and detailed imagery. Somewhere directly below them, under some unknown depth of backfilled soil and tree roots, were two structures that aligned like the twin stars from which the organisms responsible for the creation of Subject Z were believed to have originated. They just had to figure out how to reach them.

And they were running out of time.

"Anyone committed to spending the majority of their lives burying the only home they'd ever known likely wouldn't leave behind an entrance," Morgan said.

"So what do you propose we do?"

Morgan slipped off his backpack, removed a hard case roughly a foot long and half as wide, and looked at him with an impassive expression.

"We make one of our own."

Barnett offered a crooked smile. He knew exactly what was inside the case. After all, he'd personally requisitioned it on the off chance they ran up against something beyond the capabilities of traditional armaments, something that might have ended this threat way back at AREA 51 a year ago had Richards's team had access to a means of destroying the ice cavern and dropping millions of tons of ice right down on the creature's head.

"I'll start digging," he said.

While the earth was soft from the rain and held its

form reasonably well, carving a hole using only branches, rocks, and his bare hands took some doing. The shaft was maybe eight inches wide and six feet deep when he finally encountered resistance. He could barely see the flat stone at the bottom, but they wouldn't be able to tell whether it was the roof of a buried building or simply a slab of bedrock until after Morgan worked his magic.

Each of the M112 demolition blocks was eleven inches long, two inches wide, an inch and a half thick, and composed of more than a pound of C-4. The military-grade plastic explosives had the consistency of clay and were stable at just about any temperature and under any environmental conditions. The only way to trigger its explosive potential was to deliver a localized shock wave from a detonator.

Morgan removed four blocks and the corresponding detonators and handed the case to Barnett.

"Hang on to rest," he said. "You never know when they might come in handy."

Barnett shoved the case into his backpack and watched as Morgan peeled off the Mylar film backing and used the pressure-sensitive adhesive to stick the blocks to the end of an eight-foot-long sapling he'd stripped of its branches. He inserted the blasting caps so they stood from the mass like the spikes of a mace and lowered the sapling into the hole, trailing the long cords wired to the handheld detonator, which, when triggered, would convert the explosives into compressed gas that rapidly expanded outward, turning the shaft into a crater and cutting straight through the earth and the roots of the surrounding trees.

"Might want to take a few steps back," he said.

Barnett retreated about twenty feet and took cover behind the massive trunk of a kapok tree. Morgan shoved through the branches and crouched beside him. He held up the detonator and looked at Barnett, who gave the order with a nod.

For a heartbeat, the world stood still.

And then the ground dropped underneath them. The air filled with dust, dirt, and wooden shrapnel. A wall of superheated air roared past them.

Several seconds passed in silence before debris rained back down to the ground all around them.

Barnett stood, shielded his eyes from the dust and smoke, and headed toward a crater easily ten feet wide. Chunks of rock and tentacle-like roots protruded from the sloping sides. He stood at the precipice and stared down at the bottom, where a ring of broken stone blocks framed a black maw, through which he could see little more than motes swirling in the darkness. He shouldered his rifle, slid down the loose earth, and perched at the edge of the hole. Below him was a vast space of indeterminate size, from which cold air that smelled like a tomb seeped. He switched on his flashlight, but even its powerful beam illuminated little more than the faint outline of the debris cone from the explosion.

He glanced back over his shoulder and tried to catch one final glimpse of the sun through the treetops before consigning himself to the darkness, but the storm clouds denied him. It was a fitting send-off for where he was going. He slid his legs over the edge, shined his beam down between his feet, and dropped into the darkness.

38
TESS

The Hangar

Tess's wrists were bound so tightly behind her back that she'd lost all sensation in her hands. Fortunately, she could feel them against her rear end, although not as acutely as the tip of the blade Maddox had pressed into the underside of her jaw. It had found a nerve, which sent electrical currents through the entire left side of her face and head when he applied even the slightest pressure, but at least she could tell by the trickle of warmth running down her neck that he had yet to cut too deeply.

"Please . . ." she whispered and immediately regretted the movement, which sent a lightning bolt of pain from behind her eye into her skull.

Maddox shoved her down the hallway toward her office, where the illusion that she possessed critical information that he desperately needed would be quickly shattered. All he had to do was run a simple search of her computer to discover that any reference to the star Aldebaran was tangential at best. She needed to find a way to distract him. Even if she did, however, she would only be able to fool him for so long, and she had no doubt about his willingness to use the blade. The man she'd known for the past six months was gone, if he'd ever really existed at all.

"Get in there," he said and shoved her so hard that she lost her balance. With her arms bound behind her, she had no way of bracing for impact. She landed squarely on her chest. Barely turned her head in time to keep from cracking her chin on the floor. Hit her forehead instead. Felt her eyebrow split. "Stand her up."

Unseen hands gripped her by either shoulder and lifted her to her feet, where she struggled to find her equilibrium while blinking the blood from her eye. She caught Maddox's stare and understood with complete certainty that this was where she was going to die.

"Aldebaran means 'The Follower' in Arabic," he said, becoming increasingly animated as he spoke. "It was given that name because it rises in the sky after the Pleiades star cluster, which features prominently in ancient Mesopotamian and Native American creation myths. It's the eye of Taurus, the second symbol of the Zodiac. Two of twelve. It appears to be the same color of red as Mars when they pass in the night sky. Two spheres, side by side. That was the message you sent to Roche. What's its significance? Tell me what it means!"

Tess glanced up at the row of monitors on the wall, hoping to God that Aldebaran aligned with an ancient Egyptian structure, anything other than the open desert.

Maddox caught her looking. Gripped her by the back of her neck. Squeezed. Jerked her around behind her desk and shoved her face right in front of the satellite image of Giza.

She prayed for strength, for him not to see her pain and fear, but her cheeks were already damp with tears, and her chest hitched with every word she spoke.

"I haven't been able to identify it on the map yet."

"Well, now's your chance. And you'd better make it count because it's the only one you're going to get."

Tess strained against his grip.

"I need my keyboard."

"If you make so much as a single errant keystroke, you'll experience pain beyond anything you've ever imagined."

He released her and, with a flick of his wrist, sliced her cheek. Blood welled to the surface before she even felt the sting of the blade parting her flesh. She clasped her hand over it to stem the bleeding, took a seat at her desk, and struggled to manipulate her system with a single trembling hand.

The overlay of Orion appeared on the satellite map of Giza, the archer's belt aligning with the pyramids. She scaled the constellation of Taurus to match and mentally tried to predict where Aldebaran would align.

Footsteps pounded down the corridor. The man in the camouflage tactical mask burst through the doorway.

"We've picked up a Black Hawk heading straight toward us," he said. "ETA: two minutes and counting."

"Is everything in place?" Maddox asked.

"Yes, sir."

"Then give the order for the men to assume their positions and let me know the moment it touches down. I want you to personally monitor remote access to the system. We need them to be able to get past the firewalls, but not too easily. Make them work for it."

"I'll start the five-minute countdown at the first sign of cyber intrusion," Camo Mask said and hustled back in the direction from which he'd appeared.

Maddox turned to face her, again with that horrible smile on his face.

"You heard him, Dr. Clarke. You're on the clock. You have less than seven minutes to figure out the location in Giza that corresponds with Aldebaran, or you're going to bleed to death in that very chair."

ROCHE

Roche's stomach lurched as the helicopter rapidly descended. It barely pulled up in time to settle gracefully onto the tarmac between the derelict buildings concealing the Hangar. He was still trying to don his Kevlar vest when the leader of the special ops team threw open the sliding door and hopped out onto the cracked concrete.

"I'm coming with you," Kelly said.

"The hell you are." Roche exchanged his headset for a tactical helmet, unbuckled his harness, and headed for the open door. He had to raise his voice so she could hear him over the rotors. "You need to stay on this chopper. It'll take you to central command for debriefing. We need someone with knowledge of the inner workings of the Hangar on the outside."

"I'm not letting you go in there alone!" she shouted.

"These guys are special ops. I couldn't be safer."

He could tell how badly she wanted to argue with him, but he leaned in and kissed her before she could. The simple truth of the matter was that one of them needed to go with the team to bypass the retinal scanner and voice recognition system so they could access the elevator, and Roche was infinitely more qualified to assume the risk than she was.

"They don't need you down there," she said. "I need you up here. With me."

"I need to know you're safe."

"But you just said—"

He kissed her again and took a quick step toward the door. She caught him by the hand and looked him dead in the eyes.

"When this is over, we're out of here," she said. "Just the two of us. We're leaving this place and starting over from scratch. I want things to be like they were in England. Let these people save themselves for a change."

He smiled and squeezed her hand.

"There's nothing in the world I want more."

While he meant every word, he could tell by the tears in her eyes that she didn't believe him, and it broke his heart.

Roche released Kelly's hand, climbed out, and pulled the door closed. He didn't look back for fear of losing his resolve. These men were going to need his help to circumvent the Hangar's physical defenses while the cyber team attempted to regain control of the system. Both teams needed to be perfectly synchronized or the elevator's incineration system would render them ashes before they reached the first sublevel.

The men ran low along the front of the Hangar and disappeared through the lone ingress. By the time Roche caught up with them, they were nearly to the end of the maze of decrepit crates and rusted airplane parts. They crouched near the final approach to the elevator, where they'd be visible on any number of closed-circuit cam-

eras. Command had been able to override external surveillance and loop the live feed preceding the helicopter's
arrival. Unfortunately, they'd only had time to acquire
five minutes of footage and were struggling to access the
partitioned internal security system.

"Walk me through it," the team leader whispered through
the speakers in their tactical helmets.

"The elevator's armed with multiple countermeasures,"
Roche said. "The retina and voice scanners are fairly
standard, but once we're inside, we have to contend with
aerial dispersion systems armed with a biological inca-
pacitant capable of putting you down for the count and a
chemical accelerant that burns at nearly five thousand degrees Kelvin."

*"Leave those to us. You just be prepared to do exactly
what I say, when I say it. Without hesitation."*

Roche nodded. He would have felt a whole lot more
comfortable if he were carrying an M4A1 rifle like the
others, but he was content to let someone else take the
lead for once.

The rotors thupped outside as the Black Hawk prepared to lift off. The sooner Kelly was safely in the air,
the better he'd feel.

"We're in the system," Command said. *"Prepare to
move on my mark."*

Roche racked his brain in an effort to anticipate what
Maddox would do. He knew even more than Roche did
about the technical capabilities of the base and had undoubtedly set a trap for anyone attempting to breach its
security. Whether or not he knew they were already here
was irrelevant; he knew they were coming and would be
ready and waiting.

"Now," Command said.

The men sprinted out into the open, toward the elevator.

A thunderous explosion nearly knocked them off their feet.

Roche turned and saw a blinding light passing through the maze of crates. Flames raced up the front wall from the doorway and spread across the ceiling. Thick black smoke roiled into the building.

"No . . ." he whispered and sprinted toward the conflagration. "Kelly!"

TESS

Tess watched Maddox from the corner of her eye as she manipulated the digital overlay of Taurus. While he seemed distracted by whatever was happening aboveground that had caused the entire bunker to shudder, he never diverted his attention from her for anywhere near long enough for her to resize the image. As it was, he undoubtedly knew just as well as she did that Aldebaran aligned with a swatch of open desert riddled with barchan dunes that made it look like the surface of the moon from the satellite.

A pair of men in matching featureless black tactical masks wheeled a cart carrying a laptop and various wires and electrical components into the elevator. A pneumatic ratchet screamed as they bolted it to the floor.

"Time's up, Dr. Clarke," Maddox said.

She could tell by the tone of his voice that he'd seen through her ruse. She placed the overlay of Taurus in its proper place and looked away from him.

"Aldebaran is meaningless, isn't it?" he said. "You used it to send a coded message to Roche. That's how he figured things out so quickly."

Tess stared blankly at the screen in front of her as though in the hope that a matching structure might miraculously rise from the sand.

"Rigel's our destination after all," he said. "Not that it makes much difference anyway. Our team is already en route from Turkey and should be on the ground within the hour. Even if Dr. Evans's team somehow managed to survive, there's no way they'll be able to get there before it's too late."

"Why are you doing this?" she asked, her voice little more than a whisper. The adrenaline had faded, leaving her physically depleted and mentally resigned to the inevitability of her fate. "You were one of us."

"But I'm not," Maddox said and looked her right in the eyes. "I'm something vastly superior."

Tess searched his startlingly blue eyes for any sign of humanity but found none. He pulled her chair back from the desk and hauled her to her feet.

"You gambled and lost," he said. "There's no shame in that. I would have killed you in the stairwell if you hadn't, so you succeeded in buying yourself a few extra minutes of life. I should probably even thank you for leading the team outside into our ambush. I guess if time is all you want, I can reward you with a little bit more."

He shoved her ahead of him. Out of the office, across the corridor, and into the elevator. His men had removed the panel and hardwired the laptop to the inner workings. Its screen displayed systems and functions she didn't immediately recognize, but the red bars presumably indicated they'd been disabled.

"Any moment now," Maddox said.

39
JADE

The roar of the propellers was so loud she could barely hear the scream of wind shear. Jade would have felt a lot more comfortable if she could tell where the armed men were, or even if she could stretch out her legs. She'd removed the battery from her cell phone with the intention of drying out the two pieces. All she needed was a single phone call or, failing that, just enough charge that her GPS beacon would pop up on the screens back at the Hangar, where, hopefully, Roche and Maddox were in a panic trying to find them, but so far it had been a complete waste of time. At least it gave her something to think about other than the fact that they were undoubtedly hurtling toward certain death, whether by the gun of whoever discovered them hiding inside the cargo hold of this truck or by the catastrophic end the being that had once been Hollis Richards had told her to stop.

The notion of the apocalypse seemed absurd to her; however, no less so than the idea that the giant cloaked figure wearing the feathered serpent mask was somehow the mummified corpse they'd found at the center of the maze beneath Teotihuacan. She was a trained medical professional, an academic steeped in logic, and yet she could no more deny the physical similarities than she could the fact that the organisms that had caused Richards to mutate into Subject A had survived inside his lifeless brain to infect the MRI technologist who'd committed hara-kiri on the jagged shards of the vessel that had once contained it. She understood on a primal level, at the insistence of millions of years of evolutionary instincts, that if she was going to survive the coming cataclysm, she was going to have to embrace the irrationality of the situation. Or perhaps simply find a way to rationalize events that seemed to have no basis in the world as she understood it.

She knew nothing about celestial phenomena. While there was evidence to support the full moon having a labor-inducing effect on pregnant women, she still considered it largely pseudoscientific. Obviously, its proximity affected the tides, but that was a consequence of gravitational forces that could be charted with complete accuracy, not some magical alignment that heralded the end of humanity, and yet here she was hiding inside a plane filled with people who'd already tried to kill her on more than one occasion, heading on what she believed to be a southwesterly bearing, toward an unknown destination she figured had to be somewhere in Northern Africa. Considering the last time she was in Nigeria she'd come face-to-face with the drone that had begged her to release Subject Z before wading to its death in a river filled with crocodiles, she was hoping to land just about anywhere else.

"We're starting to descend," Evans whispered directly into her ear.

Jade was simultaneously grateful for his arms around

her and angry at herself for feeling that way. And while there had been plenty of men in her life, she'd never allowed herself to be in a position of being dependent upon one, especially one like Evans, who stimulated all sorts of feelings inside her, from exasperation to . . . whatever the hell this was.

She leaned her head back into the nook of his neck and raised her lips to his ear.

"If we're right about which direction we're traveling, we ought to be somewhere over the Mediterranean."

His cheek grazed hers as he turned to align his mouth with her ear. She felt the warmth of his breath when he spoke.

"We'll need to be on the ground soon if they intend to reach their destination before the lunar eclipse. For my money, that puts us landing somewhere in Egypt, likely either within range of Memphis or Giza, both of which are near El-Amarna, where I first discovered the remains of a creature like Zeta."

"You think the two are related?"

"God, I hope not, but I'm struggling to figure out their endgame. I mean, what's down there that could possibly bring about the end of the world, even theoretically, within what little time is left?"

"We have to assume they have the virus and intend to release it, presumably at some symbolic location."

"There are definitely more strategic locations to serve as the epicenter of a pandemic, though."

He was right. If Enigma wanted to do serious damage with the virus, this plane would be headed in just about any other direction. Into the heart of Europe to the northwest or China to the east, population centers through which the virus would spread like wildfire. It would have been a quick jaunt from Turkey to Dubai International Airport, the third-busiest transportation hub in the world, from which the virus could have reached every point around the globe within a matter of hours. No, these people had gone to great lengths to acquire the virus and confirm its efficacy. They had to have a different plan for it, although she simply couldn't see it.

"It must have something to do with the pyramids," Anya said. "From the one we found in Antarctica to the others in Teotihuacan, everything seems to revolve around them. It makes sense we'd be heading toward the most famous pyramids in the world, don't you think?"

Jade had to admit that her theory made perfect sense.

"But what could they possibly hope to accomplish?" she asked.

"The pyramid in Antarctica was responsible for the physical transformation of Zeta," Evans said.

"You think one of the others could serve the same function?"

"I don't know, but the thought of turning that giant with the feathered serpent mask into one of those creatures scares the hell out of me."

"Even if that was their goal, what does it have to do with the virus?" Jade asked.

The entire plane shuddered. Turbulence. They were definitely descending.

She heard voices. Indistinct at first, but coming closer.

They scooted as far back as they could into the corner, where they'd managed to shove aside the boxes to create just enough room to fully conceal one of them, and partially hide the other two, but if anyone opened the back flaps and took more than a passing glance . . .

The door of one of the trucks ahead of theirs opened

with a squeal. Jade closed her eyes and pressed herself deeper into Evans's embrace.

". . . drei Kilometer nordwestlich von Khufu," a man said. His voice was distant, barely audible over the cacophony of noise inside the plane. *"Du wirst die Führung übernehmen—"*

The words were silenced by the *thunk* of the closing door.

She'd learned just enough German to muddle her way through a few rudimentary conversations, but only recognized a few of the words.

"We're going three kilometers northwest of something," she whispered.

"Khufu," Evans said. "It's the largest of the Great Pyramids."

"So what's out there?"

"Nothing but desert, as far as I know. It's been at least five years since I was in Giza, though."

"Are you certain that's our destination?"

"Assuming they're referring to the pyramid," Evans said. "It was built to serve as Khufu's tomb, but archeologists have yet to find his body. The only thing they found in the burial chamber was a broken stone sarcophagus."

"Like the one in Mexico?" Jade asked.

"And the one in Antarctica. Only on a much grander scale."

"You don't think another of these beings—?" Jade started to ask, but she fell silent when she heard another voice. Female. Presumably the blond woman in the golden mask, but she was too far away to decipher her words.

A third voice. Baritone. So deep she could feel its vibrations in her chest, like the rumble of thunder.

"Ana Harrani Sa Alaktasa La Tarat." Jade froze. Goosebumps rippled up the backs of her arms. There was something about the voice, about the words . . . During her tenure at the United Nations' International Criminal Court, she'd been exposed to just about every language spoken throughout the civilized world, and yet she'd never heard anything like this one.

She knew exactly who—or rather what—was speaking. She caught Evans's stare, clutched his arm even tighter, and prayed it didn't come any closer.

The truck in front of theirs started with a grumble and a blast of exhaust. They must have been running way behind schedule, if readying the vehicles to roll while they were still in the air was any indication. It made a series of knocking sounds and threatened to stall, but the driver revved the engine several times and let it idle. She wasn't sure if she should be grateful she couldn't hear the voices anymore or terrified that she no longer knew where their enemies were.

She tried not to think about the Great Pyramid or the being that had been entombed inside, one for whom nothing shy of the greatest architectural marvel ever built would suffice, a structure vastly superior to the Temple of the Feathered Serpent, where they'd found the body of the man bearing its likeness, and the Antarctic Pyramid, from which Subject Z had liberated the remains of UNSUB X. Giza was the precise center of the Earth's landmass, the point where all geomagnetic ley lines converged, and ground zero for a potential global pandemic.

It was from these sands that humanity first arose, and to them that it would return.

Whether or not these masked people were delusional

was irrelevant. They genuinely believed they'd found the final resting place of another of these giants, possibly even their supreme god, a deity whose body had been stolen from its stone coffin and hidden elsewhere, a being whose resurrection heralded the end of the world.

They needed to find the body first, and they needed to destroy it.

She just hoped Enigma didn't release the virus first.

40
ROCHE

The Hangar

"**S**tay on mission!" the team leader shouted.

Roche didn't even break stride. He knew exactly what had happened before he emerged from the Hangar and saw the wreckage of the Black Hawk. Smoke billowed from the shattered windows of the cockpit, through which he could see what was left of the bodies of the pilots slumped forward in their seats, their carcasses actively burning. A ragged hole where the side door had been issued gouts of black smoke and flames that reached up over the roof and engulfed the warped rotors.

"Kelly!" he shouted.

"We lost Roche," a voice said through his headset. *"We're going to need a way around that retinal scanner."*

Roche shielded his face and fought through the intense heat toward the chopper. He could barely get close enough to see the tangled metal that had once been seats through the smoke.

There was no way she could have survived.

"Kelly!"

He fell to his knees and bellowed up into the sky. Tears

blurred his vision and dampened his cheeks. It was his fault she'd been on the chopper. She'd wanted to come with him, but he'd insisted she remain onboard.

And now she was gone.

He struggled back to his feet and turned toward the Hangar.

Maddox.

He was responsible for all of this. He'd lied to him, betrayed him, and taken from him the only thing in the world that mattered. He had to pay for what he'd done. Had to suffer. And even if it cost Roche his life, he intended to make sure that Maddox never left this base.

"We're going to kill the power," Command said. *"If we knock out the internal power supply at the same time we take down the grid, you'll have three seconds to get through that door and into the shaft. The car is on the second sublevel, so you'll be able to slide down the cables and access the first sublevel."*

Roche struggled to piece together what had happened. He hadn't heard the scream of a missile or gunfire of any kind. The Air Force would have intercepted any rocket fire or incoming fighter jets long before they were within range of the base, which meant the explosive device had to have been inside the helicopter itself. Had it been on board when they left for USAMRIID, then surely whoever set it would have taken down the chopper with the entire special ops team inside, unless . . .

"Charges placed," one of the men said. *"We're all set to demo the false wall on your go ahead."*

". . . one of them is in on it," Roche said, finishing his thought aloud.

"They know we're here," Team Leader said. *"It's now or never!"*

"Our team's been compromised!" Roche shouted as he ran back into the building. "Don't give the order!"

"We're detecting a localized anomaly," Command said. *"Someone's attempting to override the controls to the elevator."*

"Kill the power!" Team Leader shouted.

"Blow the door! Now!"

An explosion ripped through the interior, filling the building with smoke.

The power died with a thud Roche felt through the ground beneath his feet.

He was too late.

"No!" he shouted, a heartbeat before he heard the crackle of gunfire.

TESS

The overhead lights snapped off and the emergency lights flooded the corridor with a crimson glare.

"And now the backup systems," Maddox said.

The hallway suddenly darkened, abandoning them to the faint glow from the laptop.

"Disabling the safety brakes," the man in the camouflage mask said. "Three seconds," Maddox said. He gripped the railing with both hands and turned to Tess. "You might want to hang on to something."

The floor dropped out from underneath them and the elevator plummeted down the shaft.

Tess screamed and caught Maddox's sleeve with one hand and the railing with the other. Her feet left the floor and she rose into midair.

"Two," Maddox said.

The screen of the laptop displayed their depth in feet

as they passed the second sublevel and accelerated even deeper. She regained her balance and managed to at least get her feet back underneath her. Maddox stared at the monitor, transfixed.

"One."

Every muscle in Tess's body tensed in anticipation of impact. She tried not to think about how fast they were going, or what would happen when they slammed into the bottom of the shaft.

"Electromagnetic lock disabled," Camo Mask said.

"Now," Maddox said.

Camo Mask hit a button and the red bars changed to green. The elevator's brakes clamped down in the rails with a deafening shriek.

The ground lurched underneath her before she was fully ready. Her legs crumpled and she barely turned her head in time to absorb the collision with her shoulder.

Thoom!

The entire elevator shook. The side walls buckled inward.

Hydraulics whined in time with the repeated thumping against the walls, as though something was attempting to crush the car from the outside.

The light snapped back on. The cables jerked in an effort to take up the slack.

Maddox stepped up onto the cart and punched open the hatch in the ceiling, which swung open and clattered against the metal directly overhead. He climbed out and vanished from sight.

"Out you go," one of the remaining men said and boosted her up onto the cart, beside the laptop.

Tess caught a glimpse of the shaft extending upward beyond the range of sight before Maddox leaned down through the hole and offered his hands. She stared at him for several seconds before reaching up. He clasped her wrists and dragged her through the hole, onto the top of the elevator, where two enormous black duffel bags were strapped to the framework.

The entire car shook again and she heard the crunch of buckling metal. She cried out and grabbed for the nearest cable.

"Relax," Maddox said. He guided her to the edge of the roof and pointed down toward where a massive steel contraption was embedded in the side of the car. The hydraulic pistons shook with each attempted compression. "What you see here is half of what essentially amounts to a cross between the door of a bank vault and a car crusher. The two halves are designed to clamp together with a hundred tons of force, completing an electromagnetic seal strong enough to literally withstand a nuclear detonation. Of course, we just needed three seconds without power to jam the elevator right in its mouth."

The pneumatic ratchet whined as the other men bolted a trio of winches to the frame. They were already wearing harnesses identical to the one Maddox removed from his bag. He stepped through the leg holes and looped the straps up over his shoulders.

"It would have been a million times easier with Barnett's retinal scan and voice imprint, but considering he's still chasing his white whale down in Mexico, we had to improvise," he said. "Fortunately, whoever designed this elevator had the foresight to install a Faraday cage around it to block electromagnetic signals so no one could remotely override its controls and disarm its defenses. Had they not turned it into an armored vehicle, it might not have been able to withstand the force of the hydraulics."

He fastened the harness across his hips and chest, un-raveled a few feet of metal cord from the winch, and latched himself to it.

Tess leaned out over the rear of the elevator and stared down into the fathomless darkness. She'd never sus-pected the shaft had a false bottom, let alone that there was something hidden beneath what she assumed to be the lowest sublevel. Of course, knowing how Barnett worked, she shouldn't have been surprised.

"What's down there?" she asked.

Maddox offered his hand.

"What do you say we find out?"

ROCHE

Roche sprinted back into the building. He could barely see a thing through all of the smoke. The flicker of flames beckoned from somewhere beyond the maze of junk. He slowed as he neared the terminus and approached more cautiously. The gunfire had stopped as suddenly as it started, which, unfortunately, only confirmed his suspi-cions.

He found the first man near the final turn, facedown on the ground with entry wounds to his shoulder, neck, and the base of his skull, below the rim of his helmet. Despite all of the blood and the exit wound that had destroyed his lower jaw, Roche recognized the team leader. The traitor had shot him in the back while he was attempting to es-cape.

The barrel of a rifle protruded from underneath the dead man. Roche knelt and tried to slide it out, but the strap caught on something. A gentle tug produced a clat-tering sound. He peered around the corner to make sure he hadn't attracted any unwanted attention. The body of another soldier lay maybe five feet away, his rifle resting on the ground near his feet. He'd never seen the point-blank shot to the temple coming.

Roche commandeered the weapon and crouched behind a stack of crates at the edge of the clearing surrounding the craterous ruin of the elevator, from which thick black smoke gushed.

It took every last ounce of his strength to focus on the situation at hand, and not the death of the woman he loved. He'd have the rest of his life to beat himself up over the role he'd played in her incineration, but he fully intended to make sure that those responsible paid for what they'd done first.

The saboteur had undoubtedly either taken up position outside the elevator to prevent anyone from getting inside or headed down the shaft to join the rest of his crew. Unless there was a way out of the Hangar that no one else knew about, neither option held the slightest chance of survival. This man knew he was going to die, which made him infinitely more dangerous.

Roche had to believe that reinforcements were already on their way, but he simply couldn't afford to wait. He crept out into the open, sweeping the barrel of the rifle through the smoke. Flames still licked at the scorched maw in the opposite wall, through which he could see little more than a roiling mass of cinders and soot. There was another body to his left, sprawled on the bare concrete in a wash of blood, facing away from him. He was halfway to the elevator when he saw another soldier off to his right. On his chest, a trail of smeared blood leading away from him, as though he had survived the initial attack only long enough to drag himself off to die.

But if there were four dead soldiers, then he must have been wrong about the betrayal. He couldn't have been, though. He'd been so certain. And the drone hadn't detected any thermal signatures inside the hangar.

He followed the trail of blood across the ground, past the elevator, toward where the third man—

"Drop your weapon," a voice said from directly behind him.

—had been lying only a few seconds prior.

The smoldering barrel of a rifle pressed against the base of his skull. If he ducked and turned around in one quick motion, he just might be fast enough to—

Crack.

A blow to the back of his head and Roche collapsed to his knees. Fell forward onto his hands. The world tilted underneath him. He felt the warmth of blood on his neck, soaking into his collar. The pain of a laceration behind his left ear, followed by the pressure of the hot barrel once more.

"It's too bad you won't live long enough to see the end of your species," the man said.

The rattle of automatic gunfire.

Roche ducked and covered his head. Bullets ricocheted from the ground all around him. Blood spattered his hand and cheek.

The man fell on him from behind, driving him to the ground.

Roche rolled out from underneath the man, whose blood was still hot on his face, and looked up—

Kelly stood in the swirling smoke, the rifle he'd bypassed seated against her shoulder. She had dark smudges on her cheeks and the knees of her jeans were torn, but otherwise she looked none the worse for wear.

"I said I was coming with you," she said.

Roche pushed himself up from the ground, walked unsteadily toward her, and wrapped his arms around her.

"I thought," he started. "I thought you . . ."

"You can't get rid of me that easily."

"But how . . . ?"

"I got out of the helicopter right before it took off. If you'd looked back while you were running into the building, you would have seen me trying to catch up with you. I wasn't even halfway there when the bomb went off right above my head and the force of the explosion threw me across the tarmac."

"Kelly, I—"

"Shh." She placed her hand on the back of his neck and drew him down to her. This time, she kissed him. When she finally withdrew, there was a smile on her face, at least until she realized her hand was covered with blood. "We need to get you to a hospital."

"There's no time." He took her by the hand and pulled her toward the elevator. He wasn't about to let her out of his sight again, not for anything in the world. "We can't let them have whatever they think is down there."

They stood at the edge of the shaft and looked down into the impenetrable darkness and smoke. "How well can you climb?" he asked.

BOOK III

Darkness of slumber and death, forever sinking and sinking.
—HENRY WADSWORTH LONGFELLOW

41
BARNETT

La Venta

Spiderwebs cast bizarre shadows ahead of Barnett into the darkness. They crackled as he pushed through them, falling aside against walls that at first appeared spattered with blood, but upon closer inspection revealed that the mortared stones had once been concealed behind red plaster, which had crumbled to dust upon the bare earth. Chunks of stone had broken loose from the low ceiling and now formed a rugged path deeper into the structure.

A narrow opening led into the adjacent structure, which was roughly the same size, although that was the only thing the two had in common. A section of the roof had collapsed, leaving a massive mound in the center and barely enough space to crawl around it. The walls featured elaborate stone reliefs that appeared to have been carved from single granite slabs. The deities depicted were in the traditional, blocky Mesoamerican style and featured faces that were half-human and half-animal. A man with large square earrings and his tongue sticking out from below a nose like the beak of an eagle, which meshed with the eyes and feathered headdress. Another with only his nose and mouth visible inside of what appeared to be the open mouth of a dragon, from the sides of which feathers flared. There was a woman with a narrow face and a rack of antlers, a man with the head of a jaguar, and another woman with some sort of skeletal construct that appeared almost canine. Barnett glanced at Dr. Clarke's hybrid map one last time and committed it to memory. While his tablet was nowhere near finished uploading the satellite data and creating its digital elevation model, he didn't have anything resembling a signal down here to access further updates. At least what he had showed a general pattern of buildings aligned to both sides of a central plaza, with the pyramid lording over them to the north.

"You remember what they used to guard the other sites, right?" Morgan whispered.

Barnett didn't need the reminder. He wouldn't soon forget the feathered serpents he and his team had encountered in Antarctica and the others had found within the maze mere miles from where they stood now.

There were three rectangular doorways, only one of which remained passable, if only barely. They climbed over the rubble and entered a plaza framed by ornate pillars. The roof had fallen in sections, and the dirt the Olmec had used to bury the city had formed giant dunes, one of which partially concealed the great stone megalith set right in the very center. Like the heads on the surface, this one was easily nine feet tall, only there was no mistaking the species it was designed to represent. Its facial architecture was deformed, its eyes too large, its mouth and nose too small, and its cranium decidedly conical in shape.

It looked just like Subject Z.

He suddenly realized that this temple had been built to venerate the creature.

It was coming home.

And with the genetic memory passed down through the hive mind of the alien organisms, it probably already knew every inch of this place. Whatever advantage they might have held was now lost. There was something here that it wanted, though, and their only hope was to find it first. And if, as he suspected, what they were looking for was a canister containing a deadly virus, the only thing capable of stopping it, he'd be damned if he wouldn't seal this place with all of them inside and release it himself.

The ground was paved with rectangular stones as green as emeralds, only dulled by the accumulation of dust and dirt. They formed elaborate patterns and designs, which led them to the end of the colonnade and out from beneath the roof. A narrow corridor remained between the fallen pillars, just large enough to crawl through. Roots dangled from the earthen ceiling. This wasn't a natural space, he knew. Something had invested considerable effort into digging it after the entire city was buried, something that had been sealed in here while it was still alive.

Morgan obviously recognized the same thing. He turned around and scooted backward into the opening, swiveling both his light and his rifle behind him to make sure that nothing was able to sneak up on them.

The tunnel grew steeper, revealing just the hint of the stone blocks that formed a short staircase, at the top of which was a dark orifice positively riddled with spider webs. The ground leveled off in front of what Barnett now recognized as a man-made doorway. The stones that had once sealed it had toppled forward to form a mound of granite and crumbled mortar the consistency of gravel. The stone lining the threshold was the same green serpentine as the walkway. The packed dirt beside it had fallen away to reveal the carvings of skulls, one on top of the other, all of which showed the same facial mutations and cranial deformities as the megalith, only these were significantly more detailed. Almost lifelike. It wasn't until he touched one that he understood that they were actual skulls set into the stone, discolored by the soil and hardened to the density of rocks by the centuries.

"We're heading in the wrong direction to reach the pyramid," Barnett whispered.

"Then where do you think we're going?" Morgan asked.

Barnett tore straight down through the web and shined his light into the narrow corridor.

"Only one way to find out," he said and ducked inside.

The passage wasn't tall enough for him to stand fully upright, so he walked in a crouch, tracing the walls and floor with the beam of his flashlight. The ground was composed of utilitarian granite slabs. They were scored with deep gouges, and a shallow trench had been worn into them from centuries of use. The walls were painted in arches and random patterns with some sort of ocher that turned to powder when he touched it. Blood. The discolorations were from ancient arterial spatters.

The Olmec had barricaded this tunnel before burying their entire civilization. It didn't take a genius to figure out why.

He'd been so focused on the walls that he nearly stepped right over a ledge in the middle of the walkway. There was a square hole that spanned the width of the passage. He shined his light down at least thirty feet into what almost looked like a well, only the area at the bottom was larger than the shaft. The water was black and reflected his beam, which made it impossible to estimate its depth, or how many skeletons were concealed beneath it. The ends of long bones and ribs protruded from below the surface, which only added to the chill radiating from the depths. There were humans and animals alike, with the antlers of deer and the skulls of crocodiles jumbled with the claws and horns of beasts he didn't immediately recognize. The mortar and stones lining the chute were positively riddled with scratch marks.

Barnett took a few steps backward so he could get a running start and jumped across the pit. The tunnel ahead of him continued far beyond the reach of his light.

"Jesus," Morgan whispered, then followed him across the gap.

Barnett tightened his grip on his rifle. It had taken a flamethrower to awaken the feathered serpents from where they were frozen in solid ice beneath the South Pole and an influx of water to revive them inside the tomb in Teotihuacan. In both cases, they'd been coiled inside the carcasses of the animals that had been trapped with them, presumably to serve as a source of food. They needed to steer clear of any remotely intact remains and pray the creatures hadn't somehow entered a state of cryobiosis out in the open.

By the time they neared the end of the corridor, the temperature had dropped a good twenty degrees. Their footsteps echoed from the vast space ahead of them. Barnett slowed and scrutinized the end of the tunnel, where the walls abruptly gave way to darkness. Only the floor continued onward and formed a ledge barely wide enough to accommodate his feet. The roof overhead was flat and featureless, supported by columns that emerged from the flooded darkness below. A slope of rubble that had once been a staircase extended all the way down to the bottom, at the center of which was a square two-story building made of the green stones. Even from this height, he could tell they'd been carved with elaborate designs, if not what they were.

It was a giant tomb.

"The necropolis," Barnett whispered.

He scooted along the wall, turned the sharp corner, and headed for what was left of the stairs. Rocks clattered down into the water as he carefully descended, pausing every few vertical feet to inspect his surroundings along the sightline of his rifle. There was no sign that they weren't alone, let alone that anyone had been here in thousands of years, but he'd learned the hard way not to take anything for granted.

When he reached the bottom, he waited for Morgan to catch up with him before wading out into the frigid water. The stones underfoot were slick with sludge that produced a wretched stench with every step. A greenish film had formed upon the stagnant water, which swirled and eddied around their waists as they approached the structure. The lower tier was framed on all four sides by columns, each of which had been carved to resemble an anthropomorphic figure wearing a loincloth and holding its belly. There was nothing remotely human about their heads, which were entirely animalian and projected from the flat roof, above which they could see the second tier, which featured an ornate cornice, but not a single exterior entrance.

They found a narrow orifice, nearly concealed by the shadows of the columns, which led into a small enclosure. There was a single pillar, right in the middle, striped with rust. The reliefs carved into the stone walls surrounding them depicted the gods they'd encountered upon entering the underground city and told stories they had neither the time nor the patience to decipher. A single opening granted access to the inner sanctum, which was barely large enough to accommodate the staircase that led up one wall, across another, and finally to a square hole in the ceiling above the third.

Barnett ascended from the cold water onto the narrow steps, ducking a little more with each step until he was forced to crawl from the top stair into a short chimney of sorts, which turned out to be little more than a two-foot-tall frame around the orifice. He climbed up into a chamber that smelled like a tomb. In the center was a great stone cube with petrified wooden posts protruding from both sides. The mural on the front of it was nearly identical to the one that led them here in the first place. It showed a man holding a container and a feathered serpent wrapped around him, its reptilian head raised above his, its jaws open as though preparing to strike.

His stomach sank with the realization that it was more than a decoration.

It was a warning.

Barnett leaned back and shined his light straight up. Enormous, teardrop-shaped casings reminiscent of the egg sacs of praying mantises hung from the ceiling. There had to be at least twenty of them, all crammed together like a bunch of balloons. The desiccated appendages of men and animals protruded from the gaps between the fibrous strands. They were the same nests he'd encountered back in Antarctica, after the feathered serpents had overrun FOB Atlantis.

He knew exactly what was inside of them.

And what would happen if he inadvertently woke them up.

42
ANYA

Giza, Egypt

Anya had never been so terrified in her life. Not even being stalked through the Antarctic research station or being hunted by men and creatures alike inside the flooded maze in Teotihuacan could compare, largely because, as horrifying as both experiences had been, she'd always maintained some small amount of control, infinitesimal though it had been. There had always been choices—which way she could turn, where she could hide—none of which applied to her current predicament. She was trapped inside the cargo hold of a panel truck, surrounded by men who would kill her without a second thought, in the belly of the plane thousands of feet above what they believed to be Egypt. And somehow even worse was the fact that Evans and Jade had found comfort in each other's arms, while she'd never felt so alone.

A gust of wind buffeted the plane. Her entire world bucked up and down. She felt a sinking sensation in her stomach. They were definitely descending in altitude. She wanted nothing more than to be on the ground, where at least she had a remote chance of escaping, but she couldn't shake the feeling that the worst was yet to come.

She sensed movement all around her. Indistinct shadows passed across the canvas siding. A car door opened with a squeal. She heard voices, although not clearly enough to make out their words. More doors opening. One closed with a sound like a gunshot, and it was all she could do to keep from screaming. She glanced back at the others, but could barely see their silhouettes. Jade gave her shoulder a reassuring squeeze, but her trembling hand betrayed her. If even the normally unflappable forensic anthropologist was scared—

The truck's engine roared to life, ready to drive down the ramp the moment they touched down. Exhaust filtered through the gaps around the bed.

Anya felt the pressure change, the rumble of the landing gear lowering. She closed her eyes and prayed for them to survive whatever nightmare awaited them, but realized that it didn't matter. If they failed to prevent the release of the virus, then they were dead anyway. And not just them, but everyone they'd ever known—their families and friends—would suffer a violent and painful end. Everyone on the planet. It would be an extinction-level event, a cataclysm beyond anything the world had ever known. She'd devoted her life to studying the evolution of the human species—from its auspicious descent from the trees to its first tenuous steps on two legs to entire branches of the hominin tree that withered and died so that a single branch could survive—and its seemingly eternal quest to eradicate itself. There was no way on this planet she was going to let that happen on her watch.

The wheels bounced beneath them. Their momentum slowed so rapidly that she slid right up into Jade's lap and had to brace the crate beside her to keep it from falling onto her legs.

She clenched her hands into fists. Drew a deep, shuddering breath.

"You can do this," she whispered.

The plane touched down hard, the ground beneath them rugged and uneven, causing the truck to rock sideways on its creaking suspension. This wasn't like any runway she'd ever landed on; it must have been a smaller airstrip, if not a road like the one from which they'd taken off.

The din of the propellers diminished as the plane juddered to a halt.

Hydraulics whined and light flooded the dim interior as the ramp lowered. She saw the terror on her friends' faces and nearly lost what little resolve she'd been able to summon.

A loud beeping sound filled the air. She recognized what it meant even before the truck started backing up.

"Brace yourselves," Evans whispered and pressed his arms against the boxes stacked to either side of him.

Anya tried to do the same, but she wasn't fast enough. She slid toward the tailgate as the truck descended the ramp. Struck metal with her heels. Caught a glimpse of first the ramp, then a dirt road through the slim gap below the canvas. She smelled dust, tasted it in her mouth. Felt grit in her sinuses. The sudden influx of heat elicited goosebumps, which quickly faded as the temperature climbed by the second.

The truck leveled off. She saw a withered brown bramble growing from a rippled dune and, past it, a rock formation the color of chalk, and then they were moving once more, trailing a wake of dust that immediately found its way into the hold. She pulled her shirt up over her mouth and nose. Clenched her hand over them to muffle the sound of her coughing.

The beeping from the other trucks faded behind her as they accelerated. The grille of the vehicle behind them occasionally materialized from the dust. She could tell from the reddish glint on its hood that the sun was somewhere off to the left, suggesting they were traveling north. It was already setting, which meant that if they were headed for Giza like they suspected, it wouldn't be very long before they arrived.

"If we get the chance, we need to jump out before we reach our destination," Evans whispered.

"With the other trucks right behind us?" Jade said. "We have to be going at least fifty miles an hour."

"We can use the dust as cover and climb out the side."

"We'll be plainly visible to every one of the vehicles behind us."

"What do you propose then? We can't just wait for them to open the flaps. We don't have a single weapon between us, and even if we did, we're outnumbered at least three to one."

"They won't check back in here," Anya whispered. "They'll be too distracted by what's in front of them, which will open a short window for us to get out of here."

"That's one hell of an assumption," Evans said.

He was right, but she felt strangely confident. The crates surrounding them likely contained all of the artifacts they'd pillaged from the caverns beneath Göbekli Tepe. They only brought them because they wouldn't have another opportunity to return for them, and there was always a chance they could potentially prove useful. While the masked men always seemed to know more than they did, she had to believe that when it came right down to it, they had no better idea what they were walking into than Anya and her friends did.

"We just have to be ready to make our move when the time comes," she whispered.

She closed her eyes to keep the dust out of them, although it somehow found a way in regardless. It clung to her damp shirt, beneath which dribbles of sweat trickled down her flesh. Her tongue felt like it was coated with sandpaper, and her chest was heavy. It was no wonder people wore those scarves that covered everything but their eyes out here.

The truck bounded down. Bounced back up. Toppled the crates sideways. Onto them. Several broke open, disgorging packing materials and heavy stone artifacts. Something struck her head, careened from it.

She struggled out from underneath it just in time to see the road falling away behind them. The tires spun in the sand, sending it ricocheting from the wheel wells, before gaining traction and propelling them across the bumpy terrain.

Anya was momentarily surprised by the sensation of dampness on her forehead. At least until the pain kicked in. She smeared away the blood with the back of her hand. Glanced down to find a whole lot more of it than she'd expected.

Jade shoved aside a broken crate and rolled a headless stone idol from her lap. Her eyes widened when she saw the younger woman's face and she gestured for Anya to come closer.

The blood dripped from the tip of her nose, past her lips. She could taste it, warm and metallic, and did her best not to panic.

"The fibrous fascia prevents vasoconstriction of the superficial capillaries," Jade whispered. "Scalp lacerations bleed profusely, but tend to look considerably worse than they actually are."

Evans climbed over the fallen cargo and scurried to the back of the truck. Peered outside through the gap.

"This isn't a road," he whispered. "We're cutting straight through the desert."

Jade rummaged through the contents of the crates until she found a foam-lined box containing what appeared to be a handful of teeth. She tore out the lining and pressed it against the wound along Anya's hairline.

"Hold this," she said.

Anya did as she was instructed and shouldered up to Evans. The trucks behind them were nearly invisible through the dust. There was nothing but seamless sand to either side, marred only by sporadic dunes crowned with tufts of dead grasses.

"We have to be getting close," he said. "Look how long the shadow of the truck is getting. They're running out of time."

"Then we should probably hide . . ."

Her words trailed off as the truck decelerated, allowing the dust to catch up and wash over them. The driver killed the engine, which continued to tick well after he'd opened the door and climbed out into the desert. The other trucks converged upon them.

"Get ready," Evans whispered.

Anya's heartbeat accelerated. Her mouth became even drier.

They would only get one shot at this, so they'd better make it count.

43

TESS

The Hangar

Tess clung for dear life to Maddox's harness. A part of her wished their combined weight would be more than it could bear and they'd both end up plummeting into the abyss, but the better part of her desperately wanted to live. She had to believe that if he wanted her dead, he would have killed her the moment he saw through her deception, and yet she couldn't figure out any logical reason for him to have spared her even this long. Maybe there was a small amount of humanity left in him after all, one she could potentially exploit to get herself out of this alive.

"You don't have to do this," she whispered. "It's not too late to turn back."

"You don't have the slightest idea what's down there, do you?" Maddox said.

"Why don't you tell me, then?"

His smile when he responded was full of teeth.

"You'll find out soon enough."

The winch lowered them at a staggeringly slow pace, like spiders descending from their webs. The other two men were maybe five feet below them, the under-barrel beams mounted to their rifles plumbing the depths. What little light reached around the elevator car wedged in the electromagnetic lock was a faint aura above them.

"Passing fifty feet," one of the men said from below her.

Stained concrete materialized at the farthest reaches of his beam. The rails running straight down the walls terminated beside massive coiled springs and a collection of mechanical components, one of which appeared to have a pressure-sensitive plate. She didn't have any desire to find out what it might be armed with.

Stainless-steel doors appeared in the wall below her feet. The two masked men leveraged them open and held them in place while Maddox floated to the ground between them. He released Tess, who stumbled forward into the dark sublevel and landed on all fours. The floor was made of polished concrete, the walls stainless steel that reflected their lights.

Maddox strode past her through the short corridor, which terminated at another stainless-steel door without any visible means of opening it. What secrets had Barnett hidden down here, and why the hell hadn't he told any of them about it?

It automatically opened when Maddox was within range. The pass-through chamber inside was barely large enough for all four of them. The moment the outer door whooshed shut behind them, the inner door opened with a popping sound and a hiss of pressurized air. Banks of overhead lights bloomed ahead of them as though leading the way. *Thoom-thoom-thoom.*

Tess's jaw dropped as she walked slowly into the vast space. It was like a museum unto itself, with each of the displays sealed within Plexiglas cases adorned with computer screens that monitored temperature, pressure, and humidity. Each one had its own climate-control unit, and no two of the readouts were the same. She assumed each containment unit had been calibrated to precisely match the environment where the artifacts, displayed beneath low-wavelength archival lights that made them appear blue, had been collected.

She walked by a massive stone upon which a petroglyph had been sculpted in the style of ancient Egypt, only the pharaoh's face resembled Subject Z's. Another was in the Mayan style and showed the same face wearing a headdress adorned with a skull. She passed several others to either side, all ancient, and all demonstrating the face of the creature in the various styles of many primitive cultures on stones and murals and sculptures, from Mesopotamia to Mesoamerica to the Pacific islands and everywhere in between.

On the other side of the main aisle were petroglyphs of the bearded man she had seen so many times recently, holding a pinecone and a canister, wearing the cloak of a fish or the heads of various animals. Only it wasn't a single figure, but many, male and female alike. With human bodies and the heads of animals, in unmistakable styles ranging from the Assyrians to the Egyptians, the Olmec to the Anasazi, and civilizations she couldn't even identify. And seemingly lost among them were scattered depictions of the same figures, only with reptilian faces, on statues and carvings, idols and murals, beings whose likeness she'd never seen before.

The central aisle branched to both sides. To the left were more sculptures and petroglyphs featuring figures wearing space suits, only from time frames long before men even dreamed of the wheel, let alone travel beyond the atmosphere. To the right were cases upon cases of metallic mechanisms, green with oxidation and red with rust. Complicated gears and dials whose functions eluded her, ranging in size from the palm of her hand to a polished number that resembled a cross between a rocket and a gigantic oxygen tank.

The corridor straight ahead was lined with physical remains. One side housed countless elongated skulls of the kind that had initially led Unit 51 to Antarctica, the kind with distorted facial architecture, enlarged orbital sockets and narrow chins, just like Subject Z. All of them the color of the dirt from which they were exhumed, some still bearing grave wax from their liquefied flesh. And on the other side were skulls considerably larger and elongated not in the posterior direction, but rather in the vertical. Nearly all were missing their front teeth. A few retained their rear molars, but only one skull retained a single canine, which was long and hooked, like the fang of a snake.

She finally made sense of the order. To the left were artifacts related to the creatures colloquially termed Grays, and to the right were beings like the ones they'd found entombed beneath Teotihuacan and Mosul, giants revered as gods by societies ranging from the Fertile Crescent to northern Africa and even as far away as South America, beings to whom countless temples and pyramids had been devoted, gods depicted wearing the heads of animals to conceal their true reptilian visages.

"We have to be getting close," Camo Mask said.

The hall of skeletal remains opened upon a space the size of a four-car garage, which featured displays of an entirely different order. The skulls had offered a degree of both physical and temporal separation, a means of distancing herself from the fact that they'd once been living, breathing organisms, but in the flesh? That was something else entirely.

"They're magnificent," Maddox said.

He ran his fingers along the Plexiglas as he passed creatures like Subject Z in various stages of mummification. They'd shriveled in upon themselves and were now little more than desiccated skin adhering to the bony framework, skin that retained its grayish cast even beyond the grave. The touchscreen monitors affixed to their cases displayed everything from detail and magnification images to 3-D reconstructions digitized from CT scans.

"Over here," Camo Mask said.

Maddox nudged Tess toward his subordinate, who stood facing a case the size of her bedroom back home at her parents' house, which had been preserved in much the same way, a snapshot of a time long gone, but one she would have recognized anywhere. It was the tomb from Mosul, from the petroglyphs on the walls to the plinth in the center, on top of which was bound the giant with the tattoo on his chest and the eagle mask on his face.

She should have known Barnett would never have allowed it to be destroyed, but she couldn't fathom why he had risked bringing it here.

"Open it," Maddox said.

The two men raised their rifles and riddled the front of the cage with bullets.

Tess screamed and covered her ears.

The sound of gunfire was deafening in such close confines. Bullets ricocheted in every direction. The Plexiglas pitted and cracked, then shattered into a cascade of shards that washed across the ground and over their feet.

Maddox took her by the hand and led her into the display case. The stone walls were now broken and pocked with bullet holes, and beneath the scent of gunpowder were the smells of age and decomposition, the stench of the tomb they'd somehow managed to secretly bring back from Iraq.

"Look at him," Maddox whispered. He traced the contours of the body with his fingertips, only he couldn't seem to bring himself to actually touch it. "Is he not the most amazing specimen you've ever seen?"

This sublevel was easily the size of the ones above it, if not larger. If Tess could break away from her captors, she could potentially elude them through the maze of artifacts and find someplace to hide, but she needed to create a distraction. Since this body was what the men had obviously come for, she needed to be ready to seize her opportunity the moment it presented itself.

"Look upon him, Dr. Clark. When will you ever have another chance to be in the presence of a god?"

Maddox walked past where the man's wrist was bound to his ankle, past where his shoulder girdle was broken along the edge of the plinth, and to the head of the altar. He reached for the massive beak of the mask. Retracted his trembling hands. Clenched them to fists. Tried again. He took hold of the beak and gently removed the mask from the corpse's face, revealing features that were simultaneously human and not.

The other men entered the case and made their way around the plinth. Tess looked down the corridor toward the nearest branch. It was maybe twenty-five feet away. Four seconds at a dead sprint. Plenty of time for them to draw their weapons and put a bullet in her back.

Maddox gripped her by the back of the neck and thrust

her face down toward the dead man's, close enough that she could see his flattened nose and angular nostrils, his shrunken eye sockets, his broad mouth, and the psoriatic texture of his mummified skin.

"I said look upon the face of God!"

She glanced up from the face, beyond its outstretched body, and toward the hallway that would lead her to freedom. The moment he relaxed his grip, she was just going to have to take her chances—

Something sharp passed across her neck. She felt its coldness inside of her, felt the sting of its passage. Glanced down to see crimson fluid spattering the ancient body.

She jerked free of Maddox's grasp and managed to take a single step before the realization of what had just happened stopped her in her tracks.

This was why he hadn't killed her when he saw through her lie.

She clasped both hands around her throat. Felt the pulsating flow of blood, the severed muscles and tendons inside the wound.

Maddox caught her by the hair and dragged her back over the body.

Tess got one final look at the hallway before her chin fell to her chest. She watched her blood wash over the face of the creature, its flesh eagerly absorbing it like a sponge. Its eyes snapped open. She saw irises marbled with red and yellow and slit pupils that widened in response to the spluttering sound of blood flooding through the wound in her trachea and into her lungs.

And then she saw no more.

44
KELLY

The Hangar

Kelly tried not to think about how far down the bottom of the shaft was. She wrapped both arms and legs around the cable and held on for all she was worth. The metal braids of the cables bit painfully into her palms, but she didn't dare risk so much as adjusting her grip. She moved in maddeningly small increments, praying that the elevator didn't start to rise. As it was, the sudden jerking on the cable by some force far below her threatened to shake her off.

Roche reached the first sublevel, readjusted his grip, and grabbed a bracket on the wall. He used it as leverage to cross the gap from the cable to the narrow ledge beside the closed doors. The release mechanism was inside the emergency panel; a flip of the switch and he was able to use the bar mounted beside it to manually open them.

He scooted sideways until he was able to step into the hallway and turned around to face her.

"You can do this," he whispered.

He secured a grip beside the elevator door and extended his arm toward her. She slid another three feet down and he gave her ankle a reassuring squeeze. Two more and he was able to touch her hand.

Kelly reached for him. Felt herself slipping. She grabbed onto the cable once more, even tighter this time.

"I won't let you fall," he whispered. "I promise."

She squeezed her eyes shut. Summoned every last ounce of courage. Blew out a long breath. Reached for him once more. Her eyes met his. Focused on nothing else. He clasped his hand around her wrist, while she, in turn, gripped his.

"One big step is all you need. You've got this."

She nodded, swung her right leg out over the nothingness, and pushed off from the cable. Her toes grazed the edge and she started to fall. Roche pulled her with such force that they stumbled backward down the hallway. He lost his balance and dragged her down on top of him.

Their eyes lingered for several seconds before she finally climbed to her feet and unslung the rifle from her back. It was a similar model to the one she'd used in FOB Atlantis, so she was at least familiar with its basic operation. While she didn't have the skill to use it at long range, up close she could do some serious damage. She just hoped she didn't run out of ammo since she didn't have the slightest clue how to do anything more than disengage the safety, pull the charging handle, and squeeze the trigger.

They advanced, side by side, into the dimly lit hallway. The emergency lights cast an eerie red glow over everything. Roche signaled for her to stay where she was while he quickly confirmed that Barnett's anteroom and office were empty. They turned the other way and passed the office she shared with Tess. There was a broken chair and what looked like blood on the floor. The monitor behind Tess's desk displayed an aerial view readily recognizable as Giza, only the pyramids were off-center, near the bottom right, while the focus of the image was a dot labeled Rigel, the foot of Orion the Hunter, which fell squarely upon an amoeboid white shape she interpreted as a low-lying mesa surrounded by miles of open desert.

The other two monitors showed a map of Göbekli Tepe with the overlay of the constellation Cygnus and what appeared to be ancient ruins just south of the Gulf of Mexico, which was barely visible at the top of the screen. A constellation labeled Reticulum had been placed over the top of the overgrown site.

"She deciphered the locations from the crop circles," Kelly whispered.

"Can you access the GPS log to see if you can locate our field teams?"

"I've never tried, but assuming that function hasn't been disabled, I should be able to figure it out."

Roche stood sentry in the doorway while she accessed her terminal. It took her several minutes to find what she was looking for. Coordinates and times appeared on the screen beside encrypted identification tags. She transferred them to a different monitor with a mapping function, but there wasn't a single active beacon.

"Nothing," she said.

"Try running their last known locations."

Kelly clicked on each of the data sets individually.

"Two signals within the ruins in Mexico," she said. "Although they disappeared about forty-five minutes ago."

They had to belong to Barnett and his team, or at least what was left of it. Either they were no longer within broadcast range of the satellite, or their tracking beacons had been disabled.

"What about the others?" Roche asked.

The most recent coordinates corresponded with Göbekli Tepe, but the last logged time was within hours of their arrival. Nothing since. Something was definitely wrong. It wasn't like—

"Wait," she said. "I have a single point of geolocation on Jade's phone. It looks like . . . that can't be right."

Kelly transferred the data to the screen and a dot surrounded by pulsating, concentric rings appeared over the Mediterranean Sea.

"How did she get all the way out there?" Roche asked.

"It's just a blip, little more than a single piece of data, but if you extrapolate a line through the beacon and her last known location, it leads straight to—"

"Giza," he finished for her.

A buzzing sound arose from the elevator shaft, long and sustained.

"We need to keep moving," Roche said and started down the hallway.

Kelly hurried to catch up with him. The open elevator doors behind her made her nervous, especially with that constant grinding noise emanating from it. She turned around every few feet to make sure no one was able to sneak up on them.

They passed offices that didn't appear to have been disturbed in the slightest, save for one in which an engineer sat in his desk chair, his head leaned back, a starburst of blood and brain matter on the wall behind him. She had to stifle a whimper at the thought of what would likely have happened to Roche and her had Friden not called them to his lab.

She prayed that Tess was still alive, wherever she was now.

Roche cleared the stairwell and guided her down, around the bend, and into the second sublevel. The doors to the Arcade and the Teleportation Room remained open. A quick glance inside confirmed there was no one inside, although judging by the bullet holes and blood spatters on the drone consoles, the pilots hadn't so much as sensed the danger.

A shifting light source beckoned them down the hallway toward the command center. A shadow passed across the floor, stretching nearly out into the corridor. There was definitely someone inside.

Roche pantomimed for her to duck to the side and into the nearest doorway. He shouldered the opposite wall. Lowered to a crouch. Cleared the computer lab through the window before passing low across it. He pressed his back against the wall beside the doorway of the command center.

Kelly heard a voice in the distance. It utilized the same kind of cadence Roche employed when he was coordinating the footage on the monitors, only she couldn't quite make out the words. He waved her closer. Her heart thundered in her ears as she sprinted along the near wall and took up position on the opposite side of the doorway. He spoke in a voice so soft she had to read his lips to understand what he was saying.

"I'm going in. You stay here. Anyone gets past me? You shoot them. No hesitation. If anything happens to me—"

"It won't."

"Listen to me, Kelly. If anything does, I want you to hide, okay? Somewhere no one can find you."

Kelly had no intention of hiding, but she nodded for his benefit.

He took a sharp breath and went into the command center, low and fast.

A shout of recognition. The rattle of gunfire. Bullets pounded the wall of the interior corridor.

Before she even realized what she intended to do, Kelly was running into the room, the rifle bouncing unsteadily against her shoulder. She stepped out onto the bridge and took everything in at a glance.

A uniformed man was sprawled on his chest in front of her in an expanding puddle of his own blood. There was a pile of what looked like bodies under a tarp to her left. Roche dove behind one of the workstations to her right and popped back up in time to nearly take a fusillade of bullets to the face. They tore through everything on the desktop. The computer monitors, stacks of books, and electrical components. Ricocheted from the steel front.

The two men manning the stations at the front of the room ducked back down behind the ledge that hid their recessed posts. She caught a glimpse of the back of one of their heads as the man made a break to the right. A chair toppled to her left.

They were moving to outflank Roche, who crawled cautiously around to the far side of the desk. From that angle, he wouldn't be able to see the second man working back toward him from the left, where he peeked around the landing at the top of the short staircase, raised his rifle, braced his forearm on the ground, and aligned his sights with the point where Roche would be emerging from behind the desk at any moment.

The man on the right came up fast, his weapon sighted squarely at—

Roche's shot hit him high in the chest. The impact lifted him from his feet and tossed him backward onto the console. Roche swiveled to his left as though in slow motion. Tried to get a bead on the man leaning over the top of the staircase, whose face cracked into a smile of victory.

Kelly fired blindly. Bullets ricocheted from the ground all around him. He jerked back his rifle, ducked down—

A stray bullet punched through his shoulder. He grabbed for it and looked up at Kelly.

She gasped in recognition. Lucas O'Reilly. She'd worked with him every day over the past six months, traded stories with him, shared coffee with him. He smirked and raised his weapon toward her.

Kelly pulled the trigger and his face crumpled into a crater of blood and bone fragments. He hovered momentarily before toppling backward.

Roche ran to her. Grabbed her by the arm. Dragged her toward the door.

She glanced up at the screens, where she saw the satellite image of Giza, the white mesa surrounded by men disgorging from a small fleet of panel trucks. The image of the Mexican jungle featured a Black Hawk chopper landing in the middle of an open field, near a giant peaked knoll, its rotor wash beating back the jungle.

Both of their field teams were walking into a trap.

"We have to warn the others," she said.

"We have to clear this place first," Roche said. "Maddox is still down here somewhere."

The grinding sound from the elevator shaft was louder now. There was a thumping sound, like a sheet of metal buckling.

There was a single entryway to the third sublevel, invisible unless you knew exactly what you were looking for. Roche found the hidden retina scanner through the gaps in the overhead vent, spoke his name out loud, and held perfectly still as the red laser shined straight down into his eye.

"How did you know—?"

"Now's not the time," Roche interrupted and pulled her toward the terminus of the dead-end corridor.

The outer panel slid back into the wall, followed by the pressurized stainless-steel door, which closed behind them the moment they passed through. Kelly barely recognized they were inside a pass-through chamber like the one at USAMRIID before the interior door opened and she was buffeted in the face with air that smelled almost like the intensive care ward in a hospital.

"We have to hurry," Roche said.

He preceded her down a narrow staircase that wound back upon itself and let off onto a landing overlooking a vast display reminiscent of a museum gallery. Even from this height, she could tell it was a collection of artifacts like those Hollis Richards had taken with him to AREA 51. She even recognized several that had been collected inside the Antarctic pyramid.

They descended another set of stairs to the main floor, where Roche guided her through the exhibits. It was an homage of sorts to the man who had spent his entire life accruing the strange and inexplicable anomalies. There were fragments of meteorites under Lucite. Inca stones from Peru. Photographs of the Nazca Lines and jars containing samples of the sand that formed them. Carvings of flying saucers and spaceman. The silver Betz sphere, which even now produced a faint humming sound. It reminded her of a sideshow exhibit in many ways, a collection of curiosities of no real scientific or anthropological value, mere trinkets a lonely old man had picked up along his way to finding the trail of mutated skulls that led him to the discovery of alien life at the bottom of the world.

It struck her that this was a sentimental place, not unlike a scrapbook full of memories, its exhibits designed to be relived anytime Hollis Richards had wanted. This was his level, but certainly not one of more than personal value. The real treasures must have been housed somewhere else.

"Where's the rest of it?" Kelly asked

"If that bunker's still down there," Roche said, "then I have a hunch that's where everything else is stored."

"Then that's where we need to go."

The elevator doors were all the way across the display floor to her left. She strode straight toward them before she lost her nerve. She'd barely been able to hang on to the cable long enough to descend a single story; the prospect of sliding some unknown distance down into the waiting arms of the enemy terrified her, and yet she could think of no way around it.

She reached the doors first, squeezed her fingertips into the seam, and tried to pry them apart. They didn't budge in the slightest, at least not until Roche caught up with her and used a length of metal he'd broken from one of the display stands to lever them open.

They stood together at the precipice and stared down at the crumpled elevator. The hydraulic pistons of the electromagnetic flaps continued to drive and release, drive and release, in their vain attempt to close. The roof of the car had buckled and mechanical components spit scalding oil in every direction. There was no telling how long the car would hold, let alone what would happen when it finally lost its battle.

"Are you sure you want to do this?" Roche said.

"No," Kelly said, "but what choice do we have?"

45
BARNETT

La Venta

Barnett studied the nests above him for the slightest sign of movement, listened for the crinkling sound of something squirming around inside, but everything was perfectly silent and still. He had to believe that as long as they didn't do anything to cause a change in the environment, there was no risk of rousing the feathered serpents from their state of cryobiosis, and yet he couldn't shake the feeling that he was preparing to spring a trap.

"What do you think?" Morgan whispered.

"I say we get what we came for and get the hell out of here. Zeta has to be getting close by now."

"And what do we do when it arrives with all of those drones?"

"One problem at a time," Barnett said. "Let's get this thing open and hope to God we're right about what's inside, because if we're not, we're in a world of hurt."

Barnett stared at the design on the side of the stone case for several seconds, searching for any indication that something other than the canister was inside, but there was only one way to know for sure. He gripped the wooden handles on the near side and waited for Morgan to assume his position on the opposite side. Their eyes met across the top of the stone slab. Barnett gave the go-ahead with a nod and together they raised the slab. It was far heavier than either of them had expected, but they managed to slide it several feet to the side, revealing the dark interior.

They stepped around to the side and shined their beams inside. The circular canister rested at the bottom of a hollow in the stone block. It was roughly eight inches tall and six inches in diameter, with a handle affixed to either side of a lid with an inset grip. It looked like it was made of silver, although there was no sign of tarnishing, even after all these years. There were faint markings on the sides, like laser engravings. Symbols of some kind, only he didn't recognize any of them.

Barnett reached inside and took it by the handle. Lifted it, but it didn't budge in the slightest. He let go, leaned into the stone cube, and shined his light around the base. There was no ring of rust, as he'd anticipated. In fact, there was no indication of corrosion at all. He couldn't see a single reason why it wouldn't come out—

And then he saw it.

The canister wasn't sitting on the bottom; it was fitted into it. A circular hole had been carved into the bottom, the exact same size as the container itself. It could have easily rusted down there, or perhaps thousands of years of humidity, temperature, and pressure changes had simply caused the metal to expand just far enough for it to become stuck.

"Let me try," Morgan said.

Barnett made room for his partner, who set his feet, gripped the handle, and pulled as hard as he could. He growled through his bared teeth with the exertion. The tendons stood out in his neck. Veins bulged in his arms. And yet it didn't move even a single millimeter.

"It's more than just stuck," Morgan said. "Something's physically holding it in there."

Barnett glanced up at the nest overhead filled with the bodies of the dead and the creatures curled up inside their remains. He didn't like this. Applying such significant mechanical force had to be the means of springing the trap, a fail-safe designed by the ancient Olmec to eliminate whoever tried to steal the artifact.

He looked down again, scooted into position, and gripped the handle. The construction of the vessel was beyond anything even the most advanced society of the time could have manufactured. The lid itself appeared to have a pressurized seal, one that could only be broken by gripping the inset handle, pushing down, and turning . . .

That was it.

He tried to turn the handle, but it still didn't budge. He tried again, this time putting his shoulders into it.

Crack.

Barnett froze. Looked straight up. Nothing.

He tried turning again. This time it moved without nearly as much effort. He could see now that the bottom of the canister was threaded, like a screw. Such a simple concept, and yet one that would have confounded everyone on the planet so long ago. Several more turns and he could see the seal of rust he'd broken. The outer ring must have been made from a different kind of metal than the canister, one more susceptible to oxidation and humidity. Two more twists and he felt it start to give—

Pressure from underneath.

He wasn't fast enough.

Water fired straight up out of the hole. It struck the underside of the lid and flipped it over the side, where it shattered on the ground with a thunderous crash. The flume struck the ceiling, knocking the nests in every direction, tearing them apart, and releasing the dead bodies trapped inside. Water rained back down on them with such force they could barely keep their eyes open. It accumulated so quickly around them that it already nearly covered their feet.

The nature of the trap hit him.

The cavern had been deliberately flooded to create the necessary pressure to fill the hollow column in the room below them, the one with the rust stains. They'd used the canister to seal it and the geyser to revive the hibernating creatures, hidden inside the corpses that were already nearly invisible beneath the water, which had risen to the lip around the lone egress in the floor.

"Go!" Barnett shouted and pushed his partner ahead of him.

Morgan splashed through the frigid water, climbed up onto the ledge, and dropped straight down into the chamber below.

Barnett glanced back in time to see the carcass of a jaguar roll onto its side. Something ripped through its desiccated fur and flagellated through the water.

He tucked the canister under his arm like a football, jumped through the hole, and landed with water pouring down on him from seemingly everywhere at once.

Morgan had already cleared the structure and sloshed madly toward the rocky slope. With as treacherous as the descent had been, the ascent would be infinitely worse.

They crawled upward as fast as they could, their wet boots slipping on the stones and sending them clattering down into the water. Every splash conjured an image of a dragon-like creature bursting from the surface of the water, but Barnett couldn't risk looking back. He and Morgan had to be a quarter of a mile from where they'd entered the underground complex and at the end of a narrow earthen maze presumably carved by these very creatures, which had been entombed down here with the sacrifices that had served first as sustenance, and then as shelter for this extant species of dinosaur.

Barnett passed Morgan about halfway up. The path ahead remained clear, although the ledge looked a whole lot narrower than it had on the way in.

A clacking sound, like one stone striking another.

He instinctively looked down, expecting to see feathered bodies ascending the rubble in almost serpentine fashion, but the pool at the bottom remained strangely placid, at least directly underneath them. The only ripples were faint and originated from somewhere in the distance.

If the creatures were only now emerging from inside the structure, then maybe there was still a chance he and Morgan would be able to reach the entrance with enough time to restack the collapsed barricade that had originally been used to seal them inside. It obviously wouldn't last forever, but they didn't need it to. All they needed was enough time to escape the ruins and call for retrieval—

Clack-clack-clack-clack.

The sound was even louder now, but, again, there was nothing scaling the crumbled staircase behind him. He recognized it, though. From the assault on FOB Atlantis beneath the ice cap. The creatures were closing the gap on them, but, for the life of him, he simply couldn't see them.

"Hurry!" he called down at Morgan, who paused only long enough to indiscriminately fire several rounds to deter their pursuit.

The echo of the reports reverberated all around them. It hadn't even faded when the clicking sounds returned.

Clack-clack-clack-clack.

"Where the hell are they?" Morgan shouted.

Barnett crawled from the loose stones onto the narrow ledge. Caught movement from the corner of his eye. A shifting of the darkness. He turned and shined his light—

The walls of the necropolis were positively alive with creatures scurrying straight up the stacked stones, their long, feathered tails swishing behind them, their necks writhing like sidewinders.

"They're coming!" Barnett shouted.

Several of them were already nearly to the same height as they were and on a course to intercept them before they reached the solitary doorway at the end of the ledge.

Barnett shouted and fired at them as he ran, bracing his shoulder against the wall and praying he kept his feet close enough together that he didn't step off over the open air.

One of the creatures screamed and lost its grip on the wall. It plummeted into the darkness, trailing a ribbon of blood. Another creature struck at it and caught it by the throat, the momentum wrenching it from its perch. It started tearing apart the other one before they hit the water.

The gunfire drove back the others, clearing a gap to the opening, for however long it might last.

Barnett rounded the bend, launched himself toward the crevice, and slid across the bare stone. He was already scrambling to his feet when he heard the clatter of claws on the walls again.

Morgan blew through the orifice behind him and waved him on. Barnett crouched and ran in the opposite direction. He was nearly to the pit when he heard Morgan bellow and start firing. The discharge flickered behind him, limning the passageway and reflecting from the water way down at the bottom as he jumped across the gap. He lowered his head and sprinted toward the entrance to the necropolis.

The moment he was clear, he threw himself to the ground and started restacking the heavy stones in the opening. He needed to leave enough room for Morgan to get out, but not so much that they wouldn't be able to wall the tunnel closed behind them in a hurry.

Morgan swung his light ahead of him as he ran. His footsteps echoed from the corridor, punctuated by the clattering sound of claws striking rock. He fired back over his shoulder, his bullets sparking from the floor, ceiling, and walls, revealing fleeting glimpses of the feathered creatures streaking toward him. Not on the ground, but from directly over his head.

"Down!" Barnett shouted.

He raised his weapon and pulled the trigger. Morgan dove onto his chest as the barrage sailed over his head and struck the wave of creatures. They screamed and dropped from the ceiling. He caught a flurry of feathers and claws in the flash of discharge. Spatters of blood. Creatures turning upon their brethren even as they tried to overtake Morgan, who crawled on his hands and knees toward the hole. He stopped before he reached it, rounded on the creatures, and lit them up. Feathers and blood filled the air. Bullets struck their flanks and exposed breasts with sounds like a butcher tenderizing meat. The siege lasted mere seconds, yet left behind utter stillness in the haze of gun smoke.

Morgan explored the darkness behind him with his light. Downy feathers settled to the ground like snow-flakes. There wasn't the slightest hint of movement what-soever.

Barnett wasn't taking any chances. He resumed stack-ing the rocks and had the opening halfway barricaded by the time Morgan started moving. Scooting backward to make sure nothing could overtake him from the rear.

Beneath the clamor of stones, Barnett heard a rapid-fire clicking sound.

Clack-clack-clack-clack.

"Get out of there!" he shouted.

"I can't see them!"

"Just keep moving!"

"How long do you think that pile of rocks is going to hold? We have a tactical advantage—"

"But they have the numbers!"

Clack-clack-clack-clack.

Barnett risked a peek, but couldn't see anything in Morgan's light. Regardless, the clacking sounds increased in volume and proximity. The creatures were definitely gaining on them, but from where?

Barnett recognized their mistake at the same time as Morgan, who turned around and shined his light straight down the shaft, toward the collection of bones protruding from the water.

He shouted and started shooting.

The feathered serpents burst from the hole in the strobe of discharge, teeth snapping, claws striking. Like the hounds of hell themselves, only with quill-like feathers bristling from their carapaces.

Morgan's carbine whirred. He cast aside his spent magazine, but they were upon him before he could reload. Latching onto his clothing. Nails sinking into the meat of his shoulders. Tearing into the side of his neck, his face.

Morgan looked straight at Barnett. Their eyes locked across the distance. Even with his cheek torn back to his ear, he could tell his old friend was smiling.

A warrior to the end.

Morgan wrapped his arms around the flailing creatures, whose slashing talons decorated the surrounding walls with his blood, and toppled forward into the pit, taking the feathered serpents with him.

Avian shrieks followed him into the abyss before they were abruptly silenced by a crack of breaking bones and a splash.

46
EVANS

Giza, Egypt

Evans unlatched one of the straps on the side of the truck. Squeezed between two overturned crates so he could get close enough to see out. Pressed his face right up against the canvas flap.

He had a clear view of the enclosed bed of the vehicle beside theirs, but the darkness and the settling dust obscured most everything else. He could barely see fifty feet across the rolling barchan dunes to where a low sandstone butte flitted in and out of the dust.

He froze at the sound of voices behind the truck, the squeal of its suspension as someone leaned against the tailgate.

Jade placed her hand on top of his. He could feel her shaking, see little more than her wide eyes staring at him from the shadows behind the crates.

Another squeal and whoever was out there walked around to the other side of the bed, his footsteps scuffing on the dirt.

"Ich mag das nicht," he said to someone out of sight. Their footsteps continued onward together.

A gentle breeze rippled the canvas siding. It was only a matter of time before the dust settled. If Evans and his team weren't gone by then, they'd be visible for miles in every direction.

"We need to go now," Evans whispered. He loosened several other straps and held the canvas in place until Jade was right next to him. "There's a rock formation out there. Straight ahead. Once you hit the ground, start running and don't look back."

"What about the virus?"

"We won't be able to stop them from releasing it if they kill us. And that's exactly what they'll do if they catch us in here."

The voices outside grew louder and more animated. There was no time to waste.

"Go," Evans whispered and raised the flap.

Jade crawled over the side of the bed and dropped down into the sand with a soft thump. Evans cringed and prayed no one had heard. Anya was already out when he heard Jade's footsteps heading away from the vehicle and caught a glimpse of her silhouette against the darkness. The moment Anya was clear, he dove through the gap behind her, landed on all fours to muffle the sound, and launched himself to his feet.

The sand was deep in places and windswept in others, making it difficult to maintain his stride. He risked a glance over his shoulder and saw the men gathered in the wash of their combined headlights. There was no way any of them could possibly see him through the glare. As long as they didn't hear him—

He tripped and hit the sand, tumbled down a dune. Pushed himself back up and raced after the others, who had already vanished around the side of the rock formation. He found them on the far side, crouching in the shadows and trying to catch their breath.

The first hint of the Earth's shadow appeared at the edge of the full moon. He had no idea how long it would take to fully eclipse it, but he was definitely running out of time to come up with a plan. They had no clue which truck the virus was in, let alone which of the hundreds of crates. They couldn't risk taking any form of action until they knew exactly where it was.

Evans gestured for the others to follow him and climbed up on top of the rock formation. He pressed his chest to the ground to minimize his profile and dragged himself all the way to the opposite side. From this vantage point, he could clearly see the trucks and the people stationed around them. A group broke away from the others. Two of the men carried a large wooden crate the size of a coffin between them.

Anya and Jade slithered up to either side of Evans.

"What do you think they're doing?" Anya whispered.

Evans could only shake his head. He counted nine enemies, but couldn't tell them apart well enough from this distance to be confident of that number. With all of them wearing masks and the same dark fatigues, it could have easily been twice that many.

The men carried the case to the foot of the distant mesa, dropped it unceremoniously onto the ground, and used a pair of crowbars to pry off the lid.

It took Evans several minutes to locate the blond woman, who stood at the periphery of the aura of the headlights. He might not have seen her at all had he not caught a reflection from her golden mask when she turned at just the right angle. The giant in the cloak towered over her, more at home in the darkness than the light.

His crocodilian snout protruded from within his hood. He raised it straight up into the air. Turned first one way, and then the other, as though scenting the air for prey.

"What is that?" Anya whispered.

Evans followed her line of sight to where the men had removed a large tripod from the crate and were in the process of affixing an enormous black disc that looked like a cross between a satellite dish and a spotlight to the top of it. They swiveled it to face the mesa and angled it slightly upward.

The first man made a final calibration to its alignment, appraised his work, and then shouted to the others. The blond woman responded in a voice too soft to make out her words and headed in his direction.

When Evans looked back, the man with the feathered serpent mask was gone.

"Wait," Jade whispered. "I can't be sure, but I think I've seen something like that before."

The man who'd erected the device met the woman halfway. The two exchanged words while the second man walked past them, trailing a long electrical cord. He opened the hood of the nearest truck and appeared to attach the cable to the battery.

"What is it?" Evans asked. He couldn't figure out where the cloaked man had gone, which made him more than a little uneasy. "We need to know what we're dealing with."

"It looks like an LRAD. A long-range acoustic device. I'm familiar with its use as a crowd-dispersal agent, but I haven't seen one in person before, at least not one that big."

The woman in the golden mask waved the others back

to the line of trucks. They wasted no time climbing inside the vehicles.

"Cover your ears," Jade whispered.

"Why—?" Anya started to ask.

"It's an ultrasonic weapon. You need to—"

Evans's reaction was a millisecond too slow. While he didn't hear anything, it felt like someone simultaneously clapped their hands over both of his ears. The air itself seemed to shiver around him. His chest quivered. His heart skipped a beat. The roots of his teeth vibrated in his jaws. He felt sick to his stomach, like he was about to explode from both ends.

Cracks raced through the rock formation underneath them. The entire world shuddered.

A headache came on without warning, multiplied exponentially until it felt like his skull couldn't contain it. His eyes went out of focus and he tasted blood in the back of his throat.

Shockwaves rippled through the distant mesa as though it were made of liquid. Some sections rose, while others collapsed. Then, all at once and with a sound like thunder, it fractured into a million pieces.

It was over as quickly as it had begun.

There was a residual high-pitched ringing sound in his head, one against which he had to fight to keep his eyes from crossing and the world from tilting. It felt like needles were lancing his eardrums.

Anya retched, but only brought up a mouthful of saliva and stomach acid.

Evans felt something warm on his ear. He dabbed at it and pulled his fingertips away bloody.

Jade scooted away from the edge and smeared the blood

from her nose with the back of her hand. She opened her mouth as if about to speak, but only shook her head.

The masked figures climbed out of their vehicles and approached the mesa, several sections of which had collapsed in upon themselves, revealing sinkholes of unknown depth. The outermost portion appeared to form a rectangular frame, while the inside—

"Hier drüben!" one of the men shouted.

He stood on top of a crumbled mound of stones and shined his flashlight down into the dark hole, from which a cloud of dust billowed.

"There's something down there," Jade whispered. "A structure of some kind."

"We need to get down there first," Evans said. "We can't afford to let them—"

Anya screamed.

Evans turned around. A hunched shape crouched near her feet. It appeared to be made of the darkness itself, until its cloak drew contrast from the night sky. A crocodilian snout protruded from within its hood, framed by brittle, broken feathers. The eyes staring out at them through the empty sockets were reptilian, the irises marbled, the pupils vertically slit. Within them he saw the fate that awaited them all, and realized there was nothing they could do to stop it.

47
ROCHE

The Hangar

Roche released the cable, alighted on the concrete pad at the bottom of the elevator shaft, and sighted the dimly lit corridor ahead of him down the barrel of his rifle while he waited for Kelly to catch up with him. He listened to her descend without taking his eyes off the stainless-steel door. The occasional curtain of sparks cascaded down the wall from the snarl of machinery overhead. He figured it was only a matter of time before either the jaws of the electromagnetic lock chewed through the elevator or their hydraulic pistons failed. Either way, some portion of that elevator was going to come careening down that shaft, and he didn't want to be anywhere nearby when it did.

Kelly dropped down behind him with a clap of her shoes striking the floor and a whimper of pain, presumably caused by her blistered palms. If hers were anything like his, she'd be lucky to be able to hold her rifle steady. She ducked her head and rushed to his side.

"Once we open those doors," he whispered, "they're going to know we're here."

"How many of them do you think there are?"

"There's no way of knowing, but we have to assume they have Tess, which means they hold all of the cards."

"Then we'll just have to hope they don't hear us."

A thunking sounded from above them, followed by the pinging of something metallic ricocheting from the walls.

Roche boosted Kelly over the lip and climbed up behind her a heartbeat before a massive gear struck the concrete behind them. Scalding fluids spattered the ground beside one of the springs with a sizzling sound.

He shouldered his rifle and advanced slowly toward the door, which whispered open when he triggered the unseen sensor. A quick glance confirmed there was no one hiding inside the chamber.

His pulse thumped in his ears.

Once the inner door opened, there'd be nowhere for them to hide. They'd be completely and utterly exposed. If anyone was waiting for them on the other side, they wouldn't stand a chance.

The outer door shushed closed behind them. He held his breath. Tightened his finger on the trigger. Mentally prepared himself. The inner door receded into the wall, revealing an empty hallway.

Roche released his breath. He glanced back at Kelly, gestured for her to keep her eyes open, and started down the hallway beneath overhead lights that reflected from the polished concrete. He placed each foot cautiously, silently, rolling from heel to toe. He slowly moved his barrel from one side of the hallway to the other as they passed between artifacts contained in climate-controlled cases, the faint hiss and rumble of their inner workings masking the subtle sounds he desperately needed to hear.

He studied them in his peripheral vision, but couldn't afford to be distracted. Gunmen could be posted to either side of the central corridor at the branch ahead, just waiting for them to walk through their crossfire.

"Stay here," he whispered.

He pressed his shoulder against the display case to his left, lowered to a crouch, and approached the juncture slowly. Listened for the sound of breathing, the click of a disengaging safety, any sound to betray the presence of the men waiting for them ahead. If he looked past the corner to his right, he could see a reflection from the cases on the other side. While it wasn't perfect, it at least confirmed there was no one lying in wait. He dashed across the hall, pressed his back flat against the opposite side, and similarly used the glass cases diagonally across the intersecting aisle to confirm there was no one on that side either.

Where were they? Had they found another way out? A single man with little more than average ability with a rifle could have prevented them from penetrating the sublevel beyond the door from the pass-through chamber.

Roche went low around the corner. Sighted his weapon first down the corridor to his left, then to his right. Both sides terminated at T-junctures, but there was no sign of anyone stationed in between.

He advanced into the continuation of the main aisle, his own reflection stalking him from the glass cases to either side, inside of which were figurines that seemed to watch him as he passed, but not nearly as closely as the skulls in the case ahead of him.

A crunching sound.

Roche froze and surveyed the deserted hallway. The sound had originated from deeper in the substructure. There was something on the floor, near where the corridor met with a display case. Broken Plexiglas. Maddox and his men must have found what they were searching for, and based upon the progression of the artifacts, he had a pretty good idea of what it was.

Damn Barnett for bringing it back here.

Another crunch.

There was definitely someone back there, somewhere out of sight, near the terminus. If he and Kelly continued walking straight ahead, they risked a direct confrontation, one that would come down to who could fire their weapons first. It was a chance they didn't have to take.

Roche glanced to his right, at a monitor displaying the 3-D reconstruction of the mummified remains partially contained within the discolored funereal bundle in the case. The digital representation of the body rotated on an invisible horizontal axis, then turned and spun on the vertical, but it wasn't the imagery, specifically, that caught his eye.

He stepped up onto the armature that supported the monitor and used it to climb on top of the display case. The gap beneath the ceiling was barely high enough for him to squirm inside, forcing him to remain on his chest. Grates vented recycled air and heat from the light sources against his belly. Cords and tubes snaked away from him, toward the recesses that housed the electrical components.

From up here, he could see all the way across the substructure in every direction. It was far vaster than he ever would have guessed. Undoubtedly, Barnett and Richards had expanded upon the original bunker, which meant there was a good chance they'd installed another egress in the process. And if that were the case, then it was possible that Maddox was already long gone.

A soft sucking sound, like a subtle release of pressure.

He crawled forward, mere inches at a time. It almost looked like there was an enclosed area ahead, a cul-de-sac of sorts.

Footsteps. Nearby. Faint. Little more than a shifting of weight.

He contorted his body so he could look behind him. Kelly was right at his heels, her rifle similarly resting on her forearms as she pulled with her palms and pushed with her toes. She nodded to let him know that she'd heard it, too.

Another ten feet and he'd be close enough to look down upon whoever was there.

Motion from the corner of his eye. By the time he looked, it was gone. Something had moved across the reflection on the glass case. Something black and human-shaped.

"Das dauert zu lange."

The speaker was practically right below him. And while he didn't understand the words, he definitely recognized the voice.

Maddox.

"Was soll ich tun?"

A second voice, farther to the right.

There were at least two of them, likely more. Roche had to believe they wouldn't be deliberately giving away their locations by talking if they had the slightest clue that they weren't alone, which gave Kelly and him a slight advantage. Even if Maddox's men were prepared to defend their position, they wouldn't expect the attack to come from above.

Roche maneuvered his rifle into the closest thing to a natural shooting position he could manage and used his elbows to drag himself toward the edge.

Just a little farther.

A shadow passed across the Plexiglas shards covering the floor below him. The footsteps sounded strange. Sticky. Like the person had stepped in spilled soda.

He pushed with his toes and craned his neck. Maddox stood below him and slightly off to his left. While Roche couldn't see his former friend's face, he could read his body language. Maddox was nervous, more so than Roche had ever seen him.

The man beside Maddox had blond hair and an urban camouflage tactical mask. He paced restlessly, glancing every few seconds into the corner of the open space, to Roche's right. A third man passed behind Maddox, but Roche couldn't see any details beyond his black fatigues and featureless tactical mask.

A crunching sound, from slightly to his right and straight down.

All three men looked toward the source in unison.

A shadow moved on the floor directly underneath Roche, a hunched shape, rising and falling, and then it was gone.

Kelly scooted up beside him. With the lights above the walkways being so bright, the two of them would be invisible in the shadows to anyone who looked up from below.

Roche needed to know what the men were watching in the back corner. He and Kelly could easily hit all three of the men below them before they could raise their weapons in their defense, but a fourth man outside of the range of sight provided a variable for which they couldn't account. If he had an automatic weapon, he could strafe the top of the display case before either of them could get a bead on him. And while Roche didn't like the man's odds of hitting them from that angle, he wasn't about to gamble with Kelly's life.

He scooted just a little bit farther, tried to lean over the edge without his face emerging from the darkness. He saw the shadow on the floor again, rising and falling almost rhythmically across a mess of broken glass and smeared footprints. Crimson and wet. Blood. No doubt about it. He took a chance and leaned out over the edge, saw the reflection of the overhead lights from a puddle of blood, beside which were handprints and smudges leading toward the shape crouching in the corner. It was a man. His back was bare, the knobs of his spine tenting gray, scabrous skin that appeared far too tight. He was emaciated, skeletal. He lowered his shoulders between his flexed knees and made a slurping sound. His entire body was covered with open lacerations. Not a single drop of blood flowed from within the puckered edges.

All at once, it dawned on Roche what he was looking at.

The eagle mask lay on the floor beside Tess's body. Her clothing was torn, her pale flesh cut clear to the bone in places, her lifeless eyes staring blankly at the ceiling. Her blood was positively everywhere.

"No," Kelly whispered.

The naked man ceased his rhythmic movements and abruptly looked up, his eyes inhuman, his face a mask of shimmering blood.

48
BARNETT

La Venta

While Morgan had given his life so that Barnett might escape, it would only buy him so much time. He refused to let his old friend's sacrifice be in vain.

He piled the last of the rocks in the entrance, shoved a stone block up against the barricade, and took aim at the earthen roof directly above it. A few well-placed shots brought down piles of dirt and debris, but not nearly as much as he'd hoped. Considering the tunnel leading here from the buried colonnade had undoubtedly been carved by these same creatures eons ago while they were starving and in search of food, he knew it wouldn't take them long to get through. He couldn't afford to waste any more bullets or time, especially not with the army of drones that could be converging upon the ruins at that very moment.

There was no way on this planet he was leaving here alive.

He looked down at the canister in his grasp.

"This had better be worth it," he whispered.

Barnett struck off into the tunnel, heading back toward

the surface. He ducked under the low ceiling, swatted away the roots, and navigated the uneven terrain until he reached a narrowing so small he was forced to crawl. He emerged from a crevice between a pair of fallen pillars, entered the colonnade, and blew past the giant megalithic head that resembled Subject Z's. Climbed through the doorway and into the chamber with the collapsed roof. Squeezed around the rubble, beneath the watchful eyes of the hybridized gods carved into the walls. Scurried through the slender opening into the room with the spiderwebs. A slanted column of light shined down onto the dirt floor.

He didn't even slow down. He hit the wall at a sprint, braced his foot against the crumbling plaster, and propelled himself upward. Caught the edge of the stone slab, covertly evaluated his surroundings, and pulled himself out into the world he'd been certain he would never see again.

The sun had already set, leaving behind a red stain to the west that made the jungle appear to burn. Scattered stars had materialized from the gloaming, against which the branches rustled ever so gently on the breeze. If he turned his head just right, he could see the moon, the Earth's shadow only now taking its first tentative bite from the edge.

He scrambled up the slope and threw himself into the thicket. He heard the trickling sound of loose dirt sliding down through the hole in the roof of the structure and alighting on the ground, but nothing else. No birds chirped or monkeys shrieked. Nothing scampered across the moldering leaves or flitted through the dense canopy.

Barnett knew exactly what that meant.

He remained perfectly silent while he surveilled the ancient site, or at least what he could see of it. Surely if the creatures were out there, he would have seen at least some sign of their presence, or if they had already arrived, then undoubtedly they would have made short work of him.

Something wasn't right.

He crept through the jungle, conscious of every crunch of the detritus and crackle of twigs underfoot. Even the gentle scraping of the wet leaves across his jacket made a sound he was certain would betray him, assuming the whining of the gathering mosquitoes didn't do so first. He slowed his heartbeat, felt the trickle of sweat rolling down his cheek, squeezed the trigger of his rifle into the sweet spot, where even the slightest addition of pressure would release a triple burst. Every one of his senses, every aspect of his being, was attuned to the world around him.

A scraping sound. Distant. Coming from somewhere to the northwest.

The sky grew darker by the second, storm clouds advancing from the horizon snuffing out the stars one by one. A faint flicker of lightning announced a soft grumble of thunder.

When he reached the edge of the forest, he lowered himself to the ground, smeared handfuls of mud onto his face, and squirmed into the underbrush until he could see into the clearing.

The wet grass shimmered in the moonlight, which seemed to diminish with each passing second. He drew his satellite phone from his pack, turned down the volume, and pressed the button to transmit.

"If anyone can hear me," he whispered, "this is Cameron Barnett, I have secured the package and—"

Something caught his eye.

There was a pattern in the grass ahead of him, a massive circular design where the blades were flattened into the ground, at the center of which were several deep impressions. He looked up to find bowed and broken branches. Tattered and torn leaves.

The forest hadn't gone silent because Subject Z's armada had arrived, but rather because someone else had.

He merged back into the jungle and advanced through the densest cover he could find, pausing every few feet to listen for the men who'd arrived on the helicopter while he was underground.

Again, he heard the scraping sound. Louder now. And, perhaps, if he held his breath, the faint whisper of voices.

Unless he'd completely lost his bearings, he was approximately a hundred feet due east of what archeologists considered the main plaza, roughly even with the Stirling acropolis and the grove of palm trees that divided the site, which placed the pyramid a quarter-mile diagonally to the northwest, on the other side of the flooded necropolis he'd narrowly escaped. He turned in that direction and closed his eyes to better concentrate on his sense of hearing. The scraping sounds were definitely coming from somewhere over there.

The forest thinned incrementally, forcing him to take a circuitous approach toward the pyramid, the very top of which he occasionally glimpsed through the canopy. It was strangely well lit, despite the diminishing moon. Another fifty feet and he was able to see the banks of portable lights directed at the base of the mound and the source of the scraping sounds.

Half a dozen men wearing black fatigues and tactical masks attacked the ground with pickaxes and shovels. They'd already created a pit large enough to reveal the discolored stones buried underneath, which formed what almost looked like the trapezoidal frame of a doorway. Like the entrance to the necropolis, it had been sealed, only in a much more permanent manner. The barricade was perfectly fitted and mortared in place. There was no way they were getting through it with anything shy of a—

As if on cue, a man wearing a tactical mask with a flaming skull removed bricks of C-4 from a satchel and commenced attaching them to the barricade.

A crashing sound. Only this time from back to his left.

Barnett glanced back in the direction from which he came but couldn't see anything through the trees.

The men in the clearing must have heard it, too. A pair of them struck off in that direction, their assault rifles seated against their shoulders.

Surely, they hadn't solved the riddle of La Venta by themselves, which meant they'd gained control of the Hangar and had access to Dr. Clarke's program. That would explain how they knew precisely where to dig to find the entrance to the pyramid, if not why they were intent on breaking in.

The remaining men ducked behind the banks of lights.

"Feuer im loch!" one of them shouted.

The explosion shook the ground.

Barnett seized the opportunity to sprint through the jungle to the north in hopes of getting a better view.

Smoke billowed from the orifice and rolled over the men. Rocks rained down onto the leaves overhead with a sound like hail.

Barnett saw a massive kapok tree to his left and made a split-second decision. He kicked off the trunk, grabbed the lowest bough, and hauled himself up into the canopy. He was nearly twenty feet off the ground when the smoke finally cleared. From where he crouched with his back against the trunk, he had a perfect view of the clearing through the branches.

The pair who'd broken away from the others were nearly to the palm grove. Several of the trees still swayed from the explosion.

Spotlights illuminated the mouth of a dark tunnel, in front of which the man with the flaming skull mask crouched, shining the beam affixed to the barrel of his rifle inside.

A crashing sound from the south.

The men in the field slowed and advanced more cautiously.

Straight ahead, the other three masked men joined their leader at the entrance, prepared to crawl into the darkness.

Barnett seated his rifle against his shoulder, watched them down the barrel. If any of them so much as turned in his direction—

Gunfire to his left. He whirled in time to see shadows streaking across the plaza toward the two men, who managed to get off a few more shots before the feathered serpents swarmed over them, tails thrashing and long necks striking, tearing them apart with their teeth. Their feathers shimmered with a strange iridescence in the moonlight as their prey bled the field red.

A high-pitched whine and a streak of light.

The projectile struck in their midst. The explosion tore through the creatures, swallowing them in a swirling mass of smoke, flames, and charred appendages. He turned in time to see the men near the pyramid reload the rocket launcher and take aim again.

A whoosh and the rocket screamed across the clearing, striking the edge of the forest and throwing dirt and debris into the air. Several trees toppled forward into the smoke and hit the ground hard enough to make it tremble.

The four men formed a line and advanced toward the conflagration, their rifles raised, discharge spitting from the barrels.

Barnett glanced at the entrance to the pyramid.

This was his chance.

He jumped down to the bough below him. Wrapped his arms around it and swung his legs over the side. Let go and fell to the ground. Rolled to cushion the impact and used his momentum to accelerate into the clearing. He broke the cover of the trees and sprinted toward the pyramid. Caught one last glimpse of the moon, little more than a sliver, and dove through the opening into the darkness.

49
JADE

Giza, Egypt

Jade drew her legs away from the creature, but Anya wasn't fast enough. It caught her by the ankle and dragged her across the bare stone. Grabbed her by the shirt and lifted her into the air. She screamed and thrashed to no avail, her toes nearly two feet off the ground.

It cocked its head from one side to the other as though appraising her. Raised its crocodilian snout and drew in a deep inhalation. Produced a deep rumbling sound that resonated from inside its chest.

Anya clawed at its eyes but only succeeded in tearing off its mask, which clattered to the ground at its cloaked feet.

The being that looked upon her was only human in form. Its eyes reflected the moonlight with an iridescence all their own. Its skin was dry and scaled, like a dead fish left to rot on the shore. There was no hair on its head or brow, only areas where the scales appeared to have sloughed off, exposing the bare bone in places. Horizontal folds stretched from the edges of its wide, thin-lipped mouth all the way to ears that were little more than membranes framed by a vaguely human-shaped conch. The scales on its chin were longer and sharper, almost like a beard.

It opened its jaws wide enough to reveal sharp teeth that lowered from where they'd been flattened to the roof of its mouth. They extended from flesh sockets, long and hooked, like the fangs of a rattlesnake. The fold in its cheeks allowed it to open its mouth even wider, stretching its lower jaw past its apparent limits.

Anya screamed as it brought her face to within inches of its own. It savored a breath through its teardrop-shaped nostrils and extended a tongue with the slightest fork at the tip. She turned her face away, but there was nothing she could do to prevent it from licking the open wound across her hairline.

Its slit pupils widened and it issued a hissing sound. Extended its fangs even farther from its gums.

"Get away from her!" Jade shouted.

She grabbed Anya around the waist and attempted to pry her from the creature's grasp.

Evans lunged at it, but it moved in a blur, driving its elbow into the side of his head without so much as loosening its grip on Anya's shirt. He pushed himself up from the rock, dribbling blood from his mouth.

"Enlil bitaltu!" The woman in the golden mask shouted. She stood at the base of the rock formation, staring up at them from the sand. *"Kima parsi labiruti!"*

The creature bared its fangs, gripped Anya by the throat, and drew her to its chest.

"Mine," it said in a deep voice that resonated from its core.

"She belongs to Anu."

The being hissed and tossed Anya to the ground. Jade

rushed to her side and scooped her up before the beast changed its mind.

"Doctors Evans, Liang, and Fleming," the woman in the golden mask said. "How fortunate you could be here to bear witness to the end of your world. And the birth of ours."

"If you release that virus, every single one of us will die," Jade said.

"Not every one of us."

The woman turned without another word and struck off across the desert. Jade had been so preoccupied with the creature that she hadn't heard the masked men climb up onto the rocks behind them. She felt the barrel of a rifle against the base of her skull.

"Do not try anything you will regret," a man said from behind her and shoved her toward the edge of the cliff.

He aimed his weapon at her the entire way down to the ground, where a man in a featureless tan tactical mask was waiting with a zip tie to bind her wrists behind her back. Anya and Evans were similarly restrained and driven out into the desert ahead of the men, who walked behind them with their rifles raised. Two others flanked them, bringing the total number of armed escorts to five, plus the woman in the golden mask. She'd already lost sight of the cloaked figure.

"Are you all right?" she whispered.

Anya walked with her head down and tears dripping from her cheeks. She nodded her head, but couldn't seem to find the voice to answer.

"Why do you think they didn't kill us right then and there?" Evans whispered.

Jade glanced up in time to see the cloaked figure ascend the rubble off to her right. Its face was once more concealed beneath the mask. She could only imagine how terrifying this Anu had to be to frighten such a ferocious creature.

"They need us for something, but I'm in no hurry to find out what."

"Silence!" one of the men behind them shouted.

A sharp blow to her lower back and her legs went out from underneath her. She cried out and collapsed to the sand.

Evans rounded on their captors.

"If you touch her again—"

He took the butt of a rifle to the gut and folded in half with an expulsion of air. The man stood over him, as though daring him to try to get back up.

"What will you do about it?"

Evans struggled to his knees, his face suffused with the blood. It took him several seconds and superhuman effort to rise to his feet. He thrust out his chin, refilled his lungs with air, and looked the man dead in the eyes when he spoke.

"I'll kill you."

The men started to laugh, but the woman in the golden mask cut them off.

"Enough!" she snapped. "We are running out of time."

Jade glanced over her shoulder at the moon, which was barely visible along the outside edge of Earth's shadow. The surrounding stars had become brighter in response to the advancing darkness.

Evans knelt in front of Jade, helped her to her feet, and together they picked their way up the loose rocks that had once formed the mesa. What had looked like a frame from above turned out to be a collection of massive rectangular stones stacked one on top of the other, staggered just enough to form a staircase pattern. She couldn't believe she hadn't recognized it from the start.

It was the base of a pyramid.

Either it had never been completed or the upper tiers had been demolished so long ago that the desert had conspired to bury it.

A man wearing a tactical mask reminiscent of a medieval knight's helmet crawled out of the ground at the woman's feet. His voice trembled with excitement.

"Wir haben es gefunden," he said.

Jade didn't let on that she understood what he'd said, which took some doing considering she was curious to know what they'd found.

"Zeige mir," the woman said and practically shoved him back down the hole in her hurry to descend.

The creature watched them through the holes where the dead croc's eyes had once been. The hunger radiating from it was palpable. Given the opportunity, she had no doubt it would rip all of them apart and wallow in their blood. These people had no idea the kind of evil they had unleashed upon the world.

"Down," the man behind her said and shoved her over the edge.

Jade barely regained her balance in time to keep from tumbling down a stone staircase so steep she had to jump from one step to the next. The rocks that had been used to seal the stairwell left little room to pass and nearly eclipsed the tunnel at the bottom.

A faint aura of light limned the top of the mound of debris, where the woman in the golden mask had flattened herself to her chest in an effort to squirm through the opening.

Two other men followed her, although with much greater difficulty. They were waiting on the other side when Jade finally managed to propel herself through the narrow gap using only her feet. One of them grabbed her by the sleeve and dragged her down the rocky slope to the floor, just outside of an elaborate doorway. A pair of giant statues stood sentry on either side, their arms crossed over their chests, a crook in one hand and an ankh in the other. They wore traditional striped head cloths with sun discs wrapped inside coiling cobras on top. The features of a falcon covered the upper halves of their faces, while the lower halves remained human. False beards projected from their chins. Coneheaded beings were carved into the walls beside them, their arms raised in adoration.

"The Tomb of Ra," Evans whispered, his voice redolent with awe.

Jade walked through the doorway and into an enormous chamber filled with a maze of pillars crowned with lotus blossoms and covered with hieroglyphics. The walls were similarly decorated, only not all of the paint had flaked off, leaving behind scattered areas of brown, blue, and gold. It wasn't the magnificence of the structure or the elaborate artwork that held her enrapt, but rather the plain stone sarcophagus at the far end of the room.

The woman stood at the head, while several of the men were already struggling to slide off the heavy lid. It took multiple tries, but with a screech, it finally slid over the edge and hit the ground with a thunderous boom that caused dust to shiver from the ceiling. It sparkled like glitter as it descended into their combined lights, all of which were shining down into the sarcophagus.

"Anu," the woman whispered and reached tentatively into the stone coffin.

She stroked the cheek of the solid-gold death mask almost lovingly. It reminded Jade of King Tutankhamun's, only the facial features were an amalgam of man and reptile. The body was even taller than that of the giant wearing the mask of the feathered serpent, who pushed his way to the sarcophagus, stared down at the body, and then turned to face Jade.

"Sharaku," he said, his voice reverberating throughout the chamber.

The woman in the golden mask walked around the sarcophagus to where Jade stood with Anya and Evans.

"He says we must make an offering." She stood before each of them in turn and looked them dead in the eyes through her mask. "But which one of you shall it be?"

50
KELLY

The Hangar

Kelly ducked back into the shadows, bit her lip to keep from crying, and prayed it hadn't seen her. She tried not to think about what that awful monster had done to Tess, but she couldn't shake the image of it crouching over her body. Worse, she feared what it would do to them if it discovered they were here.

"Wir müssen gehen," Maddox said. *"Bring ihn mit."*

The man in the camouflage mask took a step toward the naked, vaguely human creature. It rounded on him, bared a mouthful of fangs, and climbed up on top of Tess's body, like a lion defending its kill.

"We don't have time for this," Maddox said. "For the love of God, would you just grab him already."

Camo Mask hesitated, then took a tentative step toward the creature, which moved so quickly that he never saw it coming. He screamed as it tore a mouthful of flesh from the side of his neck, carving through muscles and tendons, severing the carotid, which pulsed arcs of blood into its scaled face.

Black Mask raised his rifle, but Maddox swatted it

aside as he pulled the trigger. The bullets flew wide and shattered the case underneath Kelly and Roche.

The creature leaped up from the floor, lifted Black Mask from his feet, and slammed his head into the paneled ceiling mere feet from Kelly's face. She was certain her eyes met the man's through the lenses in his mask, but he didn't have a chance to alert the others. The reptilian beast slammed him to the ground with a crack of breaking bones and buried its face into his neck, shaking back and forth like a dog until it ripped out enough soft tissue to reveal a glimpse of the man's spine.

To Kelly's left, Roche eased the barrel of his rifle over the edge of the case and took aim.

"Enki nahu," Maddox said and held up his open palms in a placating manner.

The creature he believed to be the ancient Assyrian god Enki shifted its weight as though preparing to strike at Maddox, but it never had the chance.

Gunfire boomed in Kelly's ear and bullets punched through the side of the monster's head.

The impact cleaved its body from the ground and tossed it sideways. It slid across the concrete in a wash of its own blood and came to rest at Maddox's feet, the contents of its skull pouring out onto the shards of Plexiglas.

"No!" Maddox shouted and started firing.

"Get back!" Roche said and shoved Kelly away from the edge.

Bullets pounded the ceiling above their heads. Kelly screamed and scooted backward as fast as she could. Shots continued to ring out, blasting straight up through the top of the display cases all around them. She pointed her weapon over the side and squeezed off a few rounds in an effort to drive Maddox out of range.

Silence descended upon the bunker. Gun smoke swirled in the columns of light rising from inside the cabinets.

She heard soft footsteps, even softer breathing.

Roche's eyes sought hers. Held them. He waved for her to crawl over the back side of the row of display cases, into the recess where the climate-control systems were housed.

She nodded her understanding, slid her legs over the edge, and quietly lowered herself into a narrow aisle barely wider than her shoulders. The hum of the equipment drowned out all but the most ambitious noises. She seated her rifle against her shoulder and headed back in the direction of the elevator. Roche lowered himself down behind her without making a sound.

A crackle of gunfire and bullets sang past over their heads.

"Do you have any idea what you've done?" Maddox shouted.

Again, he fired a fusillade of bullets straight over the top of the cabinets.

His footsteps echoed from all around them at once. He tossed aside a spent magazine and slammed a fresh one home.

The recess branched to the left and paralleled the intersecting hallway. She started in that direction but pulled up short when a flurry of bullets punched through the back of the cabinet right in front of her face. It took every last ounce of restraint to keep from screaming.

Shattered glass rained to the ground and crunched beneath Maddox's tread as he walked.

"You dare murder the god who saved humanity from the Great Flood, the deity who would save us from extinction and usher in the next phase in mankind's evolution?"

Maddox fired again, only this time farther ahead. He didn't know where they were. He was testing them, trying to get them to give away where they were hiding.

Kelly glanced back at Roche in time to see his feet disappear over the top of the case. Maybe he'd be able to line up a clear shot, but if Maddox even sensed he'd gone back up there, he was in big trouble.

"Show yourselves!"

Another barrage. Bullets ricocheted from the floor, hammered the ceiling, shattered glass. Maddox was losing his patience, firing indiscriminately.

More crunching of shards as he walked past the case in front of her, toward the main corridor, presumably right into Roche's line of—

Maddox fired wildly again, seemingly in all directions at once. She dropped to her knees as bullets streaked past over her head.

A grunt from somewhere above her.

Maddox must have heard it, too. He remained silent and still, listening for a repeat occurrence so he could line up the kill shot.

She looked up toward where she's last seen Roche. A rivulet of blood slowly trickled over the edge and ran down the back of the display case. He's been hit, but she had no idea how badly. For all she knew, he could already be dead or in desperate need of immediate medical attention. She couldn't afford to wait any longer.

Subtle crunching sounds.

Kelly pressed her back against the case behind her, aimed her weapon at the rear wall of the case in front of her, toward the source of the sounds on the other side.

Crunching, barely audible over the hum of machinery.

Maddox stopped moving. She kept the barrel aligned with where she'd heard him last.

Roche's blood dripped to the floor with a faint *plat . . . plat . . . plat . . .*

The crunching commenced again.

She tightened her finger on the trigger, imagined Maddox walking just on the other side of the case, maybe three feet away.

He stopped again. Right on the other side of the cabinet, directly beneath where Roche was hiding.

"There you are," he said. "Why don't you come down from there so we—?"

Kelly screamed and pulled the trigger. She swung the barrel from side to side and up and down until the magazine ran dry and the carbine whirred. The back of the case was destroyed, but all she could see through it was an empty corridor, its concrete floor covered with broken glass.

A pool of blood slowly expanded into view.

She dropped the rifle and climbed up on top of the case as fast as she could. Roche had squirmed to the edge and aimed his rifle down at the ground, where she could see Maddox sprawled on his back in a wash of blood. There had to be half a dozen entry wounds on his chest, so many it looked almost like his rib cage had been cracked open for surgery.

"I think you got him," Roche said.

Kelly threw herself on top of him and nearly knocked him right over the edge. Wrapped her arms around his neck and kissed him over and over. She felt him tense and recoiled just far enough to see the rictus of pain on his face. There was a spatter of blood on his cheek, which called attention to the gunshot wound near his clavicle, just inside his shoulder girdle.

"Oh, God," she said. "We need to get you to the surface."

She climbed over the other side and dropped to the ground with a crunch of the broken glass that had saved them. Roche swung his legs over the edge and made it halfway down before losing his grip. His heels hit first, and he toppled backward to the floor. The front of his shirt was positively drenched with blood. When he didn't immediately try to stand, she knew he was in trouble.

He groaned and cradled his injured arm to his chest. She grabbed his free hand and tried to pull him to his feet. He made it to a sitting position before needing to battle through a wave of pain. She ducked her head underneath his arm, held onto his wrist, and strained to stand up with his weight draped over her shoulders.

"You have to help me," she said.

"I won't be able to climb the cable like this," he said. "You're going to have to go without me."

"I'm not leaving you here."

"You don't have a choice."

She guided him into the main walkway. The pass-through doors seemed so far away. She glanced back the other way, toward the cul-de-sac where—

Her breath caught in her chest. The blood rushed in her ears.

Thoosh-thoosh-thoosh.

There was blood all over the floor where Roche had hit the creature in the head at such close range that he'd nearly decapitated it, but the body was gone.

A trail of bare footprints led to one of the few intact display cases. A smear of blood covered the glass, from behind which mummified alien corpses stared down at them. Droplets of blood swelled from the top edge of the case and dripped to the ground.

"Get out of here," Roche whispered.

"Not without you."

He removed his arm from her shoulder, cupped the back of her head, and drew her face to within inches of his.

"I need you to do this for me."

"Two of us stand a better chance—"

"Kelly . . ."

"Don't you dare tell me goodbye," she said.

"You have to go."

"You promised we'd go anywhere in the world I wanted, that we'd start over. Together. You promised me!"

"We can't let this thing get out of here. You have to make sure they seal off this building. You're the only one who can do it."

In her mind, she knew he was right, but in her heart . . .

Kelly kissed him. Leaned her forehead against his. Felt tears flowing down her cheeks. She pushed away before she could change her mind and ran for the elevator.

She couldn't bring herself to look back.

51
BARNETT

La Venta

Barnett scurried through the darkness, parting curtains of roots and spiderwebs, navigating the narrow stone corridor. He was out of time, and he knew it. Regardless of which side won the battle being waged outside, the victor would be hot on his heels, bringing with it either an overwhelming amount of firepower or an insatiable hunger. Either way, it wouldn't be long before his head start evaporated and confrontation became a foregone conclusion. He needed to make every second count.

The rattle of gunfire faded behind him as he reached the first fork in the tunnel. One branch led upward, while the other slanted downward into depths from which a bitter cold radiated. He stopped in his tracks when he realized how similar it was to the layout of the pyramid in Antarctica, where, if he continued downward, he would have found the ancient machinery that powered the device that had transformed Dale Rubley into the creature now known as Subject Z. In fact, if he listened closely, he was certain he heard the sound of running water, felt the thrum of the subterranean aquifer flowing beneath his feet. If this structure served the same purpose . . .

He ducked his head and started up the ascending corridor until he reached an enormous vaulted chamber, inside of which he found himself surrounded by anthropomorphic statues of winged beings with the heads of animals. While those at the bottom of the world had been classical in design, sculpted with the precision of Michelangelo's *David,* these were blocky and abstract, reflecting the style of the ancient Maya, despite which he clearly recognized that they depicted the same beings. It was as though the Olmec had followed the same blueprints as the Atlanteans who crafted this pyramid's Antarctic twin. If he was right, once he passed through the statuary, he would find—

There. A hole in the far wall. He ran toward it, dove inside, and crawled until he emerged into exactly what he'd expected to find, right down to the spiral pattern set into the floor, winding outward from the lone column in the center. Both were greenish-blue with oxidation, although he had no doubt that the copper filaments would still carry an electrical charge.

A thumping sound, followed by a rumble that shook the entire structure. He felt more than heard the clanking of the primitive lodestone gears coming to life in the bowels of the pyramid.

This entire region of Mexico was one giant karst formation, a limestone platform sitting on top of a veritable underground network of rivers and lakes in a continual state of erosion, opening sinkholes the Mayans believed were sacred, cenotes that granted them access to the underworld. It was more than that, though; it was a massive landlocked ocean subject to the same gravitational forces that controlled the rise and fall of the tides, making it especially sensitive to the alignment of the planets, which, under the right conditions, would cause that water table to rise high enough to perform its designated task. In this case, that meant turning a water wheel attached to a series of gears that caused a magnetized stone ring to spin around a metallic post wrapped with copper wiring, creating a changing magnetic field that stimulated an electrical current to flow through the windings and—

The inset spiral started to glow. Faint, but unmistakable. It wouldn't be long now before the aquifer flowed fast enough to charge the capacitors in the chamber underneath him, generating enough power to turn on the machine.

He thought about Subject Z and its desperate flight to reach this site, about UNSUB X, the creature it had brought with it all the way from the South Pole. And suddenly everything made sense. If there was one trait Subject Z had demonstrated above all others, it was an uncanny ability to survive. From the subzero temperatures of the lake trapped beneath the ice cap to the surge of electricity and scalding steam that should have cooked its host body in the process of assimilation to its escape from FOB Atlantis and subsequent northward track across the entire southern hemisphere, everything it had done had been to ensure its survival. It was the human part of its biology that made it susceptible to the virus the Assyrians had released inside the tomb in Mosul, one that had wiped out all of the mutated creatures, and yet left the giant masked man to rot on the plinth. He now understood why Subject Z had risked being recaptured and drowning in the floodwaters to save the mummified remains from the stone sarcophagus, why it had continued heading toward Mexico when it could have vanished into the high Andes or the hundreds of thousands of unexplored acres of the Amazon rainforest.

This giant being was its means of surviving the release of the virus.

Its goal had never been to beat them here so that it could destroy the one thing that could kill it; this was about upgrading to a host body that could withstand the coming apocalypse. And if it achieved its goal of sub-suming the body of a god, there was nothing in the world that would be able to stop it from supplanting mankind as the dominant form of life on the planet.

He couldn't allow that to happen.

The rising electrical currents caused the hairs on his arms to stand on end.

Barnett sprinted across the room to another small open-ing. Crawled until he reached the dead end. Stood up into the vertical shaft. Climbed the diagonal stone staircase lead-ing upward into the darkness until he reached the opening to the room he knew would be there.

He entered the transformation chamber, where a silver toroid had been set into the middle of the floor to distrib-ute the current to the green bands of oxidized copper that radiated outward and ascended the walls. When the elec-trical charge reached the terminal threshold, it would va-porize the water at the bottom of the shaft, filling this room with steam at the same moment it became electri-fied.

This was where Subject Z needed to go, and it was running out of time to get here. The sparkle of current passing through the wiring meant that the lunar eclipse was now at hand.

The grinding of gears grew louder. The vibrations passing through the stone structure intensified. Dust shivered from the ceiling. Mortar crumbled from the walls.

There was nowhere to hide in here. No place to set an ambush.

He hurried back down the stairs and out into the room with the spiral floor. Blue bolts of energy spit and popped from the central column. He felt the heat coursing through the floor. Crawled back into the gallery with its giant statues. Stepped into the shadows between two gods and pressed his back against the wall.

Barnett heard the clamor of nails striking stone. Distant, but coming in fast.

He opened his backpack and removed the silver canister. Turned it over in his hands, surprised by how steady they were. There was something liberating about knowing he was about to die.

Skree!

Barnett gripped the handle set into the top of the case, pushed down, and then turned. A hiss of air escaped from inside on a breath of mist. The lid popped up ever so slightly. He pulled it open, retracting the attached contents from what appeared to be a cryogenic chamber, from which pure white smoke rose. Six vials were mounted in a ring around a central post, like bullets in a speed loader for a revolver. They were etched with frost, and yet the fluid inside remained in a liquid state. He removed one from its holster, cradled it in his palm, and felt its awesome weight.

Skree!

He shoved the vial into his front pocket. It was bitterly cold against his thigh. He unslung his rifle. Leaned around

the side of the statue. Aimed into the mouth of the ascending corridor. Blew out his breath to steady his nerves.
Tightened his finger on the—

The feathered serpents appeared from seemingly everywhere at once. Scurrying across the floor. The walls.
From the ceiling of the tunnel.

He fired as fast as he could. Caught a glimpse of a
creature streaking toward him along the ground. It
opened its jaws, exposing its razor-sharp teeth. The first
shot took it straight through the back of its throat. The
second punched a hole through its forehead. He was already shooting at one climbing up the face of a statue
when the first slid through a mess of blood and came to
rest at his feet.

A crimson starburst decorated the statue and the creature lost its grip. He detected a blur of movement in the
flicker of discharge and hit one streaking at him across
the vaulted ceiling. Swung his rifle to the right and lit up
the belly of the beast lunging at him. Pounded its chest
with enough force to reverse its momentum, causing its
feathered tail to nearly whip him in the face.

Another was on top of him before he could aim. He
managed to get his elbow under its chin. Thrust the barrel
of his rifle into its mouth and blew out the back of its
feathered cranium.

He shrugged it aside, but there were too many.

Talons sank into his back. Another creature pounced
on him from the wall to his right, driving him to the
ground onto the one behind him. It scrabbled to free itself
from underneath him, snapped at his ear, the stench of its
carrion breath all around him.

He fired blindly at the ground beside his head, the sound

simultaneously deafening him and producing a high-pitched whine inside his skull. He felt warmth on his cheek, draining from his ear, but couldn't tell if it was the creature's blood or his.

The feathered serpent on top of him slashed his chest, slicing through cloth and flesh alike. He bellowed in agony, momentarily exposing his throat. Raised his forearm to ward off the attack. Its teeth passed through his flesh and struck the bone, sending pain rocketing straight down into his hand. It crunched down and he heard bone break. Stuffed the rifle between them and kept pulling the trigger until the firing pin clicked on an empty chamber.

It continued to scratch at his legs, even as its blood flooded onto his abdomen.

He gingerly flopped it off of him. His broken arm bent in a way it was never meant to bend, forcing him to use his other hand to pry its jaws from the wound.

Feathers hung in the air all around him. He heard the trickle of blood passing through the gaps between stones in the floor and, beneath it, the sound of footsteps.

Barnett cradled his useless arm to his chest, struggled to his feet, and stumbled backward, away from the ascending corridor. He shrugged off his backpack, let it fall to the ground, and rummaged around in search of a fresh magazine. Furrowed his brow when he found a rectangular case. He heard Morgan's voice in his head.

You never know when they might come in handy.

He shoved the case down the back of his pants, under his waistband, and continued searching until he found a full magazine. Loaded it one-handed and raised it just in time to witness the silhouette of a being he would have recognized anywhere materialize from the dark tunnel.

"Cameron Barnett," Subject Z said in a voice that re-verberated throughout the gallery. *"How fitting that you should be here to witness the end."*

Barnett reached into his pocket and shattered the small vial.

"I wouldn't have missed it for anything in the world."

52
ANYA

Giza, Egypt

The blond woman stood in front of Anya, their stares meeting through the mesh of the Celtic cross concealing her bright blue eyes.

"What about you, little one?" the woman said. "Would you like the honor of giving your life so that your god might live?"

Anya sensed the men standing behind her, felt them preparing to restrain her. She looked at Jade and Evans. If her death could buy them more time—

The man wearing the medieval knight mask charged into the room, breathing heavily.

"Das musst du sehen," he said and gestured toward the entrance from which he'd appeared. *"Eile!"*

A faint tremor passed through the ground, causing sand to cascade from the between the stone blocks overhead.

"It's happening," the woman whispered. *"Bring den körper mit."*

Anya had worked with German archeologists at various digs all around the world. While she was nowhere close to being fluent, in her line of work it wasn't uncommon for someone to request that the body be brought with them.

"Do not worry, little one. You will still have your chance."

The woman turned and rushed through the doorway. A handful of masked men converged on the sarcophagus. They reached reverently inside, slid their arms beneath the desiccated remains, and loaded them carefully into a silver body bag.

A shove from behind and Anya stumbled toward a sloped stone passageway leading down into the darkness. She had to duck to keep from hitting her head on the low ceiling, which made it nearly impossible to maintain her balance with her arms restrained behind her back. She slipped several times, but somehow managed to keep from falling.

The ramp leveled off before opening into a natural formation, only one unlike any she'd ever seen before. The walls were as smooth and polished as glass, almost as if the surrounding sand had been superheated. Stone blocks had been set into the slick earth to provide a means to reach the bottom of the steep formation, where the walls seemed to absorb the light, illuminating the entire cavern with an ethereal glow.

The vibrations grew stronger as they descended. Anya detected a humming sound coming from somewhere ahead of her. The cavern tapered until they reached a small hole barely two feet wide.

Knight Mask shined his beam inside for the woman in the golden mask, who crouched at the edge for several seconds before crawling into what appeared to be a man-made structure, and the source of both the sound and the sensation.

Anya watched several others slither into the darkness before being prodded with the barrel of a rifle. Wriggling through without the use of her hands took some doing, but she accomplished the feat and found herself inside a chamber reminiscent of an industrial boiler room, the slanted floor of which was paneled with metal grates that had broken in places and revealed the thick pipes running underneath them. The walls were rusted, like the interior of a scuttled submarine. A row of cabinets that almost looked like breaker boxes were mounted to the wall beside parallel rows of conduits and metal tubes concealed beneath the accumulation of dust. A long hose dangled from the ceiling, frayed wires protruding from the end. Bands of copper wiring, green with oxidation, traversed every available surface. There were four giant cylindrical units from which pipes thicker than her thighs originated. They went straight down into the ground to some unknown depth.

The blond woman raised the golden mask from her face to better take in everything around her. There were tears on her cheeks. Her resemblance to Maddox was uncanny, with the exception of her nose and brow, which were broad and flat. Her nostrils were teardrop-shaped, like those of a lizard. The deformities were plainly apparent, and undoubtedly the reason she wore the mask. Considering the others had the same eyes, Anya could only assume they shared similar physical abnormalities.

The men carrying the mummified corpse shoved past Anya. They hadn't been able to zip the bag closed because of the elaborate, solid gold hawk mask, which concealed the upper half of the being's face. She caught a glimpse of the lower half, noticed its flattened nose and angled nostrils, its broad, thin-lipped mouth.

As an evolutionary anthropologist, Anya was accustomed to looking for the origins of the people she met in their facial features, but she'd never expected to find them in a place like this.

She looked back at the woman, who traced her fingertips almost lovingly over the exposed portion of the corpse's face. There was no denying the resemblance.

They followed the macabre pallbearers down the slope and toward a crumpled hole in the wall, where it looked like an explosion had torn through the metal siding, leaving behind a ragged crater lined with sharp protrusions, on the other side of which was a bare stone room that appeared to have been excavated around the more modern structure, and yet had to be as old as the pyramids themselves.

Anya's mind reeled as she attempted to make sense of everything. The sand fused to glass. The modern technology. The ancient chamber built upon the ruins of a structure that couldn't possibly have existed during the same time frame. There was only one explanation for how this anomaly could have gotten here, but she couldn't rationalize it, let alone speak the words out loud.

"It's some kind of aircraft," Jade said.

"*Spacecraft*," the woman said.

"*Wir müssen uns beeilen,*" Knight Mask said. There was no mistaking the tone of desperation in his voice. "*Wir haben keine zeit mehr.*"

The woman grabbed Anya by the upper arm and dragged her through the ragged orifice into a room adorned with intricate hieroglyphics featuring animal-faced gods

with sun discs balanced on their heads, humans and creatures with oblong heads raising their arms in adoration,
and behind them, saucerlike objects cutting across the
sky. The designs were covered with grayish-green flecks
reminiscent of lichen and striated with horizontal lines
that almost looked like a series of high-water marks.

The vibrations intensified. The humming became louder.

"Faster," the woman said and shoved her up a narrow
staircase, the steps covered with dust the same color as
the lichen. It let out upon a narrow stone passageway that
extended a seemingly infinite distance ahead of them.
The men carrying the body were already several hundred
feet away, silhouetted by the flashlight of the man leading
them into the darkness.

It struck Anya that they were heading to the southeast,
which meant that if they continued on their present heading, they would eventually reach the pyramids.

Another rumble and a stone block fell from the roof,
admitting a mound of sand.

They had to slow to climb over it, which allowed
Evans to catch up with her.

"Look at the walls," he whispered.

He'd noticed the sedimentary lines on the block walls,
too. Worse, he'd made the connection that she'd missed
until that precise moment. If the pyramid ahead of them
functioned like the one in Antarctica, then it would need a
means of generating power. She recalled the contraptions
with the thick pipes extending down into the ground, ma-
chines that had looked almost like industrial water pumps,
and felt sick to her stomach.

They were in big trouble.

The ground shuddered and more sand cascaded from
above. She felt a sudden change in pressure, followed by

a sensation of sound she felt more than heard, a deep res-
onance like distant thunder.

The blond woman stopped. Held perfectly still. She
slowly turned and looked at Anya. No, past her. Her inhumanly blue eyes widened in recognition.

"*Lauf!*" she shouted, and broke into a sprint in the opposite direction.

Anya ran as fast as she could and prayed it would be
fast enough. Their footsteps echoed from the confines
until they were eventually drowned out by the rumbling
sound, which grew louder and louder until it became a
roar.

She glanced back and wished to God she hadn't. It
looked like a black wall had formed behind them, only
when it rushed into the range of their lights, she could see
the whitecaps and debris churning before it.

"Go!" Evans shouted and waved her on.

Anya pushed herself harder than she ever had in her
life, despite repeatedly scraping her head against the ceiling.

Ahead of them, the light ceased moving, shined back
in their direction, then into an opening in the wall. The
men transporting the body disappeared inside of it. Anya
was practically on top of it when she finally saw the steep
staircase and the square opening at the top, through which
the men dragged the body.

The woman shoved aside the man with the knight mask
and started climbing. He shined his beam past Anya and
into the tunnel as the leading edge of the floodwaters
raced past his feet.

Anya jumped onto the bottom stair, braced her shoulder against the wall, and ascended the steep steps.

The thunder of the advancing water was deafening,

like a subway train speeding through a tunnel. Waves broke against the wall beside her, filling the air with frigid spray.

Knight Mask shoved her to the ground. Climbed over her in his hurry to reach the top.

It took everything she had left to stand without the use of her hands and stagger upward through the rising water, the current driving her sideways against the wall.

She glanced back to see Evans putting his shoulder into Jade's lower back, trying to push her above the level of the water, which had already risen past his waist. It raced onward behind him, getting deeper by the second. She caught a blur of movement and the tail end of a scream as one of the masked men was carried away.

Anya reached the top of the staircase and stumbled into a chamber straight out of her worst nightmares. A waterwheel spun in the mouth of the well to her right, flinging water into the air and splashing it out onto the floor. Stone gears turned, driving a lodestone ring around an iron post, slowly at first, but incrementally faster as it broke through thousands of years' worth of dust and dirt.

The chamber was nearly identical to the machine room beneath the pyramid in Antarctica, with the notable distinction that there were bones everywhere, human and animal alike. Broken long bones hollowed of their marrow. Skulls with fractured craniums where something had bitten through them to consume the brains. Every surface of every bone was scarred and pitted from being scraped by teeth, just like those in the nest Subject Z had made for itself in the tunnels beneath the Antarctic research station, only there were so many more that they'd been piled against the walls all around the room.

The woman in the golden mask commandeered a flashlight from one of her subordinates and shined it across the carpet of dusty remains. While she said nothing, her body language hinted at a rising level of doubt that hadn't been there before. The loss of her ordinarily unflappable confidence made Anya realize that the woman was no longer in complete control of the situation. Whatever lay ahead of them would be as much a surprise to her as it was to the rest of them.

She caught Anya looking and shined the beam directly into her eyes, forcing her to turn away.

"Start walking," she said.

The entrance to the descending corridor had been completely sealed with rubble and packed earth and largely hidden behind a drift of broken bones, but there was an earthen orifice on the other side, where the Antarctic pyramid had shown signs of unfinished construction. Anya battled toward it through the sunspots staining her vision and climbed over mounds of remains so old they'd hardened into solid masses. The rocky walls were coarse and irregular. Recesses had been carved into them to display deformed humanoid skulls with vaguely reptilian aspects, only the majority of them were considerably smaller, with cranial sutures that had yet to fuse.

"These are the remains of children," Jade whispered.

Anya recognized the implications and glanced back at her.

"The majority of embryos are nonviable," the woman in the golden mask said. "Even those who reach full term rarely survive for very long."

She wanted to ask how the woman knew this, but she didn't have to; she'd seen the evidence in the woman's face when she removed her mask.

The pieces started to fall into place. She remembered

the wreckage of the submarine they'd discovered in Antarctica, at the end of the underground river leading to an abandoned listening station rumored to be the fabled Base 211, where the Nazis had retreated to regroup after the war; the maps and artifacts on the walls; the stickpin bearing the insignia of the Ahnenerbe—the pseudoscientific branch of the SS dedicated to tracing the Aryan roots of the German people. She recalled the story Hollis Richards had told them about the "Fuhrer's Convoy"—the pair of submarines that arrived unheralded in Mar Del Plata and surrendered to the Argentinian authorities—and their cargo of heavily bandaged passengers and priceless relics, among them the anthropomorphic face cast of a creature like Subject Z, which might have still been alive when it was created. There'd been signs of an attack on the Germans at Snow Fell and Anya had witnessed the recovery from the hidden chamber inside the pyramid of the savaged bodies of the Americans who'd been dispatched to hunt them.

Something had killed them, something that hadn't been there when Richards's team arrived decades later, something that must have been alive to inflict grievous injuries upon what was left of the Nazi army, something that had scared them so badly they'd headed straight to the nearest port to turn themselves in, something that hadn't been on board when they arrived.

All of these people had the same blond hair and blue eyes underneath their masks. Masks they'd been forced to wear because of their startling deformities. She thought about the scars on Maddox's face, from the reconstructive surgery he claimed to have endured in Afghanistan.

Anya understood exactly what had happened.

"Jesus," she whispered. She looked at the woman's back when he spoke. "They took it with them, didn't they?"

The woman stopped walking but didn't turn around.

"The Nazis . . ." Anya said. "What did they find in Antarctica?"

"A being unlike any they had ever encountered before."

53
ROCHE

The Hangar

Roche walked in a shooter's stance. The pressure of the butt on the gunshot wound to his shoulder was more than he could bear. He could hardly move that arm, let alone hold it extended and steady for any length of time. Both hands were slick with blood, his index finger wet on the trigger. Presumably, the creature was in worse shape than he was, having taking a bullet to the head, but he couldn't afford to assume anything. He had no idea how quickly the regenerative properties worked, and he most definitely didn't possess any abilities like that. He was losing blood at a staggering rate. If he didn't end this quickly, he might not be able to do so at all.

He sighted along the top of the row of cases, barely able to see into the shadowed region beneath the ceiling. For all he knew, the being could have climbed over the back side and fallen into the slender walkway housing the climate-control units. The problem was that it wasn't a wounded animal slinking off to die. He needed to find it—and find it fast—before it regained the advantage. While he had no intention of dying down here, the most important thing was that he bought Kelly enough time to reach the upper levels, where she'd be able to coordinate the response with the tactical teams that had to be converging on the Hangar at that very moment.

A smear of blood on the ledge.

Roche stepped back and tried to see into the shadows, but he simply didn't have the angle. He fired a single shot into the gap and heard the bullet ricochet from something before striking a wall in the far distance.

A crashing sound from the shaft behind him. He prayed the elevator held long enough for Kelly to get past it.

He walked sideways, one foot carefully stepping across the other, never taking his sights from the darkness above the display cases. At the end of the row, he turned down the intersecting aisle and searched for any indication that the creature had attempted to cross it, but there wasn't so much as a single drop of blood.

A narrow hinged door granted access to the hollow space between the backs of the rows of cases. He steadied himself, grabbed the handle, and blew out his breath. A wounded animal was infinitely more dangerous. If it was in there, he needed to be prepared for it to attack. He pulled the handle, raised his rifle, and aimed at—

Nothing.

Machinery idled and air pumps hissed. He could see all the way to the end of the row, but there was no sign—

A faint crimson smear. On the very edge of the cabinet halfway down, on his left.

Again, Roche walked sideways until he reached the next hallway. Sighted straight down another empty corridor. There was no movement in the shadows. No blood on the floor or dripping down the glass cases. It had to be up there in the shadows. He fired another shot, which ca-

reened off into the distance. Beneath the echo of the report, he heard a slapping sound, followed by a series of
rapid footsteps.

He headed down the row to the next aisle, turned—

There was a mess of blood on the ground where it had
landed, a smudged palm print where it had pushed itself
back up, and a trail of partial footprints. They disappeared around the side of a display case housing an idol
made from the bones of various animals. He rushed to
catch up, heard the sigh of pressurized air.

"No," he whispered and broke into a sprint.

The footprints turned down the main aisle and led
straight to the pass-through chamber. He ran as fast as he
could and nearly collided with the door when it didn't automatically open, which could mean only one thing: the
creature was still inside.

A swishing sound from the other side, as the outer door
opened.

The inner door receded into the wall several seconds
later, and Roche hurried inside. Waited seemingly forever
for it to close behind him and the outer door to open.
Stepped out into the stainless-steel corridor.

He moved his rifle slowly from one side to the other,
absorbing everything around him from his peripheral vision. Massive partial footprints on the floor. An occasional palm print on the wall. Sparks rained across the
open mouth of the elevator shaft. Fluid positively poured
from above, spattering the concrete pad loud enough to
mask the lower registers of sound.

The floor tilted underneath him. He felt his grip on
consciousness start to slip. His arm tingled with pins and
needles and his finger was nearly numb on the trigger.
The blood loss was catching up with him.

The hallway led to a small landing. He approached slowly, cautiously, clearing the dead space to either side of him before stepping out into the open.

Where was it?

The footprints became less distinct with every step, but they were still clear enough to lead him toward the shaft.

A rumble and a clanking sound. A long metal beam broke loose from high above and rebounded from the walls. Struck the bottom of the shaft. Slammed against the lip in front of him. The smell of smoke grew more intense; the heat emanating from above him was now palpable.

He could only see the bare concrete walls and the cables running straight down them through the open doorway. The spaces directly to either side of the opening and below the ledge wouldn't be visible until he was right on top of them.

A groan from somewhere overhead. More sparks rained down. The patter of fluid grew louder. He could think of only one source. The hydraulics. And when they failed—

A silver panel screamed down the shaft and landed right on top of the beam with a resounding clang.

Roche advanced upon the shaft from the left side of the corridor. Cleared the front corner to his right. Stepped quickly across the opening and cleared the left.

Where the hell was it?

He leaned just far enough into the shaft to see the floor. Nothing but rubble and puddles of fluid that reflected the flickering glow from above him. He followed the cables upward with his eyes, toward where the distant elevator—

A shadow eclipsed his view.

It struck his shoulders before he could duck out of range, pulled him over the edge into the shaft.

Roche landed beneath the creature's weight, tumbled down the warped metal plate. Landed squarely on his wounded arm. A bolt of pain struck straight into his hand, deadening it.

He drew his knees to his chest and used his left arm to push the creature away. It snapped at his face with serpentine fangs, flinging droplets of blood onto his cheeks. Its eyes were animalian, feral. The side of its cranium where the bullets had exited was a craterous ruin, exposing what little of its cerebrum remained. It was now a creature of instinct, a beast at the mercy of its hindbrain. A being victimized by its primitive impulses. A killing machine.

Roche pushed it up just far enough to roll out from underneath it.

A girder banged from the wall and slammed down between them.

He used the distraction to scurry out of reach. Onto the rifle. He grabbed it with his left hand. Made a break for the opening.

The creature dove onto his back. Drove him to his chest. Rolled him over. Buried its face into his shoulder.

Roche shouted in agony as its fangs burrowed into the entrance wound.

The rush of blood only seemed to drive it into a frenzy.

He jammed the barrel of the rifle into its chest. Pulled the trigger. The bullet hit the wall behind it a split second before a high-velocity spatter of its blood, but the pain didn't even seem to faze it.

It pinned down his shoulders. Shifted its weight onto his hips. Leaned in toward his exposed neck.

Roche raised the rifle and fired as fast as he could. The bullets streaked past its rib cage and flank, straight up into the shaft, striking the bottom of the elevator and the electromagnetic jaws.

The creature swatted the rifle from his hand and it clattered outside of his reach. Even in the dim light, he could see the corners of its mouth curl upward into a smile, mocking him for missing it at such close range. It opened its mouth inhumanly wide to reveal its horrible fangs.

A loud crashing sound, followed by a thunderous boom.

Roche locked eyes with the monster.

"I wasn't aiming at you," he said and looked up the shaft, drawing the creature's stare.

The electromagnetic jaws released the elevator with a shriek of shearing metal. It plummeted straight down toward them, its couplings sparking from the rails.

Roche pushed the creature with everything he had left. Scrambled out from underneath it. Dove for the ledge and pulled himself up onto the landing.

The elevator screamed and rattled.

The creature scurried up the rubble. Pounced at the landing.

"Enki!" Roche shouted.

It raised its reptilian eyes to meet his, issued a horrible hissing sound.

The elevator slammed down on top of it with a deafening crash, billowing smoke out into the corridor.

Roche waved it away and approached the shaft. Flames had taken root in the mangled metal. In the flickering glare, he caught a glimpse of a hand lying on the floor, severed just shy of the wrist. A second one twitched several feet away, near where the creature's head had rolled.

It rested on its face in the blood flooding from the severed arteries at the base of its neck.

He nudged it over with the toe of his boot. Stared into its hideous eyes as its jaws snapped uselessly at the air. Crouched over what was left of this being that had been worshiped as a god and had nearly been released upon an unsuspecting world by the masked faction that wished to destroy it.

"Let's see you recover from that," he said and kicked the head into the burning shaft.

54

BARNETT

La Venta

Barnett fired into the mouth of the ascending corridor as a dozen more creatures like Subject Z poured into the gallery. Streaking into the shadows between the statues, climbing the walls, hurtling straight at him.

He hit the lead drone squarely between the eyes. Its feet went out from underneath it, but two others had already passed it before its body hit the ground. He could feel them trying to outflank him from the shadowed perimeter, leaving him with only one viable option.

Retreat.

Barnett hit the two converging upon him. Fired indiscriminately to either side. Ran and hurled himself toward the hole in the wall. Landed on his chest, spun while he was sliding, and went feet-first through the orifice.

The broken glass in his pocket lanced into his thigh. He could already feel the infection moving through him in hot waves, tracing the patterns of his vessels in such a way that he felt the course of each and every one of them, from the smallest capillaries to the deep femoral artery.

He scooted backward as fast as he could. Shot straight

through the tunnel to drive them back. And yet they just kept coming.

The moment he was clear, he jumped to his feet and ran across the spiral design on the floor, past the wire-wrapped post, into the opposite opening. He whirled and fired toward the tunnel from which he'd just emerged. Hit a drone in the forehead, right above the brow line of its deformed skull. Another crawled over its back and scurried out of the way before Barnett's next shot struck the creature behind it.

He threw himself into the hole and crawled for his life. He could already hear the footsteps striking the floor behind him, the nails clattering from the stone. Caught a glimpse of its alien face entering the tunnel as he twisted his torso up into the vertical chute and started up the stairs.

Uhr-uhr-uhr-uhr-uhr-uh.

The vocalization nearly stopped him in his tracks. He glanced down the stairs, waited for it to poke its head up through the opening, and drilled it right through its elongated skull. Took off before the others could shove its body out of the way.

A fiery pain radiated from his groin to his lower abdomen, nearly doubling him over. His waistband was already wet with blood, the legs of his pants sapped to his legs.

The clatter of nails on the steps.

He shot blindly behind him. Heard the bullets ricochet. Prayed it would hold them off for just a few more seconds. He burst into the transformation chamber, from which there was no other way out.

This was where he would die.

He pulled the box from the back of his pants, grabbed

one of the M112 demolition blocks, and peeled the backing as he ran toward the tarnished silver ring in the floor. Stuck it right in the middle, stepped on it for good measure, and walked backward toward the far side of the room until he met with the rear wall.

A faint current crackled from the copper conduits all around him.

His chest felt heavy, as though his lungs were filling with fluid. He tasted blood in his mouth, felt it flooding throughout his abdomen, distending his stomach.

"What are you waiting for?" he shouted.

Uhr-uhr-uhr-uhr-uhr-uh.

A drone appeared in silhouette through the narrow opening. His rifle spat one final triple burst before the carbine whirred, announcing its empty magazine for all to hear. He let it fall from his grasp and clatter to the ground at his feet. He stared down at it, watched the blood dripping from his nose pattern its stock. When he looked back up, there were already four drones inside with him, moving stealthily around the room to flank him. They crouched, planted their hands on the floor, and tensed in anticipation of sprinting at him and ripping him to shreds.

Subject Z emerged from the shadows and stepped into the chamber in halting, disjointed movements. He saw his reflection in the surface of its wide black eyes.

Another much larger shape appeared behind the creature, its shape decidedly female. She'd been forced to remove the stag's skull from her head to pass through the narrow tunnels. He almost would have preferred it to her true visage, which was no more human than Subject Z's.

"So what's the plan?" Barnett said. "Trading in that ugly body for a better one?"

The creature smiled, its teeth a nest of razors.

"Even gods can evolve," it said in a voice that filled the chamber, deep and resonant.

"You're still singing that same tired tune, huh? You think that gray husk is an improvement over human flesh?"

"This form is weak."

"If hers is so much stronger, shouldn't she be able to keep you from taking it?"

"Not just weak here." The creature gestured at its spindly body, then tapped its conical head. "Here."

It took a step forward into the room. Blue bolts of electricity rippled through the copper bands in the floor. The toroid crackled.

Barnett bit his lip to keep from betraying his rising level of pain. It felt like his brain was expanding, causing the pressure inside his skull to multiply exponentially. He felt blood welling in his ears, wiped it from his upper lip with his sleeve.

"And you're just going to let him have your body, is that it? You, who fancy yourself a god, would willingly become a supplicant to this collection of microscopic germs?"

The woman revealed her long fangs. Her cheeks stretched all the way back to her ears. He realized it was her attempt at a smile.

"Inanna is supplicant to no one," she said in a sexless voice, one Barnett felt reverberate in his chest. "She is the daughter of Anu and the bringer of his divine wrath."

"She's about to become host to a soul-sucking parasite, and all so it can survive the release of this . . ."

He removed his backpack, took out the silver canister, and held it up for her to see.

Subject Z bared its teeth and lowered its body to the ground.

The giant woman strode across the chamber, stepping over copper bands buzzing with current, and closed her hand around the canister. She crushed it in her palm like an aluminum can. He heard the glass vials shatter inside and realized his mistake. He remembered the debriefings of the survivors of the disaster at AREA 51 he'd conducted aboard the *Aurora Borealis,* recalled how they'd described Hollis Richards's final confrontation with Subject Z. It had told him that all species served the gods in different capacities, that mankind's purpose was to build, while the role of the organisms collectively responsible for transforming Dale Rubley into Subject Z was to do "what is required," a purpose he now understood wasn't to subsume the form of this Inanna, but rather to sacrifice itself to her so she could become something far greater.

She tossed aside the canister, which bounced from the floor and struck the wall.

The ground shook beneath their feet. Electricity sparked from the toroid.

Not much longer now.

Barnett started to laugh. He couldn't help himself.

Inanna gripped him by the throat and lifted him from his feet. He felt the vessels in his eyes rupture and for a moment saw only red, felt the heat of blood flowing down his cheeks like tears.

"He infected himself," she said. "We must hurry."

She dropped Barnett into a heap on the floor. He barely had the strength left to roll over onto his side so the blood would drain from his mouth. The cold stone felt good against his forehead. He clung to that sensation as his insides dissolved. The pain was beyond anything he'd ever imagined. He prayed for the release of death, but not yet.

Not . . . quite . . . yet . . .

The creatures surrounding him raced toward him with the clicking of nails.

Clack-clack-clack.

Inanna and Subject Z converged at the center of the room. Electricity shot from the silver ring. Steam filtered into the room through the cracks between stones.

Barnett fought to keep his eyes open, through the pain inflicted by both the hemorrhagic disease and the teeth of the drones, just long enough to see this through to the end.

The current finally reached the threshold charge of the blasting cap.

Inanna looked down at the demolition block and then at Barnett, who managed one final smile.

She knelt and reached for the—

A blinding light.

Searing heat—

55
EVANS

Giza, Egypt

The tunnel terminated at a small square chamber. Evans recognized it as one of the previously unexplored structural voids discovered inside the Pyramid of Khufu on the muographic scan—an imaging technique that created three-dimensional volumetric renderings of solid structures using cosmic radiation that passed through matter in the same manner as X-rays were used to image the human body. A single doorway to his right granted access to a corridor that ascended toward the heart of the pyramid. The men carrying the body bag had already reached a point where the passage appeared to double back upon itself. They struggled to maneuver the stiff remains around the sharp turn, before vanishing from sight.

If Evans was right about where this was leading, he had a pretty good idea what they'd find when they arrived.

The ground quivered, forcing him to lean against the wall for balance. He stepped aside and allowed the blond woman to pass him.

"The being the Nazis found . . . was it like the creature

that killed your men in Mexico or like that guy back there?" Evans asked.

The hulking beast with the mask of the feathered serpent followed them at a distance, as though wary of something none of the rest of them sensed.

"Both," she said. "The people living in Antarctica before the crustal displacement not only built that pyramid, they figured out how to use it."

Evans recalled his first impression of the gallery with the elaborate statuary and how it had been designed to be seen, a ceremonial space created to impress upon a large number of people the might of the gods. At the time, he hadn't had a clue as to what this theoretical audience had been gathered to witness, but suddenly it all made sense.

"They put one of these beings they believed to be a god inside and used the machine to mutate it, didn't they?"

"They used it to evolve him, much like our progenitors used him to evolve us."

"Then they obviously didn't adhere to Nazi ideologies," Jade said. "The basic tenet of their entire Aryan philosophy was that their blood was pure, superior to lesser forms of humanity."

"Not everyone shared the vision of my forebears. The commanding officer of the Antarctic expedition demanded that he be taken to Argentina with the intention of using him as collateral to broker a deal for their freedom and the absolution of the war crimes for which they were being hunted, like many prominent scientists had already done. My ancestors, however, were true believers in the cause, apostles of the Ahnenerbe, who trusted in the inherent superiority of our Aryan genes, but, more than that, dreamed of elevating them to superhuman levels. They escaped from the submarine on a lifeboat, spent the next two years working their way home, and set about not just rebuilding the Reich, but creating a new one. A stronger one."

"Using this being as foundation stock?" Evans said.

"This was no mere being. We are talking about the god Utu. Enforcer of divine judgment. Brother of Enki and Enlil. Twin of Inanna. Son of Anu, lord of all creation, father of all mankind. An to the Sumerians. Ahura Mazda to the Zoroastrians. Quetzalcoatl to the Olmec. Zeus to the Greeks. Ra to the Egyptians. God to the Christians."

"You believe that corpse up there with the hawk mask is the body of God," Jade said, incredulous.

"We *know* it is."

They rounded the bend and struck off uphill toward exactly what Evans had expected to find. He could see the post wrapped in copper wires, the faint glow emanating from the copper spiral in the floor.

"So then you believe you're demigods."

"We are not their offspring; we are something far greater. The skulls of the children we passed on the walls are the result of attempted hybridization, human mules capable of little more than eating and sleeping. Even with their advanced scientific knowledge, the Ahnenerbe's early attempts at selective breeding and in vitro fertilization failed to produce a single individual capable of higher orders of thought and functionality. My brothers and I were the first. We are their crowning achievement, marvels of genetic engineering, the product of splicing together the most advantageous genes from both species."

"They must have messed up somewhere along the way," Anya said. "Have you looked in a mirror?"

"We shall see how you fare when we release the virus. We have already demonstrated that our immune systems can fight off the virus. Will your species be able to say the same?"

"So what do you intend to do?" Evans asked. "Use the pyramid on this Anu?"

"We will use it to evolve him." She paused at the entryway to the chamber and turned to look at him. "And ourselves right along with him."

"You want to become a monster like Subject Zeta?" Anya said.

The blond woman spoke over her shoulder as she crossed the room toward the hole in the wall, through which the men ferrying the remains had already crawled.

"No, we shall become gods, the fulfillment of our Aryan destiny."

"And then you'll release the virus."

"We will have no further use for your kind."

She crawled through the hole, climbed up into the shaft, and ascended the stairs to the transformation chamber.

Evans followed in mute silence. They were running out of time. He understood on a primal level that once they crossed this threshold, they would never come out again. They would be sacrificed and their blood used to resurrect this Anu, or perhaps they'd be deliberately infected with the virus and used to spread the disease. He couldn't allow either to happen. If this was where the road ended for him, so be it, but the hell if he wasn't taking these monsters with him.

Lightning crackled from the toroid, shot straight through the floor and up the walls, converging at the center of the ceiling.

"Das müssen wir jetzt tun," Knight Mask said and crouched over the body of Anu. They'd removed it from

the body bag and stripped it of its death mask and robes. *"Ich weiss nicht, wie lange das noch dauern wird."*

"Kneel," the woman said.

The men behind Anya, Evans, and Jade drove them to their knees beside the corpse.

"Who will be first?" the woman asked.

Evans looked first at Anya, then at Jade. He stared deeply into her eyes when he spoke.

"I'll do it. Just, please, let the others go."

"How very noble," the woman said, "but this is not a negotiation."

A wet *thuck*.

Jade's eyes widened. Her lips parted. She made a gurgling sound and blood dribbled from her lower lip.

Evans glanced down at her chest. Caught a fleeting glimpse of the tip of the blade protruding from between her breasts before the woman retracted it.

"No," he cried. "Please God, no."

Jade toppled forward onto the remains, the light already fading from her eyes as her blood washed over the desiccated flesh of the creature.

Evans tried to roll her over with his shoulder, pressed his cheek against hers, searched for any sign—

A sharp blow to the back of his head. His eyes crossed. Darkness gathered in his peripheral vision. He struggled to remain conscious. Fought through the pain and nausea to get to his feet. Brayed like a wounded animal and lunged at the woman.

The men caught him by the arms and dragged him backward, against the wall. The butt of a rifle to the gut and he was again on his knees, gasping for breath he couldn't seem to catch. They hurled Anya to the ground beside him, her face awash with tears.

"Do not think you have been spared," a man in a reflective mask said. "Anu will be hungry when he awakens."

Faint wisps of steam erupted from between the stones. The air grew hotter by the second.

"Beeile dich!" the woman shouted, her voice barely audible over the rumbling.

She held out her open hand to the man in the knight mask, who placed the handle of the silver canister in her palm. It looked just like it did in the petroglyphs, far too plain for the awesome might it contained. She set it down in the center of the toroid, where the electromagnetic forces caused it to slowly start spinning, faster and faster with every revolution until it levitated from the floor. The lid popped open and the contents rose above the rim. A blur of vials, spinning as though in an invisible centrifuge.

Evans slipped his bound wrists under his rear end, fed his legs through.

"It is working!" the woman cried.

She rejoined the others and the seven of them formed a circle around the room, halfway between the toroid and the walls. They cast aside their masks and revealed their true faces. The creature with the crocodilian face crouched in the doorway, watching the chest of the body on the floor rise and fall ever so slightly and the vessels plump beneath its skin.

Evans made fists, pressed them together. Bit the tail end of the zip tie, tightened it until it cut into the flesh of his wrists. Raised his arms above his head. Brought them down against his hips as hard as he could, drawing his shoulder blades together, his elbows back and away.

Unable to withstand the directional force, the tie snapped, and he jumped to his feet.

The creature with the feathered serpent mask turned to face him, its eyes locking onto his. It recognized what he intended to do and attempted to cut him off.

Evans grabbed Anya and shoved her toward the opening in the wall.

"Get out of here!"

The creature nearly struck at her as it raced past, losing its crocodilian mask in the process.

Lightning bolts crackled and snapped, filling the room. The scalding steam turned everyone around him into flickering silhouettes. A blossom of pure energy bloomed from the toroid. Started to swirl. It assumed a helical form, like the beam that had erupted from the top of the pyramid in Antarctica, only this one wouldn't merely serve to catalyze the transformation, it would disperse the virus into the air.

Electricity licked at him, passed through him. It shot outward from the toroid and impaled the seven figures, lifting them from the ground. Anu floated between them, his body stiff and frail. His eyes opened and his lips peeled back from his long teeth.

Evans ran past the blond woman, the current singing his skin, the alien organisms flooding his chest on the steam, bringing with them memories not his own.

The creature bore down on him from the other side of the room.

Evans threw himself into the vortex of energy as it rocketed toward the point of convergence overhead. Caught the canister against his chest. Forced the lid closed.

The creature reached for him, but it was too late.

The disrupted flow of energy expanded outward, setting the suspended bodies on fire. They screamed and thrashed. Arched backward with electricity snapping from their eyes and mouths.

Evans hit the ground. Glanced back. Watched the ball of energy collapse in upon itself, sucking in all of the steam and the suspended bodies.

Jade's lifeless form slid past him. He caught her by the hand. Rolled on top of her. Wrapped her in his arms—

56
KELLY

The Hangar

The flashing emergency lights turned the night into a red-and-blue mockery of day. Helicopters streaked across the sky, securing the perimeter around the abandoned hangars. They'd already found the vehicle belonging to Maddox's team off-base, but there had been no fingerprints or any other means of identifying the men, whose bodies were in the process of being collected at that very moment, or so she had heard over the walkie-talkies the men topside used to communicate with the investigative teams down below, none of whom had yet to find Roche. They'd seen what was hidden beneath the masks, however, so the remains were being sent to Friden at USAM-RIID instead of the office of the medical examiner, whose men had already left with the bodies of her unsuspecting colleagues who'd been killed at their stations. They promised to send another unit for Tess when they finally recovered her remains. They all owed her a debt of gratitude, not just for sending the warning to Roche, but for solving the riddle of the crop circles, which had likely prevented the extinction of mankind.

With the help of the field teams that still hadn't checked in yet, of course.

Kelly had already been informed about the explosions that had been detected by satellite in La Venta and Giza, which didn't bode well for anyone who might have been within the archeological sites at the time. The information specialists were sorting through every available source of imaging at that very moment in hopes of finding her friends, but they didn't sound overly optimistic. While the Middle Eastern team had fallen out of contact nearly a full day ago, Barnett had remained in close communication clear up until the moment that Maddox had seized the Hangar. She had to figure that if he were still alive, he would have found a way to contact them.

"Make way," one of the sentries guarding the entrance to the Hangar shouted.

Kelly pushed past the officer who'd been debriefing her in the back of the ambulance, climbed down from the tailgate, and rushed toward the point where a pair of soldiers wheeled a gurney toward the waiting helicopter. She was nearly upon it when she realized that it wasn't Roche and slowed to watch Maddox's body blow past. His pale face was spattered with blood from the point-blank gunshot wounds that had destroyed his chest. The scars along the sides of his nose and cheeks looked like worms. His men followed on separate gurneys, their faces concealed inside pillowcases, to conceal the truth of their lineage from those unprepared to handle the truth. She watched the soldiers slide them through the side door of a cargo chopper.

The rotors ramped up with a high-pitched whine and

flattened the surrounding weeds. The helicopter lifted off and thundered low over the rooftops. She followed it with her eyes until it disappeared from sight.

"I wasn't expecting a parade or anything," a voice said from behind her, "but I kind of thought some kind of celebration might be in order."

"Martin!" she sobbed and rushed to his side. Like the others, he was on a gurney, but one trailed by medical specialists. She climbed on top of him and kissed him all over his face. "I didn't know if you were still—"

"Shh," he whispered and wiped the tears from her cheeks. "It'll take more than any old god to kill me. Besides, I made a promise I fully intend to keep."

"Ma'am," the medic said. "He's in stable condition, but we still need to get him to a hospital."

Kelly climbed off the gurney, grabbed Roche's hand, and ran alongside him as they wheeled him toward a second waiting chopper, this one with a red cross on its nose and another on its side door, which slid open as they neared. She stepped aside long enough for them to slide the gurney inside and started to climb in beside him—

"Ma'am, we've arranged for you to be transported by ambulance—"

"Try and stop me."

She forced her way on board, knelt beside Roche, and kissed his hand.

The medic squeezed in beside his partner on the opposite side and signaled for the pilot to take off. The ground abruptly fell away from them. Kelly glanced back down at the smoldering ruins of what had essentially been her home for the past six months and silently hoped she never saw it again.

The chopper banked to the north and offered a brief glimpse through the dissipating smoke of the Chesapeake Bay, its waves glimmering beneath the light of the full moon as the final sliver of Earth's shadow passed into oblivion.

EPILOGUE

ONE WEEK LATER

And starward drifts the stricken world,
Lone in unalterable gloom
Dead, with a universe for tomb,
Dark, and to vaster darkness whirled.
—GEORGE STERLING

ANYA

Giza, Egypt

Anya sat on the steps beside the Sphinx and stared up at the Pyramid of Khufu. The pyramidion on top had been destroyed in the explosion, leaving the structure flat-topped and nine tiers too short. It had been crafted from a different color of stone, likely after a similar accident thousands of years ago. The Egyptian Ministry of Antiquities had already located a quarry with stone that matched the old pyramidion and commissioned the masons to start cutting. Until they were finished, the desert surrounding the pyramid would remain cordoned off and the upper portion would be concealed beneath a framework of metal poles and tarps to discourage people from snapping pictures through the hole.

That was the official story, anyway.

The truth was that an entire team of specialists, financed by the DOD in cooperation with the Egyptian government, was crawling around inside like ants, and likely would be for the foreseeable future. They dressed in civilian attire and entered through the tunnel in the demolished pyramid to the northwest so as not to attract any unwanted attention. After all, they would have had a hard time explaining the logo with the twin inverted triangles on their caps and shoulders, and an even harder time trying to explain exactly which organization they represented, especially considering that no one had ever heard of Unit 51 and likely never would, despite its considerable increase in discretionary funding. As it turned out, stopping an extinction-level event was the kind of thing that opened a few eyes and checkbooks in Washington, although no amount of money or prestige was worth the price they'd paid.

Not even close.

For her part, Anya had spent the last two days at the Air Force Specialized Hospital in Cairo, receiving treatment for injuries that still hurt and probably always would. She wasn't about to complain, though, as they would be a constant reminder that others had died so that she might live. A few broken bones, a couple dozen stitches, and a complete lack of hair and eyebrows were nothing compared to what it had cost her friends.

Evans had managed to seal the container before being incinerated by the explosion. They found it a quarter-mile away, at the edge of the blast radius, amid a scattering of debris. That was all she knew about it, though. The Secretary of Defense, Grady Clayborn, had personally conducted her debriefing, but she didn't remember a word he'd said after delivering the news that she was the only survivor, crushing what little hope she'd been able to cling to during the hours slowly suffocating under the rubble, her subsequent handling by rescuers who could no more understand her then she could understand them, and the seemingly eternal convalescence. All she clearly remembered was resigning her position, signing about a million nondisclosure agreements, and waiting for Roche and Kelly to finally arrive.

It had been at their insistence that she was out here now, as close to the pyramids as she was going to get ever again. This was her chance to say goodbye, to provide herself with a small amount of closure, knowing full well that not a single day would pass without recalling what she'd found here, what she'd lost, and how close her species had come to its ultimate demise. Worse, she'd looked upon the face of a being that might have been a god, maybe even her creator, and found him wanting.

"You were right," Roche said from behind her. She'd been so lost in thought she hadn't heard him climb the stairs. "It was in the Black Forest, not far from the French border. I've made arrangements to have a plane fueled and waiting for us."

Anya nodded. She'd known it was only a matter of time before they located Enigma's base of operations. When the blond woman had said the surviving members of the Ahnenerbe had returned to Germany not just to re-build the Reich, but to pick up right where they left off, she'd meant it literally. She might as well have drawn them a map.

"Evans and Jade would have wanted you to live your life," Kelly whispered.

They would have wanted to live theirs, too, Anya thought, but refrained from saying so out loud. She knew that the best way to honor their sacrifice was to make the most of every day she'd been given; she just hoped she had the strength to do so.

"Come on," Roche said. He offered his good hand and

pulled her to her feet. He looked miserable with his other arm in a sling, but, like hers, his wounds would heal. "There's just one more thing left to do."

Anya turned her back on the pyramids and took her first steps into a new life.

ROCHE

Roche didn't know the new director of Unit 51, let alone if he could be trusted. The only thing he did know was that he was no longer a part of it and wasn't about to take the chance of anyone finding out about this final mission. The secrets contained inside the Ahnenerbe's base of operations were priceless to certain factions, people who should be prevented from ever learning of their existence at all costs, so when it came to finding the staging grounds for the organization they'd nicknamed Enigma, he'd bypassed traditional information networks and reached out to some colleagues from his old life.

While the kind of men who traveled the world documenting the crop-circle phenomenon couldn't be counted upon to keep a secret any more then they could keep a crackpot theory to themselves, he could definitely count on no one believing them if they did betray his trust. Besides, even he hadn't been sure that dispatching a group of single-prop airplanes over the nearly impenetrable Black Forest would yield any results, but Anya's theory had been proved correct on the second day of sorties when they photographed what appeared to be an exact replica of Wewelsburg Castle at the base of a mountain practically unreachable by terrestrial vehicle.

It had been designed to re-create the famed Renaissance castle built in 1609 and leased by Heinrich Himmler with the intention of converting it into a training facility for SS officers; however, it had quickly become the cult-center for the more esoteric pursuits of the Nazis—and who better to lead that charge than his pet project, the Ahnenerbe?

"Are you sure you want to do this?" Kelly whispered.

Roche wrapped his arm around her and glanced back at Anya, who stared at the ramparts with an unreadable expression on her face.

"We owe Barnett this much," he said and led them across the narrow outer bridge, through the arched entry-way, and into the triangular courtyard, where he'd stashed the tanks of gasoline he'd spent the last forty-eight hours ferrying out here by the truckload. "Besides, it'll be a relief to know that no one will ever be able to reproduce the atrocities they conducted here."

He grabbed a tank in each hand and headed up the stairs into the castle, sloshing out gasoline as he went. The others each took a different wing of the triangular structure, with the intention of dousing everything in sight. He met up with Kelly at the point where the two main wings converged at a massive circular tower, inside of which was an elaborate chamber with ornate pillars and a marble design on the floor featuring the *Schwartze Sonne,* the Black Sun, an occult symbol with twelve lightning bolts striking from a central circle to an outer ring. They finished off their tanks, discarded them on the design, and returned to the courtyard for more.

Together, they reentered the castle, climbed the staircase, and diverged once more. The toxic fumes were
overwhelming, and yet they continued to splash the accelerant onto the floor, the walls, the furniture, everything
they could find. Rooms passed in a blur as they walked
from one floor to the next, returning to the courtyard as
needed to replenish their supply of gasoline. The lower
floors were reminiscent of a college dormitory, simple
living quarters for anything but simple beings. The top
floor, however, housed scientific suites stocked with computer systems and equipment of all kinds, clean rooms
and isolation vaults, nurseries and cages, a veritable one-
stop shop for a species hell-bent on its own eradication.
The most disturbing discovery of all, though, was a room
filled with candles that had burned to puddles, only to be
replaced by others in a continual cycle of renewal that
had apparently gone on for decades. The altar in the center was made from what at first looked like aspen branches,
but upon closer examination turned out to be large bones,
human, at least to some extent. Far larger than any man
Roche had ever seen. They must have belonged to the
being whose conical head rested upon them, his deformed face hidden behind the mask of a bull, a face that
no doubt would have born a striking resemblance to the
half-breeds who'd once lived here.

As planned, they all met in the Crypt, or at least that
was what it had been called at Wewelsburg. It was the
ceremonial center of the castle, the black heart of the corrupted body, in the middle of which was a recessed pit
surrounded by a granite ring. The red light of the setting
sun passed through the angled windows of the domed
ceiling in columns that spotlighted the inset *Schwartze
Sonne* design. The blood spatters had long since dried,

but there were more than enough of them to suggest that this room had seen its fair share of use.

He closed his eyes and imagined the body of the creature with the mask of the feathered serpent, the god Enlil, lying supine in this very pit while the blood of a sacrifice spurted onto his vile remains. He wished they'd found some part of him within the blast zone, but, like the others, his physical form had surely been converted to ashes.

Roche shook the last of the gasoline into the pit and looked at the others. While this was largely a ritual performed for their own benefit, it marked the formal end of one of the evilest eras in the history of their species and a new beginning for them personally.

There were no words said, not that any would have sufficiently conveyed the gravity of the situation. They simply returned to the rutted dirt road leading into the trees, and, together, watched the castle burn.

Elsewhere

Enlil watched the men coming and going from the tunnel leading into the demolished pyramid from a distance, careful not to let them see him over the crest of the dune, although even if they had, they would have undoubtedly just wondered how a crocodile had found its way out into the desert, and then they would have thought nothing else of it. If there was one thing he had learned and his long life, it was patience, the kind of patience required for one to willingly allow himself to wither and die in order to be reborn again, to suffer the indignities of the flesh, to take a final breath, to feel the last beat of his heart.

His time would come again, of that he was certain. And when it did, he would claim what was rightfully his and inflict suffering upon this world the likes of which it had never known. For his brother and sister. For his father. And, most important, for himself.

He lowered his head and slithered across the sand to the tunnel he had painfully exhumed—while his scorched arms regrew and his blistered skin regenerated, while every nerve ending sang in electric agony and his vision slowly returned—at the base of a rock formation. It led beneath the ground to a temple where his devotees had gathered thousands of years ago to sing his praises and offer sacrifices in his name. He crawled through a crack in the wall, into the darkness and the dust, into a chamber that would, at least for now, serve as his tomb.

The feathered serpent god closed his eyes and awaited death, all the while dreaming of the day mankind would awaken him once more and he could finally take his place in the sun.

**Keep reading for an excerpt of the first
Unit 51 novel . . .**

SUBHUMAN
by Michael McBride
Bestselling author of *Burial Ground*

THEY ARE NOT HUMAN.
At a research station in Antarctica, five of the world's
top scientists have been brought together to solve one of
the greatest mysteries in human history. Their subject,
however, is anything but human . . .

THEY ARE NOT NATURAL.
Deep beneath the ice, the submerged ruins of a lost
civilization hold the key to the strange mutations that
each scientist has encountered across the globe: A
misshapen skull in Russia. The grotesque carvings of a
lost race in Peru. The mummified remains of a
humanoid monstrosity in Egypt . . .

THEY ARE NOT FRIENDLY.
When a series of sound waves trigger the ancient
organisms, a new kind of evolution begins. Latching
onto a human host—crossbreeding with human DNA—a
long-extinct life-form is reborn. Its kind has not walked
the earth for thousands of years. Its instincts are fiercer,
more savage, than any predator alive. And its prey are the
scientists who unleashed it, the humans who spawned it,
and the tender living flesh on which it feeds . . .

Look for SUBHUMAN, *on sale now.*

PROLOGUE

Man is not what he thinks he is; he is what he hides.

—ANDRÉ MALRAUX

Queen Maud Land, Antarctica
December 30, 1946

Their compasses couldn't be trusted this close to the pole. All they had were aerial photographs taken six days ago, which were useless in this storm. The wind propelled the snow with such ferocity that they could only raise their eyes from the ground for seconds at a time. They couldn't see more than five feet in any direction and had tethered themselves to each other for fear of becoming separated. Their only hope was to maintain their course and pray they didn't overshoot their target, if it was even there at all.

Sergeant Jack Barnett clawed the ice from his eyelashes and nostrils. He'd survived Guadalcanal and Saipan, two of the bloodiest battles in the Pacific campaign, with no more than a few scars to show for it, but no amount of experience could have prepared him for what he'd found down here at the bottom of the world. When his commanding officer assigned him to an elite expeditionary squad, he'd assumed he was being sent back to the South Pacific with the rest of the 2nd Marines. It wasn't until his briefing aboard the USS *Mount Olympus* that he learned he'd been drafted for Operation Highjump, whose stated mission was to establish a research base in Antarctica.

His mission, however, was something else entirely.

Jagged black peaks materialized from the storm. He'd studied the aerial reconnaissance and committed the configuration of the Drygalski Mountains to memory. They had to be nearly right on top of the anomaly they'd been dispatched to find.

The Nazis had made no secret of their interest in the South Pole, but it wasn't until eighteen months ago, when two German U-boats unexpectedly appeared off the shores of Mar del Plata and surrendered to Argentinian authorities, that the intelligence community sat up and took notice. All charts, books, and identification papers aboard had been destroyed, and the captains had refused to divulge the nature of their mission to Antarctica, the whereabouts of a jettisoned dinghy, or the reason their passengers were covered with bandages.

The Counterintelligence Corps had been tracking various networks used to smuggle SS officers out of Europe and into South America, but none of those so-called ratlines passed through the Antarctic Circle. During their investigations, however, they'd encountered rumors of a mysterious Base 211 in Queen Maud Land, a veritable fortress commissioned by Hitler in the face of inevitable defeat. They couldn't dismiss the stories out of hand and potentially allow the Nazis to regroup and lick their wounds, so nearly 5,000 men had boarded a squadron of aircraft carriers, destroyers, and icebreakers under the auspices of scientific research and embarked upon a per-

ilous four-month journey through a gauntlet of icebergs
and sheet ice. Sorties were launched in every direction in
an attempt to reconnoiter the entire continent, upon which,
in addition to vast stretches of snow and ice, the camera-
men aboard the planes photographed surprising amounts
of dry land, open water, and what appeared to be a bunker
of German design nestled in the valley ahead of them,
which was why Barnett's squad had parachuted into this
frozen wasteland.

The wind screamed and nearly drove Barnett to his
knees. The rope connecting him to the others tightened,
and he caught a fleeting glimpse of several of his men,
silhouetted against coal-black cliffs rimed with ice. Barnett shielded his field glasses from the blizzard and
strained to follow the course of the ridgeline eastward toward a peak shaped like a shark's tooth. He followed the
sheer escarpment down to where it vanished behind the
drifted snow. The ruins of a rectangular radar tower protruded from the accumulation.

Barnett lowered his binoculars, unclipped his line, and
unslung his M3 carbine. The semiautomatic assault rifle
had been equipped with an infrared spotlight and a special scope that allowed him to see in complete darkness.
The Nazis had called the soldiers who wielded them
Nachtjaegers, or night-hunters, which struck him as the
perfect name as he struck off across the windswept snow,
which broke like Styrofoam underfoot.

The twin barrels of a FlaK anti-aircraft turret stood up
from the drifted snow, beneath which a convex slab of
concrete protruded. Icicles hung from the roof of the horizontal embrasure like fangs, between which Barnett
could see only darkness.

He crouched in the lee of the bunker and waited for the

others, who were nearly upon him before they separated from the storm. Their white arctic suits would have made it impossible to tell them apart were it not for their armaments. Corporal Buck Jefferson, who'd served with him since the Solomon Islands, wore the triple tanks of his customary M2 flamethrower on his back. They'd rehearsed this scenario so many times that he didn't need to be told what to do. He stepped out into the open and raised the nozzle.

"Fire in the hole."

Jefferson switched the igniter, pulled the trigger, and sprayed molten flames through the embrasure. The icicles vaporized and liquid fire spread across the inner concrete floor. Gouts of black smoke churned from the opening.

Barnett nodded to the automatic riflemen, who stood, sighted their M1918 Browning automatic rifles through the gap, and laid down suppressing fire. The moment their magazines were empty they hit the ground in anticipation of blind return fire.

The thunderous report rolled through the valley. Smoke dissipated into the storm. The rifleman cautiously raised their heads.

Barnett waited several seconds longer before sending in the infantrymen, who climbed through the embrasure and vanished into the smoke. He rose and approached the gun slit. The flames had already nearly burned out. The intonation of their footsteps hinted at a space much larger than the unimpressive façade suggested.

He crawled into the fortification, cranked his battery pack, and seated his rifle against his shoulder. The infrared spotlight created a cone of what could only loosely be considered light. Everything within its range and the limitations of the scope appeared in shades of gray, while the periphery remained cloaked in darkness, through which his men moved like specters.

The bunker itself was little more than a storage corridor. Winter gear and camouflage fatigues hung from hooks fashioned from exposed rebar. A rack of Sturmgewehr 44 assault rifles stood beside smoldering wooden crates filled with everything from rations to ammunition. Residual puddles of burning gasoline blinded his optics, forcing him to direct his sightline toward walls spattered with what looked like oil.

"Sergeant," one of his men called.

A haze of smoke collected near the ceiling amid ductwork and pipes that led him into a cavernous space that reflected both natural and man-made architecture. To his left, concrete gave way to bare stone adorned with Nazi flags, golden swastikas and eagles, and all kinds of ornate paraphernalia. Banks of radio equipment crowded the wall to his right. He recognized radar screens, oscilloscopes, and the wheel that controlled the antenna.

"It's a listening station," Jefferson said.

There was no power to any of the relay boards. Chairs lay toppled behind desks littered with Morse keys, handsets, and crumpled notes, both handwritten and typed.

"Give me some light," Barnett said.

He lowered his weapon and snatched the nearest man's flashlight from him. He didn't read much German, but he recognized the headings *Nur für den Dienstgebrauch* and *Befehl für das Instellunggehen*. These were top-secret documents, and they weren't even encrypted.

Barnett turned and shined the light deeper into the cavern. The rear wall was plastered with maps, the majority

of which were detailed topographical representations of
South America and Antarctica, all of them riddled with
pins and notes. His beam cast the shadows of his men
across bare rock etched with all sorts of bizarre and esoteric symbols before settling upon an orifice framed with
wooden cribbing, like a mineshaft. Automatic shell casings sparkled from the ground, which was positively covered with what could only have been dried blood.

"Radioman," he said.

A baby-faced infantryman rushed to his side, the antenna from the SCR-300 transceiver on his back whip-
ping over his shoulder.

"Open a direct line to Rear Admiral Warren. Ears-
only."

A shout and the rattle of gunfire.

Discharge momentarily limned the bend in the tunnel.

Barnett killed his light and again looked through the
scope. The others followed his lead and a silent darkness
descended.

A scream reverberated from inside the mountain ahead
of them.

Barnett advanced in a shooter's stance. The tunnel
wound to his right before opening into another cavern,
where his infrared light reflected in shimmering silver
from standing fluid. Indistinct shapes stood from it like
islands. He placed each footfall gently, silently, and qui-
eted his breathing. He recognized the spotted fur of leop-
ard seals, the distinctive patterns of king penguins, and
the ruffled feathers of petrels. All of them gutted and
scavenged. The stench struck him a heartbeat before
buzzing flies erupted from the carcasses.

He turned away and saw a rifle just like his on the

ground. One of his men was sprawled beside it, his boots pointing to the ceiling, his winter gear shredded and covered with blood. Several hunched silhouettes were crouched over his torso and head. They turned as one toward Barnett, who caught a flash of eyeshine and a blur of motion.

His screams echoed into the frozen earth.

1
RICHARDS

*Two possibilities exist: either we are
alone in the Universe or we are not.
Both are equally terrifying.*

—ARTHUR C. CLARKE

Queen Maud Land, Antarctica
Modern day: January 13—8 months ago

The wind howled and assaulted the command trailer with
snow that sounded more like sleet against the steel siding. What little Hollis Richards could see through the
frost fractals on the window roiled with flakes that shifted
direction with each violent gust. The Cessna ski plane
that brought him here from McMurdo Station was somewhere out there beyond the veritable armada of red Kress
transport vehicles and Delta heavy haulers, each of them
the size of a Winnebago with wheels as tall as a full-
grown man. The single-prop plane had barely reached the
camp before being overtaken by the storm, which the
pilot had tried to use as an excuse not to fly. At least until
Richards made him an offer he couldn't refuse. There
was no way that he was going to wait so much as a single
minute longer.

It had taken four days, operating around the clock, for
the hot-water drill to bore through two miles of solid ice

to reach a lake roughly the size of the Puget Sound, which had been sealed off from the outside world for an estimated quarter of a million years. They only had another twelve hours before the hole closed on them again, so they didn't have a second to waste. They needed to evaluate all of the water samples and sediment cores before they lost the ability to replenish them. It wasn't the cost that made the logistics of the operation so prohibitive. The problem was transporting tens of thousands of gallons of purified water across an entire continent during what passed for summer in Antarctica. They couldn't just fire antifreeze into the ice cap and risk contaminating the entire site, like the Russians did with Lake Vostok.

Richards pulled up a chair beside Dr. Max Friden, who worked his magic on the scanning electron microscope and made a blurry image appear on the monitor between them. The microbiologist tweaked the focus until the magnified sample of the sediment became clear. The contrast appeared in shades of gray and at first reminded Richards of the surface of the moon.

"Tell me you see something," Richards said. His voice positively trembled with excitement.

"If there's anything here, I'll find it."

The microscope crept slowly across the slide.

"Well, well, well. What do we have here?" Friden said.

Richards leaned closer to the monitor, but nothing jumped out at him.

"Right there." Friden tapped the screen with his index finger. "Give me a second. Let me see if I can . . . zoom . . . in . . . ." The image momentarily blurred before resolving once more. "There."

Richards leaned onto his elbows and stared at what looked like a gob of spit stuck to the bark of a birch tree.

"Pretty freaking amazing, right?" Friden said.

"What is it?"

"That, my friend, is the execution of the bonus clause in my contract." The microbiologist leaned back and laced his fingers behind his head. "What you're looking at is a bacterium. A living, breathing microscopic creature. Well, it really isn't, either. We killed it when we prepared the slide and it's a single-celled organism, so it can't really breathe, but you get the gist."

"What kind?"

"No one knows exactly how many species of bacteria there are, but our best estimate suggests a minimum of 36,000 . . ."

Richards smiled patiently. He might have been the spitting image of his father, from his piercing blue eyes to his thick white hair and goatee, but fortunately that was all he'd inherited from his old man. He could thank his mother—God rest her soul—for his temperament.

Friden pushed his glasses higher on his slender nose. The thick lenses magnified his brown eyes.

"I don't know," the microbiologist said. "I haven't seen anything quite like it before."

Richards beamed and clapped him on the shoulder.

"That's exactly what I wanted to hear. Now find me something I can work with."

Richards's handheld transceiver crackled. He snatched it from the edge of the desk and already had one arm in his jacket when he spoke into it.

"Talk to me."

"We have eyes," the man on the other end of the connection said.

Richards's heart leapt into his throat, rendering him momentarily speechless.

"Don't go any farther until I get there."

He popped the seal on the door and clattered down the steps into the accumulation. The raging wind battered him sideways. He pulled up his fur-fringed hood, lowered his head, and staggered blindly toward the adjacent big red trailer, which didn't appear from the blowing snow until it was within arm's reach. The door opened as he ascended the icy stairs.

"You've got to see this," Will Connor said, and practically dragged him into the cabin. The former Navy SEAL was more than his personal assistant. He was his right-hand man, his bodyguard, and, most important, the only person in the world he trusted implicitly. The truth was he was also the closest thing Richards had to a friend.

The entire trailer was filled with monitors and electronic components fed by an external gas generator, which made the floor vibrate and provided a constant background thrum. The interior smelled of stale coffee, body odor, and an earthy dampness that brought to mind memories of the root cellar at his childhood home in Kansas, even the most fleeting memories of which required swift and forceful repression.

Connor pulled back a chair at the console for Richards, who sat beside a man he'd met only briefly two years ago, when his team of geologists first identified the topographical features suggesting the presence of a large body of water beneath the polar ice cap and he'd only just opened negotiations with the government of Norway for the land lease. Ron Dreger was the lead driller for the team from Advanced Mining Solutions, the company responsible for the feats of engineering that had brought Richards to the bottom of the Earth and the brink of realizing his lifelong dream.

The monitor above him featured a circular image of a white tube that darkened to blue at the very end.

"What you're looking at is the view from the fiber-optic camera two miles beneath our feet," Dreger said. He toggled some keys on his laptop, using only three fingers as he was missing the tips of his ring and pinkie fingers, and the camera advanced toward the bottom. The shaft was already considerably narrower than when the hot-water drill broke through, accelerated by a surprise flume of water that fired upward as a result of the sudden change in pressure, which had inhaled fluid from the surrounding network of subsurface rivers and lakes they were only now discovering.

The lead driller turned to face Richards with an enormous grin on his heavily bearded face, like a Viking preparing to pillage.

"Are you ready?"

Richards stared at the monitor and released a long, slow exhalation.

"I've been waiting for this my whole life."

The camera passed through the orifice and into a vast cavernous space, the ring of lights around the lens creating little more than a halo of illumination. The water had receded, leaving behind icicles hanging like stalactites from the vaulted ice dome. There was no way of estimating size or depth. There was only up, down, and the unfathomable darkness in between.

"Should I keep going?" Dreger asked.

Richards nodded, and the camera slowly approached the surface of the lake, which remained in a liquid state due to a combination of geothermal heat rising from beneath the mantle, insulation from the polar extremes by two vertical miles of ice, and the pressure formed by the marriage of the two. The image became fluid. When the aperture rectified, it revealed cloudy brownish water through which whitish blebs and air bubbles shivered toward the surface. A greenish shape took form from the depths, gaining focus as the camera neared. The rocky bed was covered with a layer of slimy sediment, from which tendrils of sludge wavered. It looked like the surface of some distant planet, which was exactly what Richards hoped it was.

There were countless theories regarding the origin of life on earth, but the one that truly resonated with him was called *lithopanspermia* and involved the seeding of the planet by microbes hitchhiking through space on comets and asteroids, whether having survived on debris ejected from a collapsing planet or by the deliberate usage of a meteorite to plant life on a suitable world by some higher intelligence. Fossilized bacteria of extraterrestrial origin were found on a meteorite recovered from this very continent less than twenty years ago, but it wasn't until living samples were collected from Lake Vostok that Richards realized what he needed to do.

Ever since that fateful night sixty years ago, when he'd run into the wheat fields to escape the sound of his father raining blows upon his sobbing mother, he'd known mankind wasn't alone in the universe. He remembered every detail with complete clarity, for it was that single moment in time that altered the course of his life. He recalled staring up into the sky and begging for God to answer his prayers, to take his mother and him from that horrible place. Only rather than a vision of the Almighty, he saw a triangle formed by three pinpricks of light hovering overhead. He'd initially thought they were part of a constellation he hadn't seen before until they sped off without a sound and vanished against the distant horizon.

He'd been looking for them ever since.

"What's that over there?" Connor asked.

"Where?" Dreger said.

Connor leaned over Richards's shoulder and tapped the left side of the screen. The driller typed commands into his laptop, and the camera turned in that direction.

"A little higher."

The change in angle was disorienting at first, at least until Richards saw what had caught Connor's eye.

"What in the name of God is that?"

Connect with

Us

Visit us online at
KensingtonBooks.com
to read more from your favorite authors, see books
by series, view reading group guides, and more.

Join us on social media

for sneak peeks, chances to win books and prize packs,
and to share your thoughts with other readers.

facebook.com/kensingtonpublishing
twitter.com/kensingtonbooks

Tell us what you think!

To share your thoughts, submit a review,
or sign up for our eNewsletters, please visit:
KensingtonBooks.com/TellUs.